Miss Alice Bridgenorth.

THE WAVERLEY NOVELS

BY

SIR WALTER SCOTT BART.

VOLUME XVIII

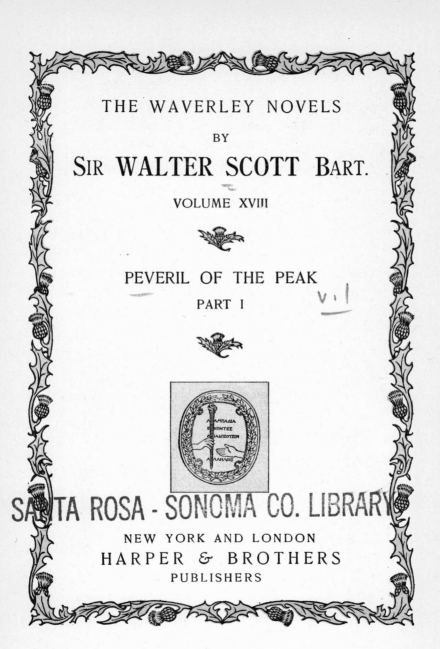

PEVERIL OF THE PEAK

PART I

NEW YORK AND LONDON

HARPER & BROTHERS

PUBLISHERS

C.S.

THE UNIVERSITY PRESS, CAMBRIDGE, U.S.A.

LIST OF ILLUSTRATIONS

Miss Alice Bridgenorth [see page 131] . . . . *Frontispiece*

"The lady of the Castle appeared at the top
    of the breach " . . . . *Facing page*   34

"Major Bridgenorth pointed to a huge oak " .   "   "   108

"Flashes of enthusiasm, too, shot along his
    conversation " . . . .   "   "   152

"He beheld beside him the little dumb maiden,
    the elfin Fenella " . . . .   "   "   200

"Julian fired at the head of the person by
    whom he was assailed " . . . . . . "   "   268

c. 1

PEVERIL OF THE PEAK

'If my readers should at any time remark that I am particularly dull, they may be assured there is a design under it.'—*British Essayist.*

INTRODUCTION TO PEVERIL OF THE PEAK

IF I had valued my own reputation, as it is said I ought in prudence to have done, I might have now drawn a line, and remained for life, or (who knows?) perhaps for some years after death, the 'ingenious author of *Waverley*.' I was not, however, more desirous of this sort of immortality, which might have lasted some twenty or thirty years, than Falstaff of the embowelling which was promised him after the field of Shrewsbury, by his patron the Prince of Wales. 'Embowel'd? If you embowel me to-day, you may powder and eat me to-morrow!'

If my occupation as a romancer were taken from me, I felt I should have at a late hour in life to find me out another; when I could hardly expect to acquire those new tricks which are proverbially said not to be learned by those dogs who are getting old. Besides, I had yet to learn from the public that my intrusions were disagreeable; and while I was endured with some patience, I felt I had all the reputation which I greatly coveted. My memory was well stored, both with historical, local, and traditional notices, and I had become almost as licensed a plague to the public as the well-remembered beggar of the ward, whom men distinguish by their favour, perhaps for no better reason than that they had been in the habit of giving him alms, as a part of the business of their daily promenade. The general fact is undeniable: all men grow old, all men must wear out; but men of ordinary wisdom, however aware of the general fact, are unwilling to admit in their own case any special instances of failure. Indeed, they can hardly be expected themselves to distinguish the effects of the Archbishop of Granada's apoplexy, and are not unwilling to pass over in their composition, as instances of mere carelessness or bad luck, what others may consider as symptoms of mortal decay. I had no choice save that of absolutely laying aside the pen, the use of which at my time of life was become a habit, or to continue its vagaries, until the public should let me plainly understand they would no more of me — a hint which I was not unlikely to meet with, and which I was determined to take without waiting for a repetition. This hint, that the reader may plainly understand me, I was determined to take when the publication of a new Waverley novel should not be the subject of some attention in the literary world.

An accidental circumstance decided my choice of a subject for the present work. It was now several years since my immediate younger brother, Thomas Scott, already mentioned in these notes, had resided for two or three seasons in the Isle of Man, and having access to the registers of that singular territory, had copied many of them, which he subjected to my perusal. These papers were put into my hands while my brother had thoughts of making some literary use of them, I do not well remember what ; but he never came to any decision on that head, and grew tired of the task of transcription. The papers, I suppose, were lost in the course of a military man's life. The tenor of them, that is, of the most remarkable, remained engraved on the memory of the Author.

The interesting and romantic story of William Christian especially struck my fancy. I found the same individual, as well as his father, particularly noticed in some memorials of the island, preserved by the Earl of Derby, and published in Dr. Peck's *Desiderata Curiosa*. This gentleman was the son of Edward, formerly governor of the island ; and William himself was afterwards one of its two Dempsters, or supreme judges. Both father and son embraced the party of the islanders, and contested some feudal rights claimed by the Earl of Derby as king of the island. When the earl had suffered death at Bolton-le-Moors, Captain Christian placed himself at the head of the Roundheads, if they might be so called, and found the means of holding communication with a fleet sent by the Parliament. The island was surrendered to the Parliament by the insurgent Manxmen. The high-spirited countess and her son were arrested and cast into prison, where they were long detained, and very indifferently treated. When the restoration took place, the countess, or by title the queen-dowager of the island, seized upon William Dhône, or Fair-haired William, as William Christian was termed, and caused him to be tried and executed, according to the laws of the

island, for having dethroned his liege mistress and imprisoned
her and her family. Romancers, and readers of romance, will
generally allow that the fate of Christian, and the contrast of his
character with that of the high-minded but vindictive Countess
of Derby, famous during the civil wars for her valiant defence
of Latham House, contained the essence of an interesting tale.
I have, however, dwelt little either on the death of William
Christian or on the manner in which Charles II. viewed that
stretch of feudal power, and the heavy fine which he imposed
upon the Derby estates for that extent of jurisdiction of which
the countess had been guilty. Far less have I given any opinion
on the justice or guilt of that action, which is to this day
judged of by the people of the island as they happen to be
connected with the sufferer, or perhaps as they may look back
with the eyes of favour upon the Cavaliers or Roundheads of
those contentious days. I do not conceive that I have done
injury to the memory of this gentleman or any of his descendants in his person; at the same time I have most willingly
given his representative an opportunity of stating in this edition
of the Novel what he thinks necessary for the vindication of
his ancestor, and the reader will find the exposition in the
Notices, for which Mr. Christian desires admission.[1] I could
do no less, considering the polite and gentlemanlike manner in
which he stated feelings concerning his ancestry, to which a
Scotsman can hardly be supposed to be indifferent.

In another respect, Mr. Christian with justice complains,
that Edward Christian, described in the romance as the brother
of the gentleman executed in consequence of the countess's
arbitrary act of authority, is pourtrayed as a wretch of un-
bounded depravity, having only ingenuity and courage to
rescue him from abhorrence, as well as hatred. Any personal
allusion was entirely undesigned on the part of the Author.
The Edward Christian of the tale is a mere creature of the
imagination. Commentators have naturally enough identified
him with a brother of William Christian, named Edward, who
died in prison after being confined seven or eight years in Peel
Castle, in the year 1650. Of him I had no access to know anything; and as I was not aware that such a person had existed,
I could hardly be said to have traduced his character. It
is sufficient for my justification that there lived at the period
of my story a person named Edward Christian, 'with whom
connected, or by whom begot,' I am a perfect stranger, but who

---

[1] See Appendix No. I.

we know to have been engaged in such actions as may imply his having been guilty of anything bad. The fact is, that upon the 5th June 1680, Thomas Blood, the famous crown-stealer, Edward Christian, Arthur O'Brien, and others, were found guilty of being concerned in a conspiracy for taking away the life and character of the celebrated Duke of Buckingham; but that this Edward was the same with the brother of William Christian is impossible, since that brother died in 1650; nor would I have used his christened name of Edward, had I supposed there was a chance of its being connected with any existing family. These genealogical matters are fully illustrated in the notes to the Appendix.

I ought to have mentioned in the former editions of this romance, that Charlotte de la Tremouille, Countess of Derby, represented as a Catholic, was, in fact, a French Protestant. For misrepresenting the noble dame in this manner, I have only Lucio's excuse : 'I spoke according to the trick.' In a story where the greater part is avowedly fiction, the author is at liberty to introduce such variations from actual fact as his plot requires, or which are calculated to enhance it; in which predicament the religion of the Countess of Derby, during the Popish Plot, appeared to fall. If I have over-estimated a romancer's privileges and immunities, I am afraid this is not the only, nor most important, case in which I have done so. To speak big words, the heroic countess has far less grounds for an action of scandal than the memory of Virgil might be liable to for his posthumous scandal of Dido.

The character of Fenella, which, from its peculiarity, made a favourable impression on the public, was far from being original. The fine sketch of Mignon in *Wilhelm Meister's Lehrjahre*, a celebrated work from the pen of Goethe, gave the idea of such a being. But the copy will be found greatly different from my great prototype; nor can I be accused of borrowing anything, save the general idea, from an author, the honour of his own country and an example to the authors of other kingdoms, to whom all must be proud to own an obligation.

Family tradition supplied me with two circumstances, which are somewhat analogous to that in question. The first is an account of a lawsuit, taken from a Scottish report of adjudged cases, quoted in Note 16, p. 601. The other — of which the editor has no reason to doubt, having often heard it from those who were witnesses of the fact — relates to the power of a female in keeping a secret, sarcastically said to be impossible, even when that secret refers to the exercise of her tongue.

In the middle of the 18th century, a female wanderer came to the door of Mr. Robert Scott, grandfather of the present author, an opulent farmer in Roxburghshire, and made signs that she desired shelter for the night, which, according to the custom of the times, was readily granted. The next day the country was covered with snow, and the departure of the wanderer was rendered impossible. She remained for many days, her maintenance adding little to the expense of a considerable household ; and by the time that the weather grew milder, she had learned to hold intercourse by signs with the household around her, and could intimate to them that she was desirous of staying where she was, and working at the wheel and other employment, to compensate for her food. This was a compact not unfrequent at that time, and the dumb woman entered upon her thrift, and proved a useful member of the patriarchal household. She was a good spinner, knitter, carder, and so forth, but her excellence lay in attending to the feeding and bringing up the domestic poultry. Her mode of whistling to call them together was so peculiarly elfish and shrill, that it was thought by those who heard it more like that of a fairy than a human being.

In this manner she lived three or four years, nor was there the slightest idea entertained in the family that she was other than the mute and deprived person she had always appeared. But in a moment of surprise she dropped the mask which she had worn so long.

It chanced upon a Sunday that the whole inhabitants of the household were at church excepting Dumb Lizzie, whose infirmity was supposed to render her incapable of profiting by divine service, and who therefore stayed at home to take charge of the house. It happened that, as she was sitting in the kitchen, a mischievous shepherd-boy, instead of looking after his flock on the lea, as was his duty, slunk into the house to see what he could pick up, or perhaps out of mere curiosity. Being tempted by something which was in his eyes a nicety, he put forth his hand unseen, as he conceived, to appropriate it. The dumb woman came suddenly upon him, and in the surprise forgot her part, and exclaimed, in loud Scotch and with distinct articulation, 'Ah, you little devil's limb!' The boy, terrified more by the character of the person who rebuked him than by the mere circumstance of having been taken in the insignificant offence, fled in great dismay to the church, to carry the miraculous news that the dumb woman had found her tongue.

The family returned home in great surprise, but found that their inmate had relapsed into her usual mute condition, would communicate with them only by signs, and in that manner denied positively what the boy affirmed.

From this time confidence was broken betwixt the other inmates of the family and their dumb, or rather silent, guest. Traps were laid for the supposed impostor, all of which she skilfully eluded; firearms were often suddenly discharged near her, but never on such occasions was she seen to start. It seems probable, however, that Lizzie grew tired of all this mistrust, for she one morning disappeared as she came, without any ceremony of leave-taking.

She was seen, it is said, upon the other side of the English Border, in perfect possession of her speech. Whether this was exactly the case or not, my informers were no way anxious in inquiring, nor am I able to authenticate the fact. The shepherd-boy lived to be a man, and always averred that she had spoken distinctly to him. What could be the woman's reason for persevering so long in a disguise as unnecessary as it was severe could never be guessed, and was perhaps the consequence of a certain aberration of the mind. I can only add, that I have every reason to believe the tale to be perfectly authentic, so far as it is here given, and it may serve to parallel the supposed case of Fenella.

ABBOTSFORD, 1st *July* 1831.

PREFATORY LETTER

THE REV. DR. DRYASDUST OF YORK

TO

CAPTAIN CLUTTERBUCK,

Residing at Fairy Lodge, near Kennaquhair, N.B.

VERY WORTHY AND DEAR SIR,

TO your last letter I might have answered, with the classic, *Haud equidem invideo, miror magis.* For though my converse, from infancy, has been with things of antiquity, yet I love not ghosts or spectres to be commentators thereon ; and truly your account of the conversation you held with our great parent, in the crypt, or most intimate recess, of the publishers at Edinburgh, had upon me much the effect of the apparition of Hector's phantom on the hero of the *Æneid* —

Obstupui, steteruntque comæ.

And, as I said above, I repeat that I wondered at the vision, without envying you the pleasure of seeing our great progenitor. But it seems that he is now permitted to show himself to his family more freely than formerly ; or that the old gentleman is turned somewhat garrulous in these latter days ; or, in short, not to exhaust your patience with conjectures of the cause, I also have seen the vision of the Author of *Waverley.* I do not mean to take any undue state on myself, when I observe, that this interview was marked with circumstances in some degree more formally complaisant than those which attended your meetings with him in our worthy publisher's ; for yours had the appearance of a fortuitous rencontre, whereas mine was preceded by the communication of a large roll of papers, containing a new history, called *Peveril of the Peak.*

I no sooner found that this manuscript consisted of a narrative, running to the length of perhaps three hundred and thirty pages in each volume, or thereabouts, than it instantly occurred to me from whom this boon came; and having set myself to peruse the written sheets, I began to entertain strong expectations that I might, peradventure, next see the Author himself.

Again, it seems to me a marked circumstance that, whereas an inner apartment of Mr. Constable's shop was thought a place of sufficient solemnity for your audience, our venerable senior was pleased to afford mine in the recesses of my own lodgings, *intra parietes*, as it were, and without the chance of interruption. I must also remark, that the features, form, and dress of the *eidolon*, as you well term the apparition of our parent, seemed to me more precisely distinct than was vouchsafed to you on the former occasion. Of this hereafter; but Heaven forbid I should glory or set up any claim of superiority over the other descendants of our common parent from such decided marks of his preference. *Laus propria sordet.* I am well satisfied that the honour was bestowed not on my person, but my cloth : that the preference did not elevate Jonas Dryasdust over Clutterbuck, but the doctor of divinity over the captain. *Cedant arma togæ* — a maxim never to be forgotten at any time, but especially to be remembered when the soldier is upon half-pay.

But I bethink me that I am keeping you all this while in the porch, and wearying you with long inductions, when you would have me *properare in mediam rem.* As you will, it shall be done; for, as his Grace is wont to say of me wittily, 'No man tells a story so well as Dr. Dryasdust, when he has once got up to the starting-post.' *Jocose hoc.* But to continue.

I had skimmed the cream of the narrative which I had received about a week before, and that with no small cost and pain ; for the hand of our parent is become so small and so crabbed that I was obliged to use strong magnifiers. Feeling my eyes a little exhausted towards the close of the second volume, I leaned back in my easy-chair, and began to consider whether several of the objections which have been particularly urged against our father and patron might not be considered as applying, in an especial manner, to the papers I had just perused. 'Here are figments enough,' said I to myself, 'to confuse the march of a whole history — anachronisms enough to overset all chronology! The old gentleman hath broken all bounds : *abiit, evasit, erupit.*'

As these thoughts passed through my mind, I fell into a fit of musing, which is not uncommon with me after dinner, when I am altogether alone, or have no one with me but my curate. I was awake, however ; for I remembered seeing, in the embers of the fire, a representation of a mitre, with the towers of a cathedral in the background ; moreover, I recollect gazing for a certain time on the comely countenance of Dr. Whiterose, my uncle by the mother's side — the same who is mentioned in *The Heart of Midlothian* — whose portrait, graceful in wig and canonicals, hangs above my mantelpiece. Farther, I remember marking the flowers in the frame of carved oak, and casting my eye on the pistols which hang beneath, being the firearms with which, in the eventful year 1746, my uncle meant to have espoused the cause of Prince Charles Edward ; for, indeed, so little did he esteem personal safety in comparison of steady High Church principle, that he waited but the news of the Adventurer's reaching London to hasten to join his standard.

Such a doze as I then enjoyed, I find compatible with indulging the best and deepest cogitations which at any time arise in my mind. I chew the cud of sweet and bitter fancy, in a state betwixt sleeping and waking, which I consider as so highly favourable to philosophy, that I have no doubt some of its most distinguished systems have been composed under its influence. My servant is, therefore, instructed to tread as if upon down ; my door-hinges are carefully oiled, and all appliances used to prevent me from being prematurely and harshly called back to the broad waking-day of a laborious world. My custom, in this particular, is so well known, that the very schoolboys cross the alley on tiptoe, betwixt the hours of four and five. My cell is the very dwelling of Morpheus. There is indeed a bawling knave of a broom-man, *quem ego*—— But this is matter for the quarter-sessions.

As my head sunk back upon the easy-chair in the philosophical mood which I have just described, and the eyes of my body began to close, in order, doubtless, that those of my understanding might be the more widely opened, I was startled by a knock at the door, of a kind more authoritatively boisterous than is given at that hour by any visitor acquainted with my habits. I started up in my seat, and heard the step of my servant hurrying along the passage, followed by a very heavy

and measured pace, which shook the long oak-floored gallery in
such a manner as forcibly to arrest my attention. ' A stranger,
sir, just arrived from Edinburgh by the north mail, desires to
speak with your reverence.'   Such were the words with which
Jacob threw the door to the wall ; and the startled tone in
which he pronounced them, although there was nothing particular in the annunciation itself, prepared me for the approach
of a visitor of uncommon dignity and importance.

The Author of *Waverley* entered, a bulky and tall man, in a
travelling great-coat, which covered a suit of snuff-brown, cut
in imitation of that worn by the great Rambler.   His flapped
hat — for he disdained the modern frivolities of a travelling-cap
— was bound over his head with a large silk handkerchief, so
as to protect his ears from cold at once and from the babble
of his pleasant companions in the public coach from which he
had just alighted.   There was somewhat of a sarcastic shrewdness and sense which sat on the heavy penthouse of his shaggy
grey eyebrow ; his features were in other respects largely shaped,
and rather heavy than promising wit or genius ; but he had a
notable projection of the nose, similar to that line of the Latin
poet —

Immodicum surgit pro cuspide rostrum.

A stout walking-stick stayed his hand ; a double Barcelona protected his neck ; his belly was something prominent, ' but that 's
not much ' ; his breeches were substantial thick-set ; and a pair
of top-boots, which were slipped down to ease his sturdy calves,
did not conceal his comfortable travelling stockings of lamb's
wool, wrought, not on the loom, but on wires, and after the
venerable ancient fashion known in Scotland by the name of
' ridge-and-furrow.'   His age seemed to be considerably above
fifty, but could not amount to threescore, which I observed
with pleasure, trusting there may be a good deal of work had
out of him yet ; especially as a general haleness of appearance
— the compass and strength of his voice, the steadiness of his
step, the rotundity of his calf, the depth of his ' hem,' and the
sonorous emphasis of his sneeze, were all signs of a constitution
built for permanence.

It struck me forcibly, as I gazed on this portly person, that
he realised, in my imagination, the Stout Gentleman in No. II.,
who afforded such subject of varying speculation to our most
amusing and elegant Utopian traveller, Master Geoffrey Crayon.
Indeed, but for one little trait in the conduct of the said Stout

Gentleman — I mean the gallantry towards his landlady, a thing which would greatly derogate from our senior's character — I should be disposed to conclude that Master Crayon had, on that memorable occasion, actually passed his time in the vicinity of the Author of *Waverley*. But our worthy patriarch, be it spoken to his praise, far from cultivating the society of the fair sex, seems, in avoiding the company of womankind, rather to imitate the humour of our friend and relation, Master Jonathan Oldbuck, as I was led to conjecture, from a circumstance which occurred immediately after his entrance.

Having acknowledged his presence with fitting thanks and gratulations, I proposed to my venerated visitor, as a refresh-ment best suited to the hour of the day, to summon my cousin and housekeeper, Miss Catharine Whiterose, with the tea-equipage ; but he rejected my proposal with disdain worthy of the Laird of Monkbarns. ' No scandal-broth,' he exclaimed —' no unidea'd woman's chatter for me. Fill the frothed tankard — slice the fatted rump ; I desire no society but yours, and no refreshment but what the cask and the gridiron can supply.'

The beefsteak, and toast, and tankard were speedily got ready ; and whether an apparition or a bodily presentation, my visitor displayed dexterity as a trencherman which might have attracted the envy of a hungry hunter after a fox-chase of forty miles. Neither did he fail to make some deep and solemn appeals not only to the tankard aforesaid, but to two decanters of London particular Madeira and old port ; the first of which I had extracted from its ripening place of deposition within reach of the genial warmth of the oven ; the other, from a deep crypt in mine own ancient cellar, which whilom may have held the vintages of the victors of the world, the arch being com-posed of Roman brick. I could not help admiring and con-gratulating the old gentleman upon the vigorous appetite which he displayed for the genial cheer of Old England. ' Sir,' was his reply, ' I must eat as an Englishman to qualify myself for taking my place at one of the most select companies of right English spirits which ever girdled in and hewed asunder a mountainous sirloin and a generous plum-pudding.'

I inquired, but with all deference and modesty, whither he was bound, and to what distinguished society he applied a description so general. I shall proceed, in humble imitation of your example, to give the subsequent dialogue in a dramatic form, unless when description becomes necessary.

Author of Waverley. To whom should I apply such a description, save to the only society to whom it can be thoroughly applicable — those unerring judges of old books and old wine — the Roxburgh Club of London? Have you not heard that I have been chosen a member of that society of select bibliomaniacs?[1]

Dryasdust. (Rummaging in his pocket.) I did hear something of it from Captain Clutterbuck, who wrote to me — ay, here is his letter — that such a report was current among the Scottish antiquaries, who were much alarmed lest you should be seduced into the heresy of preferring English beef to seven-year-old black-faced mutton, Maraschino to whisky, and turtle-soup to cock-a-leekie; in which case, they must needs renounce you as a lost man. 'But,' adds our friend, looking at the letter, his hand is rather of a military description, better used to handle the sword than the pen — 'our friend is so much upon the SHUN' — the *shun,* I think it is — 'that it must be no light temptation which will withdraw him from his incognito.'

Author. No light temptation, unquestionably; but this is a powerful one, to hob-or-nob with the lords of the literary treasures of Althorpe and Hodnet, in Madeira negus, brewed by the classical Dibdin; to share those profound debates which stamp accurately on each 'small volume, dark with tarnished gold,' its colour, not of S. S. but of R. R.; to toast the immortal memory of Caxton, Valdarar, Pynson, and the other fathers of that great art which has made all, and each of us, what we are. These, my dear son, are temptations to which you see me now in the act of resigning that quiet chimney-corner of life in which, unknowing and unknown — save by means of the hopeful family to which I have given birth — I proposed to wear out the end of life's evening grey.

So saying, our venerable friend took another emphatic touch of the tankard, as if the very expression had suggested that specific remedy against the evils of life recommended in the celebrated response of Johnson's anchorite —

Come, my lad, and drink some beer.

When he had placed on the table the silver tankard, and fetched a deep sigh to collect the respiration which the long draught had interrupted, I could not help echoing it in a note so pathetically compassionate that he fixed his eyes on me with

---

[1] The Author has pride in recording that he had the honour to be elected a member of this distinguished association, merely as the Author of *Waverley,* without any other designation; and it was an additional inducement to throw off the masque of an anonymous author, that it gives him a right to occupy the vacant chair at that festive board.

surprise. 'How is this?' said he, somewhat angrily; 'do you, the creature of my will, grudge me my preferment? Have I dedicated to you and your fellows the best hours of my life for these seven years past; and do you presume to grumble or repine because, in those which are to come, I seek for some enjoyment of life in society so congenial to my pursuits?' I humbled myself before the offended senior, and professed my innocence in all that could possibly give him displeasure. He seemed partly appeased, but still bent on me an eye of suspicion, while he questioned me in the words of old Norton, in the ballad of the *Rising in the North Country*.

> *Author.* What wouldst thou have, Francis Norton?
> Thou art my youngest son and heir;
> Something lies brooding at thy heart —
> Whate'er it be, to me declare.

Dryasdust. Craving, then, your paternal forgiveness for my presumption, I only sighed at the possibility of your venturing yourself amongst a body of critics to whom, in the capacity of skilful antiquaries, the investigation of truth is an especial duty, and who may therefore visit with the more severe censure those aberrations which it is so often your pleasure to make from the path of true history.

Author. I understand you. You mean to say these learned persons will have but little toleration for a romance or a fictitious narrative founded upon history?

Dryasdust. Why, sir, I do rather apprehend that their respect for the foundation will be such that they may be apt to quarrel with the inconsistent nature of the superstructure; just as every classical traveller pours forth expressions of sorrow and indignation when, in travelling through Greece, he chances to see a Turkish kiosk rising on the ruins of an ancient temple.

Author. But since we cannot rebuild the temple, a kiosk may be a pretty thing, may it not? Not quite correct in architecture, strictly and classically criticised; but presenting something uncommon to the eye, and something fantastic to the imagination, on which the spectator gazes with pleasure of the same description which arises from the perusal of an Eastern tale.

Dryasdust. I am unable to dispute with you in metaphor, sir; but I must say, in discharge of my conscience, that you stand much censured for adulterating the pure sources of historical knowledge. You approach them, men say, like the drunken yeoman who, once upon a time, polluted the crystal

spring which supplied the thirst of his family, with a score of
sugar loaves and a hogshead of rum; and thereby converted a
simple and wholesome beverage into a stupifying, brutifying,
and intoxicating fluid, sweeter, indeed, to the taste than the
natural lymph, but, for that very reason, more seductively
dangerous.

Author. I allow your metaphor, doctor; but yet, though
good punch cannot supply the want of spring water, it is, when
modestly used, no *malum in se;* and I should have thought it
a shabby thing of the parson of the parish had he helped to
drink out the well on Saturday night and preached against the
honest, hospitable yeoman on Sunday morning. I should have
answered him that the very flavour of the liquor should have
put him at once upon his guard; and that, if he had taken a
drop over much, he ought to blame his own imprudence more
than the hospitality of his entertainer.

Dryasdust. I profess I do not exactly see how this applies.

Author. No; you are one of those numerous disputants who
will never follow their metaphor a step farther than it goes
their own way. I will explain. A poor fellow, like myself,
weary with ransacking his own barren and bounded imagination, looks out for some general subject in the huge and bound-
less field of history, which holds forth examples of every kind;
lights on some personage, or some combination of circumstances, or some striking trait of manners, which he thinks
may be advantageously used as the basis of a fictitious narrative; bedizens it with such colouring as his skill suggests, ornaments it with such romantic circumstances as may heighten the
general effect, invests it with such shades of character as will
best contrast with each other, and thinks, perhaps, he has done
some service to the public, if he can present to them a lively
fictitious picture, for which the original anecdote or circumstance which he made free to press into his service only furnished a slight sketch. Now I cannot perceive any harm in
this. The stores of history are accessible to every one, and
are no more exhausted or impoverished by the hints thus
borrowed from them than the fountain is drained by the water
which we subtract for domestic purposes. And in reply to
the sober charge of falsehood against a narrative announced
positively to be fictitious, one can only answer by Prior's
exclamation —

Odzooks, must one swear to the truth of a song?

Dryasdust. Nay; but I fear me that you are here eluding the charge. Men do not seriously accuse you of misrepresenting history; although I assure you I have seen some grave treatises in which it was thought necessary to contradict your assertions.

Author. That certainly was to point a discharge of artillery against a wreath of morning mist.

Dryasdust. But besides, and especially, it is said that you are in danger of causing history to be neglected, readers being contented with such frothy and superficial knowledge as they acquire from your works, to the effect of inducing them to neglect the severer and more accurate sources of information.

Author. I deny the consequence. On the contrary, I rather hope that I have turned the attention of the public on various points which have received elucidation from writers of more learning and research, in consequence of my novels having attached some interest to them. I might give instances, but I hate vanity — I hate vanity. The history of the divining-rod is well known : it is a slight, valueless twig in itself, but indicates, by its motion, where veins of precious metal are concealed below the earth, which afterwards enrich the adventurers by whom they are laboriously and carefully wrought. I claim no more merit for my historical hints; but this is something.

Dryasdust. We severer antiquaries, sir, may grant that this is true; to wit, that your works may occasionally have put men of solid judgment upon researches which they would not perhaps have otherwise thought of undertaking. But this will leave you still accountable for misleading the young, the indolent, and the giddy, by thrusting into their hands works which, while they have so much the appearance of conveying information as may prove perhaps a salve to their consciences for employing their leisure in the perusal, yet leave their giddy brains contented with the crude, uncertain, and often false, statements which your novels abound with.

Author. It would be very unbecoming in me, reverend sir, to accuse a gentleman of your cloth of cant; but, pray, is there not something like it in the pathos with which you enforce these dangers? I aver, on the contrary, that, by introducing the busy and the youthful to 'truths severe in fairy fiction dressed,'[1] I am doing a real service to the more ingenious and

---

[1] The doctor has denied the Author's title to shelter himself under this quotation; but the Author continues to think himself entitled to all the shelter which, threadbare as it is, it may yet be able to afford him. The truth severe applies not to the narrative itself, but to the moral it conveys, in which the Author has not been thought deficient. The 'fairy fiction' is the conduct of the story which the tale is invented to elucidate.

the more apt among them; for the love of knowledge wants
but a beginning — the least spark will give fire when the train
is properly prepared; and having been interested in fictitious
adventures, ascribed to a historical period and characters, the
reader begins next to be anxious to learn what the facts really
were, and how far the novelist has justly represented them.

But even where the mind of the more careless reader
remains satisfied with the light perusal he has afforded to a
tale of fiction, he will still lay down the book with a degree of
knowledge, not perhaps of the most accurate kind, but such as
he might not otherwise have acquired. Nor is this limited to
minds of a low and incurious description; but, on the contrary,
comprehends many persons otherwise of high talents, who,
nevertheless, either from lack of time or of perseverance, are
willing to sit down contented with the slight information which
is acquired in such a manner. The great Duke of Marlborough,
for example, having quoted in conversation some fact of English history rather inaccurately, was requested to name his
authority. 'Shakspeare's historical plays,' answered the conqueror of Blenheim; 'the only English history I ever read in
my life.' And a hasty recollection will convince any of us
how much better we are acquainted with those parts of English
history which that immortal bard has dramatised than with
any other portion of British story.

Dryasdust. And you, worthy sir, are ambitious to render
a similar service to posterity?

Author. May the saints forefend I should be guilty of such
unfounded vanity! I only show what has been done when
there were giants in the land. We pigmies of the present day
may at least, however, do something; and it is well to keep a
pattern before our eyes, though that pattern be inimitable.

Dryasdust. Well, sir, with me you must have your own
course; and for reasons well known to you it is impossible for
me to reply to you in argument. But I doubt if all you have
said will reconcile the public to the anachronisms of your
present volumes. Here you have a Countess of Derby fetched
out of her cold grave and saddled with a set of adventures
dated twenty years after her death, besides being given up as
a Catholic, when she was in fact a zealous Huguenot.

Author. She may sue me for damages, as in the case Dido
versus Virgil.

Dryasdust. A worse fault is, that your manners are even
more incorrect than usual. Your Puritan is faintly traced in
comparison to your Cameronian.

Author. I agree to the charge; but although I still consider hypocrisy and enthusiasm as fit food for ridicule and satire, yet I am sensible of the difficulty of holding fanaticism up to laughter or abhorrence without using colouring which may give offence to the sincerely worthy and religious. Many things are lawful which, we are taught, are not convenient; and there are many tones of feeling which are too respectable to be insulted, though we do not altogether sympathise with them.

Dryasdust. Not to mention, my worthy sir, that perhaps you may think the subject exhausted.

Author. The devil take the men of this generation for putting the worst construction on their neighbour's conduct!

So saying, and flinging a testy sort of adieu towards me with his hand, he opened the door and ran hastily downstairs. I started on my feet and rang for my servant, who instantly came. I demanded what had become of the stranger. He denied that any such had been admitted. I pointed to the empty decanters, and he — he — he had the assurance to intimate that such vacancies were sometimes made when I had no better company than my own. I do not know what to make of this doubtful matter, but will certainly imitate your example in placing this dialogue, with my present letter, at the head of *Peveril of the Peak.*

I am, Dear Sir, very much,

Your faithful and obedient Servant,

JONAS DRYASDUST.

Michaelmas Day, 1822,
YORK.

PEVERIL OF THE PEAK

CHAPTER I

When civil dudgeon first grew high,
And men fell out they knew not why ;
When foul words, jealousies, and fears,
Set folk together by the ears.
BUTLER.

WILLIAM, the Conqueror of England, was, or supposed himself to be, the father of a certain William Peveril, who attended him to the battle of Hastings, and there distinguished himself. The liberal-minded monarch, who assumed in his charters the veritable title of Gulielmus Bastardus, was not likely to let his son's illegitimacy be any bar to the course of his royal favour, when the laws of England were issued from the mouth of the Norman victor, and the lands of the Saxons were at his unlimited disposal. William Peveril obtained a liberal grant of property and lordships in Derbyshire, and became the erector of that Gothic fortress which, hanging over the mouth of the Devil's Cavern, so well known to tourists, gives the name of Castleton to the adjacent village.

From this feudal baron, who chose his nest upon the principles on which an eagle selects her eyrie, and built it in such a fashion as if he had intended it, as an Irishman said of the Martello towers, for the sole purpose of puzzling posterity, there was, or conceived themselves to be, descended (for their pedigree was rather hypothetical) an opulent family of knightly rank, in the same county of Derby. The great fief of Castleton, with its adjacent wastes and forests, and all the wonders which they contain, had been forfeited in King John's stormy days by one William Peveril, and had been granted anew to the Lord Ferrers of that day. Yet this William's descendants, though no longer possessed of what they alleged to have been

their original property, were long distinguished by the proud
title of Peverils of the Peak, which served to mark their high
descent and lofty pretensions.

In Charles the Second's time, the representative of this
ancient family was Sir Geoffrey Peveril, a man who had many
of the ordinary attributes of an old-fashioned country gentleman, and very few individual traits to distinguish him from
the general portrait of that worthy class of mankind. He was
proud of small advantages, angry at small disappointments,
incapable of forming any resolution or opinion abstracted from
his own prejudices; he was proud of his birth, lavish in his
housekeeping, convivial with those kindred and acquaintances
who would allow his superiority in rank; contentious and
quarrelsome with all that crossed his pretensions; kind to the
poor, except when they plundered his game ; a Royalist in his
political opinions, and one who detested alike a Roundhead, a
poacher, and a Presbyterian. In religion, Sir Geoffrey was a
High Churchman of so exalted a strain that many thought he
still nourished in private the Roman Catholic tenets, which his
family had only renounced in his father's time, and that he had
a dispensation for conforming in outward observances to the
Protestant faith. There was at least such a scandal amongst
the Puritans, and the influence which Sir Geoffrey Peveril
certainly appeared to possess amongst the Catholic gentlemen
of Derbyshire and Cheshire seemed to give countenance to the
rumour.

Such was Sir Geoffrey, who might have passed to his grave
without farther distinction than a brass plate in the chancel,
had he not lived in times which forced the most inactive spirits
into exertion, as a tempest influences the sluggish waters of
the deadest mere. When the Civil Wars broke out, Peveril
of the Peak, proud from pedigree and brave by constitution,
raised a regiment for the King, and showed upon several occasions more capacity for command than men had heretofore given
him credit for.

Even in the midst of the civil turmoil, he fell in love with,
and married, a beautiful and amiable young lady of the noble
house of Stanley ; and from that time had the more merit in his
loyalty, as it divorced him from her society, unless at very
brief intervals, when his duty permitted an occasional visit to
his home. Scorning to be allured from his military duty by
domestic inducements, Peveril of the Peak fought on for
several rough years of civil war, and performed his part with

sufficient gallantry, until his regiment was surprised and cut to pieces by Poyntz, Cromwell's enterprising and successful general of cavalry. The defeated Cavalier escaped from the field of battle, and, like a true descendant of William the Conqueror, disdaining submission, threw himself into his own castellated mansion, which was attacked and defended in a siege of that irregular kind which caused the destruction of so many baronial residences during the course of those unhappy wars. Martindale Castle, after having suffered severely from the cannon which Cromwell himself brought against it, was at length surrendered when in the last extremity. Sir Geoffrey himself became a prisoner, and while his liberty was only restored upon a promise of remaining a peaceful subject to the Commonwealth in future, his former delinquencies, as they were termed by the ruling party, were severely punished by fine and sequestration.

But neither his forced promise nor the fear of farther unpleasant consequences to his person or property could prevent Peveril of the Peak from joining the gallant Earl of Derby the night before the fatal engagement in Wiggan Lane, where the earl's forces were dispersed. Sir Geoffrey, having had his share in that action, escaped with the relics of the Royalists after the defeat, to join Charles II. He witnessed also the final defeat of Worcester, where he was a second time made prisoner; and as, in the opinion of Cromwell and the language of the times, he was regarded as an obstinate Malignant, he was in great danger of having shared with the Earl of Derby his execution at Bolton-le-Moors, having partaken with him the dangers of two actions. But Sir Geoffrey's life was preserved by the interest of a friend, who possessed influence in the councils of Oliver. This was a Mr. Bridgenorth, a gentleman of middling quality, whose father had been successful in some commercial adventure during the peaceful reign of James I.; and who had bequeathed his son a considerable sum of money, in addition to the moderate patrimony which he inherited from his father.

The substantial, though small-sized, brick building of Moultrassie Hall was but two miles distant from Martindale Castle, and the young Bridgenorth attended the same school with the heir of the Peverils. A sort of companionship, if not intimacy, took place betwixt them, which continued during their youthful sports — the rather that Bridgenorth, though he did not at heart admit Sir Geoffrey's claims of superiority to the extent which the other's vanity would have exacted, paid deference in a reasonable degree to the representative of a family so much more ancient and important than his own, without conceiving that he in any respect degraded himself by doing so.

Mr. Bridgenorth did not, however, carry his complaisance so far as to embrace Sir Geoffrey's side during the Civil War. On the contrary, as an active justice of the peace, he rendered much assistance in arraying the militia in the cause of the Parliament, and for some time held a military commission in that service. This was partly owing to his religious principles, for he was a zealous Presbyterian, partly to his political ideas, which, without being absolutely democratical, favoured the popular side of the great national question. Besides, he was a moneyed man, and to a certain extent had a shrewd eye to his worldly interest. He understood how to improve the opportunities which civil war afforded of advancing his fortune, by a dexterous use of his capital; and he was not at a loss to perceive that these were likely to be obtained by joining the Parliament; while the King's cause, as it was managed, held out nothing to the wealthy but a course of exaction and compulsory loans. For these reasons, Bridgenorth became a decided Roundhead, and all friendly communication betwixt his neighbour and him was abruptly broken asunder. This was done with the less acrimony that, during the Civil War, Sir Geoffrey was almost constantly in the field, following the vacillating and unhappy fortunes of his master; while Major Bridgenorth, who soon renounced active military service, resided chiefly in London, and only occasionally visited the hall.

Upon these visits, it was with great pleasure he received the intelligence that Lady Peveril had shown much kindness to Mrs. Bridgenorth, and had actually given her and her family shelter in Martindale Castle when Moultrassie Hall was threatened with pillage by a body of Prince Rupert's ill-disciplined Cavaliers. This acquaintance had been matured by frequent walks together, which the vicinity of their places of residence suffered the Lady Peveril to have with Mrs. Bridgenorth, who deemed herself much honoured in being thus admitted into the society of so distinguished a lady. Major Bridgenorth heard of this growing intimacy with great pleasure, and he determined to repay the obligation, as far as he could without much hurt to himself, by interfering with all his influence in behalf of her unfortunate husband. It was chiefly owing to Major Bridgenorth's mediation that Sir Geoffrey's life was saved after the battle of Worcester. He obtained him permission to compound for his estate on easier terms than many who had been less obstinate in malignancy; and finally, when, in order to raise the money to pay the composition, the knight was obliged to sell a considerable portion of his patrimony, Major Bridgenorth became the purchaser, and that at a larger price than had been paid to any Cavalier under such circumstances by a member of the Committee for Sequestrations. It is true, the prudent committeeman did not, by any means, lose sight of his own interest in the transaction, for the price was, after all, very moderate, and the property lay adjacent to Moultrassie Hall, the value of which was at least trebled by the acquisition. But then it was also true that the unfortunate owner must have submitted to much worse conditions had the committeeman used, as others did, the full advantages which his situation gave him; and Bridgenorth took credit to himself, and received it from others, for having, on this occasion, fairly sacrificed his interest to his liberality.

Sir Geoffrey Peveril was of the same opinion, and the rather that Mr. Bridgenorth seemed to bear his exaltation with great moderation, and was disposed to show him personally the same deference in his present sunshine of prosperity which he had exhibited formerly in their early acquaintance. It is but justice to Major Bridgenorth to observe that in this conduct he paid respect as much to the misfortunes as to the pretensions of his far-descended neighbour, and that, with the frank generosity of a blunt Englishman, he conceded points of ceremony, about which he himself was indifferent, merely because he saw that his doing so gave pleasure to Sir Geoffrey.

Peveril of the Peak did justice to his neighbour's delicacy, in consideration of which he forgot many things. He forgot that Major Bridgenorth was already in possession of a fair third of his estate, and had various pecuniary claims affecting the remainder to the extent of one-third more. He endeavoured even to forget what it was still more difficult not to remember, the altered situation in which they and their mansions now stood to each other.

Before the Civil War, the superb battlements and turrets of Martindale Castle looked down on the red brick-built hall, as it stole out from the green plantations, just as an oak in Martindale Chase would have looked beside one of the stunted and formal young beech-trees with which Bridgenorth had graced his avenue; but after the siege which we have commemorated the enlarged and augmented hall was as much predominant in

the landscape over the shattered and blackened ruins of the
castle, of which only one wing was left habitable, as the youthful beech, in all its vigour of shoot and bud, would appear to
the same aged oak stripped of its boughs and rifted by lightning, one half laid in shivers on the ground, and the other
remaining a blackened and ungraceful trunk, rent and splintered,
and without either life or leaves. Sir Geoffrey could not but
feel that the situation and prospects were exchanged as disad-
vantageously for himself as the appearance of their mansions ;
and that, though the authority of the man in office under the
Parliament, the sequestrator and the committeeman, had been
only exerted for the protection of the Cavalier and the Malignant, they would have been as effectual if applied to procure
his utter ruin, and that he was become a client while his neighbour was elevated into a patron.

There were two considerations, besides the necessity of the
case and the constant advice of his lady, which enabled Peveril
of the Peak to endure, with some patience, this state of degradation. The first was, that the politics of Major Bridgenorth
began, on many points, to assimilate themselves to his own.
As a Presbyterian, he was not an utter enemy to monarchy, and
had been considerably shocked at the unexpected trial and
execution of the King ; as a civilian and a man of property, he
feared the domination of the military ; and though he wished
not to see Charles restored by force of arms, yet he arrived at
the conclusion that to bring back the heir of the royal family,
on such terms of composition as might ensure the protection of
those popular immunities and privileges for which the Long
Parliament had at first contended, would be the surest and
most desirable termination to the mutations in state affairs
which had agitated Britain. Indeed, the major's ideas on this
point approached so nearly those of his neighbour that he had
wellnigh suffered Sir Geoffrey, who had a finger in almost
all the conspiracies of the Royalists, to involve him in the unfortunate rising of Penruddock and Groves in the west, in which
many of the Presbyterian interest, as well as the Cavalier party,
were engaged. And though his habitual prudence eventually
kept him out of this and other dangers, Major Bridgenorth was
considered, during the last years of Cromwell's domination and
the interregnum which succeeded, as a disaffected person to the
Commonwealth and a favourer of Charles Stuart.

But, besides this approximation to the same political opinions,
another bond of intimacy united the families of the castle and

the hall. Major Bridgenorth, fortunate, and eminently so, in all his worldly transactions, was visited by severe and reiterated misfortunes in his family, and became, in this particular, an object of compassion to his poorer and more decayed neighbour. Betwixt the breaking out of the Civil War and the Restoration, he lost successively a family of no less than six children, apparently through a delicacy of constitution, which cut off the little prattlers at the early age when they most wind themselves around the heart of the parents.

In the beginning of the year 1658, Major Bridgenorth was childless; ere it ended, he had a daughter, indeed, but her birth was purchased by the death of an affectionate wife, whose constitution had been exhausted by maternal grief, and by the anxious and harrowing reflection that from her the children they had lost derived that delicacy of health which proved unable to undergo the tear and wear of existence. The same voice which told Bridgenorth that he was father of a living child (it was the friendly voice of Lady Peveril) communicated to him the melancholy intelligence that he was no longer a husband. The feelings of Major Bridgenorth were strong and deep, rather than hasty and vehement; and his grief assumed the form of a sullen stupor, from which neither the friendly remonstrances of Sir Geoffrey, who did not fail to be with his neighbour at this distressing conjuncture, even though he knew he must meet the Presbyterian pastor, nor the ghostly exhortations of this latter person, were able to rouse the unfortunate widower.

At length Lady Peveril, with the ready invention of a female sharpened by the sight of distress and the feelings of sympathy, tried on the sufferer one of those experiments by which grief is often awakened from despondency into tears. She placed in Bridgenorth's arms the infant whose birth had cost him so dear, and conjured him to remember that his Alice was not yet dead, since she survived in the helpless child she had left to his paternal care.

'Take her away — take her away!' said the unhappy man, and they were the first words he had spoken: 'let me not look on her; it is but another blossom that has bloomed to fade, and the tree that bore it will never flourish more!'

He almost threw the child into Lady Peveril's arms, placed his hands before his face, and wept aloud. Lady Peveril did not say 'Be comforted,' but she ventured to promise that the blossom should ripen to fruit.

'Never — never!' said Bridgenorth; 'take the unhappy child

away, and let me only know when I shall wear black for her.
Wear black!' he exclaimed, interrupting himself, 'what other
colour shall I wear during the remainder of my life?'

'I will take the child for a season,' said Lady Peveril, 'since
the sight of her is so painful to you; and the little Alice shall
share the nursery of our Julian, until it shall be pleasure and
not pain for you to look on her.'

'That hour will never come,' said the unhappy father; 'her
doom is written — she will follow the rest — God's will be done.
Lady, I thank you — I trust her to your care; and I thank God
that my eye shall not see her dying agonies.'

Without detaining the reader's attention longer on this
painful theme, it is enough to say that the Lady Peveril did
undertake the duties of a mother to the little orphan; and
perhaps it was owing, in a great measure, to her judicious
treatment of the infant that its feeble hold of life was preserved,
since the glimmering spark might probably have been altogether
smothered, had it, like the major's former children, undergone
the over-care and over-nursing of a mother rendered nervously
cautious and anxious by so many successive losses. The lady
was the more ready to undertake this charge, that she herself
had lost two infant children; and that she attributed the preservation of the third, now a fine healthy child of three years
old, to Julian's being subjected to rather a different course of
diet and treatment than was then generally practised. She
resolved to follow the same regimen with the little orphan
which she had observed in the case of her own boy; and it was
equally successful. By a more sparing use of medicine, by a
bolder admission of fresh air, by a firm, yet cautious, attention
to encourage rather than to supersede the exertions of nature,
the puny infant, under the care of an excellent nurse, gradually
improved in strength and in liveliness.

Sir Geoffrey, like most men of his frank and good-natured
disposition, was naturally fond of children, and so much compassionated the sorrows of his neighbour that he entirely forgot
his being a Presbyterian, until it became necessary that the
infant should be christened by a teacher of that persuasion.

This was a trying case: the father seemed incapable of giving
direction, and that the threshold of Martindale Castle should
be violated by the heretical step of a dissenting clergyman was
matter of horror to its orthodox owner. He had seen the famous
Hugh Peters, with a Bible in one hand and a pistol in the other,
ride in triumph through the court-door when Martindale was

surrendered; and the bitterness of that hour had entered like iron into his soul. Yet such was Lady Peveril's influence over the prejudices of her husband, that he was induced to connive at the ceremony taking place in a remote garden-house, which was not properly within the precincts of the castle wall. The lady even dared to be present while the ceremony was performed by the Reverend Master Solsgrace, who had once preached a sermon of three hours' length before the House of Commons, upon a thanksgiving occasion after the relief of Exeter. Sir Geoffrey Peveril took care to be absent the whole day from the castle, and it was only from the great interest which he took in the washing, perfuming, and as it were purification, of the summer-house that it could have been guessed he knew anything of what had taken place in it.

But, whatever prejudices the good knight might entertain against his neighbour's form of religion, they did not in any way influence his feelings towards him as a sufferer under severe affliction. The mode in which he showed his sympathy was rather singular, but exactly suited the character of both, and the terms on which they stood with each other.

Morning after morning the good baronet made Moultrassie Hall the termination of his walk or ride, and said a single word of kindness as he passed. Sometimes he entered the old parlour where the proprietor sat in solitary wretchedness and despondency; but more frequently, for Sir Geoffrey did not pretend to great talents of conversation, he paused on the terrace, and stopping or halting his horse by the latticed window, said aloud to the melancholy inmate, 'How is it with you, Master Bridgenorth? (the knight would never acknowledge his neighbour's military rank of major); I just looked in to bid you keep a good heart, man, and to tell you that Julian is well, and little Alice is well, and all are well at Martindale Castle.'

A deep sigh, sometimes coupled with 'I thank you, Sir Geoffrey; my grateful duty waits on Lady Peveril,' was generally Bridgenorth's only answer. But the news was received on the one part with the kindness which was designed upon the other; it gradually became less painful and more interesting; the lattice window was never closed, nor was the leathern easy-chair, which stood next to it, ever empty, when the usual hour of the baronet's momentary visit approached. At length the expectation of that passing minute became the pivot upon which the thoughts of poor Bridgenorth turned during all the rest of the day. Most men have known the influence of such

brief but ruling moments at some period of their lives. The
moment when a lover passes the window of his mistress, the
moment when the epicure hears the dinner-bell, is that into
which is crowded the whole interest of the day ; the hours
which precede it are spent in anticipation, the hours which
follow in reflection on what has passed ; and fancy, dwelling on
each brief circumstance, gives to seconds the duration of minutes, to minutes that of hours. Thus, seated in his lonely chair,
Bridgenorth could catch at a distance the stately step of Sir
Geoffrey, or the heavy tramp of his war-horse, Black Hastings,
which had borne him in many an action ; he could hear the hum
of 'The King shall enjoy his own again,' or the habitual whistle
of 'Cuckolds and Roundheads,' die into reverential silence, as
the knight approached the mansion of affliction ; and then came
the strong, hale voice of the huntsman-soldier with its usual
greeting.

By degrees the communication became something more pro-
tracted, as Major Bridgenorth's grief, like all human feelings,
lost its overwhelming violence, and permitted him to attend,
in some degree, to what passed around him, to discharge various
duties which pressed upon him, and to give a share of attention
to the situation of the country, distracted as it was by the contending factions, whose strife only terminated in the Restoration.
Still, however, though slowly recovering from the effects of the
shock which he had sustained, Major Bridgenorth felt himself
as yet unable to make up his mind to the effort necessary to
see his infant ; and though separated by so short a distance
from the being in whose existence he was more interested than
in anything the world afforded, he only made himself acquainted
with the windows of the apartment where little Alice was lodged,
and was often observed to watch them from the terrace, as they
brightened in the evening under the influence of the setting
sun. In truth, though a strong-minded man in most respects,
he was unable to lay aside the gloomy impression that this
remaining pledge of affection was soon to be conveyed to that
grave which had already devoured all besides that was dear to
him ; and he awaited in miserable suspense the moment when
he should hear that symptoms of the fatal malady had begun
to show themselves.

The voice of Peveril continued to be that of a comforter,
until the month of April 1660, when it suddenly assumed a
new and different tone. 'The King shall enjoy his own again,'
far from ceasing, as the hasty tread of Black Hastings came up

the avenue, bore burden to the clatter of his hoofs on the paved
courtyard, as Sir Geoffrey sprang from his great war-saddle,
now once more garnished with pistols of two feet in length, and,
armed with steel-cap, back and breast, and a truncheon in his
hand, he rushed into the apartment of the astonished major,
with his eyes sparkling and his cheek inflamed, while he called
out, ' Up ! — up, neighbour ! No time now to mope in the
chimney-corner ! Where is your buff-coat and broadsword,
man ? Take the true side once in your life, and mend past
mistakes. The King is all lenity, man — all royal nature and
mercy. I will get your full pardon.'
    ' What means all this ?' said Bridgenorth. ' Is all well with
you — all well at Martindale Castle, Sir Geoffrey ?'
    ' Well as you could wish them, Alice and Julian and all.
But I have news worth twenty of that. Monk has declared at
London against those stinking scoundrels the Rump. Fairfax
is up in Yorkshire for the King — for the King, man ! Churchmen, Presbyterians, and all, are in buff and bandelier for King
Charles. I have a letter from Fairfax to secure Derby and
Chesterfield, with all the men I can make. D—n him, fine
that I should take orders from him ! But never mind that !
all are friends now, and you and I, good neighbour, will charge
abreast, as good neighbours should. See there ! read — read —
read ; and then boot and saddle in an instant.

> Hey for cavaliers, ho for cavaliers,
> Pray for cavaliers,
>   Dub-a-dub, dub-a-dub,
>   Have at old Beelzebub,
>   Oliver shakes in his bier !'

    After thundering forth this elegant effusion of loyal enthu-
siasm, the sturdy Cavalier's heart became too full. He threw
himself on a seat, and exclaiming, ' Did ever I think to live to
see this happy day !' he wept, to his own surprise, as much as
to that of Bridgenorth.
    Upon considering the crisis in which the country was placed,
it appeared to Major Bridgenorth, as it had done to Fairfax and
other leaders of the Presbyterian party, that their frank embracing of the royal interest was the wisest and most patriotic
measure which they could adopt in the circumstances, when all
ranks and classes of men were seeking refuge from the uncertainty and varied oppression attending the repeated contests
between the factions of Westminster Hall and of Wallingford
House. Accordingly, he joined with Sir Geoffrey, with less

enthusiasm indeed, but with equal sincerity, taking such measures as seemed proper to secure their part of the country on
the King's behalf, which was done as effectually and peaceably
as in other parts of England.   The neighbours were both at
Chesterfield when news arrived that the King had landed in
England ; and Sir Geoffrey instantly announced his purpose of
waiting upon his Majesty, even before his return to the Castle
of Martindale.

'Who knows, neighbour,' he said, 'whether Sir Geoffrey
Peveril will ever return to Martindale ?   Titles must be going
amongst them yonder, and I have deserved something among
the rest.   Lord Peveril would sound well — or stay, Earl of
Martindale — no, not of Martindale — Earl of the Peak.   Meanwhile, trust your affairs to me — I will see you secured.   I
would you had been no Presbyterian, neighbour — a knight-
hood — I mean a knight-bachelor, not a knight-baronet — would
have served your turn well.'

'I leave these things to my betters, Sir Geoffrey,' said the
major, 'and desire nothing so earnestly as to find all well at
Martindale when I return.'

'You will — you will find them all well,' said the baronet —
'Julian, Alice, Lady Peveril, and all of them.   Bear my commendations to them, and kiss them all, neighbour, Lady Peveril
and all ; you may kiss a countess when I come back : all will
go well with you now you are turned honest man.'

'I always meant to be so, Sir Geoffrey,' said Bridgenorth,
calmly.

'Well — well — well, no offence meant,' said the knight, 'all
is well now ; so you to Moultrassie Hall, and I to Whitehall.
Said I well, aha ?   So ho, mine host, a stoup of canary to the
King's health ere we get to horse.   I forgot, neighbour, you
drink no healths.'

'I wish the King's health as sincerely as if I drank a gallon
to it,' replied the major ; 'and I wish you, Sir Geoffrey, all
success on your journey, and a safe return.'

CHAPTER II

Why then, we will have bellowing of beeves,
Broaching of barrels, brandishing of spigots ;
Blood shall flow freely, but it shall be gore
Of herds and flocks, and venison and poultry,
Join'd to the brave heart's-blood of John-a-Barleycorn !

Old Play.

WHATEVER rewards Charles might have condescended
to bestow in acknowledgment of the sufferings and
loyalty of Peveril of the Peak, he had none in his
disposal equal to the pleasure which Providence had reserved for
Bridgenorth on his return to Derbyshire. The exertion to which
he had been summoned had had the usual effect of restoring to
a certain extent the activity and energy of his character, and he
felt it would be unbecoming to relapse into the state of lethar-
gic melancholy from which it had roused him. Time also had
its usual effect in mitigating the subjects of his regret ; and
when he had passed one day at the hall in regretting that he
could not expect the indirect news of his daughter's health
which Sir Geoffrey used to communicate in his almost daily call,
he reflected that it would be in every respect becoming that he
should pay a personal visit at Martindale Castle, carry thither
the remembrances of the knight to his lady, assure her of his
health, and satisfy himself respecting that of his daughter.
He armed himself for the worst : he called to recollection the
thin cheeks, faded eye, wasted hand, pallid lip, which had
marked the decaying health of all his former infants.

' I shall see,' he said, ' these signs of mortality once more :
I shall once more see a beloved being to whom I have given
birth gliding to the grave which ought to inclose me long
before her. No matter ! it is unmanly so long to shrink from
that which must be — God's will be done ! '

He went accordingly, on the subsequent morning, to Martindale Castle, and gave the lady the welcome assurances of
her husband's safety, and of his hopes of preferment.

'For the first, may Almighty God be praised!' said the Lady Peveril; 'and be the other as our gracious and restored sovereign may will it. We are great enough for our means, and have means sufficient for contentment, though not for splendour. And now I see, good Master Bridgenorth, the folly of putting faith in idle presentiments of evil. So often had Sir Geoffrey's repeated attempts in favour of the Stewarts led him into new misfortunes, that when, the other morning, I saw him once more dressed in his fatal armour, and heard the sound of his trumpet, which had been so long silent, it seemed to me as if I saw his shroud and heard his death-knell. I say this to you, good neighbour, the rather because I fear your own mind has been harassed with anticipations of impending calamity, which it may please God to avert in your case as it has done in mine; and here comes a sight which bears good assurance of it.'

The door of the apartment opened as she spoke, and two lovely children entered. The eldest, Julian Peveril, a fine boy betwixt four and five years old, led in his hand, with an air of dignified support and attention, a little girl of eighteen months, who rolled and tottered along, keeping herself with difficulty upright by the assistance of her elder, stronger, and masculine companion.

Bridgenorth cast a hasty and fearful glance upon the countenance of his daughter, and, even in that glimpse, perceived, with exquisite delight, that his fears were unfounded. He caught her in his arms, pressed her to his heart, and the child, though at first alarmed at the vehemence of his caresses, presently, as if prompted by nature, smiled in reply to them. Again he held her at some distance from him, and examined her more attentively; he satisfied himself that the complexion of the young cherub he had in his arms was not the hectic tinge of disease, but the clear hue of ruddy health; and that, though her little frame was slight, it was firm and springy.

'I did not think that it could have been thus,' he said, looking to Lady Peveril, who had sat observing the scene with great pleasure; 'but praise be to God in the first instance, and next, thanks to you, madam, who have been His instrument.'

'Julian must lose his playfellow now, I suppose?' said the lady; 'but the hall is not distant, and I will see my little charge often. Dame Martha, the housekeeper at Moultrassie, has sense, and is careful. I will tell her the rules I have observed with little Alice, and ——'

'God forbid my girl should ever come to Moultrassie,' said Major Bridgenorth, hastily; 'it has been the grave of her race. The air of the low grounds suited them not; or there is perhaps a fate connected with the mansion. I will seek for her some other place of abode.'

'That you shall not, under your favour be it spoken, Major Bridgenorth,' answered the lady. 'If you do so, we must suppose that you are undervaluing my qualities as a nurse. If she goes not to her father's house, she shall not quit mine. I will keep the little lady as a pledge of her safety and my own skill; and since you are afraid of the damp of the low grounds, I hope you will come here frequently to visit her.'

This was a proposal which went to the heart of Major Bridgenorth. It was precisely the point which he would have given worlds to arrive at, but which he saw no chance of attaining.

It is too well known that those whose families are long pursued by such a fatal disease as existed in his become, it may be said, superstitious respecting its fatal effects, and ascribe to place, circumstance, and individual care much more perhaps than these can in any case contribute to avert the fatality of constitutional distemper. Lady Peveril was aware that this was peculiarly the impression of her neighbour; that the depression of his spirits, the excess of his care, the feverishness of his apprehensions, the restraint and gloom of the solitude in which he dwelt, were really calculated to produce the evil which most of all he dreaded. She pitied him, she felt for him, she was grateful for former protection received at his hands, she had become interested in the child itself. What female fails to feel such interest in the helpless creature she has tended? And to sum the whole up, the dame had a share of human vanity; and being a sort of Lady Bountiful in her way, for the character was not then confined to the old and the foolish, she was proud of the skill by which she had averted the probable attacks of hereditary malady, so inveterate in the family of Bridgenorth. It needed not, perhaps, in other cases, that so many reasons should be assigned for an act of neighbourly humanity; but civil war had so lately torn the country asunder, and broken all the usual ties of vicinage and good neighbourhood, that it was unusual to see them preserved among persons of different political opinions.

Major Bridgenorth himself felt this; and while the tear of joy in his eye showed how gladly he would accept Lady Peveril's proposal, he could not help stating the obvious incon-

veniences attendant upon her scheme, though it was in the tone
of one who would gladly hear them overruled. 'Madam,' he
said, 'your kindness makes me the happiest and most thankful
of men; but can it be consistent with your own convenience?
Sir Geoffrey has his opinions on many points which have
differed, and probably do still differ, from mine. He is high-
born, and I of middling parentage only. He uses the Church
Service, and I the catechism of the Assembly of Divines at
Westminster——'

'I hope you will find prescribed in neither of them,' said the
Lady Peveril, 'that I may not be a mother to your motherless
child. I trust, Master Bridgenorth, the joyful Restoration of
his Majesty, a work wrought by the direct hand of Providence,
may be the means of closing and healing all civil and religious
dissensions among us, and that, instead of showing the superior
purity of our faith, by persecuting those who think otherwise
from ourselves on doctrinal points, we shall endeavour to show
its real Christian tendency, by emulating each other in actions
of good-will towards man, as the best way of showing our love
to God.'

'Your ladyship speaks what your own kind heart dictates,'
answered Bridgenorth, who had his own share of the narrow-
mindedness of the time; 'and sure am I, that if all who call
themselves loyalists and Cavaliers thought like you —and like
my friend Sir Geoffrey (this he added after a moment's pause,
being perhaps rather complimentary than sincere), we, who
thought it our duty in time past to take arms for freedom of
conscience, and against arbitrary power, might now sit down in
peace and contentment. But I wot not how it may fall. You
have sharp and hot spirits amongst you; I will not say our
power was always moderately used, and revenge is sweet to the
race of fallen Adam.'

'Come, Master Bridgenorth,' said the Lady Peveril, gaily,
'these evil omenings do but point out conclusions which,
unless they were so anticipated, are most unlikely to come to
pass. You know what Shakspeare says —

> To fly the boar before the boar pursues
> Were to incense the boar to follow us,
> And make pursuit when he did mean no chase.

But I crave your pardon; it is so long since we have met that
I forgot you love no play-books.'

'With reverence to your ladyship,' said Bridgenorth, 'I were much to blame did I need the idle words of a Warwickshire stroller to teach me my grateful duty to your ladyship on this occasion, which appoints me to be directed by you in all things which my conscience will permit.'

'Since you allow me such influence, then,' replied the Lady Peveril, 'I shall be moderate in exercising it, in order that I may, in my domination at least, give you a favourable impression of the new order of things. So, if you will be a subject of mine for one day, neighbour, I am going, at my lord and husband's command, to issue out my warrants to invite the whole neighbourhood to a solemn feast at the castle on Thursday next; and I not only pray you to be personally present yourself, but to prevail on your worthy pastor and such neighbours and friends, high and low, as may think in your own way, to meet with the rest of the neighbourhood, to rejoice on this joyful occasion of the King's Restoration, and thereby to show that we are to be henceforward a united people.'

The Parliamentarian major was considerably embarrassed by this proposal. He looked upwards and downwards and around, cast his eye first to the oak-carved ceiling, and anon fixed it upon the floor; then threw it around the room till it lighted on his child, the sight of whom suggested another and a better train of reflections than ceiling and floor had been able to supply.

'Madam,' he said, 'I have long been a stranger to festivity, perhaps from constitutional melancholy, perhaps from the depression which is natural to a desolate and deprived man, in whose ear mirth is marred, like a pleasant air when performed on a mistuned instrument. But though neither my thoughts nor temperament are jovial or mercurial, it becomes me to be grateful to Heaven for the good He has sent me by the means of your ladyship. David, the man after God's own heart, did wash and eat bread when his beloved child was removed; mine is restored to me, and shall I not show gratitude under a blessing, when he showed resignation under an affliction? Madam, I will wait on your gracious invitation with acceptance, and such of my friends with whom I may possess influence, and whose presence your ladyship may desire, shall accompany me to the festivity, that our Israel may be as one people.'

Having spoken these words with an aspect which belonged more to a martyr than to a guest bidden to a festival, and having kissed and solemnly blessed his little girl, Major Bridgenorth took his departure for Moultrassie Hall.

CHAPTER III

Here 's neither want of appetite nor mouths ;
Pray Heaven we be not scant of meat or mirth !
Old Play.

EVEN upon ordinary occasions, and where means were ample, a great entertainment in those days was not such a sinecure as in modern times, when the lady who presides has but to intimate to her menials the day and hour when she wills it to take place. At that simple period, the lady was expected to enter deeply into the arrangement and provision of the whole affair ; and from a little gallery, which communicated with her own private apartment, and looked down upon the kitchen, her shrill voice was to be heard, from time to time, like that of the warning spirit in a tempest, rising above the clash of pots and stew-pans, the creaking of spits, the clattering of marrow-bones and cleavers, the scolding of cooks, and all the other various kinds of din which form an accompaniment to dressing a large dinner.

But all this toil and anxiety was more than doubled in the case of the approaching feast at Martindale Castle, where the presiding genius of the festivity was scarce provided with adequate means to carry her hospitable purpose into effect. The tyrannical conduct of husbands, in such cases, is universal ; and I scarce know one householder of my acquaintance who has not, on some ill-omened and most inconvenient season, announced suddenly to his innocent helpmate that he had invited

Some odious Major Rock,
To drop in at six o'clock,

to the great discomposure of the lady, and the discredit, perhaps, of her domestic arrangements.

Peveril of the Peak was still more thoughtless ; for he had directed his lady to invite the whole honest men of the neighbourhood to make good cheer at Martindale Castle, in honour

of the blessed Restoration of his most sacred Majesty, without
precisely explaining where the provisions were to come from.
The deer-park had lain waste ever since the siege ; the dovecot
could do little to furnish forth such an entertainment ; the
fish-ponds, it is true, were well provided (which the neighbouring Presbyterians noted as a suspicious circumstance), and
game was to be had for the shooting upon the extensive heaths
and hills of Derbyshire. But these were only the secondary
parts of a banquet ; and the house-steward and bailiff, Lady
Peveril's only coadjutors and counsellors, could not agree how
the butcher-meat — the most substantial part, or, as it were, the
main body of the entertainment — was to be supplied. The
house-steward threatened the sacrifice of a fine yoke of young
bullocks, which the bailiff, who pleaded the necessity of their
agricultural services, tenaciously resisted ; and Lady Peveril's
good and dutiful nature did not prevent her from making some
impatient reflections on the want of consideration of her absent
knight, who had thus thoughtlessly placed her in so embarrassing a situation.

These reflections were scarcely just, if a man is only responsible for such resolutions as he adopts when he is fully
master of himself. Sir Geoffrey's loyalty, like that of many
persons in his situation, had, by dint of hopes and fears, victories
and defeats, struggles and sufferings, all arising out of the same
moving cause, and turning, as it were, on the same pivot,
acquired the character of an intense and enthusiastic passion ;
and the singular and surprising change of fortune, by which
his highest wishes were not only gratified but far exceeded,
occasioned for some time a kind of intoxication of loyal rapture
which seemed to pervade the whole kingdom. Sir Geoffrey had
seen Charles and his brothers, and had been received by the
merry monarch with that graceful, and at the same time frank,
urbanity by which he conciliated all who approached him ; the
knight's services and merits had been fully acknowledged, and
recompense had been hinted at, if not expressly promised.
Was it for Peveril of the Peak, in the jubilee of his spirits, to
consider how his wife was to find beef and mutton to feast his
neighbours ?

Luckily, however, for the embarrassed lady, there existed
some one who had composure of mind sufficient to foresee this
difficulty. Just as she had made up her mind, very reluctantly,
to become debtor to Major Bridgenorth for the sum necessary
to carry her husband's commands into effect, and whilst she was

bitterly regretting this departure from the strictness of her
usual economy, the steward, who, by the by, had not been
absolutely sober since the news of the King's landing at Dover,
burst into the apartment, snapping his fingers, and showing
more marks of delight than was quite consistent with the
dignity of my lady's large parlour.

'What means this, Whitaker?' said the lady, somewhat
peevishly; for she was interrupted in the commencement of a
letter to her neighbour on the unpleasant business of the
proposed loan. 'Is it to be always thus with you? Are you
dreaming?'

'A vision of good omen, I trust,' said the steward, with a
triumphant flourish of the hand; 'far better than Pharaoh's,
though, like his, it be of fat kine.'

'I prithee be plain, man,' said the lady, 'or fetch some one
who can speak to purpose.'

'Why, odds-my-life, madam,' said the steward, 'mine errand
can speak for itself. Do you not hear them low? Do you not
hear them bleat? A yoke of fat oxen, and half a score prime
wethers. The castle is victualled for this bout, let them storm
when they will; and Gatherill may have his d—d mains
ploughed to the boot.'

The lady, without farther questioning her elated domestic,
rose and went to the window, where she certainly beheld the
oxen and sheep which had given rise to Whitaker's exultation.
'Whence come they?' said she, in some surprise.

'Let them construe that who can,' answered Whitaker; 'the
fellow who drove them was a west-countryman, and only said
they came from a friend to help to furnish out your ladyship's
entertainment. The man would not stay to drink; I am sorry
he would not stay to drink — I crave your ladyship's pardon for
not keeping him by the ears to drink; it was not my fault.'

'That I'll be sworn it was not,' said the lady.

'Nay, madam, by G—, I assure you it was not,' said the
zealous steward; 'for, rather than the castle should lose credit,
I drank his health myself in double ale, though I had had my
morning draught already. I tell you the naked truth, my lady,
by G—!'

'It was no great compulsion, I suppose,' said the lady; 'but,
Whitaker, suppose you should show your joy on such occasions
by drinking and swearing a little less, rather than a little more,
would it not be as well, think you?'

'I crave your ladyship's pardon,' said Whitaker, with much

reverence; 'I hope I know my place. I am your ladyship's poor servant; and I know it does not become me to drink and swear like your ladyship — that is, like his honour, Sir Geoffrey, I would say. But I pray you, if I am not to drink and swear after my degree, how are men to know Peveril of the Peak's steward — and I may say butler too, since I have had the keys of the cellar ever since old Spigots was shot dead on the north-west turret, with a black-jack in his hand — I say, how is an old Cavalier like me to be known from those cuckoldy Round-heads that do nothing but fast and pray, if we are not to drink and swear according to our degree?'

The lady was silent, for she well knew speech availed nothing; and, after a moment's pause, proceeded to intimate to the steward that she would have the persons whose names were marked in a written paper, which she delivered to him, invited to the approaching banquet.

Whitaker, instead of receiving the list with the mute acqui-escence of a modern major-domo, carried it into the recess of one of the windows, and, adjusting his spectacles, began to read it to himself. The first names, being those of distinguished Cavalier families in the neighbourhood, he muttered over in a tone of approbation — paused and pshawed at that of Bridge-north — yet acquiesced, with the observation, 'But he is a good neighbour, so it may pass for once.' But when he read the name and surname of Nehemiah Solsgrace, the Presbyterian parson, Whitaker's patience altogether forsook him; and he declared he would as soon throw himself into Eldon Hole [1] as consent that the intrusive old Puritan howlet, who had usurped the pulpit of a sound orthodox divine, should ever darken the gates of Martindale Castle by any message or mediation of his. 'The false, crop-eared hypocrites,' cried he, with a hearty oath, 'have had their turn of the good weather. The sun is on our side of the hedge now, and we will pay off old scores, as sure as my name is Richard Whitaker!'

'You presume on your long services, Whitaker, and on your master's absence, or you had not dared to use me thus,' said the lady.

The unwonted agitation of her voice attracted the attention of the refractory steward, notwithstanding his present state of elevation; but he no sooner saw that her eye glistened and her cheek reddened than his obstinacy was at once subdued.

---

[1] A chasm in the earth supposed to be unfathomable; one of the won-ders of the Peak.

'A murrain on me,' he said, 'but I have made my lady angry
in good earnest! and that is an unwonted sight for to see. I
crave your pardon, my lady! It was not poor Dick Whitaker
disputed your honourable commands, but only that second
draught of double ale. We have put a double stroke of malt to
it, as your ladyship well knows, ever since the happy Restoration. To be sure, I hate a fanatic as I do the cloven foot of
Satan; but then your honourable ladyship hath a right to invite
Satan himself, cloven foot and all, to Martindale Castle; and
to send me to hell's gate with a billet of invitation — and so
your will shall be done.'

The invitations were sent round accordingly, in all due form;
and one of the bullocks was sent down to be roasted whole
at the market-place of a little village called Martindale-Moultrassie, which stood considerably to the eastward both of the
castle and hall, from which it took its double name, at about
an equal distance from both; so that, suppose a line drawn from
the one manor-house to the other to be the base of a triangle,
the village would have occupied the salient angle. As the said
village, since the late transference of a part of Peveril's property, belonged to Sir Geoffrey and to Bridgenorth in nearly
equal portions, the lady judged it not proper to dispute the
right of the latter to add some hogsheads of beer to the popular
festivity.

In the meanwhile, she could not but suspect the major
of being the unknown friend who had relieved her from the
dilemma arising from the want of provisions; and she esteemed
herself happy when a visit from him, on the day preceding the
proposed entertainment, gave her, as she thought, an opportunity of expressing her gratitude.

CHAPTER IV

No, sir, I will not pledge ; I 'm one of those
Who think good wine needs neither bush nor preface
To make it welcome. If you doubt my word,
Fill the quart-cup, and see if I will choke on 't.

Old Play.

THERE was a serious gravity of expression in the disclamation with which Major Bridgenorth replied to the
thanks tendered to him by Lady Peveril for the supply
of provisions which had reached her castle so opportunely. He
seemed first not to be aware what she alluded to ; and when
she explained the circumstance, he protested so seriously that
he had no share in the benefit conferred that Lady Peveril was
compelled to believe him ; the rather that, being a man of
plain downright character, affecting no refined delicacy of sentiment, and practising almost a Quaker-like sincerity of expression,
it would have been much contrary to his general character to
have made such a disavowal, unless it were founded in truth.

'My present visit to you, madam,' said he, 'had indeed some
reference to the festivity of to-morrow.' Lady Peveril listened,
but as her visitor seemed to find some difficulty in expressing
himself, she was compelled to ask an explanation. 'Madam,'
said the major, 'you are not perhaps entirely ignorant that the
more tender-conscienced among us have scruples at certain
practices, so general amongst your people at times of rejoicing
that you may be said to insist upon them as articles of faith,
or at least greatly to resent their omission.'

'I trust, Master Bridgenorth,' said the Lady Peveril, not
fully comprehending the drift of his discourse, 'that we shall,
as your entertainers, carefully avoid all allusions or reproaches
founded on past misunderstanding.'

'We would expect no less, madam, from your candour and
courtesy,' said Bridgenorth ; 'but I perceive you do not fully
understand me. To be plain, then, I allude to the fashion of

drinking healths, and pledging each other in draughts of strong
liquor, which most among us consider as a superfluous and
sinful provoking of each other to debauchery, and the excessive
use of strong drink; and which, besides, if derived, as learned
divines have supposed, from the custom of the blinded pagans,
who made libations and invoked idols when they drank, may be
justly said to have something in it heathenish, and allied to
demon-worship.'

The lady had already hastily considered all the topics which
were likely to introduce discord into the proposed festivity; but
this very ridiculous, yet fatal, discrepancy betwixt the manners
of the parties on convivial occasions had entirely escaped her.
She endeavoured to soothe the objecting party, whose brows
were knit like one who had fixed an opinion by which he was
determined to abide.

'I grant,' she said, 'my good neighbour, that this custom is
at least idle, and may be prejudicial if it leads to excess in the
use of liquor, which is apt enough to take place without such
conversation.   But I think, when it hath not this consequence,
it is a thing indifferent, affords a unanimous mode of expressing our good wishes to our friends and our loyal duty to our
sovereign; and, without meaning to put any force upon the
inclination of those who believe otherwise, I cannot see how I
can deny my guests and friends the privilege of drinking a
health to the King, or to my husband, after the old English
fashion.'

'My lady,' said the major, 'if the age of fashion were to
command it, Popery is one of the oldest English fashions that
I have heard of; but it is our happiness that we are not be-
nighted like our fathers, and therefore we must act according
to the light that is in us, and not after their darkness.   I had
myself the honour to attend the Lord-Keeper Whitelocke,
when, at the table of the chamberlain of the kingdom of
Sweden, he did positively refuse to pledge the health of his
queen, Christina, thereby giving great offence and putting in
peril the whole purpose of that voyage; which it is not to be
thought so wise a man would have done, but that he held such
compliance a thing not merely indifferent, but rather sinful
and damnable.'

'With all respect to Whitelocke,' said the Lady Peveril, 'I
continue of my own opinion, though, Heaven knows, I am no
friend to riot or wassail.   I would fain accommodate myself to
your scruples, and will discourage all other pledges; but surely

those of the King and of Peveril of the Peak may be permitted ?'

'I dare not,' answered Bridgenorth, 'lay even the ninety-ninth part of a grain of incense upon an altar erected to Satan.'

'How, sir!' said the lady; 'do you bring Satan into comparison with our master King Charles and with my noble lord and husband ?'

'Pardon me, madam,' answered Bridgenorth, 'I have no such thoughts — indeed they would ill become me. I do wish the King's health and Sir Geoffrey's devoutly, and I will pray for both. But I see not what good it should do their health if I should prejudice my own by quaffing pledges out of quart flagons.'

'Since we cannot agree upon this matter,' said Lady Peveril, 'we must find some resource by which to offend those of neither party. Suppose you winked at our friends drinking these pledges, and we should connive at your sitting still ?'

But neither would this composition satisfy Bridgenorth, who was of opinion, as he expressed himself, that it would be holding a candle to Beelzebub. In fact, his temper, naturally stubborn, was at present rendered much more so by a previous conference with his preacher, who, though a very good man in the main, was particularly and illiberally tenacious of the petty distinctions which his sect adopted; and while he thought with considerable apprehension on the accession of power which Popery, Prelacy, and Peveril of the Peak were like to acquire by the late revolution, became naturally anxious to put his flock on their guard, and prevent their being kidnapped by the wolf. He disliked extremely that Major Bridgenorth, indisputably the head of the Presbyterian interest in that neighbourhood, should have given his only daughter to be, as he termed it, nursed by a Canaanitish woman; and he told him plainly that he liked not this going to feast in the high places with the uncircumcised in heart, and looked on the whole conviviality only as a making merry in the house of Tirzah.

Upon receiving this rebuke from his pastor, Bridgenorth began to suspect he might have been partly wrong in the readiness which, in his first ardour of gratitude, he had shown to enter into intimate intercourse with the Castle of Martindale; but he was too proud to avow this to the preacher, and it was not till after a considerable debate betwixt them that it was mutually agreed, their presence at the entertainment should depend upon the condition that no healths or pledges should be given in their presence. Bridgenorth, therefore, as the delegate and representative of his party, was bound to stand firm against all entreaty, and the lady became greatly embarrassed. She now regretted sincerely that her well-intended invitation had ever been given, for she foresaw that its rejection was to awaken all former subjects of quarrel, and perhaps to lead to new violences amongst people who had not many years since been engaged in civil war. To yield up the disputed point to the Presbyterians would have been to offend the Cavalier party, and Sir Geoffrey in particular, in the most mortal degree; for they made it as firm a point of honour to give healths and compel others to pledge them as the Puritans made it a deep article of religion to refuse both. At length the lady changed the discourse, introduced that of Major Bridgenorth's child, caused it to be sent for and put into his arms. The mother's stratagem took effect; for, though the Parliamentary major stood firm, the father, as in the case of the Governor of Tilbury, was softened, and he agreed that his friends should accept a compromise. This was that the major himself, the reverend divine, and such of their friends as held strict Puritan tenets, should form a separate party in the large parlour, while the hall should be occupied by the jovial Cavaliers; and that each party should regulate their potations after their own conscience or after their own fashion.

Major Bridgenorth himself seemed greatly relieved after this important matter had been settled. He had held it matter of conscience to be stubborn in maintaining his own opinion, but was heartily glad when he escaped from the apparently inevitable necessity of affronting Lady Peveril by the refusal of her invitation. He remained longer than usual, and spoke and smiled more than was his custom. His first care on his return was to announce to the clergyman and his congregation the compromise which he had made, and this not as a matter for deliberation, but one upon which he had already resolved; and such was his authority among them, that, though the preacher longed to pronounce a separation of the parties, and to exclaim 'To your tents, O Israel!' he did not see the chance of being seconded by so many as would make it worth while to disturb the unanimous acquiescence in their delegate's proposal.

Nevertheless, each party being put upon the alert by the consequences of Major Bridgenorth's embassy, so many points of doubt and delicate discussion were started in succession, that the Lady Peveril, the only person, perhaps, who was desirous of achieving an effectual reconciliation between them, incurred in reward for her good intentions the censure of both factions, and had much reason to regret her well-meant project of bringing the Capulets and Montagues of Derbyshire together on the same occasion of public festivity.

As it was now settled that the guests were to form two different parties, it became not only a subject of dispute betwixt themselves which should be first admitted within the Castle of Martindale, but matter of serious apprehension to Lady Peveril and Major Bridgenorth, lest, if they were to approach by the same avenue and entrance, a quarrel might take place betwixt them, and proceed to extremities, even before they reached the place of entertainment. The lady believed she had discovered an admirable expedient for preventing the possibility of such interference, by directing that the Cavaliers should be admitted by the principal entrance, while the Roundheads should enter the castle through a great breach which had been made in the course of the siege, and across which there had been since made a sort of bye-path, to drive the cattle down to their pasture in the wood. By this contrivance the Lady Peveril imagined she had altogether avoided the various risks which might occur from two such parties encountering each other, and disputing for precedence. Several other circumstances of less importance were adjusted at the same time, and apparently so much to the satisfaction of the Presbyterian teacher that, in a long lecture on the subject of the marriage garment, he was at the pains to explain to his hearers that outward apparel was not alone meant by that Scriptural expression, but also a suitable frame of mind for enjoyment of peaceful festivity; and therefore he exhorted the brethren, that, whatever might be the errors of the poor blinded Malignants, with whom they were in some sort to eat and drink upon the morrow, they ought not on this occasion to show any evil will against them, lest they should therein become troublers of the peace of Israel.

Honest Doctor Dummerar, the ejected Episcopal vicar of Martindale *cum* Moultrassie, preached to the Cavaliers on the same subject. He had served the cure before the breaking out of the Rebellion, and was in high favour with Sir Geoffrey, not merely on account of his sound orthodoxy and deep learning, but his exquisite skill in playing at bowls, and his facetious conversation over a pipe and tankard of October. For these latter accomplishments, the doctor had the honour to be recorded by old Century White amongst the roll of lewd, incompetent, profligate clergymen of the Church of England, whom he denounced to God and man, on account chiefly of the heinous sin of playing at games of skill and chance, and of occasionally joining in the social meetings of their parishioners. When the King's party began to lose ground, Doctor Dummerar left his vicarage, and, betaking himself to the camp, showed upon several occasions, when acting as chaplain to Sir Geoffrey Peveril's regiment, that his portly bodily presence included a stout and masculine heart.   When all was lost, and he himself, with most other loyal divines, was deprived of his living, he made such shift as he could ; now lurking in the garrets of old friends in the university, who shared with him, and such as him, the slender means of livelihood which the evil times had left them ; and now lying hid in the houses of the oppressed and sequestrated gentry, who respected at once his character and sufferings.   When the Restoration took place, Doctor Dummerar emerged from some one of his hiding-places, and hied him to Martindale Castle, to enjoy the triumph inseparable from this happy change.

His appearance at the castle in his full clerical dress, and the warm reception which he received from the neighbouring gentry, added not a little to the alarm which was gradually extending itself through the party which were so lately the uppermost.   It is true, Doctor Dummerar framed (honest, worthy man) no extravagant views of elevation or preferment ; but the probability of his being replaced in the living, from which he had been expelled under very flimsy pretences, inferred a severe blow to the Presbyterian divine, who could not be considered otherwise than as an intruder.   The interest of the two preachers, therefore, as well as the sentiments of their flocks, were at direct variance ; and here was another fatal objection in the way of Lady Peveril's scheme of a general and comprehensive healing ordinance.

Nevertheless, as we have already hinted, Doctor Dummerar behaved as handsomely upon the occasion as the Presbyterian incumbent had done.   It is true that, in a sermon which he preached in the castle hall to several of the most distinguished Cavalier families, besides a world of boys from the village, who went to see the novel circumstance of a parson in a cassock and surplice, he went at great length into the foulness of the various crimes committed by the rebellious party during the late evil times, and greatly magnified the merciful and peaceful

nature of the honourable lady of the manor, who condescended
to look upon, or receive into her house in the way of friendship
and hospitality, men holding the principles which had led to
the murder of the King, the slaying and despoiling his loyal
subjects, and the plundering and breaking down of the church
of God. But then he wiped all this handsomely up again with
the observation that, since it was the will of their gracious and
newly restored sovereign, and the pleasure of the worshipful
Lady Peveril, that this contumacious and rebellious race should
be, for a time, forborne by their faithful subjects, it would be
highly proper that all the loyal liegemen should, for the present,
eschew subjects of dissension or quarrel with these sons of
Shimei ; which lesson of patience he enforced by the comfortable
assurance that they could not long abstain from their old
rebellious practices ; in which case, the Royalists would stand
exculpated before God and man in extirpating them from the
face of the earth.

The close observers of the remarkable passages of the times
from which we draw the events of our history have left it
upon record that these two several sermons, much contrary,
doubtless, to the intention of the worthy divines by whom they
were delivered, had a greater effect in exasperating than in
composing the disputes betwixt the two factions. Under such
evil auspices, and with corresponding forebodings on the mind
of Lady Peveril, the day of festivity at length arrived.

By different routes, and forming each a sort of procession,
as if the adherents of each party were desirous of exhibiting
its strength and numbers, the two several factions approached
Martindale Castle ; and so distinct did they appear in dress,
aspect, and manners, that it seemed as if the revellers of a
bridal party and the sad attendants upon a funeral solemnity
were moving towards the same point from different quarters.

The Puritanical party was by far the fewer in numbers, for
which two excellent reasons might be given. In the first place,
they had enjoyed power for several years, and, of course, became
unpopular among the common people, never at any time attached
to those who, being in the immediate possession of authority,
are often obliged to employ it in controlling their humours.
Besides, the country people of England had, and still have, an
animated attachment to field sports, and a natural unrestrained
joviality of disposition, which rendered them impatient under
the severe discipline of the fanatical preachers ; while they were
not less naturally discontented with the military despotism of

Cromwell's major-generals.   Secondly, the people were fickle as
usual, and the return of the King had novelty in it, and was therefore popular.   The side of the Puritans was also deserted at this
period by a numerous class of more thinking and prudential
persons, who never forsook them till they became unfortunate.
These sagacious personages were called in that age the Waiters
upon Providence, and deemed it a high delinquency towards
Heaven if they afforded countenance to any cause longer than
it was favoured by fortune.

But, though thus forsaken by the fickle and the selfish, a
solemn enthusiasm, a stern and determined depth of principle,
a confidence in the sincerity of their own motives, and the
manly English pride which inclined them to cling to their
former opinions, like the traveller in the fable to his cloak, the
more strongly that the tempest blew around them, detained in
the ranks of the Puritans many who, if no longer formidable
from numbers, were still so from their character.   They consisted chiefly of the middling gentry, with others whom industry
or successful speculations in commerce or in mining had raised
into eminence — the persons who feel most umbrage from the
overshadowing aristocracy, and are usually the most vehement
in defence of what they hold to be their rights.   Their dress
was in general studiously simple and unostentatious, or only
remarkable by the contradictory affectation of extreme simplicity
or carelessness.   The dark colour of their cloaks, varying from
absolute black to what was called sad-coloured ; their steeple-
crowned hats, with their broad shadowy brims ; their long
swords, suspended by a simple strap around the loins, without
shoulder-belt, sword-knot, plate, buckles, or any of the other
decorations with which the Cavaliers loved to adorn their trusty
rapiers ; the shortness of their hair, which made their ears
appear of disproportioned size ; above all, the stern and gloomy
gravity of their looks, announced their belonging to that class
of enthusiasts who, resolute and undismayed, had cast down
the former fabric of government, and who now regarded with
somewhat more than suspicion that which had been so unexpectedly substituted in its stead.   There was gloom in their
countenances ; but it was not that of dejection, far less of
despair.   They looked like veterans after a defeat, which may
have checked their career and wounded their pride, but has
left their courage undiminished.

The melancholy, now become habitual, which overcast Major
Bridgenorth's countenance well qualified him to act as the

chief of the group who now advanced from the village. When they reached the point by which they were first to turn aside into the wood which surrounded the castle, they felt a momentary impression of degradation, as if they were yielding the highroad to their old and oft-defeated enemies the Cavaliers. When they began to ascend the winding path, which had been the daily passage of the cattle, the opening of the wooded glade gave them a view of the castle-ditch, half choked with the rubbish of the breach, and of the breach itself, which was made at the angle of a large square flanking-tower, one half of which had been battered into ruins, while the other fragment remained in a state strangely shattered and precarious, and seemed to be tottering above the huge aperture in the wall. A stern, still smile was exchanged among the Puritans, as the sight reminded them of the victories of former days. Holdfast Clegg, a millwright of Derby, who had been himself active at the siege, pointed to the breach, and said, with a grim smile, to Mr. Solsgrace, ' I little thought that, when my own hand helped to level the cannon which Oliver pointed against yon tower, we should have been obliged to climb like foxes up the very walls which we won by our bow and by our spear. Methought these Malignants had then enough of shutting their gates and making high their horn against us.'

' Be patient, my brother,' said Solsgrace — 'be patient, and let not thy soul be disquieted. We enter not this high place dishonourably, seeing we ascend by the gate which the Lord opened to the godly.'

The words of the pastor were like a spark to gunpowder. The countenances of the mournful retinue suddenly expanded, and, accepting what had fallen from him as an omen and a light from Heaven how they were to interpret their present situation, they uplifted, with one consent, one of the triumphant songs in which the Israelites celebrated the victories which had been vouchsafed to them over the heathen inhabitants of the Promised Land :

> ' Let God arise, and then his foes
> Shall turn themselves to flight,
> His enemies for fear shall run,
> And scatter out of sight;
>
> And as wax melts before the fire,
> And wind blows smoke away,
> So in the presence of the Lord,
> The wicked shall decay.

God's army twenty thousand is,
    Of angels bright and strong,
The Lord also in Sinai
    Is present them among.

Thou didst, O Lord, ascend on high,
    And captive led'st them all,
Who, in times past, thy chosen flock
    In bondage did enthral.'

These sounds of devotional triumph reached the joyous band
of the Cavaliers, who, decked in whatever pomp their repeated
misfortunes and impoverishment had left them, were moving
towards the same point, though by a different road, and were
filling the principal avenue to the castle with tiptoe mirth and
revelry.   The two parties were strongly contrasted ; for, during
that period of civil dissension, the manners of the different
factions distinguished them as completely as separate uniforms
might have done.   If the Puritan was affectedly plain in his
dress and ridiculously precise in his manners, the Cavalier
often carried his love of ornament into tawdry finery, and his
contempt of hypocrisy into licentious profligacy.   Gay, gallant
fellows, young and old, thronged together towards the ancient
castle, with general and joyous manifestation of those spirits
which, as they had been buoyant enough to support their
owners during the worst of times, as they termed Oliver's
usurpation, were now so inflated as to transport them nearly
beyond the reach of sober reason.   Feathers waved, lace glit-
tered, spears jingled, steeds caracoled ; and here and there a
petronel or pistol was fired off by some one, who found his own
natural talents for making a noise inadequate to the dignity of
the occasion.   Boys — for, as we said before, the rabble were
with the uppermost party, as usual — hallooed and whooped,
' Down with the Rump,' and 'Fie upon Oliver ! '   Musical instruments, of as many different fashions as were then in use,
played all at once, and without any regard to each other's
tune ; and the glee of the occasion, while it reconciled the
pride of the high-born of the party to fraternise with the
general rout, derived an additional zest from the conscious
triumph that their exultation was heard by their neighbours,
the crestfallen Roundheads.

When the loud and sonorous swell of the psalm-tune, multi-
plied by all the echoes of the cliffs and ruinous halls, came full
upon their ear, as if to warn them how little they were to
reckon upon the depression of their adversaries, at first it was

answered with a scornful laugh, raised to as much height as
the scoffers' lungs would permit, in order that it might carry
to the psalmodists the contempt of their auditors; but this
was a forced exertion of party spleen. There is something in
melancholy feelings more natural to an imperfect and suffering
state than in those of gaiety, and when they are brought into
collision the former seldom fail to triumph. If a funeral-train
and wedding-procession were to meet unexpectedly, it will
readily be allowed that the mirth of the last would be speedily
merged in the gloom of the other. But the Cavaliers, moreover, had sympathies of a different kind. The psalm-tune
which now came rolling on their ear had been heard too often,
and upon too many occasions had preceded victory gained over
the Malignants, to permit them, even in their triumph, to hear
it without emotion. There was a sort of pause, of which the
party themselves seemed rather ashamed, until the silence was
broken by the stout old knight, Sir Jasper Cranbourne, whose
gallantry was so universally acknowledged that he could afford,
if we may use such an expression, to confess emotions which
men whose courage was in any respect liable to suspicion would
have thought it imprudent to acknowledge.

'Adad,' said the old knight, 'may I never taste claret again,
if that is not the very tune with which the prick-eared villains
began their onset at Wiggan Lane, where they trowled us down
like so many ninepins! Faith, neighbours, to say truth and
shame the devil, I did not like the sound of it above half.'

'If I thought the Roundheaded rogues did it in scorn
of us,' said Dick Wildblood of the Dale, 'I would cudgel
their psalmody out of their peasantly throats with this very
truncheon'; a motion which, being seconded by old Roger
Raine, the drunken tapster of the Peveril Arms in the village,
might have brought on a general battle, but that Sir Jasper
forbade the feud.

'We'll have no ranting, Dick,' said the old knight to the
young franklin — 'adad, man, we'll have none, for three reasons:
first, because it would be ungentle to Lady Peveril; then, because it is against the king's peace; and lastly, Dick, because,
if we did set on the psalm-singing knaves, thou mightest come
by the worst, my boy, as has chanced to thee before.'

'Who, I, Sir Jasper!' answered Dick — 'I come by the worst!
I'll be d—d if it ever happened but in that accursed lane,
where we had no more flank, front, or rear than if we had been
so many herrings in a barrel.'

'That was the reason, I fancy,' answered Sir Jasper, 'that
you, to mend the matter, scrambled into the hedge and stuck
there, horse and man, till I beat thee through it with my
leading-staff; and then, instead of charging to the front, you
went right-about, and away as fast as your feet would carry you.'

This reminiscence produced a laugh at Dick's expense, who
was known, or at least suspected, to have more tongue in his
head than mettle in his bosom.   And this sort of rallying on
the part of the knight having fortunately abated the resentment
which had begun to awaken in the breasts of the Royalist cavalcade, farther cause for offence was removed by the sudden
ceasing of the sounds which they had been disposed to interpret
into those of premeditated insult.

This was owing to the arrival of the Puritans at the bottom
of the large and wide breach which had been formerly made in
the wall of the castle by their victorious cannon.   The sight of
its gaping heaps of rubbish, and disjointed masses of building,
up which slowly winded a narrow and steep path, such as is
made amongst ancient ruins by the rare passage of those who
occasionally visit them, was calculated, when contrasted with
the grey and solid massiveness of the towers and curtains which
yet stood uninjured, to remind them of their victory over the
stronghold of their enemies, and how they had bound nobles
and princes with fetters of iron.

But feelings more suitable to the purpose of their visit to
Martindale Castle were awakened in the bosoms even of these
stern sectaries when the lady of the castle, still in the very
prime of beauty and of womanhood, appeared at the top of the
breach with her principal female attendants, to receive her
guests with the honour and courtesy becoming her invitation.
She had laid aside the black dress which had been her sole
attire for several years, and was arrayed with a splendour not
unbecoming her high descent and quality.   Jewels, indeed, she
had none; but her long and dark hair was surmounted with a
chaplet made of oak-leaves, interspersed with lilies; the former
being the emblem of the King's preservation in the Royal Oak,
and the latter, of his happy Restoration.   What rendered her
presence still more interesting to those who looked on her was
the presence of the two children whom she held in either hand;
one of whom was well known to them all to be the child of
their leader, Major Bridgenorth, who had been restored to
life and health by the almost maternal care of the Lady
Peveril.

"The lady of the Castle appeared at the top of the breach."

If even the inferior persons of the party felt the healing influence of her presence, thus accompanied, poor Bridgenorth was almost overwhelmed with it. The strictness of his cast and manners permitted him not to sink on his knee and kiss the hand which held his little orphan ; but the deepness of his obeisance, the faltering tremor of his voice, and the glistening of his eye, showed a grateful respect for the lady whom he addressed, deeper and more reverential than could have been expressed even by Persian prostration. A few courteous and mild words, expressive of the pleasure she found in once more seeing her neighbours as her friends ; a few kind inquiries, addressed to the principal individuals among her guests, concerning their families and connexions, completed her triumph over angry thoughts and dangerous recollections, and disposed men's bosoms to sympathise with the purposes of the meeting.

Even Solsgrace himself, although imagining himself bound by his office and duty to watch over and counteract the wiles of the 'Amalekitish woman,' did not escape the sympathetic infection ; being so much struck with the marks of peace and good-will exhibited by Lady Peveril that he immediately raised the psalm,

> ' O what a happy thing it is,
> And joyful, for to see
> Brethren to dwell together in
> Friendship and unity ! '

Accepting this salutation as a mark of courtesy repaid, the Lady Peveril marshalled in person this party of her guests to the apartment where ample good cheer was provided for them ; and had even the patience to remain while Master Nehemiah Solsgrace pronounced a benediction of portentous length as an introduction to the banquet. Her presence was in some measure a restraint on the worthy divine, whose prolusion lasted the longer, and was the more intricate and embarrassed, that he felt himself debarred from rounding it off by his usual alliterative petition for deliverance from Popery, Prelacy, and Peveril of the Peak, which had become so habitual to him that, after various attempts to conclude with some other form of words, he found himself at last obliged to pronounce the first words of his usual formula aloud, and mutter the rest in such a manner as not to be intelligible even by those who stood nearest to him.

The minister's silence was followed by all the various sounds which announce the onset of a hungry company on a well-

furnished table ; and at the same time gave the lady an opportunity to leave the apartment, and look to the accommodation
of her other company.   She felt, indeed, that it was high time
to do so ; and that the Royalist guests might be disposed to
misapprehend, or even to resent, the prior attentions which she
had thought it prudent to offer to the Puritans.

These apprehensions were not altogether ill-founded.   It
was in vain that the steward had displayed the royal standard,
with its proud motto of *Tandem Triumphans*, on one of the
great towers which flanked the main entrance of the castle ;
while from the other floated the banner of Peveril of the Peak,
under which many of those who now approached had fought
during all the vicissitudes of civil war.   It was in vain he repeated his clamorous ' Welcome, noble Cavaliers ! — welcome,
generous gentlemen ! '   There was a slight murmur amongst
them that their welcome ought to have come from the mouth
of the colonel's lady, not from that of a menial.   Sir Jasper
Cranbourne, who had sense as well as spirit and courage, and
who was aware of his fair cousin's motives, having been indeed
consulted by her upon all the arrangements which she had
adopted, saw matters were in such a state that no time ought
to be lost in conducting the guests to the banqueting-apartment,
where a fortunate diversion from all these topics of rising dis-
content might be made, at the expense of the good cheer of all
sorts which the lady's care had so liberally provided.

The stratagem of the old soldier succeeded in its utmost extent.   He assumed the great oaken chair usually occupied by the
steward at his audits ; and Dr. Dummerar having pronounced
a brief Latin benediction, which was not the less esteemed
by the hearers that none of them understood it, Sir Jasper
exhorted the company to whet their appetites to the dinner by a
brimming cup to his Majesty's health, filled as high and as deep
as their goblets would permit.   In a moment all was bustle
with the clang of wine-cups and of flagons.   In another moment
the guests were on their feet like so many statues, all hushed
as death, but with eyes glancing with expectation, and hands
outstretched, which displayed their loyal brimmers.   The voice
of Sir Jasper, clear, sonorous, and emphatic as the sound of his
war-trumpet, announced the health of the restored monarch,
hastily echoed back by the assemblage, impatient to render it
due homage.   Another brief pause was filled by the draining of
their cups, and the mustering breath to join in a shout so loud
that not only the rafters of the old hall trembled while they

echoed it back, but the garlands of oaken boughs and flowers with which they were decorated waved wildly and rustled as if agitated by a sudden whirlwind. This rite observed, the company proceeded to assail the good cheer with which the table groaned, animated as they were to the attack both by mirth and melody, for they were attended by all the minstrels of the district, who, like the Episcopal clergy, had been put to silence during the reign of the self-entitled saints of the Commonwealth. The social occupation of good eating and drinking, the exchange of pledges betwixt old neighbours who had been fellow-soldiers in the moment of resistance, fellow-sufferers in the time of depression and subjugation, and were now partners in the same general subject of congratulation, soon wiped from their memory the trifling cause of complaint which in the minds of some had darkened the festivity of the day; so that when the Lady Peveril walked into the hall, accompanied as before with the children and her female attendants, she was welcomed with the acclamations due to the mistress of the banquet and of the castle — the dame of the noble knight who had led most of them to battle with an undaunted and persevering valour which was worthy of better success.

Her address to them was brief and matronly, yet spoken with so much feeling as found its way to every bosom. She apologised for the lateness of her personal welcome, by reminding them that there were then present in Martindale Castle that day persons whom recent happy events had converted from enemies into friends, but on whom the latter character was so recently imposed that she dared not neglect with them any point of ceremonial. But those whom she now addressed were the best, the dearest, the most faithful friends of her husband's house, to whom and to their valour Peveril had not only owed those successes which had given them and him fame during the late unhappy times, but to whose courage she in particular had owed the preservation of their leader's life, even when it could not avert defeat. A word or two of heartfelt congratulation on the happy restoration of the royal line and authority completed all which she had boldness to add, and, bowing gracefully round her, she lifted a cup to her lips as if to welcome her guests.

There still remained, and especially amongst the old Cavaliers of the period, some glimmering of that spirit which inspired Froissart, when he declares that a knight hath double courage at need when animated by the looks and words of a beautiful

and virtuous woman. It was not until the reign which was
commencing at the moment we are treating of, that the un-
bounded license of the age, introducing a general course of
profligacy, degraded the female sex into mere servants of
pleasure, and, in so doing, deprived society of that noble tone
of feeling towards the sex which, considered as a spur to 'raise
the clear spirit,' is superior to every other impulse save those
of religion and of patriotism. The beams of the ancient hall
of Martindale Castle instantly rang with a shout louder and
shriller than that at which they had so lately trembled, and the
names of the knight of the Peak and his lady were proclaimed
amid waving of caps and hats, and universal wishes for their
health and happiness.

Under these auspices the Lady Peveril glided from the hall,
and left free space for the revelry of the evening.

That of the Cavaliers may be easily conceived, since it had
the usual accompaniments of singing, jesting, quaffing of healths,
and playing of tunes, which have in almost every age and quarter
of the world been the accompaniments of festive cheer. The
enjoyments of the Puritans were of a different and less noisy
character. They neither sung, jested, heard music, nor drank
healths ; and yet they seemed not the less, in their own phrase,
to enjoy the creature-comforts which the frailty of humanity
rendered grateful to their outward man. Old Whitaker even
protested that, though much the smaller party in point of
numbers, they discussed nearly as much sack and claret as his
own more jovial associates. But those who considered the
steward's prejudices were inclined to think that, in order to
produce such a result, he must have thrown in his own by-
drinkings — no inconsiderable item — to the sum total of the
Presbyterian potations.

Without adopting such a partial and scandalous report, we
shall only say, that on this occasion, as on most others, the
rareness of indulgence promoted the sense of enjoyment, and
that those who made abstinence, or at least moderation, a point
of religious principle, enjoyed their social meeting the better
that such opportunities rarely presented themselves. If they
did not actually drink each other's healths, they at least showed,
by looking and nodding to each other as they raised their
glasses, that they all were sharing the same festive gratification
of the appetite, and felt it enhanced, because it was at the same
time enjoyed by their friends and neighbours. Religion, as it
was the principal topic of their thoughts, became also the chief

subject of their conversation, and as they sat together in small
separate knots, they discussed doctrinal and metaphysical points
of belief, balanced the merits of various preachers, compared the
creeds of contending sects, and fortified by Scriptural quotations
those which they favoured. Some contests arose in the course
of these debates, which might have proceeded farther than was
seemly but for the cautious interference of Major Bridgenorth.
He suppressed also, in the very bud, a dispute betwixt Gaffer
Hodgeson of Charnelycot and the Reverend Mr. Solsgrace upon
the tender subject of lay-preaching and lay-ministering; nor
did he think it altogether prudent or decent to indulge the
wishes of some of the warmer enthusiasts of the party, who felt
disposed to make the rest partakers of their gifts in extem-
poraneous prayer and exposition. These were absurdities that
belonged to the time, which, however, the major had sense
enough to perceive were unfitted, whether the offspring of
hypocrisy or enthusiasm, for the present time and place.

The major was also instrumental in breaking up the party
at an early and decorous hour, so that they left the castle long
before their rivals, the Cavaliers, had reached the spring-tide of
their merriment — an arrangement which afforded the greatest
satisfaction to the lady, who dreaded the consequences which
might not improbably have taken place had both parties met
at the same period and point of retreat.

It was near midnight ere the greater part of the Cavaliers,
meaning such as were able to effect their departure without
assistance, withdrew to the village of Martindale-Moultrassie,
with the benefit of the broad moon to prevent the chance of
accidents. Their shouts, and the burden of their roaring
chorus of —

'The King shall enjoy his own again,'

were heard with no small pleasure by the lady, heartily glad
that the riot of the day was over without the occurrence of any
unpleasing accident. The rejoicing was not, however, entirely
ended; for the elevated Cavaliers, finding some of the villagers
still on foot around a bonfire on the street, struck merrily in
with them, sent to Roger Raine, of the Peveril Arms, the loyal
publican whom we have already mentioned, for two tubs of
merry stingo, as it was termed, and lent their own powerful
assistance at the 'dusting' it off to the health of the King and
the loyal General Monk. Their shouts for a long time disturbed,
and even alarmed, the little village; but no enthusiasm is able

to withstand for ever the natural consequences of late hours
and potations pottle-deep.   The tumult of the exulting Royalists
at last sunk into silence, and the moon and the owl were left in
undisturbed sovereignty over the old tower of the village church,
which, rising white above a circle of knotty oaks, was tenanted
by the bird and silvered by the planet.[1]

_____

[1] See Cavaliers and Roundheads.   Note 1.

CHAPTER V

'T was when they raised, 'mid sap and siege,
The banners of their rightful liege,
    At their she-captain's call,
Who, miracle of womankind !
Lent mettle to the meanest hind
    That mann'd her castle wall.

WILLIAM S. ROSE.

ON the morning succeeding the feast, the Lady Peveril,
fatigued with the exertions and the apprehensions of
the former day, kept her apartment for two or three
hours later than her own active habits and the matutinal custom of the time rendered usual. Meanwhile, Mistress Ellesmere, a person of great trust in the family, and who assumed
much authority in her mistress's absence, laid her orders upon
Deborah, the governante, immediately to carry the children to
their airing in the park, and not to let any one enter the gilded
chamber, which usually was their sporting-place. Deborah,
who often rebelled, and sometimes successfully, against the de-
puted authority of Ellesmere, privately resolved that it was
about to rain, and that the gilded chamber was a more suitable
place for the children's exercise than the wet grass of the park
on a raw morning.

But a woman's brain is sometimes as inconstant as a popular
assembly ; and presently after she had voted the morning was
like to be rainy, and that the gilded chamber was the fittest
play-room for the children, Mistress Deborah came to the
somewhat inconsistent resolution that the park was the fittest
place for her own morning walk. It is certain that, during the
unrestrained joviality of the preceding evening, she had danced
till midnight with Lance Outram, the park-keeper ; but how
far the seeing him just pass the window in his woodland trim,
with a feather in his hat and a cross-bow under his arm, influenced the discrepancy of the opinions Mrs. Deborah formed
concerning the weather, we are far from presuming to guess.
It is enough for us that, so soon as Mistress Ellesmere's back

was turned, Mistress Deborah carried the children into the gilded chamber, not without a strict charge (for we must do her justice) to Master Julian to take care of his little wife, Mistress Alice; and then, having taken so satisfactory a precaution, she herself glided into the park by the glass-door of the still-room, which was nearly opposite to the great breach.

The gilded chamber in which the children were, by this arrangement, left to amuse themselves, without better guardianship than what Julian's manhood afforded, was a large apartment, hung with stamped Spanish leather, curiously gilded, representing, in a manner now obsolete, but far from unpleasing, a series of tilts and combats betwixt the Saracens of Grenada and the Spaniards under the command of King Ferdinand and Queen Isabella, during that memorable siege which was terminated by the overthrow of the last fragments of the Moorish empire in Spain.

The little Julian was careering about the room for the amusement of his infant friend, as well as his own, mimicking with a reed the menacing attitude of the Abencerrages and Zegris engaged in the Eastern sport of hurling the 'jerid,' or javelin; and at times sitting down beside her, and caressing her into silence and good-humour, when the petulant or timid child chose to become tired of remaining an inactive spectator of his boisterous sport; when, on a sudden, he observed one of the panelled compartments of the leather hangings slide apart, so as to show a fair hand, with its fingers resting upon its edge, prepared, it would seem, to push it still farther back. Julian was much surprised, and somewhat frightened, at what he witnessed, for the tales of the nursery had strongly impressed on his mind the terrors of the invisible world. Yet, naturally bold and high-spirited, the little champion placed himself beside his defenceless sister, continuing to brandish his weapon in her defence as boldly as if he had himself been an Abencerrage of Grenada.

The panel, on which his eye was fixed, gradually continued to slide back, and display more and more the form to which the hand appertained, until, in the dark aperture which was disclosed, the children saw the figure of a lady in a mourning dress, past the meridian of life, but whose countenance still retained traces of great beauty, although the predominant character both of her features and person was an air of almost royal dignity. After pausing a moment on the threshold of the portal which she had thus unexpectedly disclosed, and looking with some surprise at the children, whom she had not probably observed while engaged with the management of the panel, the stranger stepped into the apartment, and the panel, upon a touch of a spring, closed behind her so suddenly that Julian almost doubted it had ever been open, and began to apprehend that the whole apparition had been a delusion.[1]

The stately lady, however, advanced to him, and said, ' Are not you the little Peveril ? '

' Yes,' said the boy, reddening, not altogether without a juvenile feeling of that rule of chivalry which forbade any one to disown his name, whatever danger might be annexed to the avowal of it.

' Then,' said the stately stranger, ' go to your mother's room and tell her to come instantly to speak with me.'

' I wo'not,' said the little Julian.

' How ! ' said the lady, ' so young and so disobedient ! but you do but follow the fashion of the time. Why will you not go, my pretty boy, when I ask it of you as a favour ? '

' I would go, madam,' said the boy, ' but ———,' and he stopped short, still drawing back as the lady advanced on him, but still holding by the hand Alice Bridgenorth, who, too young to understand the nature of the dialogue, clung, trembling, to her companion.

The stranger saw his embarrassment, smiled, and remained standing fast, while she asked the child once more, ' What are you afraid of, my brave boy ; and why should you not go to your mother on my errand ? '

' Because,' answered Julian firmly, ' if I go, little Alice must stay alone with you.'

' You are a gallant fellow,' said the lady, ' and will not disgrace your blood, which never left the weak without protection.'

The boy understood her not, and still gazed with anxious apprehension, first on her who addressed him, and then upon his little companion, whose eyes, with the vacant glance of infancy, wandered from the figure of the lady to that of her companion and protector, and at length, infected by a portion of the fear which the latter's magnanimous efforts could not entirely conceal, she flew into Julian's arms, and, clinging to him, greatly augmented his alarm, and, by screaming aloud, rendered it very difficult for him to avoid the sympathetic fear which impelled him to do the same.

---

[1] See Concealment of the Countess of Derby. Note 2.

There was something in the manner and bearing of this unexpected inmate which might justify awe at least, if not fear, when joined to the singular and mysterious mode in which she had made her appearance. Her dress was not remarkable, being the hood and female riding-attire of the time, such as was worn by the inferior class of gentlewomen; but her black hair was very long, and several locks, having escaped from under her hood, hung down dishevelled on her neck and shoulders. Her eyes were deep black, keen, and piercing, and her features had something of a foreign expression. When she spoke, her language was marked by a slight foreign accent, although in construction it was pure English. Her slightest tone and gesture had the air of one accustomed to command and to be obeyed; the recollection of which probably suggested to Julian the apology he afterwards made for being frightened, that he took the stranger for an 'enchanted queen.'

While the stranger lady and the children thus confronted each other, two persons entered almost at the same instant, but from different doors, whose haste showed that they had been alarmed by the screams of the latter.

The first was Major Bridgenorth, whose ears had been alarmed with the cries of his child as he entered the hall, which corresponded with what was called the gilded chamber. His intention had been to remain in the more public apartment until the Lady Peveril should make her appearance, with the good-natured purpose of assuring her that the preceding day of tumult had passed in every respect agreeably to his friends, and without any of those alarming consequences which might have been apprehended from a collision betwixt the parties. But when it is considered how severely he had been agitated by apprehensions for his child's safety and health, too well justified by the fate of those who had preceded her, it will not be thought surprising that the infantine screams of Alice induced him to break through the barriers of form, and intrude farther into the interior of the house than a sense of strict propriety might have warranted.

He burst into the gilded chamber, therefore, by a side door and narrow passage, which communicated betwixt that apartment and the hall, and, snatching the child up in his arms, endeavoured by a thousand caresses to stifle the screams which burst yet more violently from the little girl on beholding herself in the arms of one to whose voice and manner she was, but for one brief interview, an entire stranger.

Of course, Alice's shrieks were redoubled, and seconded by those of Julian Peveril, who on the appearance of this second intruder, was frightened into resignation of every more manly idea of rescue than that which consisted in invoking assistance at the very top of his lungs.

Alarmed by this noise, which in half a minute became very clamorous, Lady Peveril, with whose apartment the gilded chamber was connected by a private door of communication opening into her wardrobe, entered on the scene. The instant she appeared, the little Alice, extricating herself from the grasp of her father, ran towards *her* protectress, and when she had once taken hold of her skirts, not only became silent, but turned her large blue eyes, in which the tears were still glistening, with a look of wonder rather than alarm towards the strange lady. Julian manfully brandished his reed, a weapon which he had never parted with during the whole alarm, and stood prepared to assist his mother if there should be danger in the encounter betwixt her and the stranger.

In fact, it might have puzzled an older person to account for the sudden and confused pause which the Lady Peveril made as she gazed on her unexpected guest, as if dubious whether she did or did not recognise in her still beautiful, though wasted and emaciated, features a countenance which she had known well under far different circumstances.

The stranger seemed to understand her cause of hesitation, for she said in that heart-thrilling voice which was peculiarly her own — 'Time and misfortune have changed me much, Margaret, that every mirror tells me ; yet methinks Margaret Stanley might still have known Charlotte de la Tremouille.'

The Lady Peveril was little in the custom of giving way to sudden emotion, but in the present case she threw herself on her knees in a rapture of mingled joy and grief, and, half embracing those of the stranger, exclaimed in broken language — 'My kind, my noble benefactress — the princely Countess of Derby — the royal Queen in Man — could I doubt your voice, your features, for a moment. Oh, forgive — forgive me !'

The countess raised the suppliant kinswoman of her husband's house with all the grace of one accustomed from early birth to receive homage and to grant protection. She kissed the Lady Peveril's forehead, and passed her hand in a caressing manner over her face as she said — 'You too are changed, my fair cousin, but it is a change becomes you, from a pretty and timid maiden to a sage and comely matron. But my own memory, which I once held a good one, has failed me strangely if this gentleman be Sir Geoffrey Peveril.'

'A kind and good neighbour only, madam,' said Lady Peveril; 'Sir Geoffrey is at court.'

'I understood so much,' said the Countess of Derby, 'when I arrived here last night.'

'How, madam!' said Lady Peveril. 'Did you arrive at Martindale Castle — at the house of Margaret Stanley, where you have such right to command, and did not announce your presence to her?'

'Oh, I know you are a dutiful subject, Margaret,' answered the countess, 'though it be in these days a rare character; but it was our pleasure,' she added with a smile, 'to travel incognito; and finding you engaged in general hospitality, we desired not to disturb you with our royal presence.'

'But how and where were you lodged, madam?' said Lady Peveril; 'or why should you have kept secret a visit which would, if made, have augmented tenfold the happiness of every true heart that rejoiced here yesterday?'

'My lodging was well cared for by Ellesmere — your Ellesmere now, as she was formerly mine; she has acted as quartermaster ere now, you know, and on a broader scale. You must excuse her — she had my positive order to lodge me in the most secret part of your castle (here she pointed to the sliding panel); she obeyed orders in that, and I suppose also in sending you now hither.'

'Indeed I have not yet seen her,' said the lady, 'and therefore was totally ignorant of a visit so joyful, so surprising.'

'And I,' said the countess, 'was equally surprised to find none but these beautiful children in the apartment where I thought I heard you moving. Our Ellesmere has become silly; your good-nature has spoiled her: she has forgotten the discipline she learned under me.'

'I saw her run through the wood,' said the Lady Peveril, after a moment's recollection, 'undoubtedly to seek the person who has charge of the children, in order to remove them.'

'Your own darlings, I doubt not,' said the countess, looking at the children. 'Margaret, Providence has blessed you.'

'That is my son,' said Lady Peveril, pointing to Julian, who stood devouring their discourse with greedy ear; 'the little girl — I may call mine too.'

Major Bridgenorth, who had in the meantime again taken

up his infant, and was engaged in caressing it, set it down as the Countess of Derby spoke, sighed deeply, and walked towards the oriel window. He was well aware that the ordinary rules of courtesy would have rendered it proper that he should withdraw entirely, or at least offer to do so; but he was not a man of ceremonious politeness, and he had a particular interest in the subjects on which the countess's discourse was likely to turn, which induced him to dispense with ceremony. The ladies seemed indeed scarce to notice his presence. The countess had now assumed a chair, and motioned to the Lady Peveril to sit upon a stool which was placed by her side. 'We will have old times once more, though there are here no roaring of rebel guns to drive you to take refuge at my side, and almost in my pocket.'

'I have a gun, madam,' said little Julian, 'and the park-keeper is to teach me how to fire it next year.'

'I will list you for my soldier, then,' said the countess.

'Ladies have no soldiers,' said the boy, looking wistfully at her.

'He has the true masculine contempt of our frail sex, I see,' said the countess; 'it is born with the insolent varlets of mankind, and shows itself as soon as they are out of their long clothes. Did Ellesmere never tell you of Latham House and Charlotte of Derby, my little master?'

'A thousand, thousand times,' said the boy, colouring; 'and how the Queen of Man defended it six weeks against three thousand Roundheads, under Rogue Harrison, the butcher.'

'It was your mother defended Latham House,' said the countess, 'not I, my little soldier. Hadst thou been there, thou hadst been the best captain of the three.'

'Do not say so, madam,' said the boy, 'for mamma would not touch a gun for all the universe.'

'Not I, indeed, Julian,' said his mother; 'there I was for certain, but as useless a part of the garrison ——'

'You forget,' said the countess, 'you nursed our hospital, and made lint for the soldiers' wounds.'

'But did not papa come to help you?' said Julian.

'Papa came at last,' said the countess, 'and so did Prince Rupert; but not, I think, till they were both heartily wished for. Do you remember that morning, Margaret, when the Roundheaded knaves, that kept us pent up so long, retreated without bag or baggage, at the first glance of the Prince's standards appearing on the hill; and how you took every high-

crested captain you saw for Peveril of the Peak, that had been
your partner three months before at the queen's mask? Nay,
never blush for the thought of it — it was an honest affection ;
and though it was the music of trumpets that accompanied
you both to the old chapel, which was almost entirely ruined
by the enemy's bullets, and though Prince Rupert, when he
gave you away at the altar, was clad in buff and bandelier, with
pistols in his belt, yet I trust these warlike signs were no type
of future discord ? '

'Heaven has been kind to me,' said Lady Peveril, 'in blessing me with an affectionate husband.'

'And in preserving him to you,' said the countess, with a
deep sigh ; 'while mine, alas! sealed with his blood his devotion to his king.[1] Oh, had he lived to see this day ! '

'Alas ! alas ! that he was not permitted ! ' answered Lady
Peveril ; 'how had that brave and noble earl rejoiced in the
unhoped-for redemption of our captivity ! '

The countess looked on Lady Peveril with an air of
surprise.

'Thou hast not then heard, cousin, how it stands with our
house ? How indeed had my noble lord wondered, had he
been told that the very monarch for whom he had laid down
his noble life on the scaffold at Bolton-le-Moors should make it
his first act of restored monarchy to complete the destruction
of our property, already wellnigh ruined in the royal cause,
and to persecute me his widow ! '

'You astonish me, madam ! ' said the Lady Peveril. 'It
cannot be that you — that you, the wife of the gallant, the
faithful, the murdered earl — you, Countess of Derby and
Queen in Man — you, who took on you even the character of a
soldier, and seemed a man when so many men proved women
— that you should sustain evil from the event which has
fulfilled — exceeded — the hopes of every faithful subject — it
cannot be ! '

'Thou art as simple, I see, in this world's knowledge as
ever, my fair cousin,' answered the countess. 'This restoration,
which has given others security, has placed me in danger ;
this change, which relieved other Royalists — scarce less zealous,
I presume to think, than I — has sent me here a fugitive, and
in concealment, to beg shelter and assistance from you, fair
cousin.'

---

[1] The Earl of Derby and King in Man was beheaded at Bolton-on-the
Moors, after having been made prisoner in a previous skirmish in Wiggan
Lane.

'From me,' answered the Lady Peveril — 'from me, whose youth your kindness sheltered — from the wife of Peveril, your gallant lord's companion in arms — you have a right to command everything; but, alas! that you should need such assistance as I can render! Forgive me, but it seems like some ill-omened vision of the night : I listen to your words as if I hoped to be relieved from their painful import by awaking.'

'It is indeed a dream — a vision,' said the Countess of Derby; 'but it needs no seer to read it : the explanation hath been long since given — "Put not your faith in princes." I can soon remove your surprise. This gentleman, your friend, is doubtless *honest ?*'

The Lady Peveril well knew that the Cavaliers, like other factions, usurped to themselves the exclusive denomination of the *honest* party, and she felt some difficulty in explaining that her visitor was not honest in that sense of the word.

'Had we not better retire, madam ?' she said to the countess, rising, as if in order to attend her.

But the countess retained her seat. 'It was but a question of habit,' she said; 'the gentleman's principles are nothing to me, for what I have to tell you is widely blazed, and I care not who hears my share of it. You remember — you must have heard, for I think Margaret Stanley would not be indifferent to my fate — that, after my husband's murder at Bolton, I took up the standard which he never dropped until his death, and displayed it with my own hand in our sovereignty of Man.'

'I did indeed hear so, madam,' said the Lady Peveril; 'and that you had bidden a bold defiance to the rebel government, even after all other parts of Britain had submitted to them. My husband, Sir Geoffrey, designed at one time to have gone to your assistance with some few followers; but we learned that the island was rendered to the Parliament party, and that you, dearest lady, were thrown into prison.'

'But you heard not,' said the countess, 'how that disaster befell me. Margaret, I would have held out that island against the knaves as long as the sea continued to flow around it. Till the shoals which surround it had become safe anchorage — till its precipices had melted beneath the sunshine — till of all its strong abodes and castles not one stone remained upon another, would I have defended against these villainous, hypocritical rebels my dear husband's hereditary dominion. The little kingdom of Man should have been yielded only when not an

arm was left to wield a sword, not a finger to draw a trigger,
in its defence. But treachery did what force could never
have done. When we had foiled various attempts upon the
island by open force, treason accomplished what Blake and
Lawson, with their floating castles, had found too hazardous an
enterprise : a base rebel, whom we had nursed in our own
bosoms, betrayed us to the enemy. This wretch was named
Christian —— '

Major Bridgenorth started and turned towards the speaker,
but instantly seemed to recollect himself, and again averted his
face. The countess proceeded, without noticing the interruption, which, however, rather surprised Lady Peveril, who was
acquainted with her neighbour's general habits of indifference
and apathy, and therefore the more surprised at his testify-
ing such sudden symptoms of interest. She would once again
have moved the countess to retire to another apartment, but
Lady Derby proceeded with too much vehemence to endure
interruption.

'This Christian,' she said, 'had eat of my lord his sovereign's
bread, and drunk of his cup, even from childhood; for his
fathers had been faithful servants to the house of Man and
Derby. He himself had fought bravely by my husband's side,
and enjoyed all his confidence ; and when my princely earl was
martyred by the rebels, he recommended to me, amongst other
instructions communicated in the last message I received from
him, to continue my confidence in Christian's fidelity. I obeyed,
although I never loved the man. He was cold and phlegmatic,
and utterly devoid of that sacred fire which is the incentive to
noble deeds, suspected too of leaning to the cold metaphysics of
Calvinistic subtilty. But he was brave, wise, and experienced,
and, as the event proved, possessed but too much interest with
the islanders. When these rude people saw themselves without
hope of relief, and pressed by a blockade, which brought want
and disease into their island, they began to fall off from the
faith which they had hitherto shown.'

'What !' said the Lady Peveril, 'could they forget what was
due to the widow of their benefactor, she who had shared with
the generous Derby the task of bettering their condition ? '

'Do not blame them,' said the countess ; 'the rude herd
acted but according to their kind : in present distress they
forgot former benefits, and, nursed in their earthen hovels, with
spirits suited to their dwellings, they were incapable of feeling
the glory which is attached to constancy in suffering. But

that Christian should have headed their revolt — that he, born a gentleman, and bred under my murdered Derby's own care in all that was chivalrous and noble — that *he* should have forgot a hundred benefits — why do I talk of benefits ? — that he should have forgotten that kindly intercourse which binds man to man far more than the reciprocity of obligation — that he should have headed the ruffians who broke suddenly into my apartment, immured me with my infants in one of my own castles, and assumed or usurped the tyranny of the island — that this should have been done by William Christian, my vassal, my servant, my friend, was a deed of ungrateful treachery which even this age of treason will scarcely parallel ! '

'And you were then imprisoned,' said the Lady Peveril, 'and in your own sovereignty ! '

'For more than seven years I have endured strict captivity,' said the countess. 'I was indeed offered my liberty, and even some means of support, if I would have consented to leave the island, and pledge my word that I would not endeavour to repossess my son in his father's rights. But they little knew the princely house from which I spring, and as little the royal house of Stanley which I uphold, who hoped to humble Charlotte of Tremouille into so base a composition. I would rather have starved in the darkest and lowest vault of Rushin Castle than have consented to aught which might diminish in one hair's breadth the right of my son over his father's sovereignty.'

'And could not your firmness, in a case where hope seemed lost, induce them to be generous, and dismiss you without conditions ? '

'They knew me better than thou dost, wench,' answered the countess ; 'once at liberty, I had not been long without the means of disturbing their usurpation, and Christian would have as soon uncaged a lioness to combat with as have given me the slightest power of returning to the struggle with him. But time had liberty and revenge in store — I had still friends and partizans in the island, though they were compelled to give way to the storm. Even among the islanders at large, most had been disappointed in the effects which they expected from the change of power. They were loaded with exactions by their new masters, their privileges were abridged, and their immunities abolished, under the pretext of reducing them to the same condition with the other subjects of the pretended republic. When the news arrived of the changes which were

current in Britain, these sentiments were privately communicated to me. Calcott and others acted with great zeal and
fidelity ; and a rising, effected as suddenly and effectually as
that which had made me a captive, placed me at liberty and
in possession of the sovereignty of Man, as regent for my
son, the youthful Earl of Derby. Do you think I enjoyed
that sovereignty long without doing justice on that traitor
Christian ?'

'How, madam?' said Lady Peveril, who, though she knew
the high and ambitious spirit of the countess, scarce anticipated
the extremities to which it was capable of hurrying her. 'Have
you imprisoned Christian ?'

'Ay, wench, in that sure prison which felon never breaks
from,' answered the countess.

Bridgenorth, who had insensibly approached them, and was
listening with an agony of interest which he was unable any
longer to suppress, broke in with the stern exclamation — 'Lady,
I trust you have not dared —— '

The countess interrupted him in her turn. 'I know
not who you are who question, and you know not me when
you speak to me of that which I dare, or dare not, do. But
you seem interested in the fate of this Christian, and you
shall hear it. I was no sooner placed in possession of my
rightful power than I ordered the Dempster of the island to
hold upon the traitor a High Court of Justice, with all the
formalities of the isle, as prescribed in its oldest records. The
court was held in the open air, before the Dempster and
the Keys of the island, assembled under the vaulted cope of
heaven, and seated on the terrace of the Zonwald Hill, where
of old Druid and Scald held their courts of judgment. The
criminal was heard at length in his own defence, which amounted
to little more than those specious allegations of public consideration which are ever used to colour the ugly front of treason.
He was fully convicted of his crime, and he received the doom
of a traitor.'

'But which, I trust, is not yet executed ?' said Lady Peveril,
not without an involuntary shudder.

'You are a fool, Margaret,' said the countess, sharply ; 'think
you I delayed such an act of justice until some wretched intrigues of the new English court might have prompted their
interference ? No, wench ; he passed from the judgment-seat
to the place of execution, with no farther delay than might be
necessary for his soul's sake. He was shot to death by a file

of musketeers in the common place of execution, called Hango Hill.'[1]

Bridgenorth clasped his hands together, wrung them, and groaned bitterly.

'As you seem interested for this criminal,' added the countess, addressing Bridgenorth, 'I do him but justice in repeating to you that his death was firm and manly, becoming the general tenor of his life, which, but for that gross act of traitorous ingratitude, had been fair and honourable. But what of that? The hypocrite is a saint, and the false traitor a man of honour, till opportunity, that faithful touchstone, proves their metal to be base.'

'It is false, woman — it is false!' said Bridgenorth, no longer suppressing his indignation.

'What means this bearing, Master Bridgenorth?' said Lady Peveril, much surprised. 'What is this Christian to you, that you should insult the Countess of Derby under my roof?'

'Speak not to me of countesses and of ceremonies,' said Bridgenorth; 'grief and anger leave me no leisure for idle observances, to humour the vanity of overgrown children. O Christian, worthy — well worthy — of the name thou didst bear! My friend — my brother — the brother of my blessed Alice — the only friend of my desolate estate! art thou then cruelly murdered by a female fury, who, but for thee, had deservedly paid with her own blood that of God's saints, which she, as well as her tyrant husband, had spilled like water! Yes, cruel murderess!' he continued, addressing the countess, 'he whom thou hast butchered in thy insane vengeance sacrificed for many a year the dictates of his own conscience to the interest of thy family, and did not desert it till thy frantic zeal for royalty had wellnigh brought to utter perdition the little community in which he was born. Even in confining thee, he acted but as the friends of the madman, who bind him with iron for his own preservation; and for thee, as I can bear witness, he was the only barrier between thee and the wrath of the Commons of England; and but for his earnest remonstrances, thou hadst suffered the penalty of thy malignancy, even like the wicked wife of Ahab.'

'Master Bridgenorth,' said Lady Peveril, 'I will allow for your impatience upon hearing these unpleasing tidings; but there is neither use nor propriety in farther urging this question. If in your grief you forget other restraints, I pray you

---

[1] See Trial and Execution of Christian. Note 3.

to remember that the countess is my guest and kinswoman, and is under such protection as I can afford her. I beseech you, in simple courtesy, to withdraw, as what must needs be the best and most becoming course in these trying circumstances.'

'Nay, let him remain,' said the countess, regarding him with composure, not unmingled with triumph ; 'I would not have it otherwise : I would not that my revenge should be summed up in the stinted gratification which Christian's death hath afforded. This man's rude and clamorous grief only proves that the retribution I have dealt has been more widely felt than by the wretched sufferer himself. I would I knew that it had but made sore as many rebel hearts as there were loyal breasts afflicted by the death of my princely Derby !'

'So please you madam,' said Lady Peveril, 'since Master Bridgenorth hath not the manners to leave us upon my request, we will, if your ladyship lists, leave him, and retire to my apartment. Farewell, Master Bridgenorth ; we will meet hereafter on better terms.'

'Pardon me, madam,' said the major, who had been striding hastily through the room, but now stood fast and drew himself up, as one who has taken a resolution — 'to yourself I have nothing to say but what is respectful ; but to this woman I must speak as a magistrate. She has confessed a murder in my presence — the murder too of my brother-in-law — as a man and as a magistrate I cannot permit her to pass from hence, excepting under such custody as may prevent her farther flight. She has already confessed that she is a fugitive, and in search of a place of concealment, until she should be able to escape into foreign parts. Charlotte, Countess of Derby, I attach thee of the crime of which thou hast but now made thy boast.'

'I shall not obey your arrest,' said the countess, composedly ; 'I was born to give, but not to receive, such orders. What have your English laws to do with my acts of justice and of government within my son's hereditary kingdom ? Am I not Queen in Man as well as Countess of Derby ? A feudatory sovereign indeed ; but yet independent so long as my dues of homage are duly discharged. What right can you assert over me ?'

'That given by the precept of Scripture,' answered Bridgenorth — ' " Whoso spilleth man's blood, by man shall his blood be spilled." Think not the barbarous privileges of ancient feudal customs will avail to screen you from the punishment

due for an Englishman murdered upon pretexts inconsistent
with the Act of Indemnity.'

'Master Bridgenorth,' said Lady Peveril, 'if by fair terms
you desist not from your present purpose, I tell you that I
neither dare nor will permit any violence against this honourable lady within the walls of my husband's castle.'

'You will find yourself unable to prevent me from executing
my duty, madam,' said Bridgenorth, whose native obstinacy
now came in aid of his grief and desire of revenge; 'I am a
magistrate, and act by authority.'

'I know not that,' said Lady Peveril. 'That you *were*
a magistrate, Master Bridgenorth, under the late usurping
powers, I know well; but till I hear of your having a commission in the name of the King, I now hesitate to obey you as
such.'

'I shall stand on small ceremony,' said Bridgenorth. 'Were
I no magistrate, every man has title to arrest for murder
against the terms of the indemnities held out by the King's
proclamations, and I will make my point good.'

'What indemnities? What proclamations?' said the Countess
of Derby, indignantly. 'Charles Stewart may, if he pleases,
and it doth seem to please him, consort with those whose
hands have been red with the blood, and blackened with the
plunder, of his father and of his loyal subjects. He may forgive them if he will, and count their deeds good service. What
has that to do with this Christian's offence against me and
mine? Born a Manxman, bred and nursed in the island, he
broke the laws under which he lived, and died for the breach
of them, after the fair trial which they allowed. Methinks,
Margaret, we have enough of this peevish and foolish magistrate; I attend you to your apartment.'

Major Bridgenorth placed himself betwixt them and the
door, in a manner which showed him determined to interrupt
their passage; when the Lady Peveril, who thought she had
already shown more deference to him in this matter than her
husband was likely to approve of, raised her voice and called
loudly on her steward, Whitaker. That alert person, who had
heard high talking, and a female voice with which he was
unacquainted, had remained for several minutes stationed in
the ante-room, much afflicted with the anxiety of his own
curiosity. Of course he entered in an instant.

'Let three of the men instantly take arms,' said his lady;
'bring them into the ante-room, and wait my farther orders.'

CHAPTER VI

You shall have no worse prison than my chamber,
Nor jailer than myself.

The Captain.

THE command which Lady Peveril laid on her domestics to arm themselves was so unlike the usual gentle acquiescence of her manners that Major Bridgenorth was astonished. 'How mean you, madam?' said he; 'I thought myself under a friendly roof.'

'And you are so, Master Bridgenorth,' said the Lady Peveril, without departing from the natural calmness of her voice and manner; 'but it is a roof which must not be violated by the outrage of one friend against another.'

'It is well, madam,' said Bridgenorth, turning to the door of the apartment. 'The worthy Master Solsgrace has already foretold that the time was returned when high houses and proud names should be once more an excuse for the crimes of those who inhabit the one and bear the other. I believed him not, but now see he is wiser than I. Yet think not I will endure this tamely. The blood of my brother — of the friend of my bosom — shall not long call from the altar, "How long, O Lord, how long?" If there is one spark of justice left in this unhappy England, that proud woman and I shall meet where she can have no partial friend to protect her.'

So saying, he was about to leave the apartment, when Lady Peveril said, 'You depart not from this place, Master Bridgenorth, unless you give me your word to renounce all purpose against the noble countess's liberty upon the present occasion.'

'I would sooner,' answered he, 'subscribe to my own dishonour, madam, written down in express words, than to any such composition. If any man offers to interrupt me, his blood be on his own head!' As Major Bridgenorth spoke, Whitaker threw open the door, and showed that, with the alertness of an old soldier, who was not displeased to see things tend once more towards a state of warfare, he had got with him four stout fellows in the knight of the Peak's livery, well armed with swords and carabines, buff-coats, and pistols at their girdles.

'I will see,' said Major Bridgenorth, 'if any of these men be so desperate as to stop me, a free-born Englishman and a magistrate, in the discharge of my duty.'

So saying, he advanced upon Whitaker and his armed assistants with his hand on the hilt of his sword.

'Do not be so desperate, Master Bridgenorth,' exclaimed Lady Peveril; and added in the same moment, 'Lay hold upon and disarm him, Whitaker, but do him no injury.'

Her commands were obeyed. Bridgenorth, though a man of moral resolution, was not one of those who undertook to cope in person with odds of a description so formidable. He half drew his sword, and offered such show of resistance as made it necessary to secure him by actual force; but then yielded up his weapon, and declared that, submitting to force which one man was unable to resist, he made those who commanded and who employed it responsible for assailing his liberty without a legal warrant.

'Never mind a warrant on a pinch, Master Bridgenorth,' said old Whitaker; 'sure enough you have often acted upon a worse yourself. My lady's word is as good a warrant, sure, as Old Noll's commission; and you bore that many a day, Master Bridgenorth, and, moreover, you laid me in the stocks for drinking the King's health, Master Bridgenorth, and never cared a farthing about the laws of England.'

'Hold your saucy tongue, Whitaker,' said the Lady Peveril; 'and do you, Master Bridgenorth, not take it to heart that you are detained prisoner for a few hours, until the Countess of Derby can have nothing to fear from your pursuit. I could easily send an escort with her that might bid defiance to any force you could muster; but I wish, Heaven knows, to bury the remembrance of old civil dissensions, not to awaken new. Once more, will you think better on it — assume your sword again, and forget whom you have now seen at Martindale Castle?'

'Never,' said Bridgenorth. 'The crime of this cruel woman will be the last of human injuries which I can forget. The last thought of earthly kind which will leave me will be the desire that justice shall be done on her.'

'If such be your sentiments,' said Lady Peveril, 'though they are more allied to revenge than to justice, I must provide for my friend's safety by putting restraint upon your person.

In this room you will be supplied with every necessary of life and every convenience ; and a message shall relieve your domestics of the anxiety which your absence from the hall is not unlikely to occasion. When a few hours, at most two days, are over, I will myself relieve you from confinement, and demand your pardon for now acting as your obstinacy compels me to do.'

The major made no answer, but that he was in her hands, and must submit to her pleasure ; and then turned sullenly to the window, as if desirous to be rid of their presence.

The countess and the Lady Peveril left the apartment arm-in-arm ; and the lady issued forth her directions to Whitaker concerning the mode in which she was desirous that Bridge-north should be guarded and treated during his temporary confinement ; at the same time explaining to him that the safety of the Countess of Derby required that he should be closely watched.

In all proposals for the prisoner's security, such as the regular relief of guards and the like, Whitaker joyfully acquiesced, and undertook, body for body, that he should be detained in captivity for the necessary period. But the old steward was not half so docile when it came to be considered how the captive's bedding and table should be supplied ; and he thought Lady Peveril displayed a very undue degree of attention to her prisoner's comforts. 'I warrant,' he said, 'that the cuckoldy Roundhead ate enough of our fat beef yesterday to serve him for a month ; and a little fasting will do his health good. Marry, for drink he shall have plenty of cold water to cool his hot liver, which, I will be bound, is still hissing with the strong liquors of yesterday. And as for bedding, there are the fine dry boards, more wholesome than the wet straw I lay upon when I was in the stocks, I trow.'

'Whitaker,' said the lady, peremptorily, 'I desire you to provide Master Bridgenorth's bedding and food in the way I have signified to you ; and to behave yourself towards him in all civility.'

'Lack-a-day ! yes, my lady,' said Whitaker ; 'you shall have all your directions punctually obeyed ; but, as an old servant, I cannot but speak my mind.'

The ladies retired after this conference with the steward in the ante-chamber, and were soon seated in another apartment, which was peculiarly dedicated to the use of the mistress of the mansion ; having, on the one side, access to the family bedroom, and on the other, to the still-room, which communicated with the garden. There was also a small door, which, ascending a few steps, led to that balcony, already mentioned, that overhung the kitchen ; and the same passage, by a separate door, admitted to the principal gallery in the chapel ; so that the spiritual and temporal affairs of the castle were placed almost at once within the reach of the same regulating and directing eye.[1]

In the tapestried room from which issued these various sallyports, the countess and Lady Peveril were speedily seated ; and the former, smiling upon the latter, said, as she took her hand, 'Two things have happened to-day which might have surprised me, if anything ought to surprise me in such times. The first is, that yonder Roundheaded fellow should have dared to use such insolence in the house of Peveril of the Peak. If your husband is yet the same honest and downright Cavalier whom I once knew, and had chanced to be at home, he would have thrown the knave out of window. But what I wonder at still more, Margaret, is your generalship. I hardly thought you had courage sufficient to have taken such decided measures, after keeping on terms with the man so long. When he spoke of justices and warrants, you looked so overawed that I thought I felt the clutch of the parish beadles on my shoulder to drag me to prison as a vagrant.'

'We owe Master Bridgenorth some deference, my dearest lady,' answered the Lady Peveril : 'he has served us often and kindly in these late times ; but neither he nor any one else shall insult the Countess of Derby in the house of Margaret Stanley.'

'Thou art become a perfect heroine, Margaret,' replied the countess.

'Two sieges and alarms innumerable,' said Lady Peveril, 'may have taught me presence of mind. My courage is, I believe, as slender as ever.'

'Presence of mind *is* courage,' answered the countess. 'Real valour consists not in being insensible to danger, but in being prompt to confront and disarm it ; and we may have present occasion for all that we possess,' she added, with some slight emotion, 'for I hear the trampling of horses' steps on the pavement of the court.'

In one moment, the boy Julian, breathless with joy, came flying into the room, to say that papa was returned with Lam-

---

[1] See Arrangement of Apartments. Note 4.

ington and Sam Brewer; and that he was himself to ride Black
Hastings to the stable. In the second, the tramp of the honest
knight's heavy jack-boots was heard, as, in his haste to see his
lady, he ascended the staircase by two steps at a time. He
burst into the room, his manly countenance and disordered
dress showing marks that he had been riding fast; and without looking to any one else, caught his good lady in his arms,
and kissed her a dozen of times. Blushing, and with some
difficulty, Lady Peveril extricated herself from Sir Geoffrey's
arms; and in a voice of bashful and gentle rebuke, bid him, for
shame, observe who was in the room.

'One,' said the countess, advancing to him, 'who is right
glad to see that Sir Geoffrey Peveril, though turned courtier
and favourite, still values the treasure which she had some share
in bestowing upon him. You cannot have forgot the raising of
the leaguer of Latham House?'

'The noble Countess of Derby!' said Sir Geoffrey, doffing
his plumed hat with an air of deep deference, and kissing with
much reverence the hand which she held out to him. 'I am
as glad to see your ladyship in my poor house as I would be
to hear that they had found a vein of lead in the Brown
Tor. I rode hard in the hope of being your escort through
the country. I feared you might have fallen into bad hands,
hearing there was a knave sent out with a warrant from the
council.'

'When heard you so? and from whom?'

'It was from Cholmondley of Vale Royal,' said Sir Geoffrey;
'he is come down to make provision for your safety through
Cheshire, and I promised to bring you there in safety. Prince
Rupert, Ormond, and other friends do not doubt the matter
will be driven to a fine; but they say the chancellor and Harry
Bennet, and some others of the over-sea counsellors, are furious
at what they call a breach of the King's proclamation. Hang
them, say I. They left us to bear all the beating, and now
they are incensed that we should wish to clear scores with those
who rode us like nightmares!'

'What did they talk of for my chastisement?' said the
countess.

'I wot not,' said Sir Geoffrey; 'some friends, as I said, from
our kind Cheshire, and others, tried to bring it to a fine; but
some, again, spoke of nothing but the Tower, and a long imprisonment.'

'I have suffered imprisonment long enough for King Charles's

sake,' said the countess, 'and have no mind to undergo it at his
hand. Besides, if I am removed from the personal superintendence of my son's dominions in Man, I know not what new
usurpation may be attempted there. I must be obliged to
you, cousin, to contrive that I may get in security to Vale
Royal, and from thence I know I shall be guarded safely to
Liverpool.'

'You may rely on my guidance and protection, noble lady,'
answered her host, 'though you had come here at midnight, and
with the rogue's head in your apron, like Judith in the Holy
Apocrypha, which I joy to hear once more read in churches.'

'Do the gentry resort much to the court ?' said the lady.

'Ay, madam,' replied Sir Geoffrey; 'and according to our
saying, when miners do begin to bore in these parts, it is "for
the grace of God, and what they there may find."'

'Meet the old Cavaliers with much countenance ?' continued
the countess.

'Faith, madam, to speak truth,' replied the knight, 'the
King hath so gracious a manner that it makes every man's
hopes blossom, though we have seen but few that have ripened
into fruit.'

'You have not yourself, my cousin,' answered the countess,
'had room to complain of ingratitude, I trust ? Few have less
deserved it at the King's hand.'

Sir Geoffrey was unwilling, like most prudent persons, to
own the existence of expectations which had proved falla-
cious, yet had too little art in his character to conceal his dis-
appointment entirely. 'Who ? I, madam ?' he said. 'Alas !
what should a poor country knight expect from the King, besides
the pleasure of seeing him in Whitehall once more, and enjoying
his own again ? And his Majesty was very gracious when I
was presented, and spoke to me of Worcester, and of my horse,
Black Hastings — he had forgot his name, though — faith, and
mine too, I believe, had not Prince Rupert whispered it to him.
And I saw some old friends, such as his Grace of Ormond, Sir
Marmaduke Langdale, Sir Philip Musgrave, and so forth ; and
had a jolly rouse or two, to the tune of old times.'

'I should have thought so many wounds received — so many
dangers risked — such considerable losses — merited something
more than a few smooth words,' said the countess.

'Nay, my lady, there were other friends of mine who had
the same thought,' answered Peveril. 'Some were of opinion
that the loss of so many hundred acres of fair land was worth

some reward of honour at least ; and there were who thought
my descent from William the Conqueror — craving your ladyship's pardon for boasting it in your presence — would not have
become a higher rank or title worse than the pedigree of some
who have been promoted.   But what said the witty Duke of
Buckingham, forsooth — whose grandsire was a Lei'stershire
knight, rather poorer, and scarcely so well-born as myself?
Why, he said that, if all of my degree who deserved well of the
King in the late times were to be made peers, the House of
Lords must meet upon Salisbury Plain!'

'And that bad jest passed for a good argument!' said the
countess ; 'and well it might, where good arguments pass for
bad jests.   But here comes one I must be acquainted with.'

This was little Julian, who now re-entered the hall, leading
his little sister, as if he had brought her to bear witness to the
boastful tale which he told his father, of his having manfully
ridden Black Hastings to the stable-yard, alone in the saddle ;
and that Saunders, though he walked by the horse's head, did
not once put his hand upon the rein, and Brewer, though he
stood beside him, scarce held him by the knee.   The father
kissed the boy heartily ; and the countess, calling him to her
so soon as Sir Geoffrey had set him down, kissed his forehead
also, and then surveyed all his features with a keen and
penetrating eye.

'He is a true Peveril,' said she, 'mixed as he should be with
some touch of the Stanley.   Cousin, you must grant me my
boon, and when I am safely established, and have my present
affair arranged, you must let me have this little Julian of yours
some time hence, to be nurtured in my house, held as my page,
and the playfellow of the little Derby.   I trust in Heaven,
they will be such friends as their fathers have been, and may
God send them more fortunate times!' [1]

'Marry, and I thank you for the proposal with all my heart,
madam,' said the knight.   'There are so many noble houses
decayed, and so many more in which the exercise and discipline
for the training of noble youths is given up and neglected,
that I have often feared I must have kept Gil to be young
master at home ; and I have had too little nurture myself to
teach him much, and so he would have been a mere hunting,
hawking knight of Derbyshire.   But in your ladyship's household, and with the noble young earl, he will have all, and
more than all, the education which I could desire.'

---

[1] See Pages.   Note 5.

'There shall be no distinction betwixt them, cousin,' said the countess; 'Margaret Stanley's son shall be as much the object of care to me as my own, since you are kindly disposed to entrust him to my charge. You look pale, Margaret,' she continued, 'and the tear stands in your eye. Do not be so foolish, my love; what I ask is better than you can desire for your boy; for the house of my father, the Duke de la Tremouille, was the most famous school of chivalry in France; nor have I degenerated from him, or suffered any relaxation in that noble discipline which trained young gentlemen to do honour to their race. You can promise your Julian no such advantages, if you train him up a mere home-bred youth.'

'I acknowledge the importance of the favour, madam,' said Lady Peveril, 'and must acquiesce in what your ladyship honours us by proposing, and Sir Geoffrey approves of; but Julian is an only child, and——'

'An only son,' said the countess, 'but surely not an only child. You pay too high deference to our masters, the male sex, if you allow Julian to engross all your affection, and spare none for this beautiful girl.'

So saying, she set down Julian, and, taking Alice Bridge-north on her lap, began to caress her; and there was, notwithstanding her masculine character, something so sweet in the tone of her voice and in the cast of her features, that the child immediately smiled, and replied to her marks of fondness. This mistake embarrassed Lady Peveril exceedingly. Knowing the blunt impetuosity of her husband's character, his devotion to the memory of the deceased Earl of Derby, and his corresponding veneration for his widow, she was alarmed for the consequences of his hearing the conduct of Bridgenorth that morning, and was particularly desirous that he should not learn it save from herself in private, and after due preparation. But the countess's error led to a more precipitate disclosure.

'That pretty girl, madam,' answered Sir Geoffrey, 'is none of ours; I wish she were. She belongs to a neighbour hard by—a good man, and, to say truth, a good neighbour, though he was carried off from his allegiance in the late times by a d—d Presbyterian scoundrel, who calls himself a parson, and whom I hope to fetch down from his perch presently, with a wannion to him! He has been cock of the roost long enough. There are rods in pickle to switch the Geneva cloak with, I can tell the sour-faced rogues that much. But this child is the daughter of Bridgenorth — neighbour Bridgenorth, of Moultrassie Hall.'

'Bridgenorth!' said the countess. 'I thought I had known all the honourable names in Derbyshire; I remember nothing of Bridgenorth. But stay — was there not a sequestrator and committeeman of that name? Sure, it cannot be he.'

Peveril took some shame to himself as he replied, 'It is the very man whom your ladyship means, and you may conceive the reluctance with which I submitted to receive good offices from one of his kidney; but had I not done so, I should have scarce known how to find a roof to cover Dame Margaret's head.'

The countess, as he spoke, raised the child gently from her lap and placed it upon the carpet, though little Alice showed a disinclination to the change of place, which the Lady of Derby and Man would certainly have indulged in a child of patrician descent and loyal parentage.

'I blame you not,' she said; 'no one knows what temptation will bring us down to. Yet I *did* think Peveril of the Peak would have resided in its deepest cavern sooner than owed an obligation to a regicide.'

'Nay, madam,' answered the knight, 'my neighbour is bad enough, but not so bad as you would make him : he is but a Presbyterian — that I must confess — but not an Independent.'

'A variety of the same monster,' said the countess, 'who hallooed while the others hunted, and bound the victim whom the Independents massacred. Betwixt such sects I prefer the Independents. They are at least bold, barefaced, merciless villains, have more of the tiger in them and less of the crocodile. I have no doubt it was that worthy gentleman who took it upon him this morning——'

She stopped short, for she saw Lady Peveril was vexed and embarrassed.

'I am,' she said, 'the most luckless of beings. I have said something, I know not what, to distress you, Margaret. Mystery is a bad thing, and betwixt us there should be none.'

'There is none, madam,' said Lady Peveril, something impatiently; 'I waited but an opportunity to tell my husband what had happened. Sir Geoffrey, Master Bridgenorth was unfortunately here when the Lady Derby and I met; and he thought it part of his duty to speak of——'

'To speak of what?' said the knight, bending his brows.

'You were ever something too fond, dame, of giving way to the usurpation of such people.'

'I only mean,' said Lady Peveril, 'that as the person — he to whom Lady Derby's story related — was the brother of his late lady, he threatened — but I cannot think that he was serious.'

'Threaten! — threaten the Lady of Derby and Man in my house! — the widow of my friend — the noble Charlotte of Latham House! By Heaven, the prick-eared slave shall answer it! How comes it that my knaves threw him not out of the window?'

'Alas! Sir Geoffrey, you forget how much we owe him,' said the lady.

'Owe him!' said the knight, still more indignant; for in his singleness of apprehension he conceived that his wife alluded to pecuniary obligations; 'if I do owe him some money, hath he not security for it? and must he have the right, over and above, to domineer and play the magistrate in Martindale Castle? Where is he? what have you made of him? I will — I must speak with him.'

'Be patient, Sir Geoffrey,' said the countess, who now discerned the cause of her kinswoman's apprehension; 'and be assured I did not need your chivalry to defend me against this discourteous faitour, as *Morte d'Arthur* would have called him. I promise you, my kinswoman hath fully righted my wrong; and I am so pleased to owe my deliverance entirely to her gallantry, that I charge and command you, as a true knight, not to mingle in the adventure of another.'

Lady Peveril, who knew her husband's blunt and impatient temper, and perceived that he was becoming angry, now took up the story, and plainly and simply pointed out the cause of Master Bridgenorth's interference.

'I am sorry for it,' said the knight; 'I thought he had more sense, and that this happy change might have done some good upon him. But you should have told me this instantly. It consists not with my honour that he should be kept prisoner in this house, as if I feared anything he could do to annoy the noble countess, while she is under my roof, or within twenty miles of this castle.'

So saying, and bowing to the countess, he went straight to the gilded chamber, leaving Lady Peveril in great anxiety for the event of an angry meeting between a temper hasty as that of her husband and stubborn like that of Bridgenorth. Her apprehensions were, however, unnecessary; for the meeting was not fated to take place.

When Sir Geoffrey Peveril, having dismissed Whitaker and his sentinels, entered the gilded chamber, in which he expected to find his captive, the prisoner had escaped, and it was easy to see in what manner. The sliding panel had, in the hurry of the moment, escaped the memory of Lady Peveril, and of Whitaker, the only persons who knew anything of it. It was probable that a chink had remained open, sufficient to indicate its existence to Bridgenorth; who, withdrawing it altogether, had found his way into the secret apartment with which it communicated, and from thence to the postern of the castle by another secret passage, which had been formed in the thickness of the wall, as is not uncommon in ancient mansions; the lords of which were liable to so many mutations of fortune, that they usually contrived to secure some lurking-place and secret mode of retreat from their fortresses. That Bridgenorth had discovered and availed himself of this secret mode of retreat was evident; because the private doors communicating with the postern and the sliding panel in the gilded chamber were both left open.

Sir Geoffrey returned to the ladies with looks of perplexity. While he deemed Bridgenorth within his reach, he was apprehensive of nothing he could do; for he felt himself his superior in personal strength, and in that species of courage which induces a man to rush, without hesitation, upon personal danger. But when at a distance, he had been for many years accustomed to consider Bridgenorth's power and influence as something formidable; and, notwithstanding the late change of affairs, his ideas so naturally reverted to his neighbour as a powerful friend or dangerous enemy, that he felt more apprehension on the countess's score than he was willing to acknowledge even to himself. The countess observed his downcast and anxious brow, and requested to know if her stay there was likely to involve him in any trouble or in any danger.

'The trouble should be welcome,' said Sir Geoffrey, 'and more welcome the danger, which should come on such an account. My plan was, that your ladyship should have honoured Martindale with a few days' residence, which might have been kept private until the search after you was ended. Had I seen this fellow Bridgenorth, I have no doubt I could have compelled him to act discreetly; but he is now at liberty, and will keep out of my reach; and, what is worse, he has the secret of the priest's chamber.'

Here the knight paused, and seemed much embarrassed.

'You can, then, neither conceal nor protect me?' said the countess.

'Pardon, my honoured lady,' answered the knight, 'and let me say out my say. The plain truth is, that this man hath many friends among the Presbyterians here, who are more numerous than I would wish them; and if he falls in with the pursuivant fellow who carries the warrant of the privy council, it is likely he will back him with force sufficient to try to execute it. And I doubt whether any of our friends can be summoned together in haste sufficient to resist such a power as they are like to bring together.'

'Nor would I wish any friends to take arms, in my name, against the King's warrant, Sir Geoffrey,' said the countess.

'Nay, for that matter,' replied the knight, 'an his Majesty will grant warrants against his best friends, he must look to have them resisted. But the best I can think of in this emergence is — though the proposal be something inhospitable — that your ladyship should take presently to horse, if your fatigue will permit. I will mount also, with some brisk fellows, who will lodge you safe at Vale Royal, though the sheriff stopped the way with a whole *posse comitatus*.'

The Countess of Derby willingly acquiesced in this proposal. She had enjoyed a night's sound repose in the private chamber, to which Ellesmere had guided her on the preceding evening, and was quite ready to resume her route, or flight. 'She scarce knew,' she said, 'which of the two she should term it.'

Lady Peveril wept at the necessity which seemed to hurry her earliest friend and protectress from under her roof, at the instant when the clouds of adversity were gathering around her; but she saw no alternative equally safe. Nay, however strong her attachment to Lady Derby, she could not but be more readily reconciled to her hasty departure, when she considered the inconvenience, and even danger, in which her presence, at such a time, and in such circumstances, was likely to involve a man so bold and hot-tempered as her husband Sir Geoffrey.

While Lady Peveril, therefore, made every arrangement which time permitted and circumstances required for the countess prosecuting her journey, her husband, whose spirits always rose with the prospect of action, issued his orders to Whitaker to get together a few stout fellows, with back and breast-pieces, and steel-caps. 'There are the two lackeys, and

Outram and Saunders, besides the other groom fellow, and
Roger Raine, and his son — but bid Roger not come drunk
again — thyself, young Dick of the Dale and his servant, and
a file or two of the tenants ; we shall be enough for any force
they can make. All these are fellows that will strike hard,
and ask no question why : their hands are ever readier than
their tongues, and their mouths are more made for drinking
than speaking.'

Whitaker, apprised of the necessity of the case, asked if he
should not warn Sir Jasper Cranbourne.

'Not a word to him, as you live,' said the knight ; 'this
may be an outlawry, as they call it, for what 1 know ; and
therefore I will bring no lands or tenements into peril saving
mine own. Sir Jasper hath had a troublesome time of it for
many a year. By my will, he shall sit quiet for the rest of 's
days.'

CHAPTER VII

Fang. A rescue ! a rescue !
Mrs. Quickly. Good people, bring a rescue or two.
Henry IV. Part I.

THE followers of Peveril were so well accustomed to the
sound of 'Boot and saddle,' that they were soon
mounted and in order; and in all the form, and with
some of the dignity, of danger proceeded to escort the Countess
of Derby through the hilly and desert tract of country which
connects the frontier of the shire with the neighbouring county
of Cheshire. The cavalcade moved with considerable precaution, which they had been taught by the discipline of the Civil
Wars. One wary and well-mounted trooper rode about two
hundred yards in advance; followed at about half that distance
by two more, with their carabines advanced, as if ready for
action. About one hundred yards behind the advance came
the main body; where the Countess of Derby, mounted on
Lady Peveril's ambling palfrey, for her own had been exhausted
by the journey from London to Martindale Castle, accompanied
by one groom of approved fidelity, and one waiting-maid, was
attended and guarded by the knight of the Peak and three files
of good and practised horsemen. In the rear came Whitaker,
with Lance Outram, as men of especial trust, to whom the
covering the retreat was confided. They rode, as the Spanish
proverb expresses it, ' with the beard on the shoulder,' — looking around, that is, from time to time, and using every precaution to have the speediest knowledge of any pursuit which
might take place.

But, however wise in discipline, Peveril and his followers
were somewhat remiss in civil policy. The knight had communicated to Whitaker, though without any apparent necessity,
the precise nature of their present expedition; and Whitaker
was equally communicative to his comrade Lance, the keeper.
'It is strange enough, Master Whitaker,' said the latter, when

he had heard the case, 'and I wish you, being a wise man, would expound it — why, when we have been wishing for the King, and praying for the King, and fighting for the King, and dying for the King, for these twenty years, the first thing we find to do on his return is to get into harness to resist his warrant!'

'Pooh! you silly fellow,' said Whitaker, 'that is all you know of the true bottom of our quarrel! Why, man, we fought for the King's person against his warrant all along from the very beginning; for I remember the rogues' proclamations, and so forth, always ran in the name of the King and Parliament.'

'Ay! was it even so?' replied Lance. 'Nay, then, if they begin the old game so soon again, and send out warrants in the King's name against his loyal subjects, well fare our stout knight, say I, who is ready to take them down in their stocking-soles. And if Bridgenorth takes the chase after us, I shall not be sorry to have a knock at him for one.'

'Why, the man, bating he is a pestilent Roundhead and Puritan,' said Whitaker, 'is no bad neighbour. What has he done to thee, man?'

'He has poached on the manor,' answered the keeper.

'The devil he has!' replied Whitaker. 'Thou must be jesting, Lance. Bridgenorth is neither hunter nor hawker; he hath not so much of honesty in him.'

'Ay, but he runs after game you little think of, with his sour, melancholy face, that would scare babes and curdle milk,' answered Lance.

'Thou canst not mean the wenches?' said Whitaker; 'why, he hath been melancholy mad with moping for the death of his wife. Thou knowest our lady took the child, for fear he should strangle it, for putting him in mind of its mother, in some of his tantrams. Under her favour, and among friends, there are many poor Cavaliers' children that care would be better bestowed upon. But to thy tale.'

'Why, thus it runs,' said Lance. 'I think you may have noticed, Master Whitaker, that a certain Mistress Deborah hath manifested a certain favour for a certain person in a certain household.'

'For thyself, to wit,' answered Whitaker; 'Lance Outram, thou art the vainest coxcomb——'

'Coxcomb!' said Lance; 'why, 'twas but last night the whole family saw her, as one would say, fling herself at my head.'

'I would she had been a brick-bat, then, to have broken it, for thy impertinence and conceit,' said the steward.

'Well, but do but hearken. The next morning — that is, this very blessed morning — I thought of going to lodge a buck in the park, judging a bit of venison might be wanted in the larder, after yesterday's wassail; and, as I passed under the nursery window, I did but just look up to see what madam governante was about; and so I saw her, through the casement, whip on her hood and scarf as soon as she had a glimpse of me. Immediately after I saw the still-room door open, and made sure she was coming through the garden, and so over the breach and down to the park; and so, thought I, "Aha, Mistress Deb, if you are so ready to dance after my pipe and tabor, I will give you a couranto before you shall come up with me." And so I went down Ivy-Tod Dingle, where the copse is tangled and the ground swampy, and round by Haxley Bottom, thinking all the while she was following, and laughing in my sleeve at the round I was giving her.'

'You deserved to be ducked for it,' said Whitaker, 'for a weather-headed puppy; but what is all this Jack-a-Lantern story to Bridgenorth?'

'Why, it was all along of he, man,' continued Lance, 'that is, of Bridgenorth, that she did not follow me. Gad, I first walked slow, and then stopped, and then turned back a little, and then began to wonder what she had made of herself, and to think I had borne myself something like a jackass in the matter.'

'That I deny,' said Whitaker, 'never jackass but would have borne him better; but go on.'

'Why, turning my face towards the castle, I went back as if I had my nose bleeding, when, just by the Copely thorn, which stands, you know, a flight-shot from the postern gate, I saw Madam Deb in close conference with the enemy.'

'What enemy?' said the steward.

'What enemy! why, who but Bridgenorth? They kept out of sight, and among the copse. "But," thought I, "it is hard if I cannot stalk you, that have stalked so many bucks. If so, I had better give my shafts to be pudding-pins." So I cast round the thicket, to watch their waters; and, may I never bend cross-bow again, if I did not see him give her gold, and squeeze her by the hand!'

'And was that all you saw pass between them?' said the steward.

'Faith, and it was enough to dismount me from my hobby,' said Lance. 'What! when I thought I had the prettiest girl in the castle dancing after my whistle, to find that she gave me the bag to hold, and was smuggling in a corner with a rich old Puritan!'

'Credit me, Lance, it is not as thou thinkest,' said Whitaker. 'Bridgenorth cares not for these amorous toys, and thou thinkest of nothing else. But it is fitting our knight should know that he has met with Deborah in secret, and given her gold; for never Puritan gave gold yet, but it was earnest for some devil's work done or to be done.'

'Nay, but,' said Lance, 'I would not be such a dog-bolt as to go and betray the girl to our master. She hath a right to follow her fancy, as the dame said who kissed her cow; only I do not much approve her choice, that is all. He cannot be six years short of fifty; and a verjuice countenance, under the penthouse of a slouched beaver, and bag of meagre dried bones, swaddled up in a black cloak, is no such temptation, methinks.'

'I tell you once more,' said Whitaker, 'you are mistaken; and that there neither is nor can be any matter of love between them, but only some intrigue, concerning, perhaps, this same noble Countess of Derby. I tell thee, it behoves my master to know it, and I will presently tell it to him.'

So saying, and in spite of all the remonstrances which Lance continued to make on behalf of Mistress Deborah, the steward rode up to the main body of their little party, and mentioned to the knight and the Countess of Derby what he had just heard from the keeper, adding at the same time his own suspicions that Master Bridgenorth of Moultrassie Hall was desirous to keep up some system of espial in the Castle of Martindale, either in order to secure his menaced vengeance on the Countess of Derby, as authoress of his brother-in-law's death, or for some unknown, but probably sinister, purpose.

The knight of the Peak was filled with high resentment at Whitaker's communication. According to his prejudices, those of the opposite faction were supposed to make up by wit and intrigue what they wanted in open force; and he now hastily conceived that his neighbour, whose prudence he always respected, and sometimes even dreaded, was maintaining, for his private purposes, a clandestine correspondence with a member of his family. If this was for the betrayal of his noble guest, it argued at once treachery and presumption; or, viewing the whole as Lance had done, a criminal intrigue with a woman so near the person of Lady Peveril was in itself, he deemed, a piece of sovereign impertinence and disrespect on the part of such a person as Bridgenorth, against whom Sir Geoffrey's anger was kindled accordingly.

Whitaker had scarce regained his post in the rear, when he again quitted it, and galloped to the main body with more speed than before, with the unpleasing tidings that they were pursued by half a score of horsemen and better.

'Ride on briskly to Hartley Nick,' said the knight, 'and there, with God to help, we will bide the knaves. Countess of Derby, one word and a short one. Farewell! you must ride forward with Whitaker and another careful fellow, and let me alone to see that no one treads on your skirts.'

'I will abide with you and stand them,' said the countess; 'you know of old, I fear not to look on man's work.'

'You *must* ride on, madam,' said the knight, 'for the sake of the young earl and the rest of my noble friend's family. There is no manly work which can be worth your looking upon : it is but child's play that these fellows bring with them.'

As she yielded a reluctant consent to continue her flight, they reached the bottom of Hartley Nick — a pass very steep and craggy, and where the road, or rather path, which had hitherto passed over more open ground, became pent up and confined, betwixt copsewood on the one side and on the other the precipitous bank of a mountain stream.

The Countess of Derby, after an affectionate adieu to Sir Geoffrey, and having requested him to convey her kind commendations to her little page-elect and his mother, proceeded up the pass at a round pace, and, with her attendants and escort, was soon out of sight. Immediately after she had disappeared, the pursuers came up with Sir Geoffrey Peveril, who had divided and drawn up his party so as completely to occupy the road at three different points.

The opposite party was led, as Sir Geoffrey had expected, by Major Bridgenorth. At his side was a person in black, with a silver greyhound on his arm ; and he was followed by about eight or ten inhabitants of the village of Martindale-Moultrassie, two or three of whom were officers of the peace, and others were personally known to Sir Geoffrey as favourers of the subverted government.

As the party rode briskly up, Sir Geoffrey called to them to halt; and as they continued advancing, he ordered his own people to present their pistols and carabines; and after assuming that menacing attitude, he repeated, with a voice of thunder, 'Halt, or we fire!'

The other party halted accordingly, and Major Bridgenorth advanced, as if to parley.

'Why, how now, neighbour,' said Sir Geoffrey, as if he had at that moment recognised him for the first time, 'what makes you ride so sharp this morning? Are you not afraid to harm your horse or spoil your spurs?'

'Sir Geoffrey,' said the major, 'I have no time for jesting: I am on the King's affairs.'

'Are you sure it is not upon Old Noll's, neighbour? You used to hold his the better errand,' said the knight, with a smile which gave occasion to a horse-laugh among his followers.

'Show him your warrant,' said Bridgenorth to the man in black formerly mentioned, who was a pursuivant. Then taking the warrant from the officer, he gave it to Sir Geoffrey. 'To this, at least, you will pay regard.'

'The same regard which you would have paid to it a month back or so,' said the knight, tearing the warrant to shreds. 'What a plague do you stare at? Do you think you have a monopoly of rebellion, and that we have not a right to show a trick of disobedience in our turn?'

'Make way, Sir Geoffrey Peveril,' said Bridgenorth, 'or you will compel me to do that I may be sorry for. I am in this matter the avenger of the blood of one of the Lord's saints, and I will follow the chase while Heaven grants me an arm to make my way.'

'You shall make no way here, but at your peril,' said Sir Geoffrey; 'this is my ground. I have been harassed enough for these twenty years by saints, as you call yourselves. I tell you, master, you shall neither violate the security of my house, nor pursue my friends over the grounds, nor tamper, as you have done, amongst my servants, with impunity. I have had you in respect for certain kind doings, which I will not either forget or deny, and you will find it difficult to make me draw a sword or bend a pistol against you; but offer any hostile movement, or presume to advance a foot, and I will make sure of you presently. And for these rascals, who come hither to annoy a noble lady on my bounds, unless you draw them off, I will presently send some of them to the devil before their time.'

'Make room at your proper peril,' said Major Bridgenorth; and he put his right hand on his holster-pistol. Sir Geoffrey closed with him instantly, seized him by the collar, and spurred

Black Hastings, checking him at the same time, so that the horse made a courbette, and brought the full weight of his chest against the counter of the other. A ready soldier might, in Bridgenorth's situation, have rid himself of his adversary with a bullet. But Bridgenorth's courage, notwithstanding his having served some time with the Parliament army, was rather of a civil than a military character; and he was inferior to his adversary, not only in strength and horsemanship, but also and especially in the daring and decisive resolution which made Sir Geoffrey thrust himself readily into personal contest. While, therefore, they tugged and grappled together upon terms which bore such little accordance with their long acquaintance and close neighbourhood, it was no wonder that Bridgenorth should be unhorsed with much violence. While Sir Geoffrey sprung from the saddle, the party of Bridgenorth advanced to rescue their leader, and that of the knight to oppose them. Swords were unsheathed and pistols presented; but Sir Geoffrey, with the voice of a herald, commanded both parties to stand back, and to keep the peace.

The pursuivant took the hint, and easily found a reason for not prosecuting a dangerous duty. 'The warrant,' he said, 'was destroyed. They that did it must be answerable to the council; for his part, he could proceed no farther without his commission.'

'Well said, and like a peaceable fellow!' said Sir Geoffrey. 'Let him have refreshment at the castle; his nag is sorely out of condition. Come, neighbour Bridgenorth, get up, man. I trust you have had no hurt in this mad affray? I was loath to lay hand on you, man, till you plucked out your petronel.'

As he spoke thus, he aided the major to rise. The pursuivant, meanwhile, drew aside; and with him the constable and head-borough, who were not without some tacit suspicion that, though Peveril was interrupting the direct course of law in this matter, yet he was likely to have his offence considered by favourable judges; and therefore it might be as much for their interest and safety to give way as to oppose him. But the rest of the party, friends of Bridgenorth and of his principles, kept their ground notwithstanding this defection, and seemed, from their looks, sternly determined to rule their conduct by that of their leader, whatever it might be.

'But it was evident that Bridgenorth did not intend to renew the struggle. He shook himself rather roughly free from the

hands of Sir Geoffrey Peveril ; but it was not to draw his sword.
On the contrary, he mounted his horse with a sullen and de-
jected air ; and, making a sign to his followers, turned back
the same road which he had come. Sir Geoffrey looked after
him for some minutes. 'Now, there goes a man,' said he,
'who would have been a right honest fellow had he not been
a Presbyterian. But there is no heartiness about them : they
can never forgive a fair fall upon the sod ; they bear malice,
and that I hate as I do a black cloak, or a Geneva skull-cap,
and a pair of long ears rising on each side on 't, like two
chimneys at the gable ends of a thatched cottage. They are
as sly as the devil to boot ; and, therefore, Lance Outram, take
two with you, and keep after them, that they may not turn
our flank, and get on the track of the countess again after
all.'

'I had as soon they should course my lady's white tame
doe,' answered Lance, in the spirit of his calling. He proceeded
to execute his master's orders by dogging Major Bridgenorth
at a distance, and observing his course from such heights as
commanded the country. But it was soon evident that no
manoeuvre was intended, and that the major was taking the
direct road homeward. When this was ascertained, Sir Geoffrey
dismissed most of his followers ; and, retaining only his own
domestics, rode hastily forward to overtake the countess.

It is only necessary to say farther, that he completed his
purpose of escorting the Countess of Derby to Vale Royal,
without meeting any farther hindrance by the way. The
lord of the mansion readily undertook to conduct the high-
minded lady to Liverpool, and the task of seeing her safely
embarked for her son's hereditary dominions, where there was
no doubt of her remaining in personal safety until the accusation
against her for breach of the royal indemnity, by the execution
of Christian, could be brought to some compromise.

For a length of time this was no easy matter. Clarendon,
then at the head of Charles's administration, considered her
rash action, though dictated by motives which the human
breast must, in some respects, sympathise with, as calculated
to shake the restored tranquillity of England, by exciting the
doubts and jealousies of those who had to apprehend the consequences of what is called, in our own days, a reaction. At the
same time, the high services of this distinguished family, the
merits of the countess herself, the memory of her gallant
husband, and the very peculiar circumstances of jurisdiction

which took the case out of all common rules, pleaded strongly in her favour ; and the death of Christian was at length only punished by the imposition of a heavy fine, amounting, we believe, to many thousand pounds, which was levied, with great difficulty, out of the shattered estates of the young Earl of Derby.

CHAPTER VIII

My native land, good-night !
BYRON.

LADY PEVERIL remained in no small anxiety for several hours after her husband and the countess had departed from Martindale Castle; more especially when she learned that Major Bridgenorth, concerning whose motions she made private inquiry, had taken horse with a party, and was gone to the westward in the same direction with Sir Geoffrey.

At length her immediate uneasiness in regard to the safety of her husband and the countess was removed by the arrival of Whitaker, with her husband's commendations, and an account of the scuffle betwixt himself and Major Bridgenorth.

Lady Peveril shuddered to see how nearly they had approached to renewal of the scenes of civil discord; and while she was thankful to Heaven for her husband's immediate preservation, she could not help feeling both regret and apprehension for the consequences of his quarrel with Major Bridgenorth. They had now lost an old friend, who had showed himself such under those circumstances of adversity by which friendship is most severely tried; and she could not disguise from herself that Bridgenorth, thus irritated, might be a troublesome, if not a dangerous, enemy. His rights as a creditor he had hitherto used with gentleness; but if he should employ rigour, Lady Peveril, whose attention to domestic economy had made her much better acquainted with her husband's affairs than he was himself, foresaw considerable inconvenience from the measures which the law put in his power. She comforted herself with the recollection, however, that she had still a strong hold on Bridgenorth, through his paternal affection, and from the fixed opinion which he had hitherto manifested that his daughter's health could only flourish while under her charge. But any expectations of reconciliation which Lady

Peveril might probably have founded on this circumstance were frustrated by an incident which took place in the course of the following morning.

The governante, Mistress Deborah, who has been already mentioned, went forth, as usual, with the children, to take their morning exercise in the park, accompanied by Rachael, a girl who acted occasionally as her assistant in attending upon them. But not as usual did she return. It was near the hour of breakfast, when Ellesmere, with an unwonted degree of primness in her mouth and manner, came to acquaint her lady that Mistress Deborah had not thought proper to come back from the park, though the breakfast-hour approached so near.

'She will come, then, presently,' said Lady Peveril, with indifference.

Ellesmere gave a short and doubtful cough, and then proceeded to say, that Rachael had been sent home with little Master Julian, and that Mistress Deborah had been pleased to say she would walk on with Miss Bridgenorth as far as Moultrassie Holt; which was a point at which the property of the major, as matters now stood, bounded that of Sir Geoffrey Peveril.

'Is the wench turned silly,' exclaimed the lady, something angrily, 'that she does not obey my orders, and return at regular hours?'

'She may be turning silly,' said Ellesmere, mysteriously; 'or she may be turning too sly; and I think it were as well your ladyship looked to it.'

'Looked to what, Ellesmere?' said the lady, impatiently. 'You are strangely oracular this morning. If you know anything to the prejudice of this young woman, I pray you speak it out.'

'I prejudice!' said Ellesmere. 'I scorn to prejudice man, woman, or child in the way of a fellow-servant; only I wish your ladyship to look about you, and use your own eyes, that is all.'

'You bid me use my own eyes, Ellesmere; but I suspect,' answered the lady, 'you would be better pleased were I contented to see through your spectacles. I charge you — and you know I will be obeyed — I charge you to tell me what you know or suspect about this girl, Deborah Debbitch.'

'*I* see through spectacles!' exclaimed the indignant abigail; 'your ladyship will pardon me in that, for I never use them, unless a pair that belonged to my poor mother, which I put on when your ladyship wants your pinners curiously wrought. No woman above sixteen ever did white-seam without barnacles. And then as to suspecting, I suspect nothing; for, as your ladyship hath taken Mistress Deborah Debbitch from under my hand, to be sure it is neither bread nor butter of mine. Only (here she began to speak with her lips shut, so as scarce to permit a sound to issue, and mincing her words as if she pinched off the ends of them before she suffered them to escape) — only, madam, if Mistress Deborah goes so often of a morning to Moultrassie Holt, why, I should not be surprised if she should never find the way back again.'

'Once more, what do you mean, Ellesmere? You were wont to have some sense; let me know distinctly what the matter is.'

'Only, madam,' pursued the abigail, 'that, since Bridgenorth came back from Chesterfield, and saw you at the castle hall, Mistress Deborah has been pleased to carry the children every morning to that place; and it has so happened that she has often met the major, as they call him, there in his walks — for he can walk about now like other folks — and I warrant you she hath not been the worse of the meeting — one way at least, for she hath bought a new hood might serve yourself, madam; but whether she hath had anything in hand besides a piece of money, no doubt your ladyship is best judge.'

Lady Peveril, who readily adopted the more good-natured construction of the governante's motives, could not help laughing at the idea of a man of Bridgenorth's precise appearance, strict principles, and reserved habits being suspected of a design of gallantry; and readily concluded that Mistress Deborah had found her advantage in gratifying his parental affection by a frequent sight of his daughter during the few days which intervened betwixt his first seeing little Alice at the castle and the events which had followed. But she was somewhat surprised when, an hour after the usual breakfast-hour, during which neither the child nor Mistress Deborah appeared, Major Bridgenorth's only man-servant arrived at the castle on horseback, dressed as for a journey; and having delivered a letter addressed to herself, and another to Mistress Ellesmere, rode away without waiting any answer.

There would have been nothing remarkable in this, had any other person been concerned; but Major Bridgenorth was so very quiet and orderly in all his proceedings, so little liable to act hastily or by impulse, that the least appearance of bustle where he was concerned excited surprise and curiosity.

Lady Peveril broke her letter hastily open, and found that it contained the following lines : —

'For the hands of the Honourable and Honoured
Lady Peveril — These :

' MADAM — Please it your Ladyship,

' I write more to excuse myself to your ladyship than to accuse either you or others, in respect that I am sensible it becomes our frail nature better to confess our own imperfections than to complain of those of others. Neither do I mean to speak of past times, particularly in respect of your worthy lady-ship, being sensible that if I have served you in that period when our Israel might be called triumphant, you have more than requited me, in giving to my arms a child, redeemed, as it were, from the vale of the shadow of death. And therefore, as I heartily forgive to your ladyship the unkind and violent measure which you dealt to me at our last meeting, seeing that the woman who was the cause of strife is accounted one of your kindred people, I do entreat you, in like manner, to pardon my enticing away from your service the young woman called Deborah Debbitch, whose nurture, instructed as she hath been under your ladyship's direction, is, it may be, indispensable to the health of my dearest child. I had purposed, madam, with your gracious permission, that Alice should have remained at Martindale Castle, under your kind charge, until she could so far discern betwixt good and evil that it should be matter of conscience to teach her the way in which she should go. For it is not unknown to your ladyship, and in no way do I speak it reproachfully, but rather sorrowfully, that a person so excellently gifted as yourself — I mean touching natural qualities — has not yet received that true light which is a lamp to the paths, but are contented to stumble in darkness, and among the graves of dead men. It has been my prayer in the watches of the night that your ladyship should cease from the doctrine which causeth to err ; but I grieve to say that, our candlestick being about to be removed, the land will most likely be involved in deeper darkness than ever ; and the return of the King, to which I and many looked forward as a manifestation of Divine favour, seems to prove little else than a permitted triumph of the Prince of the Air, who setteth about to restore his vanity fair of bishops,

deans, and such-like, extruding the peaceful ministers of the
Word, whose labours have proved faithful to many hungry souls.
So, hearing from a sure hand that commission has gone forth
to restore these dumb dogs, the followers of Laud and of
Williams, who were cast forth by the late Parliament, and that
an Act of Conformity, or rather of deformity, of worship was
to be expected, it is my purpose to flee from the wrath to come,
and to seek some corner where I may dwell in peace and enjoy
liberty of conscience. For who would abide in the sanctuary
after the carved work thereof is broken down, and when it hath
been made a place for owls and satyrs of the wilderness ? And
herein I blame myself, madam, that I went in the singleness of
my heart too readily into that carousing in the house of feasting,
wherein my love of union, and my desire to show respect to
your ladyship, were made a snare to me. But I trust it will
be an atonement, that I am now about to absent myself from
the place of my birth and the house of my fathers, as well as
from the place which holdeth the dust of those pledges of my
affection. I have also to remember, that in this land my honour,
after the worldly estimation, hath been abated, and my utility
circumscribed, by your husband, Sir Geoffrey Peveril ; and that
without any chance of my obtaining reparation at his hand,
whereby I may say the hand of a kinsman was lifted up against
my credit and my life. These things are bitter to the taste of
the old Adam ; wherefore, to prevent farther bickerings, and, it
may be, bloodshed, it is better that I leave this land for a time.
The affairs which remain to be settled between Sir Geoffrey
and myself, I shall place in the hand of the righteous Master
Joachim Win-the-Fight, an attorney in Chester, who will arrange them with such attention to Sir Geoffrey's convenience
as justice and the due exercise of the law will permit ; for, as
I trust I shall have grace to resist the temptation to make the
weapons of carnal warfare the instruments of my revenge, so I
scorn to effect it through the means of Mammon. Wishing,
madam, that the Lord may grant you every blessing, and, in
especial, that which is over all others, namely, the true knowledge of His way,

' I remain,

' Your devoted servant to command,

'RALPH BRIDGENORTH.

' Written at Moultrassie Hall, this tenth day
of July 1660.'

So soon as Lady Peveril had perused this long and singular homily, in which it seemed to her that her neighbour showed more spirit of religious fanaticism than she could have supposed him possessed of, she looked up and beheld Ellesmere with a countenance in which mortification and an affected air of contempt seemed to struggle together, who, tired with watching the expression of her mistress's countenance, applied for confirmation of her suspicions in plain terms.

'I suppose, madam,' said the waiting-woman, 'the fanatic fool intends to marry the wench? They say he goes to shift the country. Truly, it's time, indeed; for, besides that the whole neighbourhood would laugh him to scorn, I should not be surprised if Lance Outram, the keeper, gave him a buck's head to bear; for that is all in the way of his office.'

'There is no great occasion for your spite at present, Ellesmere,' replied her lady. 'My letter says nothing of marriage; but it would appear that Master Bridgenorth, being to leave this country, has engaged Deborah to take care of his child; and I am sure I am heartily glad of it, for the infant's sake.'

'And I am glad of it for my own,' said Ellesmere; 'and, indeed, for the sake of the whole house. And your ladyship thinks she is not like to be married to him? Troth, I could never see how he should be such an idiot; but perhaps she is going to do worse, for she speaks here of coming to high preferment, and that scarce comes by honest servitude nowadays; then she writes me about sending her things, as if I were mistress of the wardrobe to her ladyship—ay, and recommends Master Julian to the care of my age and experience, forsooth, as if she needed to recommend the dear little jewel to me; and then, to speak of my age. But I will bundle away her rags to the hall, with a witness!'

'Do it with all civility,' said the lady, 'and let Whitaker send her the wages for which she has served, and a broad-piece over and above; for, though a light-headed young woman, she was kind to the children.'

'I know who is kind to their servants, madam, and would spoil the best ever pinned a gown.'

'I spoiled a good one, Ellesmere, when I spoiled thee,' said the lady; 'but tell Mrs. Deborah to kiss the little Alice for me, and to offer my good wishes to Major Bridgenorth, for his temporal and future happiness.'

She permitted no observation or reply, but dismissed her attendant, without entering into farther particulars.

When Ellesmere had withdrawn, Lady Peveril began to reflect, with much feeling of compassion, on the letter of Major Bridgenorth — a person in whom there were certainly many excellent qualities, but whom a series of domestic misfortunes, and the increasing gloom of a sincere, yet stern, feeling of devotion, rendered lonely and unhappy ; and she had more than one anxious thought for the happiness of the little Alice, brought up, as she was likely to be, under such a father.   Still the removal of Bridgenorth was, on the whole, a desirable event ; for while he remained at the hall, it was but too likely that some accidental collision with Sir Geoffrey might give rise to a rencontre betwixt them, more fatal than the last had been.

In the meanwhile, she could not help expressing to Doctor Dummerar her surprise and sorrow that all which she had done and attempted to establish peace and unanimity betwixt the contending factions had been perversely fated to turn out the very reverse of what she had aimed at.

'But for my unhappy invitation,' she said, 'Bridgenorth would not have been at the castle on the morning which succeeded the feast, would not have seen the countess, and would not have incurred the resentment and opposition of my husband.   And but for the King's return, an event which was so anxiously expected as the termination of all our calamities, neither the noble lady nor ourselves had been engaged in this new path of difficulty and danger.'

'Honoured madam,' said Doctor Dummerar, 'were the affairs of this world to be guided implicitly by human wisdom, or were they uniformly to fall out according to the conjectures of human foresight, events would no longer be under the domination of that time and chance which happen unto all men, since we should, in the one case, work out our own purposes to a certainty, by our own skill, and, in the other, regulate our conduct according to the views of unerring prescience.   But man is, while in this vale of tears, like an uninstructed bowler, so to speak, who thinks to attain the jack, by delivering his bowl straight forward upon it, being ignorant that there is a concealed bias within the spheroid, which will make it, in all probability, swerve away and lose the cast.'

Having spoken this with a sententious air, the doctor took his shovel-shaped hat, and went down to the castle green to conclude a match of bowls with Whitaker, which had probably suggested this notable illustration of the uncertain course of human events.

Two days afterwards, Sir Geoffrey arrived. He had waited at Vale Royal till he heard of the countess's being safely embarked for Man, and then had posted homeward to his castle and Dame Margaret. On his way, he learned from some of his attendants the mode in which his lady had conducted the entertainment which she had given to the neighbourhood at his order; and, notwithstanding the great deference he usually showed in cases where Lady Peveril was concerned, he heard of her liberality towards the Presbyterian party with great indignation.

'I could have admitted Bridgenorth,' he said, 'for he always bore him in neighbourly and kindly fashion till this last career — I could have endured him, so he would have drunk the King's health, like a true man; but to bring that snuffling scoundrel Solsgrace, with all his beggarly, long-eared congregation, to hold a conventicle in my father's house — to let them domineer it as they listed — why, I would not have permitted them such liberty when they held their head the highest! They never, in the worst of times, found any way into Martindale Castle but what Noll's cannon made for them; and, that they should come and cant there, when good King Charles is returned, — by my hand, Dame Margaret shall hear of it!'

But, notwithstanding these ireful resolutions, resentment altogether subsided in the honest knight's breast when he saw the fair features of his lady lightened with affectionate joy at his return in safety. As he took her in his arms and kissed her, he forgave her ere he mentioned her offence.

'Thou hast played the knave with me, Meg,' he said, shaking his head, and smiling at the same time, 'and thou knowest in what manner; but I think thou art true churchwoman, and didst only act from some silly womanish fancy of keeping fair with these roguish Roundheads. But let me have no more of this. I had rather Martindale Castle were again rent by their bullets than receive any of the knaves in the way of friend-ship. I always except Ralph Bridgenorth of the hall, if he should come to his senses again.'

Lady Peveril was here under the necessity of explaining what she had heard of Master Bridgenorth — the disappearance of the governante with his daughter, and placed Bridgenorth's letter in his hand. Sir Geoffrey shook his head at first, and then laughed extremely at the idea that there was some little love-intrigue between Bridgenorth and Mistress Deborah.

'It is the true end of a dissenter,' he said, 'to marry his

own maid-servant or some other person's. Deborah is a good, likely wench, and on the merrier side of thirty, as I should think.'

'Nay — nay,' said the Lady Peveril, 'you are as uncharitable as Ellesmere ; I believe it but to be affection to his child.'

'Pshaw ! pshaw !' answered the knight, 'women are eternally thinking of children ; but among men, dame, many one caresses the infant that he may kiss the child's maid ; and where 's the wonder or the harm either, if Bridgenorth should marry the wench ? Her father is a substantial yeoman ; his family has had the same farm since Bosworth field — as good a pedigree as that of the great-grandson of a Chesterfield brewer, I trow. But let us hear what he says for himself ; I shall spell it out if there is any roguery in the letter about love and liking, though it might escape your innocence, Dame Margaret.'

The knight of the Peak began to peruse the letter accordingly, but was much embarrassed by the peculiar language in which it was couched. 'What he means by moving of candlesticks, and breaking down of carved work in the church, I cannot guess ; unless he means to bring back the large silver candlesticks which my grandsire gave to be placed on the altar at Martindale-Moultrassie, and which his crop-eared friends, like sacrilegious villains as they are, stole and melted down. And in like manner, the only breaking I know of was when they pulled down the rails of the communion-table, for which some of their fingers are hot enough by this time, and when the brass ornaments were torn down from the Peveril monuments ; and that was breaking and removing with a vengeance. However, dame, the upshot is, that poor Bridgenorth is going to leave the neighbourhood. I am truly sorry for it, though I never saw him oftener than once a-day, and never spoke to him above two words. But I see how it is — that little shake by the shoulder sticks in his stomach ; and yet, Meg, I did but lift him out of the saddle as I might have lifted thee into it, Margaret. I was careful not to hurt him ; and I did not think him so tender in point of honour as to mind such a thing much. But I see plainly where his sore lies ; and I warrant you I will manage that he stays at the hall, and that you get back Julian's little companion. Faith, I am sorry myself at the thought of losing the baby, and of having to choose another ride when it is not hunting-weather than round by the hall, with a word at the window.'

'I should be very glad, Sir Geoffrey,' said Lady Peveril,

'that you could come to a reconciliation with this worthy man, for such I must hold Master Bridgenorth to be.'

'But for his dissenting principles, as good a neighbour as ever lived,' said Sir Geoffrey.

'But I scarce see,' continued the lady, 'any possibility of bringing about a conclusion so desirable.'

'Tush, dame,' answered the knight, 'thou knowest little of such matters. I know the foot he halts upon, and you shall see him go as sound as ever.'

Lady Peveril had, from her sincere affection and sound sense, as good a right to claim the full confidence of her husband as any woman in Derbyshire; and, upon this occasion, to confess the truth, she had more anxiety to know his purpose than her sense of their mutual and separate duties permitted her in general to entertain. She could not imagine what mode of reconciliation with his neighbour Sir Geoffrey (no very acute judge of mankind or their peculiarities) could have devised, which might not be disclosed to her; and she felt some secret anxiety lest the means resorted to might be so ill chosen as to render the breach rather wider. But Sir Geoffrey would give no opening for farther inquiry. He had been long enough colonel of a regiment abroad to value himself on the right of absolute command at home; and to all the hints which his lady's ingenuity could devise and throw out, he only answered, 'Patience, Dame Margaret — patience. This is no case for thy handling. Thou shalt know enough on 't by and by, dame. Go, look to Julian. Will the boy never have done crying for lack of that little sprout of a Roundhead? But we will have little Alice back with us in two or three days, and all will be well again.'

As the good knight spoke these words, a post winded his horn in the court, and a large packet was brought in, addressed to the worshipful Sir Geoffrey Peveril, Justice of the Peace, and so forth; for he had been placed in authority as soon as the King's restoration was put upon a settled basis. Upon opening the packet, which he did with no small feeling of importance, he found that it contained the warrant which he had solicited for replacing Doctor Dummerar in the parish, from which he had been forcibly ejected during the usurpation.[1]

Few incidents could have given more delight to Sir Geoffrey. He could forgive a stout, able-bodied sectary or nonconformist, who enforced his doctrines in the field by downright blows on the casques and cuirasses of himself and other Cavaliers; but

---

[1] See Ejection of Presbyterian Clergy. Note 6.

he remembered, with most vindictive accuracy, the triumphant entrance of Hugh Peters through the breach of his castle ; and for his sake, without nicely distinguishing betwixt sects or their teachers, he held all who mounted a pulpit without war-rant from the Church of England — perhaps he might also in private except that of Rome — to be disturbers of the public tranquillity, seducers of the congregation from their lawful preachers, instigators of the late Civil War, and men well dis-posed to risk the fate of a new one.

Then, on the other hand, besides gratifying his dislike to Solsgrace, he saw much satisfaction in the task of replacing his old friend and associate in sport and in danger, the worthy Doctor Dummerar, in his legitimate rights, and in the ease and comforts of his vicarage. He communicated the contents of the packet, with great triumph, to the lady, who now perceived the sense of the mysterious paragraph in Major Bridgenorth's letter concerning the removal of the candlestick, and the extinction of light and doctrine in the land. She pointed this out to Sir Geoffrey, and endeavoured to persuade him that a door was now opened to reconciliation with his neighbour, by executing the commission which he had received in an easy and moderate manner, after due delay, and with all respect to the feelings both of Solsgrace and his congregation, which cir-cumstances admitted of. This, the lady argued, would be doing no injury whatever to Doctor Dummerar — nay, might be the means of reconciling many to his ministry, who might otherwise be disgusted with it for ever, by the premature expulsion of a favourite preacher.

There was much wisdom, as well as moderation, in this advice ; and, at another time, Sir Geoffrey would have had sense enough to have adopted it. But who can act composedly or prudently in the hour of triumph ? The ejection of Mr. Solsgrace was so hastily executed as to give it some appearance of persecution ; though, more justly considered, it was the re-storing of his predecessor to his legal rights. Solsgrace him-self seemed to be desirous to make his sufferings as manifest as possible. He held out to the last ; and on the Sabbath after he had received intimation of his ejection, attempted to make his way to the pulpit, as usual, supported by Master Bridge-north's attorney, Win-the-Fight, and a few zealous followers.

Just as their party came into the churchyard on the one side, Dr. Dummerar, dressed in full pontificals, in a sort of triumphal procession, accompanied by Peveril of the Peak, Sir

Jasper Cranbourne, and other Cavaliers of distinction, entered at the other.

To prevent an actual struggle in the church, the parish officers were sent to prevent the farther approach of the Presbyterian minister; which was effected without farther damage than a broken head, inflicted by Roger Raine, the drunken innkeeper of the Peveril Arms, upon the Presbyterian attorney of Chesterfield.

Unsubdued in spirit, though compelled to retreat by superior force, the undaunted Mr. Solsgrace retired to the vicarage ; where, under some legal pretext which had been started by Mr. Win-the-Fight (in that day unaptly named), he attempted to maintain himself — bolted gates, barred windows, and, as report said (though falsely), made provision of firearms to resist the officers. A scene of clamour and scandal accordingly took place, which being reported to Sir Geoffrey, he came in person, with some of his attendants carrying arms, forced the outer gate and inner doors of the house, and, proceeding to the study, found no other garrison save the Presbyterian parson, with the attorney, who gave up possession of the premises, after making protestation against the violence that had been used.

The rabble of the village being by this time all in motion, Sir Geoffrey, both in prudence and good-nature, saw the propriety of escorting his prisoners, for so they might be termed, safely through the tumult ; and accordingly conveyed them in person, through much noise and clamour, as far as the avenue of Moultrassie Hall, which they chose for the place of their retreat.

But the absence of Sir Geoffrey gave the rein to some disorders, which, if present, he would assuredly have restrained. Some of the minister's books were torn and flung about as treasonable and seditious trash, by the zealous parish officers or their assistants. A quantity of his ale was drunk up in healths to the King and Peveril of the Peak. And finally, the boys, who bore the ex-parson no good-will for his tyrannical interference with their games at skittles, football, and so forth, and, moreover, remembered the unmerciful length of his sermons, dressed up an effigy with his Geneva gown and band and his steeple-crowned hat, which they paraded through the village, and burned on the spot whilom occupied by a stately Maypole, which Solsgrace had formerly hewed down with his own reverend hands.

Sir Geoffrey was vexed at all this, and sent to Mr. Solsgrace,

offering satisfaction for the goods which he had lost; but the
Calvinistical divine replied, 'From a thread to a shoe-latchet,
I will not take anything that is thine. Let the shame of the
work of thy hands abide with thee.'

Considerable scandal, indeed, arose against Sir Geoffrey
Peveril, as having proceeded with indecent severity and haste
upon this occasion; and rumour took care to make the usual
additions to the reality. It was currently reported that the
desperate Cavalier, Peveril of the Peak, had fallen on a Presbyterian congregation, while engaged in the peaceable exercise of
religion, with a band of armed men, had slain some, desper-
ately wounded many more, and finally pursued the preacher to
his vicarage, which he burned to the ground. Some alleged the
clergyman had perished in the flames; and the most mitigated
report bore, that he had only been able to escape by disposing
his gown, cap, and band near a window, in such a manner as
to deceive them with the idea of his person being still surrounded by flames, while he himself fled by the back part of
the house. And although few people believed in the extent of
the atrocities thus imputed to our honest Cavalier, yet still
enough of obloquy attached to him to infer very serious consequences, as the reader will learn at a future period of our
history.

CHAPTER IX

Bessus. 'T is a challenge, sir, is it not ?
Gentleman. 'T is an inviting to the field.
                                    King and no King.

FOR a day or two after this forcible expulsion from the
vicarage, Mr. Solsgrace continued his residence at Moultrassie Hall, where the natural melancholy attendant on
his situation added to the gloom of the owner of the mansion.
In the morning, the ejected divine made excursions to different
families in the neighbourhood, to whom his ministry had been acceptable in the days of his prosperity, and from whose grateful
recollections of that period he now found sympathy and consolation. He did not require to be condoled with because he was
deprived of an easy and competent maintenance, and thrust out
upon the common of life, after he had reason to suppose he would
be no longer liable to such mutations of fortune. The piety of
Mr. Solsgrace was sincere ; and if he had many of the uncharitable prejudices against other sects which polemical controversy
had generated, and the Civil War brought to a head, he had
also that deep sense of duty by which enthusiasm is so often dignified, and held his very life little, if called upon to lay it down
in attestation of the doctrines in which he believed. But he
was soon to prepare for leaving the district which Heaven, he
conceived, had assigned to him as his corner of the vineyard ;
he was to abandon his flock to the wolf; was to forsake those
with whom he had held sweet counsel in religious communion ;
was to leave the recently converted to relapse into false doctrines, and forsake the wavering, whom his continued cares
might have directed into the right path — these were of themselves deep causes of sorrow, and were aggravated, doubtless,
by those natural feelings with which all men, especially those
whose duties or habits have confined them to a limited circle,
regard the separation from wonted scenes and their accustomed
haunts of solitary musing or social intercourse.

There was, indeed, a plan of placing Mr. Solsgrace at the head of a Nonconforming congregation in his present parish, which his followers would have readily consented to endow with a sufficient revenue. But although the Act for universal conformity was not yet passed, such a measure was understood to be impending, and there existed a general opinion among the Presbyterians that in no hands was it likely to be more strictly enforced than in those of Peveril of the Peak. Solsgrace himself considered not only his personal danger as being considerable — for, assuming perhaps more consequence than was actually attached to him or his productions, he conceived the honest knight to be his mortal and determined enemy — but he also conceived that he should serve the cause of his church by absenting himself from Derbyshire.

'Less known pastors,' he said, 'though perhaps more worthy of the name, may be permitted to assemble the scattered flocks in caverns or in secret wilds, and to them shall the gleaning of the grapes of Ephraim be better than the vintage of Abiezer. But I, that have so often carried the banner forth against the mighty — I, whose tongue hath testified, morning and evening, like the watchman upon the tower, against Popery, Prelacy, and the tyrant of the Peak — for me to abide here were but to bring the sword of bloody vengeance amongst you, that the shepherd might be smitten and the sheep scattered. The shedders of blood have already assailed me, even within that ground which they themselves call consecrated ; and yourselves have seen the scalp of the righteous broken, as he defended my cause. Therefore, I will put on my sandals and gird my loins, and depart to a far country, and there do as my duty shall call upon me, whether it be to act or to suffer, to bear testimony at the stake or in the pulpit.'

Such were the sentiments which Mr. Solsgrace expressed to his desponding friends, and which he expatiated upon at more length with Major Bridgenorth ; not failing, with friendly zeal, to rebuke the haste which the latter had shown to thrust out the hand of fellowship to the Amalekite woman, whereby he reminded him, 'He had been rendered her slave and bondsman for a season, like Samson, betrayed by Delilah, and might have remained longer in the house of Dagon, had not Heaven pointed to him a way out of the snare. Also, it sprung originally from the major's going up to feast in the high place of Baal, that he who was the champion of the truth was stricken down and put to shame by the enemy, even in the presence of the host.'

These objurgations seeming to give some offence to Major Bridgenorth, who liked no better than any other man to hear of his own mishaps, and at the same time to have them imputed to his own misconduct, the worthy divine proceeded to take shame to himself for his own sinful compliance in that matter ; for to the vengeance justly due for that unhappy dinner at Martindale Castle, 'which was,' he said, 'a crying of peace when there was no peace, and a dwelling in the tents of sin,' he imputed his ejection from his living, with the destruction of some of his most pithy and highly prized volumes of divinity, with the loss of his cap, gown, and band, and a double hogshead of choice Derby ale.

The mind of Major Bridgenorth was strongly tinged with devotional feeling, which his late misfortunes had rendered more deep and solemn ; and it is therefore no wonder that, when he heard these arguments urged again and again by a pastor whom he so much respected, and who was now a confessor in the cause of their joint faith, he began to look back with disapproval on his own conduct, and to suspect that he had permitted himself to be seduced by gratitude towards Lady Peveril, and by her special arguments in favour of a mutual and tolerating liberality of sentiments, into an action which had a tendency to compromise his religious and political principles.

One morning, as Major Bridgenorth had wearied himself with several details respecting the arrangement of his affairs, he was reposing in the leathern easy-chair, beside the latticed window — a posture which, by natural association, recalled to him the memory of former times, and the feelings with which he was wont to expect the recurring visit of Sir Geoffrey, who brought him news of his child's welfare. 'Surely,' he said, thinking, as it were, aloud, 'there was no sin in the kindness with which I then regarded that man.'

Solsgrace, who was in the apartment, and guessed what passed through his friend's mind, acquainted as he was with every point of his history, replied — 'When God caused Elijah to be fed by ravens, while hiding at the brook Cherith, we hear not of his fondling the unclean birds, whom, contrary to their ravening nature, a miracle compelled to minister to him.'

'It may be so,' answered Bridgenorth, 'yet the flap of their wings must have been gracious in the ear of the famished prophet, like the tread of his horse in mine. The ravens, doubtless, resumed their nature when the season was passed,

and even so it has fared with him. Hark!' he exclaimed,
starting, 'I hear his horse's hoof-tramp even now.'

It was seldom that the echoes of that silent house and courtyard were awakened by the trampling of horses, but such was
now the case.

Both Bridgenorth and Solsgrace were surprised at the sound,
and even disposed to anticipate some farther oppression on the
part of government, when the major's old servant introduced,
with little ceremony (for his manners were nearly as plain as
his master's), a tall gentleman on the farther side of middle
life, whose vest and cloak, long hair, slouched hat, and drooping
feather, announced him as a Cavalier. He bowed formally, but
courteously, to both gentlemen, and said, that he was 'Sir
Jasper Cranbourne, charged with an especial message to Master
Ralph Bridgenorth of Moultrassie Hall, by his honourable friend
Sir Geoffrey Peveril of the Peak, and that he requested to know
whether Master Bridgenorth would be pleased to receive his
acquittal of commission here or elsewhere.'

'Anything which Sir Geoffrey Peveril can have to say to me,'
said Major Bridgenorth, 'may be told instantly, and before my
friend, from whom I have no secrets.'

'The presence of any other friend were, instead of being
objectionable, the thing in the world most to be desired,' said
Sir Jasper, after a moment's hesitation, and looking at Mr.
Solsgrace; 'but this gentleman seems to be a sort of clergyman.'

'I am not conscious of any secrets,' answered Bridgenorth,
'nor do I desire to have any, in which a clergyman is an un-
fitting confidant.'

'At your pleasure,' replied Sir Jasper. 'The confidence,
for aught I know, may be well enough chosen, for your divines
— always under your favour — have proved no enemies to such
matters as I am to treat with you upon.'

'Proceed, sir,' answered Mr. Bridgenorth, gravely; 'and I
pray you to be seated, unless it is rather your pleasure to stand.'

'I must, in the first place, deliver myself of my small commission,' answered Sir Jasper, drawing himself up; 'and it will
be after I have seen the reception thereof that I shall know
whether I am or am not to sit down at Moultrassie Hall. Sir
Geoffrey Peveril, Master Bridgenorth, hath carefully considered with himself the unhappy circumstances which at present
separate you as neighbours. And he remembers many passages in former times — I speak his very words — which incline
him to do all that can possibly consist with his honour to

wipe out unkindness between you; and for this desirable object
he is willing to condescend in a degree which, as you could
not have expected, it will no doubt give you great pleasure to
learn.'

'Allow me to say, Sir Jasper,' said Bridgenorth, 'that this
is unnecessary. I have made no complaints of Sir Geoffrey; I
have required no submission from him. I am about to leave
this country; and what affairs we may have together can be as
well settled by others as by ourselves.'

'In a word,' said the divine, 'the worthy Major Bridgenorth
hath had enough of trafficking with the ungodly, and will no
longer, on any terms, consort with them.'

'Gentlemen both,' said Sir Jasper, with imperturbable politeness, bowing, 'you greatly mistake the tenor of my commission,
which you will do as well to hear out before making any reply
to it. I think, Master Bridgenorth, you cannot but remember
your letter to the Lady Peveril, of which I have here a rough
copy, in which you complain of the hard measure which you
have received at Sir Geoffrey's hand, and in particular when
he pulled you from your horse at or near Hartley Nick. Now,
Sir Geoffrey thinks so well of you as to believe that, were it
not for the wide difference betwixt his descent and rank and
your own, you would have sought to bring this matter to a
gentlemanlike arbitrement, as the only mode whereby your
stain may be honourably wiped away. Wherefore, in this slight
note, he gives you, in his generosity, the offer of what you, in your
modesty, for to nothing else does he impute your acquiescence,
have declined to demand of him. And withal, I bring you the
measure of his weapon; and when you have accepted the cartel
which I now offer you, I shall be ready to settle the time, place,
and other circumstances of your meeting.'

'And I,' said Solsgrace, with a solemn voice, 'should the
Author of Evil tempt my friend to accept of so bloodthirsty a
proposal, would be the first to pronounce against him sentence
of the greater excommunication.'

'It is not you whom I address, reverend sir,' replied the
envoy; 'your interest, not unnaturally, may determine you to
be more anxious about your patron's life than about his honour.
I must know from himself to which *he* is disposed to give the
preference.'

So saying, and with a graceful bow, he again tendered the
challenge to Major Bridgenorth. There was obviously a struggle
in that gentleman's bosom between the suggestions of human

honour and those of religious principle; but the latter prevailed. He calmly waived receiving the paper which Sir Jasper offered to him, and spoke to the following purpose : — 'It may not be known to you, Sir Jasper, that, since the general pouring out of Christian light upon this kingdom, many solid men have been led to doubt whether the shedding human blood by the hand of a fellow-creature be in *any* respect justifiable. And although this rule appears to me to be scarcely applicable to our state in this stage of trial, seeing that such non-resistance, if general, would surrender our civil and religious rights into the hands of whatsoever daring tyrants might usurp the same; yet I am, and have been, inclined to limit the use of carnal arms to the case of necessary self-defence, whether such regards our own person or the protection of our country against invasion; or of our rights of property, and the freedom of our laws and of our conscience, against usurping power. And as I have never shown myself unwilling to draw my sword in any of the latter causes, so you shall excuse my suffering it now to remain in the scabbard, when, having sustained a grievous injury, the man who inflicted it summons me to combat, either upon an idle punctilio or, as is more likely, in mere bravado.'

'I have heard you with patience,' said Sir Jasper; 'and now, Master Bridgenorth, take it not amiss if I beseech you to bethink yourself better on this matter. I vow to Heaven, sir, that your honour lies a-bleeding; and that in condescending to afford you this fair meeting, and thereby giving you some chance to stop its wounds, Sir Geoffrey has been moved by a tender sense of your condition, and an earnest wish to redeem your dishonour. And it will be but the crossing of your blade with his honoured sword for the space of some few minutes, and you will either live or die a noble and honoured gentleman; besides that the knight's exquisite skill of fence may enable him, as his good-nature will incline him, to disarm you with some flesh wound, little to the damage of your person, and greatly to the benefit of your reputation.'

'The tender mercies of the wicked,' said Master Solsgrace, emphatically, by way of commenting on this speech, which Sir Jasper had uttered very pathetically, 'are cruel.'

'I pray to have no farther interruption from your reverence,' said Sir Jasper; 'especially as I think this affair very little concerns you; and I entreat that you permit me to discharge myself regularly of my commission from my worthy friend.'

So saying, he took his sheathed rapier from his belt, and

passing the point through the silk thread which secured the
letter, he once more, and literally at sword-point, gracefully
tendered it to Major Bridgenorth, who again waived it aside,
though colouring deeply at the same time, as if he was putting
a marked constraint upon himself, drew back, and made Sir
Jasper Cranbourne a deep bow.

'Since it is to be thus,' said Sir Jasper, 'I must myself do
violence to the seal of Sir Geoffrey's letter, and read it to you,
that I may fully acquit myself of the charge entrusted to me,
and make you, Master Bridgenorth, equally aware of the generous intentions of Sir Geoffrey on your behalf.'

'If,' said Major Bridgenorth, 'the contents of the letter be
to no other purpose than you have intimated, methinks farther
ceremony is unnecessary on this occasion, as I have already
taken my course.'

'Nevertheless,' said Sir Jasper, breaking open the letter, 'it
is fitting that I read to you the letter of my worshipful friend.'
And he read accordingly as follows : —

'For the worthy hands of Ralph Bridgenorth, Esquire,
of Moultrassie Hall — These :

'By the honoured conveyance of the Worshipful Sir Jasper
Cranbourne, Knight, of Long Mallington.

'MASTER BRIDGENORTH —
'We have been given to understand by your letter to
our loving wife, Dame Margaret Peveril, that you hold hard construction of certain passages betwixt you and I, of a late date,
as if your honour should have been, in some sort, prejudiced
by what then took place. And although you have not thought
it fit to have direct recourse to me, to request such satisfaction
as is due from one gentleman of condition to another, yet I am
fully minded that this proceeds only from modesty, arising out
of the distinction of our degree, and from no lack of that courage
which you have heretofore displayed, I would I could say in a
good cause. Wherefore I am purposed to give you, by my
friend Sir Jasper Cranbourne, a meeting, for the sake of doing
that which doubtless you entirely long for. Sir Jasper will
deliver you the length of my weapon, and appoint circumstances and an hour for our meeting ; which, whether early or
late, on foot or horseback, with rapier or backsword, I refer to
yourself, with all the other privileges of a challenged person ;

only desiring that, if you decline to match my weapon, you
will send me forthwith the length and breadth of your own.
And nothing doubting that the issue of this meeting must
needs be to end, in one way or other, all unkindness betwixt
two near neighbours,

'I remain,

'Your humble servant to command,

'GEOFFREY PEVERIL OF THE PEAK.

'Given from my poor house of Martindale
    Castle, this same —— of —— sixteen
    hundred and sixty.'

'Bear back my respects to Sir Geoffrey Peveril,' said Major
Bridgenorth. 'According to his light, his meaning may be fair
towards me ; but tell him that our quarrel had its rise in his
own wilful aggression towards me ; and that, though I wish to
be in charity with all mankind, I am not so wedded to his
friendship as to break the laws of God, and run the risk of
suffering or committing murder, in order to regain it. And for
you, sir, methinks your advanced years and past misfortunes
might teach you the folly of coming on such idle errands.'

'I shall do your message, Master Ralph Bridgenorth,' said
Sir Jasper ; 'and shall then endeavour to forget your name, as
a sound unfit to be pronounced, or even remembered, by a man
of honour. In the meanwhile, in return for your uncivil advice,
be pleased to accept of mine — namely, that as your religion
prevents your giving a gentleman satisfaction, it ought to make
you very cautious of offering him provocation.'

So saying, and with a look of haughty scorn, first at the
major and then at the divine, the envoy of Sir Geoffrey put his
hat on his head, replaced his rapier in its belt, and left the
apartment. In a few minutes afterwards the tread of his horse
died away at a considerable distance.

Bridgenorth had held his hand upon his brow ever since his
departure, and a tear of anger and shame was on his face as he
raised it when the sound was heard no more. 'He carries this
answer to Martindale Castle,' he said. 'Men will hereafter
think of me as a whipped, beaten, dishonourable fellow, whom
every one may baffle and insult at their pleasure. It is well I
am leaving the house of my father.'

Master Solsgrace approached his friend with much sympathy,
and grasped him by the hand. 'Noble brother,' he said, with

unwonted kindness of manner, 'though a man of peace, I can
judge what this sacrifice hath cost to thy manly spirit. But
God will not have from us an imperfect obedience. We must
not, like Ananias and Sapphira, reserve behind some darling
lust, some favourite sin, while we pretend to make sacrifice of
our worldly affections. What avails it to say that we have but
secreted a little matter, if the slightest remnant of the accursed
thing remain hidden in our tent? Would it be a defence in
thy prayers to say, "I have not murdered this man for the lucre
of gain, like a robber; nor for the acquisition of power, like a
tyrant; nor for the gratification of revenge, like a darkened
savage; but because the imperious voice of worldly honour
said, 'Go forth — kill or be killed — is it not I that have sent
thee?'" Bethink thee, my worthy friend, how thou couldst
frame such a vindication in thy prayers; and if thou art forced
to tremble at the blasphemy of such an excuse, remember in
thy prayers the thanks due to Heaven, which enabled thee to
resist the strong temptation.'

'Reverend and dear friend,' answered Bridgenorth, 'I feel
that you speak the truth. Bitterer indeed, and harder, to the
old Adam is the text which ordains him to suffer shame than
that which bids him to do valiantly for the truth. But happy
am I that my path through the wilderness of this world will,
for some space at least, be along with one whose zeal and friendship are so active to support me when I am fainting in the
way.'

While the inhabitants of Moultrassie Hall thus communicated together upon the purport of Sir Jasper Cranbourne's
visit, that worthy knight greatly excited the surprise of Sir
Geoffrey Peveril by reporting the manner in which his embassy
had been received.

'I took him for a man of other metal,' said Sir Geoffrey;
'nay, I would have sworn it, had any one asked my testimony.
But there is no making a silken purse out of a sow's ear. I have
done a folly for him that I will never do for another; and that
is, to think a Presbyterian would fight without his preacher's
permission. Give them a two hours' sermon, and let them
howl a psalm to a tune that is worse than the cries of a flogged
hound, and the villains will lay on like threshers; but for a
calm, cool gentlemanlike turn upon the sod, hand to hand,
in a neighbourly way, they have not honour enough to undertake it. But enough of our crop-eared cur of a neighbour.
Sir Jasper, you will tarry with us to dine, and see how Dame

Margaret's kitchen smokes ; and after dinner I will show you a long-winged falcon fly. She is not mine, but the countess's, who brought her from London on her fist almost the whole way, for all the haste she was in, and left her with me to keep the perch for a season.'

This match was soon arranged ; and Dame Margaret over-heard the good knight's resentment mutter itself off, with those feelings with which we listen to the last growling of the thunder-storm, which, as the black cloud sinks behind the hill, at once assures us that there has been danger and that the peril is over. She could not, indeed, but marvel in her own mind at the singular path of reconciliation with his neighbour which her husband had, with so much confidence, and in the actual sincerity of his good-will to Mr. Bridgenorth, attempted to open ; and she blessed God internally that it had not terminated in bloodshed. But these reflections she locked carefully within her own bosom, well knowing that they referred to subjects in which the knight of the Peak would neither permit his sagacity to be called in question nor his will to be controlled.

The progress of the history hath hitherto been slow ; but after this period so little matter worthy of mark occurred at Martindale that we must hurry over hastily the transactions of several years.

CHAPTER X

Cleopatra. Give me to drink mandragora,
That I may sleep away this gap of time.
                        Antony and Cleopatra.

THERE passed, as we hinted at the conclusion of the last chapter, four or five years after the period we have dilated upon, the events of which scarcely require to be discussed, so far as our present purpose is concerned, in as many lines. The knight and his lady continued to reside at their castle — she, with prudence and with patience, endeavouring to repair the damages which the Civil Wars had inflicted upon their fortune ; and murmuring a little when her plans of economy were interrupted by the liberal hospitality which was her husband's principal expense, and to which he was attached, not only from his own English heartiness of disposition, but from ideas of maintaining the dignity of his ancestry — no less remarkable, according to the tradition of their buttery, kitchen, and cellar, for the fat beeves which they roasted, and the mighty ale which they brewed, than for their extensive estates and the number of their retainers.

The world, however, upon the whole, went happily and easily with the worthy couple. Sir Geoffrey's debt to his neighbour Bridgenorth continued, it is true, unabated ; but he was the only creditor upon the Martindale estate, all others being paid off. It would have been most desirable that this encumbrance also should be cleared, and it was the great object of Dame Margaret's economy to effect the discharge ; for although interest was regularly settled with Master Win-the-Fight, the Chesterfield attorney, yet the principal sum, which was a large one, might be called for at an inconvenient time. The man, too, was gloomy, important, and mysterious, and always seemed as if he was thinking upon his broken head in the churchyard of Martindale *cum* Moultrassie.

Dame Margaret sometimes transacted the necessary business

with him in person; and when he came to the castle on these occasions, she thought she saw a malicious and disobliging expression in his manner and countenance. Yet his actual conduct was not only fair but liberal; for indulgence was given, in the way of delay of payment, whenever circumstances rendered it necessary to the debtor to require it. It seemed to Lady Peveril that the agent, in such cases, was acting under the strict orders of his absent employer, concerning whose welfare she could not help feeling a certain anxiety.

Shortly after the failure of the singular negotiation for attaining peace by combat which Peveril had attempted to open with Major Bridgenorth, that gentleman left his seat of Moultrassie Hall in the care of his old housekeeper, and departed, no one knew whither, having in company with him his daughter Alice and Mrs. Deborah Debbitch, now formally installed in all the duties of a governante; to these was added the Reverend Master Solsgrace. For some time public rumour persisted in asserting that Major Bridgenorth had only retreated to a distant part of the country for a season, to achieve his supposed purpose of marrying Mrs. Deborah, and of letting the news be cold, and the laugh of the neighbourhood be ended, ere he brought her down as mistress of Moultrassie Hall. This rumour died away; and it was then affirmed that he had removed to foreign parts, to ensure the continuance of health in so delicate a constitution as that of little Alice. But when the major's dread of Popery was remembered, together with the still deeper antipathies of worthy Master Nehemiah Solsgrace, it was resolved unanimously that nothing less than what they might deem a fair chance of converting the Pope would have induced the parties to trust themselves within Catholic dominions. The most prevailing opinion was, that they had gone to New England, the refuge then of many whom too intimate concern with the affairs of the late times, or the desire of enjoying uncontrolled freedom of conscience, had induced to emigrate from Britain.

Lady Peveril could not help entertaining a vague idea that Bridgenorth was not so distant. The extreme order in which everything was maintained at Moultrassie Hall seemed — no disparagement to the care of Dame Dickens, the housekeeper, and the other persons engaged — to argue that the master's eye was not so very far off but that its occasional inspection might be apprehended. It is true, that neither the domestics nor the attorney answered any questions respecting the residence

Master Bridgenorth ; but there was an air of mystery about them when interrogated that seemed to argue more than met the ear.

About five years after Master Bridgenorth had left the country, a singular incident took place. Sir Geoffrey was absent at the Chesterfield races, and Lady Peveril, who was in the habit of walking around every part of the neighbourhood unattended, or only accompanied by Ellesmere or her little boy, had gone down one evening upon a charitable errand to a solitary hut, whose inhabitant lay sick of a fever, which was supposed to be infectious. Lady Peveril never allowed apprehensions of this kind to stop ' devoted charitable deeds ' ; but she did not choose to expose either her son or her attendant to the risk which she herself, in some confidence that she knew precautions for escaping the danger, did not hesitate to incur.

Lady Peveril had set out at a late hour in the evening, and the way proved longer than she expected ; several circumstances also occurred to detain her at the hut of her patient. It was a broad autumn moonlight when she prepared to return homeward through the broken glades and upland which divided her from the castle. This she considered as a matter of very little importance in so quiet and sequestered a country, where the road lay chiefly through her own domains, especially as she had a lad about fifteen years old, the son of her patient, to escort her on the way. The distance was better than two miles, but might be considerably abridged by passing through an avenue belonging to the estate of Moultrassie Hall, which she had avoided as she came, not from the ridiculous rumours which pronounced it to be haunted, but because her husband was much displeased when any attempt was made to render the walks of the castle and hall common to the inhabitants of both. The good lady, in consideration, perhaps, of extensive latitude allowed to her in the more important concerns of the family, made a point of never interfering with her husband's whims or prejudices ; and it is a compromise which we would heartily recommend to all managing matrons of our acquaintance ; for it is surprising how much real power will be cheerfully resigned to the fair sex for the pleasure of being allowed to ride one's hobby in peace and quiet.

Upon the present occasion, however, although the Dobby's Walk [1] was within the inhibited domains of the hall, the Lady Peveril determined to avail herself of it, for the purpose of shortening her road home, and she directed her steps accord-

---

[1] Dobby, an old English name for goblin.

ingly. But when the peasant-boy, her companion, who had hitherto followed her, whistling cheerily, with a hedge-bill in his hand, and his hat on one side, perceived that she turned to the stile which entered to the Dobby's Walk, he showed symptoms of great fear, and at length, coming to the lady's side, petitioned her, in a whimpering tone, 'Don't ye now — don't ye now, my lady — don't ye go yonder.'

Lady Peveril, observing that his teeth chattered in his head, and that his whole person exhibited great signs of terror, began to recollect the report that the first squire of Moultrassie, the brewer of Chesterfield, who had bought the estate, and then died of melancholy for lack of something to do, and, as was said, not without suspicions of suicide, was supposed to walk in this sequestered avenue, accompanied by a large headless mastiff, which, when he was alive, was a particular favourite of the ex-brewer. To have expected any protection from her escort, in the condition to which superstitious fear had reduced him, would have been truly a hopeless trust; and Lady Peveril, who was not apprehensive of any danger, thought there would be great cruelty in dragging the cowardly boy into a scene which he regarded with so much apprehension. She gave him, therefore, a silver piece, and permitted him to return. The latter boon seemed even more acceptable than the first; for, ere she could return the purse into her pocket, she heard the wooden clogs of her bold convoy in full retreat, by the way from whence they came.

Smiling within herself at the fear she esteemed so ludicrous, Lady Peveril ascended the stile, and was soon hidden from the broad light of the moonbeams by the numerous and entangled boughs of the huge elms, which, meeting from either side, totally overarched the old avenue. The scene was calculated to excite solemn thoughts; and the distant glimmer of a light from one of the numerous casements in the front of Moultrassie Hall, which lay at some distance, was calculated to make them even melancholy. She thought of the fate of that family — of the deceased Mrs. Bridgenorth, with whom she had often walked in this very avenue, and who, though a woman of no high parts or accomplishments, had always testified the deepest respect and the most earnest gratitude for such notice as she had shown to her. She thought of her blighted hopes — her premature death — the despair of her self-banished husband — the uncertain fate of their orphan child, for whom she felt, even at this distance of time, some touch of a mother's affection.

Upon such sad subjects her thoughts were turned, when, just as she attained the middle of the avenue, the imperfect and checkered light which found its way through the silvan archway showed her something which resembled the figure of a man. Lady Peveril paused a moment, but instantly advanced; her bosom, perhaps, gave one startled throb, as a debt to the superstitious belief of the times, but she instantly repelled the thought of supernatural appearances. From those that were merely mortal she had nothing to fear. A marauder on the game was the worst character whom she was likely to encounter; and he would be sure to hide himself from her observation. She advanced, accordingly, steadily; and, as she did so, had the satisfaction to observe that the figure, as she expected, gave place to her, and glided away amongst the trees on the left-hand side of the avenue. As she passed the spot on which the form had been so lately visible, and bethought herself that this wanderer of the night might, nay must, be in her vicinity, her resolution could not prevent her mending her pace, and that with so little precaution, that, stumbling over the limb of a tree, which, twisted off by a late tempest, still lay in the avenue, she fell, and, as she fell, screamed aloud. A strong hand in a moment afterwards added to her fears by assisting her to rise, and a voice, to whose accents she was not a stranger, though they had been long unheard, said, 'Is it not you, Lady Peveril?'

'It is I,' said she, commanding her astonishment and fear; 'and, if my ear deceive me not, I speak to Master Bridgenorth.'

'I was that man,' said he, 'while oppression left me a name.'

He spoke nothing more, but continued to walk beside her for a minute or two in silence. She felt her situation embarrassing; and, to divest it of that feeling, as well as out of real interest in the question, she asked him, 'How her god-daughter Alice now was?'

'Of god-daughter, madam,' answered Major Bridgenorth, 'I know nothing; that being one of the names which have been introduced to the corruption and pollution of God's ordinances. The infant who owed to your ladyship, so called, her escape from disease and death, is a healthy and thriving girl, as I am given to understand by those in whose charge she is lodged, for I have not lately seen her. And it is even the recollection of these passages which in a manner impelled me, alarmed also by your fall, to offer myself to you at this time and mode,

which in other respects is no way consistent with my present
safety.'

'With your safety, Master Bridgenorth!' said the Lady
Peveril; 'surely, I could never have thought that it was in
danger!'

'You have some news, then, yet to learn, madam,' said Major
Bridgenorth; 'but you will hear, in the course of to-morrow,
reasons why I dare not appear openly in the neighbourhood of
my own property, and wherefore there is small judgment in
committing the knowledge of my present residence to any one
connected with Martindale Castle.'

'Master Bridgenorth,' said the lady, 'you were in former
times prudent and cautious; I hope you have been misled by
no hasty impression — by no rash scheme; I hope ——'

'Pardon my interrupting you, madam,' said Bridgenorth.
'I have indeed been changed — ay, my very heart within me has
been changed. In the times to which your ladyship, so called,
thinks proper to refer, I was a man of this world, bestowing on
it all my thoughts, all my actions, save formal observances,
little deeming what was the duty of a Christian man, and how
far his self-denial ought to extend, even unto his giving all as
if he gave nothing. Hence I thought chiefly on carnal things
— on the adding of field to field, and wealth to wealth, of
balancing between party and party, securing a friend here
without losing a friend there. But Heaven smote me for my
apostasy, the rather that I abused the name of religion, as a
self-seeker, and a most blinded and carnal will-worshipper.
But I thank HIM who hath at length brought me out of Egypt.'

In our day, although we have many instances of enthusiasm among us, we might still suspect one who avowed it thus
suddenly and broadly of hypocrisy or of insanity; but, according to the fashion of the times, such opinions as those which
Bridgenorth expressed were openly pleaded as the ruling
motives of men's actions. The sagacious Vane, the brave and
skilful Harrison, were men who acted avowedly under the
influence of such. Lady Peveril, therefore, was more grieved
than surprised at the language she heard Major Bridgenorth
use, and reasonably concluded that the society and circumstances in which he might lately have been engaged had blown
into a flame the spark of eccentricity which always smouldered
in his bosom. This was the more probable, considering that
he was melancholy by constitution and descent, that he had
been unfortunate in several particulars, and that no passion is

more easily nursed by indulgence than the species of enthusiasm of which he now showed tokens. She therefore answered him by calmly hoping, 'That the expression of his sentiments had not involved him in suspicion or in danger.'

'In suspicion, madam!' answered the major; 'for I cannot forbear giving to you, such is the strength of habit, one of those idle titles by which we poor potsherds are wont, in our pride, to denominate each other. I walk not only in suspicion, but in that degree of danger that, were your husband to meet me at this instant — me, a native Englishman, treading on my own lands — I have no doubt he would do his best to offer me to the Moloch of Roman superstition who now rages abroad for victims among God's people.'

'You surprise me by your language, Major Bridgenorth,' said the lady, who now felt rather anxious to be relieved from his company, and with that purpose walked on somewhat hastily. He mended his pace, however, and kept close by her side.

'Know you not,' said he, 'that Satan hath come down upon earth with great wrath, because his time is short? The next heir to the crown is an avowed Papist; and who dare assert, save sycophants and time-servers, that he who wears it is not equally ready to stoop to Rome, were he not kept in awe by a few noble spirits in the Commons' House? You believe not this; yet in my solitary and midnight walks, when I thought on your kindness to the dead and to the living, it was my prayer that I might have the means granted to warn you, and lo! Heaven hath heard me.'

'Major Bridgenorth,' said Lady Peveril, 'you were wont to be moderate in these sentiments — comparatively moderate, at least — and to love your own religion, without hating that of others.'

'What I was while in the gall of bitterness and in the bond of iniquity, it signifies not to recall,' answered he. 'I was then like to Gallio, who cared for none of these things. I doted on creature-comforts — I clung to worldly honour and repute — my thoughts were earthward, or those I turned to heaven were cold, formal, pharisaical meditations. I brought nothing to the altar save straw and stubble. Heaven saw need to chastise me in love. I was stripped of all that I clung to on earth; my worldly honour was torn from me; I went forth an exile from the home of my fathers — a deprived and desolate man — a baffled, and beaten, and dishonoured man. But who shall

find out the ways of Providence? Such were the means by
which I was chosen forth as a champion for the truth, holding my life as nothing, if thereby that may be advanced. But
this was not what I wished to speak of. Thou hast saved
the earthly life of my child; let me save the eternal welfare of
yours.'

Lady Peveril was silent. They were now approaching the
point where the avenue terminated in a communication with a
public road, or rather pathway, running through an uninclosed
common field; this the lady had to prosecute for a little way,
until a turn of the path gave her admittance into the park of
Martindale. She now felt sincerely anxious to be in the open
moonshine, and avoided reply to Bridgenorth that she might
make the more haste. But as they reached the junction of the
avenue and the public road, he laid his hand on her arm, and
commanded, rather than requested, her to stop. She obeyed.
He pointed to a huge oak, of the largest size, which grew on the
summit of a knoll in the open ground which terminated the
avenue, and was exactly so placed as to serve for a termination
to the vista. The moonshine without the avenue was so
strong that, amidst the flood of light which it poured on the
venerable tree, they could easily discover, from the shattered
state of the boughs on one side, that it had suffered damage
from lightning. 'Remember you,' he said, 'when we last
looked together on that tree? I had ridden from London, and
brought with me a protection from the committee for your
husband; and as I passed the spot — here on this spot where
we now stand, you stood with my lost Alice — two — the last
two of my beloved infants gambolled before you. I leaped from
my horse; to her I was a husband — to those a father — to you a
welcome and revered protector. What am I now to any one?'
He pressed his hand on his brow, and groaned in agony of
spirit.

It was not in the Lady Peveril's nature to hear sorrow without an attempt at consolation. 'Master Bridgenorth,' she said,
'I blame no man's creed, while I believe and follow my own;
and I rejoice that in yours you have sought consolation for
temporal afflictions. But does not every Christian creed teach
us alike that affliction should soften our heart?'

'Ay, woman,' said Bridgenorth, sternly, 'as the lightning
which shattered yonder oak hath softened its trunk. No; the
seared wood is the fitter for the use of the workmen; the
hardened and the dried-up heart is that which can best bear

"Major Bridgenorth pointed to a huge oak."

the task imposed by these dismal times. God and man will no longer endure the unbridled profligacy of the dissolute — the scoffing of the profane — the contempt of the Divine laws — the infraction of human rights. The times demand righters and avengers, and there will be no want of them.'

'I deny not the existence of much evil,' said Lady Peveril, compelling herself to answer, and beginning at the same time to walk forward; 'and from hearsay, though not, I thank Heaven, from observation, I am convinced of the wild debauchery of the times. But let us trust it may be corrected without such violent remedies as you hint at. Surely the ruin of a second civil war, though I trust your thoughts go not that dreadful length, were at best a desperate alternative.'

'Sharp, but sure,' replied Bridgenorth. 'The blood of the Paschal lamb chased away the destroying angel; the sacrifices offered on the threshing-floor of Araunah stayed the pestilence. Fire and sword are severe remedies, but they purge and purify.'

'Alas! Major Bridgenorth,' said the lady, 'wise and moderate in your youth, can you have adopted in your advanced life the thoughts and language of those whom you yourself beheld drive themselves and the nation to the brink of ruin ? '

'I know not what I then was; you know not what I now am,' he replied, and suddenly broke off; for they even then came forth into the open light, and it seemed as if, feeling himself under the lady's eye, he was disposed to soften his tone and his language.

At the first distinct view which she had of his person, she was aware that he was armed with a short sword, a poniard, and pistols at his belt — precautions very unusual for a man who formerly had seldom, and only on days of ceremony, carried a walking rapier, though such was the habitual and constant practice of gentlemen of his station in life. There seemed also something of more stern determination than usual in his air, which indeed had always been rather sullen than affable; and ere she could repress the sentiment, she could not help saying, 'Master Bridgenorth, you are indeed changed.'

'You see but the outward man,' he replied; 'the change within is yet deeper. But it was not of myself that I desired to talk : I have already said that, as you have preserved my child from the darkness of the grave, I would willingly preserve yours from that more utter darkness which, I fear, hath involved the path and walks of his father.'

'I must not hear this of Sir Geoffrey,' said the Lady Peveril;

'I must bid you farewell for the present; and when we again meet at a more suitable time, I will at least listen to your advice concerning Julian, although I should not perhaps incline to it.'

'That more suitable time may never come,' replied Bridgenorth. 'Time wanes, eternity draws nigh. Hearken! It is said to be your purpose to send the young Julian to be bred up in yonder bloody island, under the hand of your kinswoman, that cruel murderess, by whom was done to death a man more worthy of vital existence than any that she can boast among her vaunted ancestry. These are current tidings. Are they true?'

'I do not blame you, Master Bridgenorth, for thinking harshly of my cousin of Derby,' said Lady Peveril; 'nor do I altogether vindicate the rash action of which she hath been guilty. Nevertheless, in her habitation, it is my husband's opinion and my own that Julian may be trained in the studies and accomplishments becoming his rank, along with the young Earl of Derby.'

'Under the curse of God and the blessing of the Pope of Rome,' said Bridgenorth. 'You, lady, so quick-sighted in matters of earthly prudence, are you blind to the gigantic pace at which Rome is moving to regain this country, once the richest gem in her usurped tiara? The old are seduced by gold, the youth by pleasure, the weak by flattery, cowards by fear, and the courageous by ambition. A thousand baits for each taste, and each bait concealing the same deadly hook.'

'I am well aware, Master Bridgenorth,' said Lady Peveril, 'that my kinswoman is a Catholic;[1] but her son is educated in the Church of England's principles, agreeably to the command of her deceased husband.'

'Is it likely,' answered Bridgenorth, 'that she, who fears not shedding the blood of the righteous, whether on the field or scaffold, will regard the sanction of her promise when her religion bids her break it? Or, if she does, what shall your son be the better, if he remain in the mire of his father? What are your Episcopal tenets but mere Popery, save that ye have chosen a temporal tyrant for your pope, and substitute a mangled mass in English for that which your predecessors pronounced in Latin? But why speak I of these things to one who hath ears indeed, and eyes, yet cannot see, listen to,

---

[1] I have elsewhere noticed that this is a deviation from the truth: Charlotte Countess of Derby was a Huguenot.

or understand what is alone worthy to be heard, seen, and
known ? Pity, that what hath been wrought so fair and exquisite in form and disposition should be yet blind, deaf, and
ignorant, like the things which perish ! '

'We shall not agree on these subjects, Master Bridgenorth,'
said the lady, anxious still to escape from this strange conference, though scarce knowing what to apprehend ; 'once
more, I must bid you farewell.'

'Stay yet an instant,' he said, again laying his hand on her
arm ; 'I would stop you if I saw you rushing on the brink of
an actual precipice ; let me prevent you from a danger still
greater. How shall I work upon your unbelieving mind ?
Shall I tell you that the debt of bloodshed yet remains a debt
to be paid by the bloody house of Derby ? And wilt thou send
thy son to be among those from whom it shall be exacted ? '

'You wish to alarm me in vain, Master Bridgenorth,' answered the lady ; 'what penalty can be exacted from the
countess for an action which I have already called a rash one
has been long since levied.'

'You deceive yourself,' retorted he, sternly. 'Think you a
paltry sum of money given to be wasted on the debaucheries of
Charles can atone for the death of such a man as Christian — a
man precious alike to Heaven and to earth ? Not on such terms
is the blood of the righteous to be poured forth ! Every hour's
delay is numbered down as adding interest to the grievous debt
which will one day be required from that bloodthirsty woman.'

At this moment, the distant tread of horses was heard on
the road on which they held this singular dialogue. Bridgenorth listened a moment, and then said, 'Forget that you have
seen me — name not my name to your nearest or dearest — lock
my counsel in your breast — profit by it, and it shall be well
with you.'

So saying, he turned from her, and, plunging through a gap
in the fence, regained the cover of his own wood, along which
the path still led.

The noise of horses advancing at full trot now came nearer ;
and Lady Peveril was aware of several riders, whose forms rose
indistinctly on the summit of the rising ground behind her.
She became also visible to them ; and one or two of the foremost made towards her at increased speed, challenging her as
they advanced with the cry of 'Stand ! Who goes there ? '
The foremost who came up, however, exclaimed, 'Mercy on us,
if it be not my lady ! ' and Lady Peveril, at the same moment,

recognised one of her own servants. Her husband rode up immediately afterwards, with, 'How now, Dame Margaret? What makes you abroad so far from home, and at an hour so late?'

Lady Peveril mentioned her visit at the cottage, but did not think it necessary to say aught of having seen Major Bridge-north, afraid, it may be, that her husband might be displeased with that incident.

'Charity is a fine thing, and a fair,' answered Sir Geoffrey; 'but I must tell you, you do ill, dame, to wander about the country like a quacksalver at the call of every old woman who has a colic-fit; and at this time of night especially, and when the land is so unsettled besides.'

'I am sorry to hear that it is so,' said the lady. 'I had heard no such news.'

'News!' repeated Sir Geoffrey; 'why, here has a new plot broken out among the Roundheads, worse than Venner's by a butt's length;[1] and who should be so deep in it as our old neighbour Bridgenorth? There is search for him every-where; and I promise you, if he is found, he is like to pay old scores.'

'Then I am sure I trust he will not be found,' said Lady Peveril.

'Do you so?' replied Sir Geoffrey. 'Now I, on my part, hope that he will; and it shall not be my fault if be be not; for which effect I will presently ride down to Moultrassie, and make strict search, according to my duty; there shall neither rebel nor traitor earth so near Martindale Castle, that I will assure them. And you, my lady, be pleased for once to dispense with a pillion, and get up, as you have done before, behind Saunders, who shall convey you safe home.'

The lady obeyed in silence; indeed, she did not dare to trust her voice in an attempt to reply, so much was she disconcerted with the intelligence she had just heard.

She rode behind the groom to the castle, where she awaited in great anxiety the return of her husband. He came back at length; but, to her great relief, without any prisoner. He then explained more fully than his haste had before permitted that an express had come down to Chesterfield with news from court of a proposed insurrection amongst the old Common-wealth men, especially those who had served in the army; and

---

[1] The celebrated insurrection of the Anabaptists and Fifth Monarchy men in London, in the year 1661.

that Bridgenorth, said to be lurking in Derbyshire, was one of the principal conspirators.

After some time, this report of a conspiracy seemed to die away like many others of that period. The warrants were recalled, but nothing more was seen or heard of Major Bridgenorth; although it is probable he might safely enough have shown himself as openly as many did who lay under the same circumstances of suspicion.[1]

About this time also, Lady Peveril, with many tears, took a temporary leave of her son Julian, who was sent, as had long been intended, for the purpose of sharing the education of the young Earl of Derby. Although the boding words of Bridgenorth sometimes occurred to Lady Peveril's mind, she did not suffer them to weigh with her in opposition to the advantages which the patronage of the Countess of Derby secured to her son.

The plan seemed to be in every respect successful; and when, from time to time, Julian visited the house of his father, Lady Peveril had the satisfaction to see him, on every occasion, improved in person and in manner, as well as ardent in the pursuit of more solid acquirements. In process of time, he became a gallant and accomplished youth, and travelled for some time upon the Continent with the young earl. This was the more especially necessary for the enlarging of their acquaintance with the world, because the countess had never appeared in London, or at the court of King Charles, since her flight to the Isle of Man in 1660; but had resided in solitary and aristocratic state, alternately on her estates in England and in that island.

This had given to the education of both the young men, otherwise as excellent as the best teachers could render it, something of a narrow and restricted character; but though the disposition of the young earl was lighter and more volatile than that of Julian, both the one and the other had profited, in a considerable degree, by the opportunities afforded them. It was Lady Derby's strict injunction to her son, now returning from the Continent, that he should not appear at the court of Charles. But having been for some time of age, he did not think it absolutely necessary to obey her in this particular; and had remained for some time in London, partaking the pleasures of the gay court there, with all the ardour of a young man bred up in comparative seclusion.

[1] See Persecution of the Puritans. Note 7.

In order to reconcile the countess to this transgression of her authority, for he continued to entertain for her the profound respect in which he had been educated, Lord Derby agreed to make a long sojourn with her in her favourite island, which he abandoned almost entirely to her management.

Julian Peveril had spent at Martindale Castle a good deal of the time which his friend had bestowed in London ; and at the period to which, passing over many years, our story has arrived, as it were, *per saltum*, they were both living, as the countess's guests, in the Castle of Rushin, in the venerable kingdom of Man.

CHAPTER XI

Mona, long hid from those who roam the main.
COLLINS.

THE Isle of Man, in the middle of the 17th century, was very different, as a place of residence, from what it is now. Men had not then discovered its merit as a place of occasional refuge from the storms of life, and the society to be there met with was of a very uniform tenor. There were no smart fellows, whom fortune had tumbled from the seat of their barouches, no plucked pigeons or winged rooks, no disappointed speculators, no ruined miners — in short, no one worth talking to. The society of the island was limited to the natives themselves, and a few merchants, who lived by contraband trade. The amusements were rare and monotonous, and the mercurial young earl was soon heartily tired of his dominions. The islanders also, become too wise for happiness, had lost relish for the harmless and somewhat childish sports in which their simple ancestors had indulged themselves. May was no longer ushered in by the imaginary contest between the queen of retiring winter and advancing spring; the listeners no longer sympathised with the lively music of the followers of the one or the discordant sounds with which the other asserted a more noisy claim to attention. Christmas, too, closed, and the steeples no longer jangled forth a dissonant peal. The wren, to seek for which used to be the sport dedicated to the holytide, was left unpursued and unslain. Party spirit had come among these simple people, and destroyed their good-humour, while it left them their ignorance. Even the races, a sport generally interesting to people of all ranks, were no longer performed, because they were no longer attractive. The gentlemen were divided by feuds hitherto unknown, and each seemed to hold it scorn to be pleased with the same diversions that amused those of the opposite faction. The hearts of both parties revolted from the recollection of former days, when all was peace among them, when the Earl of Derby, now slaughtered, used to bestow the prize, and Christian, since so vindictively executed, started horses to add to the amusement.[1]

Julian was seated in the deep recess which led to a latticed window of the old castle; and, with his arms crossed, and an air of profound contemplation, was surveying the long perspective of ocean, which rolled its successive waves up to the foot of the rock on which the ancient pile is founded.   The earl was suffering under the infliction of *ennui*, now looking into a volume of Homer, now whistling, now swinging on his chair, now traversing the room, till at length his attention became swallowed up in admiration of the tranquillity of his companion.

'King of men!' he said, repeating the favourite epithet by which Homer describes Agamemnon — 'I trust, for the old Greek's sake, he had a merrier office than being King of Man. Most philosophical Julian, will nothing rouse thee, not even a bad pun on my own royal dignity?'

'I wish you would be a little more the King in Man,' said Julian, starting from his reverie, 'and then you would find more amusement in your dominions.'

'What! dethrone that royal Semiramis my mother,' said the young lord, 'who has as much pleasure in playing queen as if she were a real sovereign? I wonder you can give me such counsel.'

'Your mother, as you well know, my dear Derby, would be delighted did you take any interest in the affairs of the island.'

'Ay, truly, she would permit me to be king; but she would choose to remain viceroy over me.   Why, she would only gain a subject the more, by my converting my spare time, which is so very valuable to me, to the cares of royalty.   No — no, Julian, she thinks it power to direct all the affairs of these poor Manxmen; and, thinking it power, she finds it pleasure.   I shall not interfere, unless she hold a high court of justice again. I cannot afford to pay another fine to my brother, King Charles. But I forget — this is a sore point with you.'

'With the countess, at least,' replied Julian; 'and I wonder you will speak of it.'

'Why, I bear no malice against the poor man's memory any more than yourself, though I have not the same reasons for holding it in veneration,' replied the Earl of Derby; 'and yet

---

[1] See Popular Pastimes in the Isle of Man.   Note 8.

I have some respect for it too.   I remember their bringing him
out to die.   It was the first holiday I ever had in my life, and
I heartily wish it had been on some other account.'

'I would rather hear you speak of anything else, my lord,'
said Julian.

'Why, there it goes,' answered the earl; 'whenever I talk
of anything that puts you on your mettle and warms your
blood, that runs as cold as a merman's — to use a simile of this
happy island — hey pass ! you press me to change the subject.
Well, what shall we talk of ?   O Julian, if you had not gone
down to earth yourself among the castles and caverns of Derbyshire, we should have had enough of delicious topics — the play-
houses, Julian ! both the King's house and the Duke's — Louis's
establishment is a jest to them ; and the Ring in the Park,
which beats the Corso at Naples ; and the beauties, who beat
the whole world ! '

'I am very willing to hear you speak on the subject, my
lord,' answered Julian ; 'the less I have seen of the London
world myself, the more I am likely to be amused by your
account of it.'

'Ay, my friend, but where to begin ? with the wit of Buckingham, and Sedley, and Etherege, or with the grace of Harry
Jermyn, the courtesy of the Duke of Monmouth, or with the
loveliness of La Belle Hamilton, of the Duchess of Richmond,
of Lady ——, the person of Roxalana, the smart humour of
Mrs. Nelly —— '

'Or what say you to the bewitching sorceries of Lady
Cynthia ?' demanded his companion.

'Faith, I would have kept these to myself,' said the earl,
'to follow your prudent example.   But since you ask me, I
fairly own I cannot tell what to say of them ; only I think of
them twenty times as often as all the beauties I have spoken of.
And yet she is neither the twentieth part so beautiful as the
plainest of these court beauties, nor so witty as the dullest I
have named, nor so modish — that is the great matter — as the
most obscure.   I cannot tell what makes me dote on her, except
that she is as capricious as her whole sex put together.'

'That I should think a small recommendation,' answered
his companion.

'Small, do you term it,' replied the earl, 'and write yourself
a brother of the angle ?   Why, which like you best ? to pull a
dead strain on a miserable gudgeon, which you draw ashore by
main force, as the fellows here tow in their fishing-boats ; or a

lively salmon, that makes your rod crack and your line whistle
— plays you ten thousand mischievous pranks — wearies your
heart out with hopes and fears — and is only laid panting on
the bank after you have shown the most unmatchable display
of skill, patience, and dexterity ? But I see you have a mind
to go on angling after your own old fashion. Off laced coat,
and on brown jerkin ; lively colours scare fish in the sober
waters of the Isle of Man ; faith, in London you will catch few,
unless the bait glistens a little. But you *are* going ? well,
good luck to you. I will take to the barge ; the sea and wind
are less inconstant than the tide you have embarked on.'

'You have learned to say all these smart things in London,
my lord,' answered Julian ; 'but we shall have you a penitent
for them, if Lady Cynthia be of my mind. Adieu, and pleasure
till we meet.'

The young men parted accordingly ; and while the earl
betook him to his pleasure-voyage, Julian, as his friend had
prophesied, assumed the dress of one who means to amuse himself with angling. The hat and feather were exchanged for a
cap of grey cloth ; the deeply-laced cloak and doublet for a
simple jacket of the same colour, with hose conforming ; and
finally, with rod in hand and pannier at his back, mounted
upon a handsome Manx pony, young Peveril rode briskly
over the country which divided him from one of those beautiful streams that descend to the sea from the Kirk-Merlagh
mountains.

Having reached the spot where he meant to commence his
day's sport, Julian let his little steed graze, which, accustomed
to the situation, followed him like a dog ; and now and then,
when tired of picking herbage in the valley through which the
stream winded, came near her master's side, and, as if she had
been a curious amateur of the sport, gazed on the trouts as
Julian brought them struggling to the shore. But Fairy's
master showed, on that day, little of the patience of a real
angler, and took no heed to old Isaac Walton's recommendation to fish the streams inch by inch. He chose, indeed, with
an angler's eye, the most promising casts, where the stream
broke sparkling over a stone, affording the wonted shelter to a
trout ; or where, gliding away from a rippling current to a still
eddy, it streamed under the projecting bank, or dashed from
the pool of some low cascade. By this judicious selection of
spots whereon to employ his art, the sportsman's basket was
soon sufficiently heavy to show that his occupation was not a

mere pretext; and so soon as this was the case, he walked
briskly up the glen, only making a cast from time to time, in
case of his being observed from any of the neighbouring heights.

It was a little green and rocky valley through which the
brook strayed, very lonely, although the slight track of an
unformed road showed that it was occasionally traversed, and
that it was not altogether void of inhabitants. As Peveril
advanced still farther, the right bank reached to some distance
from the stream, leaving a piece of meadow ground, the lower
part of which, being close to the brook, was entirely covered
with rich herbage, being possibly occasionally irrigated by its
overflow. The higher part of the level ground afforded a stance
for an old house, of a singular structure, with a terraced garden,
and a cultivated field or two beside it. In former times a
Danish or Norwegian fastness had stood here, called the Black
Fort, from the colour of a huge heathy hill, which, rising
behind the building, appeared to be the boundary of the valley,
and to afford the source of the brook. But the original structure had been long demolished, as, indeed, it probably only
consisted of dry stones, and its materials had been applied to
the construction of the present mansion — the work of some
churchman during the 16th century, as was evident from the
huge stonework of its windows, which scarce left room for
light to pass through, as well as from two or three heavy
buttresses, which projected from the front of the house, and
exhibited on their surface little niches for images. These had
been carefully destroyed, and pots of flowers were placed in the
niches in their stead, besides their being ornamented by creeping plants of various kinds, fancifully twined around them.
The garden was also in good order; and though the spot was
extremely solitary, there was about it altogether an air of comfort, accommodation, and even elegance, by no means generally
characteristic of the habitations of the island at the time.

With much circumspection, Julian Peveril approached the
low Gothic porch, which defended the entrance of the mansion
from the tempests incident to its situation, and was, like the
buttresses, over-run with ivy and other creeping plants. An
iron ring, contrived so as when drawn up and down to rattle
against the bar of notched iron through which it was suspended,
served the purpose of a knocker; and to this he applied himself,
though with the greatest precaution.

He received no answer for some time, and indeed it seemed
as if the house was totally uninhabited; when at length, his

impatience getting the upper hand, he tried to open the door, and, as it was only upon the latch, very easily succeeded.   He passed through a little low-arched hall, the upper end of which was occupied by a staircase, and turning to the left, opened the door of a summer parlour, wainscoted with black oak, and very simply furnished with chairs and tables of the same materials, the former cushioned with leather.   The apartment was gloomy — one of those stone-shafted windows which we have mentioned, with its small latticed panes, and thick garland of foliage, admitting but an imperfect light.

Over the chimney-piece, which was of the same massive materials with the panelling of the apartment, was the only ornament of the room — a painting, namely, representing an officer in the military dress of the Civil Wars.   It was a green jerkin, then the national and peculiar wear of the Manxmen; his short band, which hung down on the cuirass, the orange-coloured scarf, but, above all, the shortness of his close-cut hair, showing evidently to which of the great parties he had belonged.   His right hand rested on the hilt of his sword; and in the left he held a small Bible, bearing the inscription, '*In hoc signo.*'   The countenance was of a light complexion, with fair and almost effeminate blue eyes, and an oval form of face; one of those physiognomies to which, though not otherwise unpleasing, we naturally attach the idea of melancholy and of misfortune.[1]   Apparently it was well known to Julian Peveril; for, after having looked at it for a long time, he could not forbear muttering aloud, 'What would I give that that man had never been born, or that he still lived!'

'How now — how is this?' said a female, who entered the room as he uttered this reflection.   '*You* here, Master Peveril, in spite of all the warnings you have had!   You here, in the possession of folks' house when they are abroad, and talking to yourself, as I shall warrant!'

'Yes, Mistress Deborah,' said Peveril, 'I am here once more, as you see, against every prohibition, and in defiance of all danger.   Where is Alice?'

'Where you will never see her, Master Julian, you may satisfy yourself of that,' answered Mistress Deborah, for it was that respectable governante; and sinking down at the same time upon one of the large leathern chairs, she began to fan herself with her handkerchief, and complain of the heat in a most ladylike fashion.

---

[1] See Portrait of William Christian.   Note 9.

In fact, Mistress Debbitch, while her exterior intimated a
considerable change of condition for the better, and her countenance showed the less favourable effects of the twenty years
which had passed over her head, was in mind and manners
very much what she had been when she battled the opinions
of Madam Ellesmere at Martindale Castle. In a word, she
was self-willed, obstinate, and coquettish as ever, otherwise no
ill-disposed person. Her present appearance was that of a
woman of the better rank. From the sobriety of the fashion
of her dress, and the uniformity of its colours, it was plain she
belonged to some sect which condemned superfluous gaiety in
attire ; but no rules, not those of a nunnery or of a Quaker's
society, can prevent a little coquetry in that particular, where
a woman is desirous of being supposed to retain some claim to
personal attention. All Mistress Deborah's garments were so
arranged as might best set off a good-looking woman, whose
countenance indicated ease and good cheer, who called herself
five-and-thirty, and was well entitled, if she had a mind, to call
herself twelve or fifteen years older.

Julian was under the necessity of enduring all her tiresome
and fantastic airs, and awaiting with patience till she had
'prinked herself and prinned herself,' flung her hoods back and
drawn them forward, snuffed at a little bottle of essences, closed
her eyes like a dying fowl, turned them up like a duck in a
thunderstorm — when at length, having exhausted her round
of *minauderies*, she condescended to open the conversation.

'These walks will be the death of me,' she said, 'and all on
your account, Master Julian Peveril ; for if Dame Christian
should learn that you have chosen to make your visits to her
niece, I promise you Mistress Alice would be soon obliged to
find other quarters, and so should I.'

'Come now, Mistress Deborah, be good-humoured,' said
Julian ; 'consider, was not all this intimacy of ours of your
own making ? Did you not make yourself known to me the
very first time I strolled up this glen with my fishing-rod, and
tell me that you were my former keeper, and that Alice had
been my little playfellow ? And what could there be more
natural than that I should come back and see two such agreeable persons as often as I could ? '

'Yes,' said Dame Deborah ; 'but I did not bid you fall in
love with us, though, or propose such a matter as marriage
either to Alice or myself.'

'To do you justice, you never did, Deborah,' answered the

youth; 'but what of that? Such things will come out before
one is aware. I am sure you must have heard such proposals
fifty times when you least expected them.'

'Fie — fie — fie, Master Julian Peveril,' said the governante;
'I would have you to know that I have always so behaved myself
that the best of the land would have thought twice of it, and
have very well considered both what he was going to say and
how he was going to say it, before he came out with such proposals to me.'

'True — true, Mistress Deborah,' continued Julian; 'but all
the world have not your discretion. Then Alice Bridgenorth
is a child — a mere child; and one always asks a baby to be
one's little wife, you know. Come, I know you will forgive me.
Thou wert ever the best-natured, kindest woman in the world;
and you know you have said twenty times we were made for
each other.'

'Oh, no, Master Julian Peveril; no — no — no!' ejaculated
Deborah. 'I may indeed have said your estates were born
to be united; and to be sure it is natural for me, that come
of the old stock of the yeomanry of Peveril of the Peak's
estate, to wish that it was all within the ring fence again;
which sure enough it might be, were you to marry Alice Bridgenorth. But then there is the knight your father and my lady
your mother; and there is her father, that is half crazy with
his religion; and her aunt, that wears eternal black grogram for
that unlucky Colonel Christian; and there is the Countess of
Derby, that would serve us all with the same sauce if we were
thinking of anything that would displease her. And besides
all that, you have broke your word with Mistress Alice, and
everything is over between you; and I am of opinion it is
quite right it should be all over. And perhaps it may be,
Master Julian, that I should have thought so a long time ago,
before a child like Alice put it into my head; but I am so good-
natured.'

No flatterer like a lover who wishes to carry his point.

'You are the best-natured, kindest creature in the world,
Deborah. But you have never seen the ring I bought for you
at Paris. Nay, I will put it on your finger myself; what!
your foster-son, whom you loved so well, and took such
care of!'

He easily succeeded in putting a pretty ring of gold, with a
humorous affectation of gallantry, on the fat finger of Mistress
Deborah Debbitch. Hers was a soul of a kind often to be met

with, both among the lower and higher vulgar, who, without
being, on a broad scale, accessible to bribes or corruption, are
nevertheless much attached to perquisites, and considerably
biassed in their line of duty, though perhaps insensibly, by the
love of petty observances, petty presents, and trivial compli-
ments.   Mistress Debbitch turned the ring round, and round,
and round, and at length said, in a whisper, ' Well, Master
Julian Peveril, it signifies nothing denying anything to such
a young gentleman as you, for young gentlemen are always
so obstinate ! and so I may as well tell you that Mistress Alice
walked back from Kirk-Truagh along with me just now, and
entered the house at the same time with myself.'

' Why did you not tell me so before ? ' said Julian, starting
up ; ' where — where is she ? '

' You had better ask why I tell you so *now*, Master Julian,'
said Dame Deborah ; ' for, I promise you, it is against her
express commands ; and I would not have told you had you
not looked so pitiful.   But as for seeing you, that she will not ;
and she is in her own bedroom, with a good oak door shut and
bolted upon her, that is one comfort.   And so, as for any
breach of trust on my part — I promise you, the little saucy
minx gives it no less name — it is quite impossible.'

' Do not say so, Deborah — only go — only try — tell her to
hear me — tell her I have a hundred excuses for disobeying her
commands — tell her I have no doubt to get over all obstacles
at Martindale Castle.'

' Nay, I tell you it is all in vain,' replied the dame.   ' When
I saw your cap and rod lying in the hall, I did but say, " There
he is again," and she ran up the stairs like a young deer ; and I
heard key turned and bolts shot ere I could say a single word
to stop her ; I marvel you heard her not.'

' It was because I am, as I ever was, an owl — a dreaming
fool, who let all those golden minutes pass which my luckless
life holds out to me so rarely.   Well — tell her I go — go for
ever — go where she will hear no more of me — where no one
shall hear more of me ! '

' Oh, the Father ! ' said the dame, ' hear how he talks !   What
will become of Sir Geoffrey, and your mother, and of me, and
of the countess, if you were to go so far as you talk of ?   And
what would become of poor Alice too ? for I will be sworn she
likes you better than she says, and I know she used to sit and
look the way that you used to come up the stream, and now
and then ask me if the morning were good for fishing.   And

all the while you were on the Continent, as they call it, she scarcely smiled once, unless it was when she got two beautiful long letters about foreign parts.'

'Friendship, Dame Deborah — only friendship — cold and calm remembrance of one who, by your kind permission, stole in on your solitude now and then, with news from the living world without. Once, indeed, I thought — but it is all over — farewell.'

So saying, he covered his face with one hand, and extended the other, in the act of bidding adieu to Dame Debbitch, whose kind heart became unable to withstand the sight of his affliction.

'Now, do not be in such haste,' she said; 'I will go up again, and tell her how it stands with you, and bring her down, if it is in woman's power to do it.'

And so saying, she left the apartment and ran upstairs.

Julian Peveril, meanwhile, paced the apartment in great agitation, waiting the success of Deborah's intercession; and she remained long enough absent to give us time to explain, in a short retrospect, the circumstances which had led to his present situation.

CHAPTER XII

Ah me ! for aught that ever I could read,
Could ever hear by tale or history,
The course of true love never did run smooth !
Midsummer Night's Dream.

THE celebrated passage which we have prefixed to this
chapter has, like most observations of the same author,
its foundation in real experience. The period at which
love is formed for the first time, and felt most strongly, is
seldom that at which there is much prospect of its being brought
to a happy issue. The state of artificial society opposes many
complicated obstructions to early marriages ; and the chance
is very great that such obstacles prove insurmountable. In
fine, there are few men who do not look back in secret to some
period of their youth at which a sincere and early affection was
repulsed, or betrayed, or became abortive from opposing circumstances. It is these little passages of secret history which
leave a tinge of romance in every bosom, scarce permitting us,
even in the most busy or the most advanced period of life, to
listen with total indifference to a tale of true love.

Julian Peveril had so fixed his affections as to ensure the
fullest share of that opposition which early attachments are so
apt to encounter. Yet nothing so natural as that he should
have done so. In early youth, Dame Debbitch had accidentally
met with the son of her first patroness, and who had himself
been her earliest charge, fishing in the little brook already
noticed, which watered the valley in which she resided with
Alice Bridgenorth. The dame's curiosity easily discovered who
he was ; and besides the interest which persons in her condition
usually take in the young people who have been under their
charge, she was delighted with the opportunity to talk about
former times — about Martindale Castle and friends there,
about Sir Geoffrey and his good lady, and now and then about
Lance Outram, the park-keeper.

The mere pleasure of gratifying her inquiries would scarce have had power enough to induce Julian to repeat his visits to the lonely glen; but Deborah had a companion — a lovely girl — bred in solitude, and in the quiet and unpretending tastes which solitude encourages — spirited also, and inquisitive, and listening, with laughing cheek and an eager eye, to every tale which the young angler brought from the town and castle.

The visits of Julian to the Black Fort were only occasional; so far Dame Deborah showed common sense, which was, perhaps, inspired by the apprehension of losing her place, in case of discovery. She had, indeed, great confidence in the strong and rooted belief, amounting almost to superstition, which Major Bridgenorth entertained, that his daughter's continued health could only be ensured by her continuing under the charge of one who had acquired Lady Peveril's supposed skill in treating those subject to such ailments. This belief Dame Deborah had improved to the utmost of her simple cunning — always speaking in something of an oracular tone upon the subject of her charge's health, and hinting at certain mysterious rules necessary to maintain it in the present favourable state. She had availed herself of this artifice to procure for herself and Alice a separate establishment at the Black Fort; for it was originally Major Bridgenorth's resolution that his daughter and her governante should remain under the same roof with the sister-in-law of his deceased wife, the widow of the unfortunate Colonel Christian. But this lady was broken down with premature age, brought on by sorrow; and, in a short visit which Major Bridgenorth made to the island, he was easily prevailed on to consider her house at Kirk-Truagh as a very cheerless residence for his daughter. Dame Deborah, who longed for domestic independence, was careful to increase this impression by alarming her patron's fears on account of Alice's health. The mansion of Kirk-Truagh stood, she said, much exposed to the Scottish winds, which could not but be cold, as they came from a country where, as she was assured, there was ice and snow at midsummer. In short, she prevailed, and was put into full possession of the Black Fort — a house which, as well as Kirk-Truagh, belonged formerly to Christian, and now to his widow.

Still, however, it was enjoined on the governante and her charge to visit Kirk-Truagh from time to time, and to consider themselves as under the management and guardianship of Mistress Christian — a state of subjection the sense of which

Deborah endeavoured to lessen by assuming as much freedom of conduct as she possibly dared, under the influence, doubtless, of the same feelings of independence which induced her, at Martindale Hall, to spurn the advice of Mistress Ellesmere.

It was this generous disposition to defy control which induced her to procure for Alice, secretly, some means of education, which the stern genius of Puritanism would have proscribed. She ventured to have her charge taught music — nay, even dancing; and the picture of the stern Colonel Christian trembled on the wainscot where it was suspended while the sylph-like form of Alice, and the substantial person of Dame Deborah, executed French *chaussées* and *borées*, to the sound of a small kit, which screamed under the bow of Monsieur de Pigal, half smuggler, half dancing-master. This abomination reached the ears of the colonel's widow, and by her was communicated to Bridgenorth, whose sudden appearance in the island showed the importance he attached to the communication. Had she been faithless to her own cause, that had been the latest hour of Mrs. Deborah's administration. But she retreated into her stronghold.

'Dancing,' she said, 'was exercise, regulated and timed by music; and it stood to reason that it must be the best of all exercise for a delicate person, especially as it could be taken within doors, and in all states of the weather.'

Bridgenorth listened, with a clouded and thoughtful brow, when, in exemplification of her doctrine, Mistress Deborah, who was no contemptible performer on the viol, began to jangle Sellenger's round, and desired Alice to dance an old English measure to the tune. As the half-bashful, half-smiling girl, about fourteen — for such was her age — moved gracefully to the music, the father's eye unavoidably followed the light spring of her step, and marked with joy the rising colour in her cheek. When the dance was over, he folded her in his arms, smoothed her somewhat disordered locks with a father's affectionate hand, smiled, kissed her brow, and took his leave, without one single word farther interdicting the exercise of dancing. He did not himself communicate the result of his visit at the Black Fort to Mrs. Christian, but she was not long of learning it, by the triumph of Dame Deborah on her next visit.

'It is well,' said the stern old lady; 'my brother Bridgenorth hath permitted you to make a Herodias of Alice, and teach her dancing. You have only now to find her a partner for life; I shall neither meddle nor make more in their affairs.'

In fact, the triumph of Dame Deborah, or rather of Dame Nature, on this occasion, had more important effects than the former had ventured to anticipate; for Mrs. Christian, though she received with all formality the formal visits of the governante and her charge, seemed thenceforth so pettish with the issue of her remonstrance upon the enormity of her niece dancing to a little fiddle, that she appeared to give up interference in her affairs, and left Dame Debbitch and Alice to manage both education and housekeeping — in which she had hitherto greatly concerned herself — much after their own pleasure.

It was in this independent state that they lived, when Julian first visited their habitation; and he was the rather encouraged to do so by Dame Deborah, that she believed him to be one of the last persons in the world with whom Mistress Christian would have desired her niece to be acquainted — the happy spirit of contradiction superseding, with Dame Deborah, on this as on other occasions, all consideration of the fitness of things. She did not act altogether without precaution neither. She was aware she had to guard not only against any reviving interest or curiosity on the part of Mistress Christian, but against the sudden arrival of Major Bridgenorth, who never failed once in the year to make his appearance at the Black Fort when least expected, and to remain there for a few days. Dame Debbitch, therefore, exacted of Julian that his visits should be few and far between; that he should condescend to pass for a relation of her own, in the eyes of two ignorant Manx girls and a lad, who formed her establishment; and that he should always appear in his angler's dress made of the simple *lougthan*, or buff-coloured wool of the island, which is not subjected to dyeing. By these cautions, she thought his intimacy at the Black Fort would be entirely unnoticed, or considered as immaterial, while, in the meantime, it furnished much amusement to her charge and herself.

This was accordingly the case during the earlier part of their intercourse, while Julian was a lad and Alice a girl two or three years younger. But as the lad shot up to youth and the girl to womanhood, even Dame Deborah Debbitch's judgment saw danger in their continued intimacy. She took an opportunity to communicate to Julian who Miss Bridgenorth actually was, and the peculiar circumstances which placed discord between their fathers. He heard the story of their quarrel with interest and surprise, for he had only resided occasionally at Martindale Castle, and the subject of Bridgenorth's quarrel with his father had never been mentioned in his presence. His imagination caught fire at the sparks afforded by this singular story ; and, far from complying with the prudent remonstrance of Dame Deborah, and gradually estranging himself from the Black Fort and its fair inmate, he frankly declared, he considered his intimacy there, so casually commenced, as intimating the will of Heaven that Alice and he were designed for each other, in spite of every obstacle which passion or prejudice could raise up betwixt them. They had been companions in infancy ; and a little exertion of memory enabled him to recall his childish grief for the unexpected and sudden disappearance of his little companion, whom he was destined again to meet with in the early bloom of opening beauty, in a country which was foreign to them both.

Dame Deborah was confounded at the consequences of her communication, which had thus blown into a flame the passion which she hoped it would have either prevented or extinguished. She had not the sort of head which resists the masculine and energetic remonstrances of passionate attachment, whether addressed to her on her own account or on behalf of another. She lamented and wondered, and ended her feeble opposition by weeping, and sympathising, and consenting to allow the continuance of Julian's visits, provided he should only address himself to Alice as a friend ; to gain the world, she would consent to nothing more. She was not, however, so simple, but that she also had her forebodings of the designs of Providence on this youthful couple ; for certainly they could not be more formed to be united than the good estates of Martindale and Moultrassie.

Then came a long sequence of reflections. Martindale Castle wanted but some repairs to be almost equal to Chatsworth. The hall might be allowed to go to ruin ; or, what would be better, when Sir Geoffrey's time came, for the good knight had seen service, and must be breaking now, the hall would be a good dowery-house, to which my lady and Ellesmere might retreat ; while, empress of the still-room and queen of the pantry, Mistress Deborah Debbitch should reign housekeeper at the castle, and extend, perhaps, the crown-matrimonial to Lance Outram, provided he was not become too old, too fat, or too fond of ale.

Such were the soothing visions under the influence of which the dame connived at an attachment which lulled also to pleasing dreams, though of a character so different, her charge and her visitant.

The visits of the young angler became more and more frequent; and the embarrassed Deborah, though foreseeing all the dangers of discovery, and the additional risk of an explanation betwixt Alice and Julian, which must necessarily render their relative situation so much more delicate, felt completely overborne by the enthusiasm of the young lover, and was compelled to let matters take their course.

The departure of Julian for the Continent interrupted the course of his intimacy at the Black Fort, and while it relieved the elder of its inmates from much internal apprehension, spread an air of languor and dejection over the countenance of the younger, which, at Bridgenorth's next visit to the Isle of Man, renewed all his terrors for his daughter's constitutional malady.

Deborah promised faithfully she should look better the next morning, and she kept her word. She had retained in her possession for some time a letter which Julian had, by some private conveyance, sent to her charge, for his youthful friend. Deborah had dreaded the consequences of delivering it as a billet-doux, but, as in the case of the dance, she thought there could be no harm in administering it as a remedy.

It had complete effect: and next day the cheeks of the maiden had a tinge of the rose, which so much delighted her father, that, as he mounted his horse, he flung his purse into Deborah's hand, with the desire she should spare nothing that could make herself and his daughter happy, and the assurance that she had his full confidence.

This expression of liberality and trust from a man of Major Bridgenorth's reserved and cautious disposition gave full plumage to Mistress Deborah's hopes; and emboldened her not only to deliver another letter of Julian's to the young lady, but to encourage more boldly and freely than formerly the intercourse of the lovers when Peveril returned from abroad.

At length, in spite of all Julian's precaution, the young earl became suspicious of his frequent solitary fishing-parties; and he himself, now better acquainted with the world than formerly, became aware that his repeated visits and solitary walks with a person so young and beautiful as Alice might not only betray prematurely the secret of his attachment, but be of essential prejudice to her who was its object.

Under the influence of this conviction, he abstained, for an unusual period, from visiting the Black Fort. But when he next indulged himself with spending an hour in the place where he would gladly have abode for ever, the altered manner of Alice, the tone in which she seemed to upbraid his neglect, penetrated his heart, and deprived him of that power of self-command which he had hitherto exercised in their interviews. It required but a few energetic words to explain to Alice at once his feelings and to make her sensible of the real nature of her own. She wept plentifully, but her tears were not all of bitterness. She sat passively still, and without reply, while he explained to her, with many an interjection, the circumstances which had placed discord between their families ; for hitherto all that she had known was that Master Peveril, belonging to the household of the great Countess or Lady of Man, must observe some precautions in visiting a relative of the unhappy Colonel Christian. But, when Julian concluded his tale with the warmest protestations of eternal love, ' My poor father ! ' she burst forth, ' and was this to be the end of all thy precautions ? This, that the son of him that disgraced and banished thee should hold such language to your daughter ! '

' You err, Alice — you err,' cried Julian, eagerly. ' That I hold this language — that the son of Peveril addresses thus the daughter of your father — that he thus kneels to you for forgiveness of injuries which passed when we were both infants, shows the will of Heaven that in our affection should be quenched the discord of our parents. What else could lead those who parted infants on the hills of Derbyshire to meet thus in the valleys of Man ? '

Alice, however new such a scene, and, above all, her own emotions, might be, was highly endowed with that exquisite delicacy which is imprinted in the female heart, to give warning of the slightest approach to impropriety in a situation like hers.

' Rise — rise, Master Peveril,' she said ; ' do not do yourself and me this injustice ; we have done both wrong — very wrong ; but my fault was done in ignorance. O God ! my poor father, who needs comfort so much — is it for me to add to his misfortunes ? Rise ! ' she added, more firmly ; ' if you retain this unbecoming posture any longer, I will leave the room, and you shall never see me more.'

The commanding tone of Alice overawed the impetuosity of her lover, who took in silence a seat removed to some distance from hers, and was again about to speak. 'Julian,' said she, in a milder tone, 'you have spoken enough, and more than enough. Would you had left me in the pleasing dream in which I could have listened to you for ever! but the hour of wakening is arrived.' Peveril waited the prosecution of her speech as a criminal while he waits his doom; for he was sufficiently sensible that an answer, delivered not certainly without emotion, but with firmness and resolution, was not to be interrupted. 'We have done wrong,' she repeated — 'very wrong; and if we now separate for ever, the pain we may feel will be but a just penalty for our error. We should never have met. Meeting, we should part as soon as possible. Our farther intercourse can but double our pain at parting. Farewell, Julian; and forget we ever have seen each other!'

'Forget!' said Julian; 'never — never. To *you* it is easy to speak the word — to think the thought. To *me*, an approach to either can only be by utter destruction. Why should you doubt that the feud of our fathers, like so many of which we have heard, might be appeased by our friendship? You are my only friend. I am the only one whom Heaven has assigned to you. Why should we separate for the fault of others, which befell when we were but children?'

'You speak in vain, Julian,' said Alice. 'I pity you; perhaps I pity myself. Indeed, I should pity myself, perhaps, the most of the two; for you will go forth to new scenes and new faces, and will soon forget me; but I, remaining in this solitude, how shall *I* forget? That, however, is not now the question. I can bear my lot, and it commands us to part.'

'Hear me yet a moment,' said Peveril; 'this evil is not, cannot be, remediless. I will go to my father — I will use the intercession of my mother, to whom he can refuse nothing — I will gain their consent — they have no other child — and they must consent, or lose him for ever. Say, Alice, if I come to you with my parents' consent to my suit, will you again say, with that tone so touching and so sad, yet so incredibly determined — "Julian, we must part"?' Alice was silent. 'Cruel girl, will you not even deign to answer me?' said her lover.

'We answer not those who speak in their dreams,' said Alice. 'You ask me what I would do were impossibilities performed. What right have you to make such suppositions, and ask such a question?'

'Hope, Alice — hope,' answered Julian, 'the last support of the wretched, which even you surely would not be cruel enough

to deprive me of. In every difficulty, in every doubt, in every
danger, Hope will fight even if he cannot conquer. Tell me
once more, if I come to you in the name of my father — in the
name of that mother to whom you partly owe your life — what
would you answer to me ?'

'I would refer you to my own father,' said Alice, blushing,
and casting her eyes down ; but instantly raising them again,
she repeated, in a firmer and a sadder tone — 'yes, Julian, I
would refer you to my father ; and you would find that your
pilot, Hope, had deceived you, and that you had but escaped
the quicksands to fall upon the rocks.'

'I would that could be tried !' said Julian. 'Methinks I
could persuade your father that in ordinary eyes our alliance is
not undesirable. My family have fortune, rank, long descent —
all that fathers look for when they bestow a daughter's hand.'

'All this would avail you nothing,' said Alice. 'The spirit
of my father is bent upon the things of another world ; and if
he listened to hear you out, it would be but to tell you that he
spurned your offers.'

'You know not — you know not, Alice,' said Julian. 'Fire
can soften iron : thy father's heart cannot be so hard, or his
prejudices so strong, but I shall find some means to melt him.
Forbid me not — Oh, forbid me not at least the experiment !'

'I can but advise,' said Alice ; 'I can forbid you nothing ;
for to forbid implies power to command obedience. But if you
will be wise and listen to me — here, and on this spot, we part
for ever !'

'Not so, by Heaven !' said Julian, whose bold and sanguine
temper scarce saw difficulty in attaining aught which he
desired. 'We now part indeed, but it is that I may return
armed with my parents' consent. They desire that I should
marry — in their last letters they pressed it more openly — they
shall have their desire ; and such a bride as I will present to
them has not graced their house since the Conqueror gave it
origin. Farewell, Alice ! — farewell, for a brief space !'

She replied, 'Farewell, Julian ! — farewell for ever !'

Julian, within a week of this interview, was at Martindale
Castle, with the view of communicating his purpose. But the
task which seems easy at a distance proves as difficult upon a
nearer approach as the fording of a river which from afar
appeared only a brook. There lacked not opportunities of
entering upon the subject ; for, in the first ride which he took
with his father, the knight resumed the subject of his son's

marriage, and liberally left the lady to his choice; but under
the strict proviso, that she was of a loyal and an honourable
family; if she had fortune, it was good and well, or rather, it
was better than well; but if she was poor, why, 'There is still
some picking,' said Sir Geoffrey, 'on the bones of the old estate;
and Dame Margaret and I will be content with the less, that you
young folks may have your share of it. I am turned frugal
already, Julian. You see what a north-country shambling
bit of a Galloway nag I ride upon — a different beast, I wot,
from my own old Black Hastings, who had but one fault, and
that was his wish to turn down Moultrassie avenue.'

'Was that so great a fault?' said Julian, affecting indifference, while his heart was trembling, as it seemed to him,
almost in his very throat.

'It used to remind me of that base, dishonourable Presbyterian fellow, Bridgenorth,' said Sir Geoffrey; 'and I would
as lief think of a toad. They say he has turned Independent,
to accomplish the full degree of rascality. I tell you, Gill, I
turned off the cow-boy for gathering nuts in his woods. I
would hang a dog that would so much as kill a hare there.
But what is the matter with you? You look pale.'

Julian made some indifferent answer, but too well understood, from the language and tone which his father used, that
his prejudices against Alice's father were both deep and en-
venomed, as those of country gentlemen often become, who,
having little to do or think of, are but too apt to spend their
time in nursing and cherishing petty causes of wrath against
their next neighbours.

In the course of the same day, he mentioned the Bridge-
norths to his mother, as if in a casual manner. But the Lady
Peveril instantly conjured him never to mention the name,
especially in his father's presence.

'Was that Major Bridgenorth, of whom I have heard the
name mentioned,' said Julian, 'so very bad a neighbour?'

'I do not say so,' said Lady Peveril; 'nay, we were more
than once obliged to him, in the former unhappy times; but
your father and he took some passages so ill at each other's
hands, that the least allusion to him disturbs Sir Geoffrey's
temper in a manner quite unusual, and which, now that his
health is somewhat impaired, is sometimes alarming to me.
For Heaven's sake, then, my dear Julian, avoid upon all
occasions the slightest allusion to Moultrassie or any of its
inhabitants.'

This warning was so seriously given, that Julian himself saw that mentioning his secret purpose would be the sure way to render it abortive, and therefore he returned disconsolate to the isle.

Peveril had the boldness, however, to make the best he could of what had happened, by requesting an interview with Alice, in order to inform her what had passed betwixt his parents and him on her account. It was with great difficulty that this boon was obtained; and Alice Bridgenorth showed no slight degree of displeasure when she discovered, after much circumlocution, and many efforts to give an air of importance to what he had to communicate, that all amounted but to this, that Lady Peveril continued to retain a favourable opinion of her father, Major Bridgenorth, which Julian would fain have represented as an omen of their future more perfect reconciliation.

'I did not think you would thus have trifled with me, Master Peveril,' said Alice, assuming an air of dignity; 'but I will take care to avoid such intrusion in future. I request you will not again visit the Black Fort; and I entreat of you, good Mistress Debbitch, that you will no longer either encourage or permit this gentleman's visits, as the result of such persecution will be to compel me to appeal to my aunt and father for another place of residence, and perhaps also for another and more prudent companion.'

This last hint struck Mistress Deborah with so much terror, that she joined her ward in requiring and demanding Julian's instant absence, and he was obliged to comply with their request. But the courage of a youthful lover is not easily subdued; and Julian, after having gone through the usual round of trying to forget his ungrateful mistress, and again entertaining his passion with augmented violence, ended by the visit to the Black Fort the beginning of which we narrated in the last chapter.

We then left him anxious for, yet almost fearful of, an interview with Alice, which he had prevailed upon Deborah to solicit; and such was the tumult of his mind, that, while he traversed the parlour, it seemed to him that the dark, melancholy eyes of the slaughtered Christian's portrait followed him wherever he went, with the fixed, chill, and ominous glance which announced to the enemy of his race mishap and misfortune.

The door of the apartment opened at length, and these visions were dissipated.

CHAPTER XIII

Parents have flinty hearts ! No tears can move them.

OTWAY.

WHEN Alice Bridgenorth at length entered the parlour where her anxious lover had so long expected her, it was with a slow step and a composed manner. Her dress was arranged with an accurate attention to form, which at once enhanced the appearance of its Puritanic simplicity and struck Julian as a bad omen ; for although the time bestowed upon the toilet may, in many cases, intimate the wish to appear advantageously at such an interview, yet a ceremonious arrangement of attire is very much allied with formality, and a preconceived determination to treat a lover with cold politeness.

The sad-coloured gown, the pinched and plaited cap, which carefully obscured the profusion of long dark-brown hair, the small ruff, and the long sleeves, would have appeared to great disadvantage on a shape less graceful than Alice Bridgenorth's ; but an exquisite form, though not, as yet, sufficiently rounded in the outlines to produce the perfection of female beauty, was able to sustain and give grace even to this unbecoming dress. Her countenance, fair and delicate, with eyes of hazel [blue], and a brow of alabaster, had, notwithstanding, less regular beauty than her form, and might have been justly subjected to criticism. There was, however, a life and spirit in her gaiety, and a depth of sentiment in her gravity, which made Alice, in conversation with the very few persons with whom she associated, so fascinating in her manners and expression, whether of language or countenance, so touching also in her simplicity and purity of thought, that brighter beauties might have been overlooked in her company. It was no wonder, therefore, that an ardent character like Julian, influenced by these charms, as well as by the secrecy and mystery attending his intercourse with Alice, should prefer the recluse of the Black Fort to all others with whom he had become acquainted in general society.

His heart beat high as she came into the apartment, and it was almost without an attempt to speak that his profound obeisance acknowledged her entrance.

'This is a mockery, Master Peveril,' said Alice, with an effort to speak firmly, which yet was disconcerted by a slightly tremulous inflection of voice — 'a mockery, and a cruel one. You come to this lone place, inhabited only by two women, too simple to command your absence, too weak to enforce it; you come in spite of my earnest request, to the neglect of your own time, to the prejudice, I may fear, of my character; you abuse the influence you possess over the simple person to whom I am entrusted — all this you do, and think to make it up by low reverences and constrained courtesy! Is this honourable, or is it fair? Is it,' she added, after a moment's hesitation — 'is it kind?'

The tremulous accent fell especially on the last word she uttered, and it was spoken in a low tone of gentle reproach, which went to Julian's heart.

'If,' said he, 'there was a mode by which, at the peril of my life, Alice, I could show my regard — my respect — my devoted tenderness — the danger would be dearer to me than ever was pleasure.'

'You have said such things often,' said Alice, 'and they are such as I ought not to hear, and do not desire to hear. I have no tasks to impose on you — no enemies to be destroyed — no need or desire of protection — no wish, Heaven knows, to expose you to danger. It is your visits here alone to which danger attaches. You have but to rule your own wilful temper — to turn your thoughts and your cares elsewhere, and I can have nothing to ask — nothing to wish for. Use your own reason — consider the injury you do yourself — the injustice you do us — and let me, once more, in fair terms, entreat you to absent yourself from this place — till — till ——'

She paused, and Julian eagerly interrupted her. 'Till when, Alice? — till when? Impose on me any length of absence which your severity can inflict, short of a final separation. Say, "Begone for years, but return when these years are over"; and, slow and wearily as they must pass away, still the thought that they must at length have their period will enable me to live through them. Let me, then, conjure thee, Alice, to name a date — to fix a term — to say till *when!*'

'Till you can bear to think of me only as a friend and sister.'

'That is a sentence of eternal banishment indeed!' said

Julian; 'it is seeming, no doubt, to fix a term of exile, but attaching to it an impossible condition.'

'And why impossible, Julian?' said Alice, in a tone of persuasion. 'Were we not happier ere you threw the mask from your own countenance, and tore the veil from my foolish eyes? Did we not meet with joy, spend our time happily, and part cheerily, because we transgressed no duty, and incurred no self-reproach? Bring back that state of happy ignorance, and you shall have no reason to call me unkind. But while you form schemes which I know to be visionary, and use language of such violence and passion, you shall excuse me if I now, and once for all, declare that, since Deborah shows herself unfit for the trust reposed in her, and must needs expose me to persecutions of this nature, I will write to my father, that he may fix me another place of residence; and in the meanwhile I will take shelter with my aunt at Kirk-Truagh.'

'Hear me, unpitying girl,' said Peveril — 'hear me, and you shall see how devoted I am to obedience in all that I can do to oblige you! You say you were happy when we spoke not on such topics — well, at all expense of my own suppressed feelings, that happy period shall return. I will meet you — walk with you — read with you — but only as a brother would with his sister or a friend with his friend; the thoughts I may nourish, be they of hope or of despair, my tongue shall not give birth to, and therefore I cannot offend; Deborah shall be ever by your side, and her presence shall prevent my even hinting at what might displease you — only do not make a crime to me of those thoughts which are the dearest part of my existence; for, believe me, it were better and kinder to rob me of existence itself.'

'This is the mere ecstasy of passion, Julian,' answered Alice Bridgenorth; 'that which is unpleasant, our selfish and stubborn will represents as impossible. I have no confidence in the plan you propose — no confidence in your resolution, and less than none in the protection of Deborah. Till you can renounce, honestly and explicitly, the wishes you have lately expressed, we must be strangers; and could you renounce them even at this moment, it were better that we should part for a long time; and, for Heaven's sake, let it be as soon as possible; perhaps it is even now too late to prevent some unpleasant accident — I thought I heard a noise.'

'It was Deborah,' answered Julian. 'Be not afraid, Alice; we are secure against surprise.'

'I know not,' said Alice, 'what you mean by such security. I have nothing to hide. I sought not this interview; on the contrary, averted it as long as I could, and am now most desirous to break it off.'

'And wherefore, Alice, since you say it must be our last? Why should you shake the sand which is passing so fast? The very executioner hurries not the prayers of the wretches upon the scaffold. And see you not — I will argue as coldly as you can desire — see you not that you are breaking your own word, and recalling the hope which yourself held out to me?'

'What hope have I suggested? What word have I given, Julian?' answered Alice. 'You yourself build wild hopes in the air, and accuse me of destroying what had never any earthly foundation. Spare yourself, Julian — spare me — and in mercy to us both depart, and return not again till you can be more reasonable.'

'Reasonable!' replied Julian; 'it is you, Alice, who will deprive me altogether of reason. Did you not say that, if our parents could be brought to consent to our union, you would no longer oppose my suit?'

'No — no — no,' said Alice, eagerly, and blushing deeply — 'I did not say so, Julian; it was your own wild imagination which put construction on my silence and my confusion.'

'You do *not* say so, then?' answered Julian; 'and if all other obstacles were removed, I should find one in the cold, flinty bosom of her who repays the most devoted and sincere affection with contempt and dislike? Is that,' he added, in a deep tone of feeling — 'is that what Alice Bridgenorth says to Julian Peveril?'

'Indeed — indeed, Julian,' said the almost weeping girl, 'I do not say so — I say nothing, and I ought not to say anything, concerning what I might do in a state of things which can never take place. Indeed, Julian, you ought not thus to press me. Unprotected as I am — wishing you well — very well — why should you urge me to say or do what would lessen me in my own eyes? to own affection for one from whom fate has separated me for ever? It is ungenerous — it is cruel — it is seeking a momentary and selfish gratification to yourself at the expense of every feeling which I ought to entertain.'

'You have said enough, Alice,' said Julian, with sparkling eyes — 'you have said enough in deprecating my urgency, and I will press you no farther. But you overrate the impediments which lie betwixt us; they must and shall give way.'

'So you said before,' answered Alice, 'and with what probability, your own account may show. You dared not to mention the subject to your own father; how should you venture to mention it to mine?'

'That I will soon enable you to decide upon. Major Bridgenorth, by my mother's account, is a worthy and an estimable man. I will remind him that to my mother's care he owes the dearest treasure and comfort of his life; and I will ask him if it is a just retribution to make that mother childless. Let me but know where to find him, Alice, and you shall soon hear if I have feared to plead my cause with him.'

'Alas!' answered Alice, 'you well know my uncertainty as to my dear father's residence. How often has it been my earnest request to him that he would let me share his solitary abode or his obscure wanderings! But the short and infrequent visits which he makes to this house are all that he permits me of his society. Something I might surely do, however little, to alleviate the melancholy by which he is oppressed.'

'Something we might both do,' said Peveril. 'How willingly would I aid you in so pleasing a task! All old griefs should be forgotten — all old friendships revived. My father's prejudices are those of an Englishman — strong, indeed, but not insurmountable by reason. Tell me, then, where Major Bridgenorth is, and leave the rest to me; or let me but know by what address your letters reach him, and I will forthwith essay to discover his dwelling.'

'Do not attempt it, I charge you,' said Alice. 'He is already a man of sorrows; and what would he think were I capable of entertaining a suit so likely to add to them? Besides, I could not tell you if I would where he is now to be found. My letters reach him from time to time by means of my aunt Christian; but of his address I am entirely ignorant.'

'Then, by Heaven,' answered Julian, 'I will watch his arrival in this island and in this house; and ere he has locked thee in his arms he shall answer to me on the subject of my suit.'

'Then demand that answer now,' said a voice from without the door, which was at the same time slowly opened — 'demand that answer now, for here stands Ralph Bridgenorth.'

As he spoke, he entered the apartment with his usual slow and sedate step, raised his flapped and steeple-crowned hat from his brows, and, standing in the midst of the room, eyed alternately his daughter and Julian Peveril with a fixed and penetrating glance.

'Father!' said Alice, utterly astonished, and terrified besides, by his sudden appearance at such a conjuncture — 'father, I am not to blame.'

'Of that anon, Alice,' said Bridgenorth; 'meantime, retire to your apartment. I have that to say to this youth which will not endure your presence.'

'Indeed — indeed, father,' said Alice, alarmed at what she supposed these words indicated, 'Julian is as little to be blamed as I! It was chance — it was fortune, which caused our meeting together.' Then suddenly rushing forward, she threw her arms around her father, saying, 'Oh, do him no injury; he meant no wrong! Father, you were wont to be a man of reason and of religious peace.'

'And wherefore should I not be so now, Alice?' said Bridgenorth, raising his daughter from the ground, on which she had almost sunk in the earnestness of her supplication. 'Dost thou know aught, maiden, which should inflame my anger against this young man more than reason or religion may bridle? Go — go to thy chamber. Compose thine own passions; learn to rule these, and leave it to me to deal with this stubborn young man.'

Alice arose, and, with her eyes fixed on the ground, retired slowly from the apartment. Julian followed her steps with his eyes till the last wave of her garment was visible at the closing door; then turned his looks to Major Bridgenorth, and then sunk them on the ground. The major continued to regard him in profound silence; his looks were melancholy and even austere; but there was nothing which indicated either agitation or keen resentment. He motioned to Julian to take a seat, and assumed one himself; after which he opened the conversation in the following manner : —

'You seemed but now, young gentleman, anxious to learn where I was to be found. Such I at least conjectured from the few expressions which I chanced to overhear; for I made bold, though it may be contrary to the code of modern courtesy, to listen a moment or two in order to gather upon what subject so young a man as you entertained so young a woman as Alice in a private interview.'

'I trust, sir,' said Julian, rallying spirits in what he felt to be a case of extremity, 'you have heard nothing on my part which has given offence to a gentleman whom, though unknown, I am bound to respect so highly.'

'On the contrary,' said Bridgenorth, with the same formal gravity, 'I am pleased to find that your business is, or appears to be, with me, rather than with my daughter. I only think you had done better to have entrusted it to me in the first instance, as my sole concern.'

The utmost sharpness of attention which Julian applied could not discover if Bridgenorth spoke seriously or ironically to the above purpose. He was, however, quick-witted beyond his experience, and was internally determined to endeavour to discover something of the character and the temper of him with whom he spoke. For that purpose, regulating his reply in the same tone with Bridgenorth's observation, he said that, not having the advantage to know his place of residence, he had applied for information to his daughter.

'Who is now known to you for the first time?' said Bridgenorth. 'Am I so to understand you?'

'By no means,' answered Julian, looking down; 'I have been known to your daughter for many years; and what I wished to say respects both her happiness and my own.'

'I must understand you,' said Bridgenorth, 'even as carnal men understand each other on the matters of this world. You are attached to my daughter by the cords of love; I have long known this.'

'You, Master Bridgenorth?' exclaimed Peveril — '*you* have long known it?'

'Yes, young man. Think you that, as the father of an only child, I could have suffered Alice Bridgenorth — the only living pledge of her who is now an angel in Heaven — to have remained in this seclusion without the surest knowledge of all her material actions? I have, in person, seen more both of her and of you than you could be aware of; and when absent in the body, I had the means of maintaining the same superintendence. Young man, they say that such love as you entertain for my daughter teaches much subtilty; but believe not that it can overreach the affection which a widowed father bears to an only child.'

'If,' said Julian, his heart beating thick and joyfully — 'if you have known this intercourse so long, may I not hope that it has not met your disapprobation?'

The major paused for an instant, and then answered, 'In some respects, certainly not. Had it done so — had there seemed

aught on your side or on my daughter's to have rendered your
visits here dangerous to her or displeasing to me — she had not
been long the inhabitant of this solitude, or of this island.   But
be not so hasty as to presume that all which you may desire
in this matter can be either easily or speedily accomplished.'

'I foresee, indeed, difficulties,' answered Julian; 'but, with
your kind acquiescence, they are such as I trust to remove.
My father is generous; my mother is candid and liberal.   They
loved you once; I trust they will love you again.   I will be
the mediator betwixt you; peace and harmony shall once more
inhabit our neighbourhood, and ——'

Bridgenorth interrupted him with a grim smile; for such
it seemed, as it passed over a face of deep melancholy.   'My
daughter well said, but short while past, that you were a
dreamer of dreams — an architect of plans and hopes fantastic
as the visions of the night.   It is a great thing you ask of me
— the hand of my only child — the sum of my worldly sub-
stance, though that is but dross in comparison.   You ask the
key of the only fountain from which I may yet hope to drink
one pleasant draught; you ask to be the sole and absolute
keeper of my earthly happiness; and what have you offered, or
what have you to offer, in return for the surrender you require
of me?'

'I am but too sensible,' said Peveril, abashed at his own
hasty conclusions, 'how difficult it may be.'

'Nay, but interrupt me not,' replied Bridgenorth, 'till I
show you the amount of what you offer me in exchange for a
boon which, whatever may be its intrinsic value, is earnestly
desired by you, and comprehends all that is valuable on earth
which I have it in my power to bestow.   You may have heard
that in the late times I was the antagonist of your father's
principles and his profane faction, but not the enemy of his
person.'

'I have ever heard,' replied Julian, 'much the contrary;
and it was but now that I reminded you that you had been his
friend.'

'Ay.   When he was in affliction and I in prosperity, I was
neither unwilling nor altogether unable to show myself such.
Well, the tables are turned — the times are changed.   A peaceful and unoffending man might have expected from a neighbour,
now powerful in his turn, such protection, when walking in the
paths of the law, as all men, subjects of the same realm, have
a right to expect even from perfect strangers.   What chances?

I pursue, with the warrant of the king and law, a murderess, bearing on her hand the blood of my near connexion, and I had, in such a case, a right to call on every liege subject to render assistance to the execution. My late friendly neighbour, bound, as a man and a magistrate, to give ready assistance to a legal action — bound, as a grateful and obliged friend, to respect my rights and my person — thrusts himself betwixt me — me, the avenger of blood — and my lawful captive; beats me to the earth, at once endangering my life, and, in mere human eyes, sullying mine honour; and, under his protection, the Midianitish woman reaches, like a sea-eagle, the nest which she hath made in the wave-surrounded rocks, and remains there till gold, duly administered at court, wipes out all memory of her crime, and baffles the vengeance due to the memory of the best and bravest of men. But,' he added, apostrophising the portrait of Christian, 'thou art not yet forgotten, my fair-haired William! The vengeance which dogs thy murderers is slow, but it is sure!'

There was a pause of some moments, which Julian Peveril, willing to hear to what conclusion Major Bridgenorth was finally to arrive, did not care to interrupt. Accordingly, in a few minutes, the latter proceeded. 'These things,' he said, 'I recall not in bitterness, so far as they are personal to me — I recall them not in spite of heart, though they have been the means of banishing me from my place of residence, where my fathers dwelt, and where my earthly comforts lie interred. But the public cause sets farther strife betwixt your father and me. Who so active as he to execute the fatal edict of black St. Bartholomew's day, when so many hundreds of Gospel-preachers were expelled from house and home — from hearth and altar — from church and parish, to make room for belly-gods and thieves? Who, when a devoted few of the Lord's people were united to lift the fallen standard, and once more advance the good cause, was the readiest to break their purpose — to search for, persecute, and apprehend them? Whose breath did I feel warm on my neck, whose naked sword was thrust within a foot of my body, whilst I lurked darkling, like a thief in concealment, in the house of my fathers? It was Geoffrey Peveril's — it was your father's! What can you answer to all this, or how can you reconcile it with your present wishes?'

Julian, in reply, could only remark, 'That these injuries had been of long standing; that they had been done in heat of times and heat of temper, and that Master Bridgenorth, in

Christian kindness, should not entertain a keen resentment of them, when a door was open for reconciliation.'

'Peace, young man,' said Bridgenorth, 'thou speakest of thou knowest not what. To forgive our human wrongs is Christian-like and commendable; but we have no commission to forgive those which have been done to the cause of religion and of liberty; we have no right to grant immunity, or to shake hands with those who have poured forth the blood of our brethren.' He looked at the picture of Christian, and was silent for a few minutes, as if he feared to give too violent way to his own impetuosity, and resumed the discourse in a milder tone.

'These things I point out to you, Julian, that I may show you how impossible, in the eyes of a merely worldly man, would be the union which you are desirous of. But Heaven hath at times opened a door, where man beholds no means of issue. Julian, your mother, for one to whom the truth is unknown, is, after the fashion of the world, one of the best and one of the wisest of women; and Providence, which gave her so fair a form, and tenanted that form with a mind as pure as the original frailty of our vile nature will permit, means not, I trust, that she shall continue to the end to be a vessel of wrath and perdition. Of your father I say nothing — he is what the times and example of others, and the counsels of his lordly priest, have made him; and of him, once more, I say nothing, save that I have power over him, which ere now he might have felt, but that there is one within his chambers who might have suffered in his suffering. Nor do I wish to root up your ancient family. If I prize not your boast of family honours and pedigree, I would not willingly destroy them; more than I would pull down a moss-grown tower, or hew to the ground an ancient oak, save for the straightening of the common path, and the advantage of the public. I have, therefore, no resentment against the humbled house of Peveril — nay, I have regard to it in its depression.'

He here made a second pause, as if he expected Julian to say something. But, notwithstanding the ardour with which the young man had pressed his suit, he was too much trained in ideas of the importance of his family, and in the better habit of respect for his parents, to hear, without displeasure, some part of Bridgenorth's discourse.

'The house of Peveril,' he replied, 'was never humbled.'

'Had you said the sons of that house had never been *humble*,'

answered Bridgenorth, 'you would have come nearer the truth.
Are *you* not humbled? Live you not here, the lackey of a
haughty woman, the play-companion of an empty youth? If
you leave this isle and go to the court of England, see what
regard will there be paid to the old pedigree that deduces your
descent from kings and conquerors. A scurril or obscene jest,
an impudent carriage, a laced cloak, a handful of gold, and the
readiness to wager it on a card or a die, will better advance
you at the court of Charles than your father's ancient name,
and slavish devotion of blood and fortune to the cause of *his*
father.'

'That is, indeed, but too probable,' said Peveril; 'but the
court shall be no element of mine. I will live like my
fathers, among my people, care for their comforts, decide their
differences ——'

'Build Maypoles, and dance around them,' said Bridgenorth,
with another of those grim smiles which passed over his features
like the light of a sexton's torch, as it glares and is reflected
by the window of the church, when he comes from locking a
funeral vault. 'No, Julian, these are not times in which, by
the dreaming drudgery of a country magistrate and the petty
cares of a country proprietor, a man can serve his unhappy
country. There are mighty designs afloat, and men are called
to make their choice betwixt God and Baal. The ancient superstition — the abomination of our fathers — is raising its head
and flinging abroad its snares, under the protection of the
princes of the earth ; but she raises not her head unmarked or
unwatched : the true English hearts are as thousands which
wait but a signal to arise as one man, and show the kings of
the earth that they have combined in vain ! We will cast
their cords from us ; the cup of their abominations we will not
taste.'

'You speak in darkness, Master Bridgenorth,' said Peveril.
'Knowing so much of me, you may, perhaps, also be aware
that I at least have seen too much of the delusions of Rome
to desire that they should be propagated at home.'

'Else, wherefore do I speak to thee friendly and so free?'
said Bridgenorth. 'Do I not know with what readiness of
early wit you baffled the wily attempts of the woman's priest
to seduce thee from the Protestant faith ? Do I not know
how thou wast beset when abroad, and that thou didst both
hold thine own faith and secure the wavering belief of thy
friend? Said I not, "This was done like the son of Margaret

Peveril"? Said I not, "He holdeth, as yet, but the dead letter; but the seed which is sown shall one day sprout and quicken"? Enough, however, of this. For to-day this is thy habitation. I will see in thee neither the servant of that daughter of Eshbaal nor the son of him who pursued my life and blemished my honours; but thou shalt be to me, for this day, as the child of her without whom my house had been extinct.'

So saying, he stretched out his thin, bony hand and grasped that of Julian Peveril; but there was such a look of mourning in his welcome that, whatever delight the youth anticipated spending so long a time in the neighbourhood of Alice Bridgenorth, perhaps in her society, or however strongly he felt the prudence of conciliating her father's good-will, he could not help feeling as if his heart was chilled in his company.

CHAPTER XIV

This day at least is friendship's ; on the morrow
Let strife come an she will.

Otway.

DEBORAH DEBBITCH, summoned by her master, now
made her appearance, with her handkerchief at her
eyes, and an appearance of great mental trouble. 'It
was not my fault, Major Bridgenorth,' she said ; 'how could I
help it ? like will to like — the boy would come — the girl would
see him.'

'Peace, foolish woman,' said Bridgenorth, 'and hear what I
have got to say.'

'I know what your honour has to say well enough,' said
Deborah. 'Service, I wot, is no inheritance nowadays — some
are wiser than other some — if I had not been wheedled away
from Martindale, I might have had a house of mine own by
this time.'

'Peace, idiot !' said Bridgenorth ; but so intent was Deborah
on her vindication, that he could but thrust the interjection,
as it were edgewise, between her exclamations, which followed
as thick as is usual in cases where folks endeavour to avert
deserved censure by a clamorous justification ere the charge
be brought.

'No wonder she was cheated,' she said, 'out of sight of her
own interest, when it was to wait on pretty Miss Alice. All
your honour's gold should never have tempted me, but that I
knew she was but a dead castaway, poor innocent, if she were
taken away from my lady or me. And so this is the end on 't !
— up early and down late, and this is all my thanks ! But
your honour had better take care what you do ; she has the
short cough yet sometimes, and should take physic, spring
and fall.'

'Peace, chattering fool !' said her master, so soon as her
failing breath gave him an opportunity to strike in ; 'thinkest
thou I knew not of this young gentleman's visits to the Black

Fort, and that, if they had displeased me, I would not have known how to stop them ? '

'Did I know that your honour knew of his visits ! ' exclaimed Deborah, in a triumphant tone — for, like most of her condition, she never sought farther for her defence than a lie, however inconsistent and improbable — '*did* I know that your honour knew of it ?   Why, how should I have permitted his visits else ?   I wonder what your honour takes me for !   Had I not been sure it was the thing in this world that your honour most desired, would I have presumed to lend it a hand forward ?   I trust I know my duty better.   Hear if I ever asked another youngster into the house, save himself, for I knew your honour was wise, and quarrels cannot last for ever, and love begins where hatred ends ; and, to be sure, they look as if they were born one for the other ; and then the estates of Moultrassie and Martindale suit each other like sheath and knife.'

'Parrot of a woman, hold your tongue ! ' said Bridgenorth, his patience almost completely exhausted ; ' or, if you will prate, let it be to your playfellows in the kitchen, and bid them get ready some dinner presently, for Master Peveril is far from home.'

'That I will, and with all my heart,' said Deborah ; ' and if there are a pair of fatter fowls in Man than shall clap their wings on the table presently, your honour shall call me goose as well as parrot.'   She then left the apartment.

'It is to such a woman as that,' said Bridgenorth, looking after her significantly, ' that you conceived me to have abandoned the charge of my only child ?   But enough of this subject ; we will walk abroad, if you will, while she is engaged in a province fitter for her understanding.'

So saying, he left the house, accompanied by Julian Peveril, and they were soon walking side by side, as if they had been old acquaintances.

It may have happened to many of our readers, as it has done to ourselves, to be thrown by accident into society with some individual whose claims to what is called a *serious* character stand considerably higher than our own, and with whom, therefore, we have conceived ourselves likely to spend our time in a very stiff and constrained manner ; while, on the other hand, our destined companion may have apprehended some disgust from the supposed levity and thoughtless gaiety of a disposition so different from his own.   Now, it has frequently happened that, when we, with that urbanity and good-humour which is

our principal characteristic, have accommodated ourself to our
companion, by throwing as much seriousness into our conversation as our habits will admit, he, on the other hand, moved by
our liberal example, hath divested his manners of a part of their
austerity; and our conversation has, in consequence, been of
that pleasant texture, betwixt the useful and agreeable, which
best resembles 'the fairy-web of night and day,' usually called
in prose the twilight.   It is probable both parties may, on such
occasions, have been the better for their encounter, even if it
went no farther than to establish for the time a community of
feeling between men who, separated more perhaps by temper
than by principle, are too apt to charge each other with profane
frivolity on the one hand or fanaticism on the other.

It fared thus in Peveril's walk with Bridgenorth, and in the
conversation which he held with him.

Carefully avoiding the subject on which he had already
spoken, Major Bridgenorth turned his conversation chiefly on
foreign travel, and on the wonders he had seen in distant
countries, and which he appeared to have marked with a
curious and observant eye.   This discourse made the time fly
light away; for, although the anecdotes and observations thus
communicated were all tinged with the serious and almost
gloomy spirit of the narrator, they yet contained traits of
interest and of wonder, such as are usually captivating to a
youthful ear, and were particularly so to Julian, who had in his
disposition some cast of the romantic and adventurous.

It appeared that Bridgenorth knew the south of France, and
could tell many stories of the French Huguenots, who already
began to sustain those vexations which a few years afterwards
were summed up by the revocation of the Edict of Nantz.
He had even been in Hungary, for he spoke as from personal
knowledge of the character of several of the heads of the great
Protestant insurrection, which at this time had taken place
under the celebrated Tekeli; and laid down solid reasons why
they were entitled to make common cause with the Great Turk,
rather than submit to the Pope of Rome.   He talked also of
Savoy, where those of the Reformed religion still suffered a cruel
persecution; and he mentioned, with a swelling spirit, the protection which Oliver had afforded to the oppressed Protestant
churches; 'therein showing himself,' he added, 'more fit to
wield the supreme power than those who, claiming it by right
of inheritance, use it only for their own vain and voluptuous
pursuits.'

'I did not expect,' said Peveril, modestly, 'to have heard
Oliver's panegyric from you, Master Bridgenorth.'

'I do not panegyrise him,' answered Bridgenorth; 'I speak
but truth of that extraordinary man, now being dead, whom,
when alive, I feared not to withstand to his face. It is the
fault of the present unhappy King if he make us look back
with regret to the days when the nation was respected abroad,
and when devotion and sobriety were practised at home. But
I mean not to vex your spirit by controversy. You have lived
amongst those who find it more easy and more pleasant to
be the pensioners of France than her controllers; to spend
the money which she doles out to themselves than to check
the tyranny with which she oppresses our poor brethren
of the religion. When the scales shall fall from thine eyes,
all this thou shalt see; and seeing, shalt learn to detest and
despise it.'

By this time they had completed their walk, and were
returned to the Black Fort by a different path from that which
had led them up the valley. The exercise and the general tone
of conversation had removed, in some degree, the shyness and
embarrassment which Peveril originally felt in Bridgenorth's
presence, and which the tenor of his first remarks had rather
increased than diminished. Deborah's promised banquet was
soon on the board; and in simplicity, as well as neatness and
good order, answered the character she had claimed for it. In
one respect alone there seemed some inconsistency, perhaps
a little affectation. Most of the dishes were of silver, and the
plates were of the same metal; instead of the trenchers and
pewter which Peveril had usually seen employed on similar
occasions at the Black Fort.

Presently, with the feeling of one who walks in a pleasant
dream from which he fears to awake, and whose delight is
mingled with wonder and with uncertainty, Julian Peveril found
himself seated between Alice Bridgenorth and her father — the
being he most loved on earth, and the person whom he had
ever considered as the great obstacle to their intercourse! The
confusion of his mind was such, that he could scarcely reply
to the importunate civilities of Dame Deborah, who, seated with
them at table in her quality of governante, now dispensed the
good things which had been prepared under her own eye.

As for Alice, she seemed to have formed a resolution to
play the mute; for she answered not, excepting briefly, to the
questions of Dame Debbitch; nay, even when her father, which

happened once or twice, attempted to bring her forward in the conversation, she made no farther reply than respect for him rendered absolutely necessary.

Upon Bridgenorth himself, then, devolved the task of entertaining the company ; and, contrary to his ordinary habits, he did not seem to shrink from it. His discourse was not only easy, but almost cheerful, though ever and anon crossed by some expressions indicative of natural and habitual melancholy, or prophetic of future misfortune and woe. Flashes of enthusiasm, too, shot along his conversation, gleaming like the sheet-lightning of an autumn eve, which throws a strong, though momentary, illumination across the sober twilight, and all the surrounding objects, which, touched by it, assume a wilder and more striking character. In general, however, Bridgenorth's remarks were plain and sensible ; and as he aimed at no graces of language, any ornament which they received arose out of the interest with which they were impressed on his hearers. For example, when Deborah, in the pride and vulgarity of her heart, called Julian's attention to the plate from which they had been eating, Bridgenorth seemed to think an apology necessary for such superfluous expense.

'It was a symptom,' he said, 'of approaching danger, when such men, as were not usually influenced by the vanities of life, employed much money in ornaments composed of the precious metals. It was a sign that the merchant could not obtain a profit for the capital, which, for the sake of security, he invested in this inert form. It was a proof that the noblemen or gentlemen feared the rapacity of power, when they put their wealth into forms the most portable and the most capable of being hidden ; and it showed the uncertainty of credit, when a man of judgment preferred the actual possession of a mass of silver to the convenience of a goldsmith's or a banker's receipt. While a shadow of liberty remained,' he said, 'domestic rights were last invaded ; and, therefore, men disposed upon their cupboards and tables the wealth which in these places would remain longest, though not perhaps finally, sacred from the grasp of a tyrannical government. But let there be a demand for capital to support a profitable commerce, and the mass is at once consigned to the furnace, and, ceasing to be a vain and cumbrous ornament of the banquet, becomes a potent and active agent for furthering the prosperity of the country.'

'In war, too,' said Peveril, 'plate has been found a ready resource.'

" Flashes of enthusiasm, too, shot along his conversation."

'But too much so,' answered Bridgenorth. 'In the late times, the plate of the nobles and gentry, with that of the colleges, and the sale of the crown jewels, enabled the King to make his unhappy stand, which prevented matters returning to a state of peace and good order, until the sword had attained an undue superiority both over King and Parliament.'

He looked at Julian as he spoke, much as he who proves a horse offers some object suddenly to his eyes, then watches to see if he starts or blenches from it. But Julian's thoughts were too much bent on other topics to manifest any alarm. His answer referred to a previous part of Bridgenorth's discourse, and was not returned till after a brief pause. 'War, then,' he said — 'war, the grand impoverisher, is also a creator of the wealth which it wastes and devours?'

'Yes,' replied Bridgenorth, 'even as the sluice brings into action the sleeping waters of the lake, which it finally drains. Necessity invents arts and discovers means; and what necessity is sterner than that of civil war? Therefore, even war is not in itself unmixed evil, being the creator of impulses and energies which could not otherwise have existed in society.'

'Men should go to war, then,' said Peveril, 'that they may send their silver plate to the mint, and eat from pewter dishes and wooden platters?'

'Not so, my son,' said Bridgenorth. Then checking himself, as he observed the deep crimson in Julian's cheek and brow, he added, 'I crave your pardon for such familiarity; but I meant not to limit what I said even now to such trifling consequences, although it may be something salutary to tear men from their pomps and luxuries, and teach those to be Romans who would otherwise be Sybarites. But I would say, that times of public danger, as they call into circulation the miser's hoard and the proud man's bullion, and so add to the circulating wealth of the country, do also call into action many a brave and noble spirit, which would otherwise lie torpid, give no example to the living, and bequeath no name to future ages. Society knows not, and cannot know, the mental treasures which slumber in her bosom, till necessity and opportunity call forth the statesman and the soldier from the shades of lowly life to the parts they are designed by Providence to perform, and the stations which nature had qualified them to hold. So rose Oliver — so rose Milton — so rose many another name which cannot be forgotten — even as the tempest summons forth and displays the address of the mariner.'

'You speak,' said Peveril, 'as if national calamity might be, in some sort, an advantage.'

'And if it were not so,' replied Bridgenorth, 'it had not existed in this state of trial, where all temporal evil is alleviated by something good in its progress or result, and where all that is good is close coupled with that which is in itself evil.'

'It must be a noble sight,' said Julian, 'to behold the slumbering energies of a great mind awakened into energy, and to see it assume the authority which is its due over spirits more meanly endowed.'

'I once witnessed,' said Bridgenorth, 'something to the same effect; and as the tale is brief, I will tell it you, if you will : —

'Amongst my wanderings, the Transatlantic settlements have not escaped me; more especially the country of New England, into which our native land has shaken from her lap, as a drunkard flings from him his treasures, so much that is precious in the eyes of God and of his children. There thousands of our best and most godly men — such whose righteousness might come between the Almighty and His wrath, and prevent the ruin of cities — are content to be the inhabitants of the desert, rather encountering the unenlightened savages than stooping to extinguish, under the oppression practised in Britain, the light that is within their own minds. There I remained for a time, during the wars which the colony maintained with Philip, a great Indian chief, or sachem, as they were called, who seemed a messenger sent from Satan to buffet them. His cruelty was great — his dissimulation profound ; and the skill and promptitude with which he maintained a destructive and desultory warfare inflicted many dreadful calamities on the settlement. I was, by chance, at a small village in the woods, more than thirty miles from Boston, and in its situation exceedingly lonely, and surrounded with thickets. Nevertheless, there was no idea of any danger from the Indians at that time, for men trusted to the protection of a considerable body of troops who had taken the field for protection of the frontiers, and who lay, or were supposed to lie, betwixt the hamlet and the enemy's country. But they had to do with a foe whom the devil himself had inspired at once with cunning and cruelty. It was on a Sabbath morning, when we had assembled to take sweet counsel together in the Lord's house. Our temple was but constructed of wooden logs ; but when shall the chant of trained hirelings, or the sounding of tin and brass tubes amid

the aisles of a minster, arise so sweetly to Heaven as did the
psalm in which we united at once our voices and our hearts!
An excellent worthy, who now sleeps in the Lord, Nehemiah
Solsgrace, long the companion of my pilgrimage, had just begun
to wrestle in prayer, when a woman, with disordered looks and
dishevelled hair, entered our chapel in a distracted manner,
screaming incessantly, "The Indians! The Indians!" In that
land no man dares separate himself from his means of defence,
and whether in the city or in the field, in the ploughed land or
the forest, men keep beside them their weapons, as did the
Jews at the rebuilding of the Temple. So we sallied forth with
our guns and pikes, and heard the whoop of these incarnate
devils, already in possession of a part of the town, and exercising
their cruelty on the few whom weighty causes or indisposition
had withheld from public worship; and it was remarked as a
judgment that, upon that bloody Sabbath, Adrian Hanson, a
Dutchman, a man well enough disposed towards man, but
whose mind was altogether given to worldly gain, was shot and
scalped as he was summing his weekly gains in his warehouse.
In fine, there was much damage done; and although our arrival
and entrance into combat did in some sort put them back, yet
being surprised and confused, and having no appointed leader of
our band, the devilish enemy shot hard at us, and had some
advantage. It was pitiful to hear the screams of women and
children amid the report of guns and the whistling of bullets,
mixed with the ferocious yells of these savages, which they term
their war-whoop. Several houses in the upper part of the village
were soon on fire; and the roaring of the flames, and crackling of
the great beams as they blazed, added to the horrible confusion;
while the smoke which the wind drove against us gave farther
advantage to the enemy, who fought, as it were, invisible, and
under cover, whilst we fell fast by their unerring fire. In this
state of confusion, and while we were about to adopt the desperate project of evacuating the village, and, placing the women
and children in the centre, of attempting a retreat to the nearest
settlement, it pleased Heaven to send us unexpected assistance.
A tall man of a reverend appearance, whom no one of us had
ever seen before, suddenly was in the midst of us, as we hastily
agitated the resolution of retreating. His garments were of the
skin of the elk, and he wore sword and carried gun; I never
saw anything more august than his features, overshadowed by
locks of grey hair, which mingled with a long beard of the same
colour. "Men and brethren," he said, in a voice like that which

turns back the flight, "why sink your hearts? and why are you thus disquieted? Fear ye that the God we serve will give you up to yonder heathen dogs? Follow me, and you shall see this day that there is a captain in Israel!" He uttered a few brief but distinct orders, in the tone of one who was accustomed to command; and such was the influence of his appearance, his mien, his language, and his presence of mind, that he was implicitly obeyed by men who had never seen him until that moment. We were hastily divided, by his orders, into two bodies; one of which maintained the defence of the village with more courage than ever, convinced that the Unknown was sent by God to our rescue. At his command they assumed the best and most sheltered positions for exchanging their deadly fire with the Indians; while, under cover of the smoke, the stranger sallied from the town, at the head of the other division of the New England men, and, fetching a circuit, attacked the red warriors in the rear. The surprise, as is usual amongst savages, had complete effect; for they doubted not that they were assailed in their turn, and placed betwixt two hostile parties by the return of a detachment from the provincial army. The heathens fled in confusion, abandoning the half-won village, and leaving behind them such a number of their warriors that the tribe hath never recovered its loss. Never shall I forget the figure of our venerable leader, when our men, and not they only, but the women and children of the village, rescued from the tomahawk and scalping-knife, stood crowded around him, yet scarce venturing to approach his person, and more minded, perhaps, to worship him as a descended angel than to thank him as a fellow-mortal. "Not unto me be the glory," he said: "I am but an implement, frail as yourselves, in the hand of Him who is strong to deliver. Bring me a cup of water, that I may allay my parched throat, ere I essay the task of offering thanks where they are most due." I was nearest to him as he spoke, and I gave into his hand the water he requested. At that moment we exchanged glances, and it seemed to me that I recognised a noble friend whom I had long since deemed in glory; but he gave me no time to speak, had speech been prudent. Sinking on his knees and signing us to obey him, he poured forth a strong and energetic thanksgiving for the turning back of the battle, which, pronounced with a voice loud and clear as a war-trumpet, thrilled through the joints and marrow of the hearers. I have heard many an act of devotion in my life, had Heaven vouchsafed me grace to profit by them;

but such a prayer as this, uttered amid the dead and the dying, with a rich tone of mingled triumph and adoration, was beyond them all : it was like the song of the inspired prophetess who dwelt beneath the palm-tree between Ramah and Bethel. He was silent; and for a brief space we remained with our faces bent to the earth, no man daring to lift his head. At length we looked up, but our deliverer was no longer amongst us ; nor was he ever again seen in the land which he had rescued.'

Here Bridgenorth, who had told this singular story with an eloquence and vivacity of detail very contrary to the usual dryness of his conversation, paused for an instant, and then resumed — 'Thou seest, young man, that men of valour and of discretion are called forth to command in circumstances of national exigence, though their very existence is unknown in the land which they are predestined to deliver.'

' But what thought the people of the mysterious stranger ? ' said Julian, who had listened with eagerness, for the story was of a kind interesting to the youthful and the brave.

' Many things,' answered Bridgenorth, ' and, as usual, little to the purpose. The prevailing opinion was, notwithstanding his own disclamation, that the stranger was really a super-natural being ; others believed him an inspired champion, transported in the body from some distant climate, to show us the way to safety ; others, again, concluded that he was a recluse, who, either from motives of piety or other cogent reasons, had become a dweller in the wilderness, and shunned the face of man.'

' And, if I may presume to ask,' said Julian, ' to which of these opinions were you disposed to adhere ? '

' The last suited best with the transient though close view with which I had perused the stranger's features,' replied Bridgenorth ; ' for although I dispute not that it may please Heaven, on high occasions, even to raise one from the dead in defence of his country, yet I doubted not then, as I doubt not now, that I looked on the living form of one who had indeed powerful reasons to conceal him in the cleft of the rock.'

' Are these reasons a secret ? ' asked Julian Peveril.

' Not properly a secret,' replied Bridgenorth ; ' for I fear not thy betraying what I might tell thee in private discourse ; and besides, wert thou so base, the prey lies too distant for any hunters to whom thou couldst point out its traces. But the name of this worthy will sound harsh in thy ear, on account of one action of his life — being his accession to a great measure which made the extreme isles of the earth to tremble. Have you never heard of Richard Whalley ? ' [1]

' Of the regicide ? ' exclaimed Peveril, starting.

' Call his act what thou wilt,' said Bridgenorth ; ' he was not less the rescuer of that devoted village, that, with other leading spirits of the age, he sat in the judgment-seat when Charles Stewart was arraigned at the bar, and subscribed the sentence that went forth upon him.'

' I have ever heard,' said Julian, in an altered voice, and colouring deeply, ' that you, Master Bridgenorth, with other Presbyterians, were totally averse to that detestable crime, and were ready to have made joint cause with the Cavaliers in preventing so horrible a parricide.'

' If it were so,' replied Bridgenorth, ' we have been richly rewarded by his successor ! '

' Rewarded ! ' exclaimed Julian. ' Does the distinction of good and evil, and our obligation to do the one and forbear the other, depend on the reward which may attach to our actions ? '

' God forbid ! ' answered Bridgenorth ; ' yet those who view the havoc which this house of Stewart have made in the church and state — the tyranny which they exercise over men's persons and consciences — may well doubt whether it be lawful to use weapons in their defence. Yet you hear me not praise, or even vindicate, the death of the King, though so far deserved, as he was false to his oath as a prince and magistrate. I only tell you what you desired to know, that Richard Whalley, one of the late King's judges, was he of whom I have just been speaking. I knew his lofty brow, though time had made it balder and higher ; his grey eye retained all its lustre ; and though the grizzled beard covered the lower part of his face, it prevented me not from recognising him. The scent was hot after him for his blood ; but, by the assistance of those friends whom Heaven had raised up for his preservation, he was concealed carefully, and emerged only to do the will of Providence in the matter of that battle. Perhaps his voice may be heard in the field once more, should England need one of her noblest hearts.'

' Now, God forbid ! ' said Julian.

' Amen,' returned Bridgenorth. ' May God avert civil war, and pardon those whose madness would bring it on us ! '

There was a long pause, during which Julian, who had scarce lifted his eyes towards Alice, stole a glance in that direction,

---

[1] See Note 10.

and was struck by the deep cast of melancholy which had stolen over features to which a cheerful, if not gay, expression was most natural. So soon as she caught his eye, she remarked, and, as Julian thought, with significance, that the shadows were lengthening and evening coming on.

He heard; and although satisfied that she hinted at his departure, he could not, upon the instant, find resolution to break the spell which detained him. The language which Bridgenorth held was not only new and alarming, but so contrary to the maxims in which he was brought up, that, as a son of Sir Geoffrey Peveril of the Peak, he would, in another case, have thought himself called upon to dispute its conclusions, even at the sword's point. But Bridgenorth's opinions were delivered with so much calmness — seemed so much the result of conviction — that they excited in Julian rather a spirit of wonder than of angry controversy. There was a character of sober decision and sedate melancholy in all that he said which, even had he not been the father of Alice (and perhaps Julian was not himself aware how much he was influenced by that circumstance), would have rendered it difficult to take personal offence. His language and sentiments were of that quiet yet decided kind upon which it is difficult either to fix controversy or quarrel, although it be impossible to acquiesce in the conclusions to which they lead.

While Julian remained as if spell-bound to his chair, scarce more surprised at the company in which he found himself than at the opinions to which he was listening, another circumstance reminded him that the proper time of his stay at Black Fort had been expended. Little Fairy, the Manx pony, which, well accustomed to the vicinity of Black Fort, used to feed near the house while her master made his visits there, began to find his present stay rather too long. She had been the gift of the countess to Julian whilst a youth, and came of a high-spirited mountain breed, remarkable alike for hardiness, for longevity, and for a degree of sagacity approaching to that of the dog. Fairy showed the latter quality by the way in which she chose to express her impatience to be moving homewards. At least such seemed the purpose of the shrill neigh with which she startled the female inmates of the parlour, who, the moment afterwards, could not forbear smiling to see the nose of the pony advanced through the opened casement.

'Fairy reminds me,' said Julian, looking to Alice and rising, 'that the term of my stay here is exhausted.'

'Speak with me yet one moment,' said Bridgenorth, with-drawing him into a Gothic recess of the old-fashioned apartment, and speaking so low that he could not be overheard by Alice and her governante, who, in the meantime, caressed, and fed with fragments of bread, the intruder Fairy.

'You have not, after all,' said Bridgenorth, 'told me the cause of your coming hither.' He stopped, as if to enjoy his embarrassment, and then added, 'And indeed it were most unnecessary that you should do so. I have not so far for-gotten the days of my youth, or those affections which bind poor frail humanity but too much to the things of this world. Will you find no words to ask of me the great boon which you seek, and which, peradventure, you would not have hesitated to have made your own without my knowledge and against my con-sent? Nay, never vindicate thyself, but mark me farther. The patriarch bought his beloved by fourteen years' hard service to her father, Laban, and they seemed to him but as a few days. But he that would wed my daughter must serve, in compari-son, but a few days, though in matters of such mighty import, that they shall seem as the service of many years. Reply not to me now, but go, and peace be with you.'

He retired so quickly, after speaking, that Peveril had liter-ally not an instant to reply. He cast his eyes around the apartment, but Deborah and her charge had also disappeared. His gaze rested for a moment on the portrait of Christian, and his imagination suggested that his dark features were illumi-nated by a smile of haughty triumph. He started and looked more attentively; it was but the effect of the evening beam, which touched the picture at the instant. The effect was gone, and there remained but the fixed, grave, inflexible features of the republican soldier.

Julian left the apartment as one who walks in a dream; he mounted Fairy, and, agitated by a variety of thoughts which he was unable to reduce to order, he returned to Castle Rushin before the night sat down.

Here he found all in movement. The countess, with her son, had, upon some news received or resolution formed during his absence, removed, with a principal part of their family, to the yet stronger castle of Holm-Peel, about eight miles' dis-tance across the island; and which had been suffered to fall into a much more dilapidated condition than that of Castle-town, so far as it could be considered as a place of residence. But as a fortress Holm-Peel was stronger than Castletown;

nay, unless assailed regularly, was almost impregnable ; and was always held by a garrison belonging to the Lords of Man. Here Peveril arrived at nightfall. He was told in the fishing-village that the night-bell of the castle had been rung earlier than usual, and the watch set with circumstances of unusual and jealous precaution.

Resolving, therefore, not to disturb the garrison by entering at that late hour, he obtained an indifferent lodging in the town for the night, and determined to go to the castle early on the succeeding morning. He was not sorry thus to gain a few hours of solitude, to think over the agitating events of the preceding day.

CHAPTER XV

What seem'd its head,
The likeness of a kingly crown had on.
Paradise Lost.

SODOR, or Holm-Peel,[1] so is named the castle to which our
Julian directed his course early on the following morning,
is one of those extraordinary monuments of antiquity with
which this singular and interesting island abounds. It occupies
the whole of a high rocky peninsula, or rather an island, for it is
surrounded by the sea at high-water, and scarcely accessible
even when the tide is out, although a stone causeway of great
solidity, erected for the express purpose, connects the island
with the mainland. The whole space is surrounded by double
walls of great strength and thickness; and the access to the
interior, at the time which we treat of, was only by two flights
of steep and narrow steps, divided from each other by a strong
tower and guard-house, under the former of which there is an
entrance arch. The open space within the walls extends to
two acres, and contains many objects worthy of antiquarian
curiosity. There were, besides the castle itself, two cathedral
churches, dedicated, the earlier to St. Patrick, the latter to
St. Germain, besides two smaller churches; all of which had
become, even in that day, more or less ruinous. Their decayed
walls, exhibiting the rude and massive architecture of the most
remote period, were composed of a ragged greystone, which
formed a singular contrast with the bright red freestone of
which the window-cases, corner-stones, arches, and other ornamental parts of the building were composed.

Besides these four ruinous churches, the space of ground
inclosed by the massive exterior walls of Holm-Peel exhibited
many other vestiges of the olden time. There was a square
mound of earth, facing, with its angles to the points of the

[1] See Note 11.

compass, one of those motes, as they were called, on which, in ancient times, the Northern tribes elected or recognised their chiefs, and held their solemn popular assemblies, or *comitia*. There was also one of those singular towers, so common in Ireland as to have proved the favourite theme of her antiquaries, but of which the real use and meaning seem yet to be hidden in the mist of ages. This of Holm-Peel had been converted to the purpose of a watch-tower. There were, besides, Runic monuments, of which the legends could not be deciphered; and later inscriptions to the memory of champions of whom the names only were preserved from oblivion. But tradition and superstitious eld, still most busy where real history is silent, had filled up the long blank of accurate information with tales of sea-kings and pirates, Hebridean chiefs and Norwegian resolutes, who had formerly warred against, and in defence of, this famous castle. Superstition, too, had her tales of goblins, ghosts, and spectres, her legends of saints and demons, of fairies and of familiar spirits, which in no corner of the British empire are told and received with more absolute credulity than in the Isle of Man.

Amidst all these ruins of an older time arose the castle itself, now ruinous; but in Charles II.'s reign well garrisoned, and, in a military point of view, kept in complete order. It was a venerable and very ancient building, containing several apartments of sufficient size and height to be termed noble. But, in the surrender of the island by Christian, the furniture had been, in a great measure, plundered or destroyed by the Republican soldiers; so that, as we have before hinted, its present state was ill adapted for the residence of the noble proprietor. Yet it had been often the abode, not only of the Lords of Man, but of those state prisoners whom the Kings of Britain sometimes committed to their charge.

In this castle of Holm-Peel the great King-Maker, Richard Earl of Warwick, was confined during one period of his eventful life, to ruminate at leisure on his farther schemes of ambition. And here, too, Eleanor, the haughty wife of the good Duke of Gloucester, pined out in seclusion the last days of her banishment. The sentinels pretended that her discontented spectre was often visible at night, traversing the battlements of the external walls, or standing motionless beside a particular solitary turret of one of the watch-towers with which they are flanked; but dissolving into air at cock-crow, or when the bell tolled from the yet remaining tower of St. Germain's church.

Such was Holm-Peel, as records inform us, till towards the end of the 17th century.

It was in one of the lofty but almost unfurnished apartments of this ancient castle that Julian Peveril found his friend the Earl of Derby, who had that moment sat down to a breakfast composed of various sorts of fish. 'Welcome, most imperial Julian,' he said — 'welcome to our royal fortress; in which, as yet, we are not like to be starved with hunger, though well-nigh dead for cold.'

Julian answered by inquiring the meaning of this sudden movement.

'Upon my word,' replied the earl, 'you know nearly as much of it as I do. My mother has told me nothing about it, supposing, I believe, that I shall at length be tempted to in-quire; but she will find herself much mistaken. I shall give her credit for full wisdom in her proceedings, rather than put her to the trouble to render a reason, though no woman can render one better.'

'Come — come, this is affectation, my good friend,' said Julian. 'You should inquire into these matters a little more curiously.'

'To what purpose?' said the earl. 'To hear old stories about the Tinwald laws, and the contending rights of the lords and the clergy, and all the rest of that Celtic barbarism, which, like Burgess's thorough-paced doctrine, enters at one ear, paces through, and goes out at the other?'

'Come, my lord,' said Julian, 'you are not so indifferent as you would represent yourself: you are dying of curiosity to know what this hurry is about; only you think it the courtly humour to appear careless about your own affairs.'

'Why, what should it be about,' said the young earl, 'unless some factious dispute between our Majesty's minister, Governor Nowel, and our vassals? or perhaps some dispute betwixt our Majesty and the ecclesiastical jurisdictions? for all which, our Majesty cares as little as any king in Christendom.'

'I rather suppose there is intelligence from England,' said Julian. 'I heard last night in Peeltown that Greenhalgh is come over with unpleasant news.'

'He brought me nothing that was pleasant, I wot well,' said the earl. 'I expected something from St. Evremond or Hamilton, some new plays by Dryden or Lee, and some waggery or lam-poons from the Rose Coffee-house; and the fellow has brought me nothing but a parcel of tracts about Protestants and Papists, and a folio play-book, one of the conceptions, as she calls them, of that old madwoman the Duchess of Newcastle.'

'Hush, my lord, for Heaven's sake,' said Peveril; 'here comes the countess; and you know she takes fire at the least slight to her ancient friend.'

'Let her read her ancient friend's works herself, then,' said the earl, 'and think her as wise as she can; but I would not give one of Waller's songs or Denham's satires for a whole cart-load of her Grace's trash. But here comes our mother, with care on her brow.'

The Countess of Derby entered the apartment accordingly, holding in her hand a number of papers. Her dress was a mourning-habit, with a deep train of black velvet, which was borne by a little favourite attendant, a deaf and dumb girl, whom, in compassion to her misfortune, the countess had educated about her person for some years. Upon this unfortunate being, with the touch of romance which marked many of her proceedings, Lady Derby had conferred the name of Fenella, after some ancient princess of the island. The countess herself was not much changed since we last presented her to our readers. Age had rendered her step more slow, but not less majestic; and while it traced some wrinkles on her brow, had failed to quench the sedate fire of her dark eye. The young men rose to receive her with the formal reverence which they knew she loved, and were greeted by her with equal kindness.

'Cousin Peveril,' she said, for so she always called Julian, in respect of his mother being a kinswoman of her husband, 'you were ill abroad last night, when we much needed your counsel.'

Julian answered with a blush which he could not prevent, 'That he had followed his sport among the mountains too far, had returned late, and, finding her ladyship was removed from Castletown, had instantly followed the family hither; but as the night-bell was rung and the watch set, he had deemed it more respectful to lodge for the night in the town.'

'It is well,' said the countess; 'and, to do you justice, Julian, you are seldom a truant neglecter of appointed hours, though, like the rest of the youth of this age, you sometimes suffer your sports to consume too much of time that should be spent otherwise. But for your friend Philip, he is an avowed contemner of good order, and seems to find pleasure in wasting time, even when he does not enjoy it.'

'I have been enjoying my time just now at least,' said the

earl, rising from table, and picking his teeth carelessly. 'These
fresh mullets are delicious, and so is the Lachrymæ Christi.   I
pray you to sit down to breakfast, Julian, and partake the
goods my royal foresight has provided.   Never was King of
Man nearer being left to the mercy of the execrable brandy of
his dominions.   Old Griffiths would never, in the midst of our
speedy retreat of last night, have had sense enough to secure a
few flasks, had I not given him a hint on that important subject.
But presence of mind amid danger and tumult is a jewel I have
always possessed.'

'I wish, then, Philip, you would exert it to better purpose,'
said the countess, half smiling, half displeased ; for she doted
upon her son with all a mother's fondness, even when she was
most angry with him for being deficient in the peculiar and
chivalrous disposition which had distinguished his father, and
which was so analogous to her own romantic and high-minded
character.   'Lend me your signet,' she added with a sigh ;
'for it were, I fear, vain to ask you to read over these despatches
from England, and execute the warrants which I have thought
necessary to prepare in consequence.'

'My signet you shall command with all my heart, madam,'
said Earl Philip ; 'but spare me the revision of what you are
much more capable to decide upon.   I am, you know, a most
complete *roi fainéant*, and never once interfered with my
maire de palais in her proceedings.'

The countess made signs to her little train-bearer, who
immediately went to seek for wax and a light, with which she
presently returned.

In the meanwhile, the countess continued, addressing Peveril
— 'Philip does himself less than justice.   When you were absent,
Julian, for if you had been here I would have given you the
credit of prompting your friend, he had a spirited controversy
with the bishop, for an attempt to enforce spiritual censures
against a poor wretch, by confining her in the vault under the
chapel.'[1]

'Do not think better of me than I deserve,' said the earl to
Peveril ; 'my mother has omitted to tell you the culprit was
pretty Peggy of Ramsey, and her crime what in Cupid's courts
would have been called a peccadillo.'

'Do not make yourself worse than you are,' replied Peveril,
who observed the countess's cheek redden ; 'you know you
would have done as much for the oldest and poorest cripple in

[1] See Prison under Church.   Note 12.

the island. Why, the vault is under the burial-ground of the chapel, and, for aught I know, under the ocean itself, such a roaring do the waves make in its vicinity. I think no one could remain there long and retain his reason.'

'It is an infernal hole,' answered the earl, 'and I will have it built up one day, that is full certain. But hold — hold; for God's sake, madam, what are you going to do? Look at the seal before you put it to the warrant; you will see it is a choice antique cameo, Cupid riding on a flying fish. I had it for twenty zechins from Signor Furabosco at Rome — a most curious matter for an antiquary, but which will add little faith to a Manx warrant.'

'How can you trifle thus, you simple boy?' said the countess, with vexation in her tone and look. 'Let me have your signet; or rather, take these warrants and sign them yourself.'

'My signet — my signet. Oh! you mean that with the three monstrous legs, which I suppose was devised as the most preposterous device to represent our most absurd Majesty of Man. The signet — I have not seen it since I gave it to Gibbon, my monkey, to play with. He did whine for it most piteously. I hope he has not gemmed the green breast of ocean with my symbol of sovereignty!'

'Now, by Heaven,' said the countess, trembling and colouring deeply with anger, 'it was your father's signet, the last pledge which he sent, with his love to me and his blessing to thee, the night before they murdered him at Bolton!'

'Mother — dearest mother,' said the earl, startled out of his apathy, and taking her hand, which he kissed tenderly, 'I did but jest : the signet is safe — Peveril knows that it is so. Go fetch it, Julian, for Heaven's sake, here are my keys; it is in the left-hand drawer of my travelling-cabinet. Nay, mother, forgive me, it was but a *mauvaise plaisanterie* — only an ill-imagined jest — ungracious, and in bad taste, I allow, but only one of Philip's follies. Look at me, dearest mother, and forgive me!'

The countess turned her eyes towards him, from which the tears were fast falling.

'Philip,' she said, 'you try me too unkindly and too severely. If times are changed, as I have heard you allege — if the dignity of rank, and the high feelings of honour and duty, are now drowned in giddy jests and trifling pursuits — let *me* at least, who live secluded from all others, die without perceiving the change which has happened, and, above all, without perceiving it in mine own son.   Let me not learn the general prevalence of this levity, which laughs at every sense of dignity or duty, through your personal disrespect.   Let me not think that when I die —— '

'Speak nothing of it, mother,' said the earl, interrupting her affectionately.   'It is true, I cannot promise to be all my father and his fathers were ; for we wear silk vests for their steel coats, and feathered beavers for their crested helmets. But believe me, though to be an absolute Palmerin of England is not in my nature, no son ever loved a mother more dearly, or would do more to oblige her.   And that you may own this, I will forthwith not only seal the warrants, to the great endangerment of my precious fingers, but also read the same from end to end, as well as the despatches thereunto appertaining.'

A mother is easily appeased, even when most offended ; and it was with an expanding heart that the countess saw her son's very handsome features, while reading these papers, settle into an expression of deep seriousness, such as they seldom wore. It seemed to her as if the family likeness to his gallant but unfortunate father increased when the expression of their countenances became similar in gravity.   The earl had no sooner perused the despatches, which he did with great attention, than he rose and said, 'Julian, come with me.'

The countess looked surprised.   'I was wont to share your father's counsels, my son,' she said ; 'but do not think that I wish to intrude myself upon yours.   I am too well pleased to see you assume the power and the duty of thinking for yourself, which is what I have so long urged you to do.   Nevertheless, my experience, who have been so long administrator of your authority in Man, might not, I think, be superfluous to the matter in hand.'

'Hold me excused, dearest mother,' said the earl, gravely. 'The interference was none of my seeking ; had you taken your own course, without consulting me, it had been well ; but since I have entered on the affair — and it appears sufficiently important — I must transact it to the best of my own ability.'

'Go, then, my son,' said the countess, 'and may Heaven enlighten thee with its counsel, since thou wilt have none of mine.   I trust that you, Master Peveril, will remind him of what is fit for his own honour ; and that only a coward abandons his rights, and only a fool trusts his enemies.'

The earl answered not, but, taking Peveril by the arm, led him up a winding stair to his own apartment, and from thence into a projecting turret, where, amidst the roar of waves and sea-mews' clang, he held with him the following conversation : —

'Peveril, it is well I looked into these warrants. My mother queens it at such a rate as may cost me not only my crown, which I care little for, but perhaps my head, which, though others may think little of, I would feel it an inconvenience to be deprived of.'

'What on earth is the matter ? ' said Peveril, with considerable anxiety.

'It seems,' said the Earl of Derby, 'that Old England, who takes a frolicsome brain-fever once every two or three years, for the benefit of her doctors, and the purification of the torpid lethargy brought on by peace and prosperity, is now gone stark staring mad on the subject of a real or supposed Popish Plot. I read one programme on the subject, by a fellow called Oates, and thought it the most absurd foolery I ever perused. But that cunning fellow Shaftesbury, and some others amongst the great ones, have taken it up, and are driving on at such a rate as makes harness crack and horses smoke for it. The King, who has sworn never to kiss the pillow his father went to sleep on, temporises and gives way to the current ; the Duke of York, suspected and hated on account of his religion, is about to be driven to the Continent ; several principal Catholic nobles are in the Tower already ; and the nation, like a bull at Tutbury running, is persecuted with so many inflammatory rumours and pestilent pamphlets that she has cocked her tail, flung up her heels, taken the bit betwixt her teeth, and is as furiously unmanageable as in the year 1642.'

'All this you must have known already,' said Peveril ; 'I wonder you told me not of news so important.'

'It would have taken long to tell,' said the earl ; 'moreover, I desired to have you *solus* ; thirdly, I was about to speak when my mother entered ; and, to conclude, it was no business of mine. But these despatches of my politic mother's private correspondent put a new face on the whole matter ; for it seems some of the informers — a trade which, having become a thriving one, is now pursued by many — have dared to glance at the countess herself as an agent in this same plot — ay, and have found those that are willing enough to believe their report.'

'On mine honour,' said Peveril, 'you both take it with great coolness. I think the countess the more composed of the two ;

for, except her movement hither, she exhibited no mark of alarm, and, moreover, seemed no way more anxious to communicate the matter to your lordship than decency rendered necessary.'

'My good mother,' said the earl, 'loves power, though it has cost her dear. I wish I could truly say that my neglect of business is entirely assumed in order to leave it in her hands, but that better motive combines with natural indolence. But she seems to have feared I should not think exactly like her in this emergency, and she was right in supposing so.'

'How comes the emergency upon you?' said Julian; 'and what form does the danger assume?'

'Marry, thus it is,' said the earl: 'I need not bid you remember the affair of Colonel Christian. That man, besides his widow, who is possessed of large property — Dame Christian of Kirk-Truagh, whom you have often heard of, and perhaps seen — left a brother called Edward Christian, whom you never saw at all. Now this brother — but I daresay you know all about it?'

'Not I, on my honour,' said Peveril; 'you know the countess seldom or never alludes to the subject.'

'Why,' replied the earl, 'I believe in her heart she is something ashamed of that gallant act of royalty and supreme jurisdiction, the consequences of which maimed my estate so cruelly. Well, cousin, this same Edward Christian was one of the dempsters at the time, and, naturally enough, was unwilling to concur in the sentence which adjudged his *aîné* to be shot like a dog. My mother, who was then in high force, and not to be controlled by any one, would have served the dempster with the same sauce with which she dressed his brother, had he not been wise enough to fly from the island. Since that time, the thing has slept on all hands; and though we knew that Dempster Christian made occasionally secret visits to his friends in the island, along with two or three other Puritans of the same stamp, and particularly a prick-eared rogue called Bridgenorth, brother-in-law to the deceased, yet my mother, thank Heaven, has hitherto had the sense to connive at them, though, for some reason or other, she holds this Bridgenorth in especial disfavour.'

'And why,' said Peveril, forcing himself to speak, in order to conceal the very unpleasant surprise which he felt — 'why does the countess now depart from so prudent a line of conduct?'

'You must know the case is now different. The rogues are not satisfied with toleration: they would have supremacy.

They have found friends in the present heat of the popular mind. My mother's name, and especially that of her confessor, Aldrick the Jesuit, have been mentioned in this beautiful maze of a plot, which, if any such at all exists, she knows as little of as you or I. However, she is a Catholic, and that is enough ; and I have little doubt that, if the fellows could seize on our scrap of a kingdom here, and cut all our throats, they would have the thanks of the present House of Commons, as willingly as old Christian had those of the Rump for a similar service.'

'From whence did you receive all this information ? ' said Peveril, again speaking, though by the same effort which a man makes who talks in his sleep.

' Aldrick has seen the Duke of York in secret, and his Royal Highness, who wept while he confessed his want of power to protect his friends — and it is no trifle will wring tears from him — told him to send us information that we should look to our safety, for that Dempster Christian and Bridgenorth were in the island, with secret and severe orders ; that they had formed a considerable party there, and were likely to be owned and protected in anything they might undertake against us. The people of Ramsey and Castletown are unluckily discontented about some new regulation of the imposts ; and, to tell you the truth, though I thought yesterday's sudden remove a whim of my mother's, I am almost satisfied they would have blockaded us in Rushin Castle, where we could not have held out for lack of provisions. Here we are better supplied, and, as we are on our guard, it is likely the intended rising will not take place.'

' And what is to be done in this emergency ? ' said Peveril.

'That is the very question, my gentle coz,' answered the earl. ' My mother sees but one way of going to work, and that is by royal authority. Here are the warrants she had pre-pared, to search for, take, and apprehend the bodies of Edward Christian and Robert — no, Ralph Bridgenorth, and bring them to instant trial. No doubt, she would soon have had them in the castle court, with a dozen of the old matchlocks levelled against them — that is her way of solving all sudden difficulties.'

' But in which, I trust, you do not acquiesce, my lord,' answered Peveril, whose thoughts instantly reverted to Alice, if they could ever be said to be absent from her.

' Truly, I acquiesce in no such matter,' said the earl. ' Wil-liam Christian's death cost me a fair half of my inheritance ; I

have no fancy to fall under the displeasure of my royal brother,
King Charles, for a new escapade of the same kind. But how
to pacify my mother, I know not. I wish the insurrection
would take place, and then, as we are better provided than
they can be, we might knock the knaves on the head; and yet,
since they began the fray, we should keep the law on our side.'

'Were it not better,' said Peveril, 'if by any means these
men could be induced to quit the island ?'

'Surely,' replied the earl; 'but that will be no easy matter:
they are stubborn on principle, and empty threats will not
move them. This storm-blast in London is wind in their sails,
and they will run their length, you may depend on it. I have
sent orders, however, to clap up the Manxmen upon whose
assistance they depended, and if I can find the two worthies
themselves, here are sloops enough in the harbour : I will take
the freedom to send them on a pretty distant voyage, and I
hope matters will be settled before they return to give an
account of it.'

At this moment a soldier belonging to the garrison approached the two young men, with many bows and tokens of
respect. 'How now, friend ?' said the earl to him. 'Leave off
thy courtesies and tell thy business.'

The man, who was a native islander, answered in Manx that
he had a letter for his honour, Master Julian Peveril. Julian
snatched the billet hastily, and asked whence it came.

'It was delivered to him by a young woman,' the soldier
replied, 'who had given him a piece of money to deliver it into
Master Peveril's own hand.'

'Thou art a lucky fellow, Julian,' said the earl. 'With that
grave brow of thine, and thy character for sobriety and early
wisdom, you set the girls a-wooing, without waiting till they
are asked; whilst I, their drudge and vassal, waste both language and leisure, without getting a kind word or look, far less
a billet-doux.'

This the young earl said with a smile of conscious triumph,
as in fact he valued himself not a little upon the interest
which he supposed himself to possess with the fair sex.

Meanwhile, the letter impressed on Peveril a different train
of thoughts from what his companion apprehended. It was in
Alice's hand, and contained these few words : —

'I fear what I am going to do is wrong ; but I must see
you. Meet me at noon at Goddard Crovan's Stone, with as
much secrecy as you may.'

The letter was signed only with the initials ' A. B.' ; but Julian had no difficulty in recognising the handwriting, which he had often seen, and which was remarkably beautiful. He stood suspended, for he saw the difficulty and impropriety of withdrawing himself from the countess and his friend at this moment of impending danger ; and yet to neglect this invitation was not to be thought of. He paused in the utmost perplexity.

'Shall I read your riddle ? ' said the earl. ' Go where love calls you — I will make an excuse to my mother ; only, most grave anchorite, be hereafter more indulgent to the failings of others than you have been hitherto, and blaspheme not the power of the little deity.'

'Nay, but, cousin Derby —— ' said Peveril, and stopped short, for he really knew not what to say. Secured himself by a virtuous passion from the contagious influence of the time, he had seen with regret his noble kinsman mingle more in its irregularities than he approved of, and had sometimes played the part of a monitor.

Circumstances seemed at present to give the earl a right of retaliation. He kept his eye fixed on his friend, as if he waited till he should complete his sentence, and at length exclaimed, 'What ! cousin, quite *à la mort !* Oh, most judicious Julian ! Oh, most precise Peveril ! have you bestowed so much wisdom on me that you have none left for yourself ? Come, be frank — tell me name and place, or say but the colour of the eyes of the most emphatic she, or do but let me have the pleasure to hear thee say, "I love !" Confess one touch of human frailty, conjugate the verb *amo,* and I will be a gentle schoolmaster, and you shall have, as father Richards used to say, when we were under his ferule, " *licentia exeundi.*" '

'Enjoy your pleasant humour at my expense, my lord,' said Peveril. 'I fairly will confess thus much, that I would fain, if it consisted with my honour and your safety, have two hours at my own disposal, the more especially as the manner in which I shall employ them may much concern the safety of the island.'

'Very likely, I daresay,' answered the earl, still laughing. 'No doubt you are summoned out by some Lady Politic Wouldbe of the isle, to talk over some of the breast-laws ; but never mind — go, and go speedily, that you may return as quick as possible. I expect no immediate explosion of this grand conspiracy. When the rogues see us on our guard, they will

be cautious how they break out. Only, once more, make
haste.'

Peveril thought this last advice was not to be neglected;
and, glad to extricate himself from the raillery of his cousin,
walked down towards the gate of the castle, meaning to cross
over to the village, and there take horse at the earl's stables
for the place of rendezvous.

CHAPTER XVI

Acasto. Can she not speak ?
Oswald. If speech be only in accented sounds,
Framed by the tongue and lips, the maiden's dumb ;
But if by quick and apprehensive look,
By motion, sign, and glance, to give each meaning,
Express as clothed in language, be term'd speech,
She hath that wondrous faculty ; for her eyes,
Like the bright stars of heaven, can hold discourse,
Though it be mute and soundless.

Old Play.

AT the head of the first flight of steps which descended towards the difficult and well-defended entrance of the Castle of Holm-Peel, Peveril was met and stopped by the countess's train-bearer. This little creature — for she was of the least and slightest size of womankind — was exquisitely well formed in all her limbs, which the dress she usually wore, a green silk tunic of a peculiar form, set off to the best advantage. Her face was darker than the usual hue of Europeans ; and the profusion of long and silken hair which, when she undid the braids in which she commonly wore it, fell down almost to her ankles, was also rather a foreign attribute. Her countenance resembled a most beautiful miniature ; and there was a quickness, decision, and fire in Fenella's look, and especially in her eyes, which was probably rendered yet more alert and acute because, through the imperfection of her other organs, it was only by sight that she could obtain information of what passed around her.

The pretty mute was mistress of many little accomplishments, which the countess had caused to be taught to her in compassion for her forlorn situation, and which she learned with the most surprising quickness. Thus, for example, she was exquisite in the use of the needle, and so ready and ingenious a draughtswoman, that, like the ancient Mexicans, she sometimes made a hasty sketch with her pencil the means of conveying her ideas, either by direct or emblematical representation. Above all, in the art of ornamental writing, much studied at that period, Fenella was so great a proficient as to rival the fame of Messrs. Snow, Shelley, and other masters of the pen, whose copy-books, preserved in the libraries of the curious, still show the artists smiling on the frontispiece in all the honours of flowing gowns and full-bottomed wigs, to the eternal glory of calligraphy.

The little maiden had, besides these accomplishments, much ready wit and acuteness of intellect. With Lady Derby and with the two young gentlemen she was a great favourite, and used much freedom in conversing with them by means of a system of signs which had been gradually established amongst them, and which served all ordinary purposes of communication.

But, though happy in the indulgence and favour of her mistress, from whom indeed she was seldom separate, Fenella was by no means a favourite with the rest of the household. In fact, it seemed that her temper, exasperated perhaps by a sense of her misfortune, was by no means equal to her abilities. She was very haughty in her demeanour, even towards the upper domestics, who in that establishment were of a much higher rank and better birth than in the families of the nobility in general. These often complained, not only of her pride and reserve, but of her high and irascible temper and vindictive disposition. Her passionate propensity had been indeed idly encouraged by the young men, and particularly by the earl, who sometimes amused himself with teazing her, that he might enjoy the various singular motions and murmurs by which she expressed her resentment. Towards him, these were of course only petulant and whimsical indications of pettish anger. But when she was angry with others of inferior degree — before whom she did not control herself — the expression of her passion, unable to display itself in language, had something even frightful, so singular were the tones, contortions, and gestures to which she had recourse. The lower domestics, to whom she was liberal almost beyond her apparent means, observed her with much deference and respect, but much more from fear than from any real attachment ; for the caprices of her temper displayed themselves even in her gifts ; and those who most frequently shared her bounty seemed by no means assured of the benevolence of the motives which dictated her liberality.

All these peculiarities led to a conclusion consonant with Manx superstition. Devout believers in all the legends of fairies so dear to the Celtic tribes, the Manx people held it for certainty that the elves were in the habit of carrying off mortal children before baptism, and leaving in the cradle of the new-born babe one of their own brood, which was almost always imperfect in some one or other of the organs proper to humanity. Such a being they conceived Fenella to be ; and the smallness of her size, her dark complexion, her long locks of silken hair, the singularity of her manners and tones, as well as the caprices of her temper, were to their thinking all attributes of the irritable, fickle, and dangerous race from which they supposed her to be sprung. And it seemed that, although no jest appeared to offend her more than when Lord Derby called her in sport the Elfin Queen, or otherwise alluded to her supposed connexion with ' the pigmy folk,' yet still her perpetually affecting to wear the colour of green, proper to the fairies, as well as some other peculiarities, seemed voluntarily assumed by her, in order to countenance the superstition, perhaps because it gave her more authority among the lower orders.

Many were the tales circulated respecting the countess's elf, as Fenella was currently called in the island ; and the malcontents of the stricter persuasion were convinced that no one but a Papist and a Malignant would have kept near her person a creature of such doubtful origin. They conceived that Fenella's deafness and dumbness were only towards those of this world, and that she had been heard talking, and singing, and laughing most elvishly with the invisibles of her own race. They alleged, also, that she had a ' double,' a sort of apparition resembling her, which slept in the countess's ante-room, or bore her train, or wrought in her cabinet, while the real Fenella joined the song of the mermaids on the moonlight sands, or the dance of the fairies in the haunted valley of Glenmoy, or on the heights of Snaefell and Barool. The sentinels, too, would have sworn they had seen the little maiden trip past them in their solitary night-walks, without their having it in their power to challenge her, any more than if they had been as mute as herself. To all this mass of absurdities the better informed paid no more attention than to the usual idle exaggerations of the vulgar, which so frequently connect that which is unusual with what is supernatural.[1]

Such, in form and habits, was the little female who, holding in her hand a small, old-fashioned ebony rod, which might have passed for a divining-wand, confronted Julian on the top of the flight of steps which led down the rock from the castle court.

---

[1] See Manx Superstitions. Note 13.

We ought to observe that, as Julian's manner to the unfortunate girl had been always gentle, and free from those teazing jests in which his gay friend indulged, with less regard to the peculiarity of her situation and feelings, so Fenella, on her part, had usually shown much greater deference to him than to any of the household, her mistress, the countess, always excepted.

On the present occasion, planting herself in the very midst of the narrow descent, so as to make it impossible for Peveril to pass by her, she proceeded to put him to the question by a series of gestures, which we will endeavour to describe. She commenced by extending her hand slightly, accompanied with the sharp, inquisitive look which served her as a note of interrogation. This was meant as an inquiry whether he was going to a distance. Julian, in reply, extended his arm more than half, to intimate that the distance was considerable. Fenella looked grave, shook her head, and pointed to the countess's window, which was visible from the spot where they stood. Peveril smiled and nodded, to intimate there was no danger in quitting her mistress for a short space. The little maiden next touched an eagle's feather which she wore in her hair, a sign which she usually employed to designate the earl, and then looked inquisitively at Julian once more, as if to say, ' Goes he with you ? ' Peveril shook his head, and, somewhat wearied by these interrogatories, smiled, and made an effort to pass. Fenella frowned, struck the end of her ebony rod perpendicularly on the ground, and again shook her head, as if opposing his departure. But finding that Julian persevered in his purpose, she suddenly assumed another and a milder mood, held him by the skirt of his cloak with one hand, and raised the other in an imploring attitude, whilst every feature of her lively countenance was composed into the like expression of supplication ; and the fire of the large dark eyes, which appeared in general so keen and piercing as almost to over-animate the little sphere to which they belonged, seemed quenched, for the moment, in the large drops which hung on her long eyelashes, but without falling.

Julian Peveril was far from being void of sympathy towards the poor girl, whose motives in opposing his departure appeared to be her affectionate apprehensions for her mistress's safety. He endeavoured to reassure her by smiles, and, at the same time, by such signs as he could devise, to intimate that there was no danger, and that he would return presently ; and having

succeeded in extricating his cloak from her grasp and in passing
her on the stair, he began to descend the steps as speedily as
he could, in order to avoid farther importunity.

But with activity much greater than his, the dumb maiden
hastened to intercept him, and succeeded by throwing herself,
at the imminent risk of life and limb, a second time into the
pass which he was descending, so as to interrupt his purpose.
In order to achieve this, she was obliged to let herself drop a
considerable height from the wall of a small flanking battery,
where two patereroes were placed to scour the pass, in case
any enemy could have mounted so high. Julian had scarce
time to shudder at her purpose, as he beheld her about to spring
from the parapet, ere, like a thing of gossamer, she stood light
and uninjured on the rocky platform below. He endeavoured,
by the gravity of his look and gesture, to make her understand
how much he blamed her rashness; but the reproof, though
obviously quite intelligible, was entirely thrown away. A hasty
wave of her hand intimated how she contemned the danger and
the remonstrance; while at the same time she instantly resumed,
with more eagerness than before, the earnest and impressive
gestures by which she endeavoured to detain him in the
fortress.

Julian was somewhat staggered by her pertinacity. 'Is it
possible,' he thought, 'that any danger can approach the
countess, of which this poor maiden has, by the extreme acuteness of her observation, obtained knowledge which has escaped
others?'

He signed to Fenella hastily to give him the tablets and
the pencil which she usually carried with her, and wrote on
them the question, 'Is there danger near to your mistress, that
you thus stop me?'

'There is danger around the countess,' was the answer
instantly written down; 'but there is much more in your own
purpose.'

'How! what! what know you of my purpose?' said Julian,
forgetting, in his surprise, that the party he addressed had
neither ear to comprehend nor voice to reply to uttered language. She had regained her book in the meantime, and
sketched, with a rapid pencil, on one of the leaves, a scene which
she showed to Julian. To his infinite surprise, he recognised
Goddard Crovan's Stone, a remarkable monument, of which she
had given the outline with sufficient accuracy; together with a
male and female figure, which, though only indicated by a few

slight touches of the pencil, bore yet, he thought, some resemblance to himself and Alice Bridgenorth.

When he had gazed on the sketch for an instant with surprise, Fenella took the book from his hand, laid her finger upon the drawing, and slowly and sternly shook her head, with a frown which seemed to prohibit the meeting which was there represented.   Julian, however, though disconcerted, was in no shape disposed to submit to the authority of his monitress.   By whatever means she, who so seldom stirred from the countess's apartment, had become acquainted with a secret which he thought entirely his own, he esteemed it the more necessary to keep the appointed rendezvous, that he might learn from Alice, if possible, how the secret had transpired.   He had also formed the intention of seeking out Bridgenorth ; entertaining an idea that a person so reasonable and calm as he had shown himself in their late conference might be persuaded, when he understood that the countess was aware of his intrigues, to put an end to her danger and his own by withdrawing from the island.   And could he succeed in this point, he should at once, he thought, render a material benefit to the father of his beloved Alice, remove the earl from his state of anxiety, save the countess from a second time putting her feudal jurisdiction in opposition to that of the crown of England, and secure quiet possession of the island to her and her family.

With this scheme of mediation in his mind, Peveril determined to rid himself of the opposition of Fenella to his departure with less ceremony than he had hitherto observed towards her ; and suddenly lifting up the damsel in his arms before she was aware of his purpose, he turned about, set her down on the steps above him, and began to descend the pass himself as speedily as possible.   It was then that the dumb maiden gave full course to the vehemence of her disposition ; and, clapping her hands repeatedly, expressed her displeasure in a sound, or rather a shriek, so extremely dissonant, that it resembled more the cry of a wild creature than anything which could have been uttered by female organs.   Peveril was so astounded at the scream as it rung through the living rocks, that he could not help stopping and looking back in alarm, to satisfy himself that she had not sustained some injury.   He saw her, however, perfectly safe, though her face seemed inflamed and distorted with passion.   She stamped at him with her foot, shook her clenched hand, and, turning her back upon him without farther adieu, ran up the rude steps as lightly as

a kid could have tripped up that rugged ascent, and paused for
a moment at the summit of the first flight.

Julian could feel nothing but wonder and compassion for
the impotent passion of a being so unfortunately circumstanced,
cut off, as it were, from the rest of mankind, and incapable of
receiving in childhood that moral discipline which teaches us
mastery of our wayward passions, ere yet they have attained
their meridian strength and violence. He waved his hand to
her, in token of amicable farewell; but she only replied by once
more menacing him with her little hand clenched; and then
ascending the rocky staircase with almost preternatural speed,
was soon out of sight.

Julian, on his part, gave no farther consideration to her
conduct or its motives, but hastening to the village on the
mainland, where the stables of the castle were situated, he
again took his palfrey from the stall, and was soon mounted
and on his way to the appointed place of rendezvous, much
marvelling, as he ambled forward with speed far greater than
was promised by the diminutive size of the animal he was
mounted on, what could have happened to produce so great a
change in Alice's conduct towards him, that, in place of enjoining his absence as usual, or recommending his departure from
the island, she should now voluntarily invite him to a meeting.
Under impression of the various doubts which succeeded each
other in his imagination, he sometimes pressed Fairy's sides
with his legs; sometimes laid his holly rod lightly on her neck;
sometimes incited her by his voice, for the mettled animal
needed neither whip nor spur; and achieved the distance betwixt
the Castle of Holm-Peel and the stone at Goddard Crovan at
the rate of twelve miles within the hour.

The monumental stone, designed to commemorate some feat
of an ancient king of Man which had been long forgotten, was
erected on the side of a narrow, lonely valley, or rather glen,
secluded from observation by the steepness of its banks, upon
a projection of which stood the tall, shapeless, solitary rock,
frowning, like a shrouded giant, over the brawling of the small
rivulet which watered the ravine.

CHAPTER XVII

This a love-meeting? See, the maiden mourns,
And the sad suitor bends his looks on earth.
There's more hath pass'd between them than belongs
To love's sweet sorrows.

Old Play.

AS he approached the monument of Goddard Crovan,
Julian cast many an anxious glance to see whether any
object visible beside the huge grey stone should ap-
prise him whether he was anticipated, at the appointed place of
rendezvous, by her who had named it. Nor was it long before
the flutter of a mantle, which the breeze slightly waved, and the
motion necessary to replace it upon the wearer's shoulders, made
him aware that Alice had already reached their place of meeting. One instant set the palfrey at liberty, with slackened
girths and loosened reins, to pick its own way through the dell
at will; another placed Julian Peveril by the side of Alice
Bridgenorth.

That Alice should extend her hand to her lover, as with the
ardour of a young greyhound he bounded over the obstacles of
the rugged path, was as natural as that Julian, seizing on the
hand so kindly stretched out, should devour it with kisses, and,
for a moment or two, without reprehension; while the other
hand, which should have aided in the liberation of its fellow,
served to hide the blushes of the fair owner. But Alice, young
as she was, and attached to Julian by such long habits of kindly
intimacy, still knew well how to subdue the tendency of her
own treacherous affections.

'This is not right,' she said, extricating her hand from
Julian's grasp — 'this is not right, Julian. If I have been too
rash in admitting such a meeting as the present, it is not you
that should make me sensible of my folly.'

Julian Peveril's mind had been early illuminated with that
touch of romantic fire which deprives passion of selfishness, and
confers on it the high and refined tone of generous and dis-

interested devotion. He let go the hand of Alice with as much
respect as he could have paid to that of a princess ; and when
she seated herself upon a rocky fragment, over which nature
had stretched a cushion of moss and lichen, interspersed with
wild-flowers, backed with a bush of copsewood, he took his
place beside her, indeed, but at such distance as to intimate
the duty of an attendant, who was there only to hear and to
obey. Alice Bridgenorth became more assured as she observed
the power which she possessed over her lover ; and the self-
command which Peveril exhibited, which other damsels in her
situation might have judged inconsistent with intensity of
passion, she appreciated more justly, as a proof of his respectful
and disinterested sincerity. She recovered, in addressing him,
the tone of confidence which rather belonged to the scenes of
their early acquaintance than to those which had passed
betwixt them since Peveril had disclosed his affection, and
thereby had brought restraint upon their intercourse.

'Julian,' she said, 'your visit of yesterday — your most ill-
timed visit — has distressed me much. It has misled my father
— it has endangered you. At all risks, I resolved that you
should know this, and blame me not if I have taken a bold and
imprudent step in desiring this solitary interview, since you are
aware how little poor Deborah is to be trusted.'

'Can you fear misconstruction from me, Alice ?' replied
Peveril, warmly — 'from me, whom you have thus highly
favoured — thus deeply obliged ? '

'Cease your protestations, Julian,' answered the maiden,
'they do but make me the more sensible that I have acted
over boldly. But I did for the best. I could not see you,
whom I have known so long — you, who say you regard me
with partiality ——'

'*Say* that I regard you with partiality !' interrupted Peveril
in his turn. 'Ah, Alice, what a cold and doubtful phrase you
have used to express the most devoted, the most sincere
affection ! '

'Well, then,' said Alice, sadly, 'we will not quarrel about
words ; but do not again interrupt me. I could not, I say, see
you, who, I believe, regard me with sincere, though vain and
fruitless, attachment, rush blindfold into a snare, deceived and
seduced by those very feelings towards me.'

'I understand you not, Alice,' said Peveril ; 'nor can I see
any danger to which I am at present exposed. The sentiments
which your father has expressed towards me are of a nature

irreconcilable with hostile purposes. If he is not offended with
the bold wishes I may have formed, and his whole behaviour
shows the contrary, I know not a man on earth from whom I
have less cause to apprehend any danger or ill-will.'

'My father,' said Alice, 'means well by his country, and
well by you ; yet I sometimes fear he may rather injure than
serve his good cause; and still more do I dread that, in attempting to engage you as an auxiliary, he may forget those
ties which ought to bind you, and I am sure which will bind
you, to a different line of conduct from his own.'

'You lead me into still deeper darkness, Alice,' answered
Peveril. 'That your father's especial line of politics differs
widely from mine, I know well ; but how many instances have
occurred, even during the bloody scenes of civil warfare, of
good and worthy men laying the prejudice of party affections
aside, and regarding each other with respect, and even with
friendly attachment, without being false to principle on either
side ? '

'It may be so,' said Alice ; 'but such is not the league
which my father desires to form with you, and that to which
he hopes your misplaced partiality towards his daughter may
afford a motive for your forming with him.'

'And what is it,' said Peveril, 'which I would refuse, with
such a prospect before me ? '

'Treachery and dishonour ! ' replied Alice — ' whatever would
render you unworthy of the poor boon at which you aim — ay,
were it more worthless than I confess it to be.'

'Would your father,' said Peveril, as he unwillingly received
the impression which Alice designed to convey — 'would he,
whose views of duty are so strict and severe — would he wish to
involve me in aught to which such harsh epithets as treachery
and dishonour can be applied with the slightest shadow of
truth ? '

'Do not mistake me, Julian,' replied the maiden ; 'my father
is incapable of requesting aught of you that is not to his
thinking just and honourable ; nay, he conceives that he only
claims from you a debt which is due as a creature to the
Creator, and as a man to your fellow-men.'

'So guarded, where can be the danger of our intercourse ? '
replied Julian. 'If he be resolved to require, and I determined
to accede to, nothing save what flows from conviction, what
have I to fear, Alice ? And how is my intercourse with your
father dangerous ? Believe not so ; his speech has already

made impression on me in some particulars, and he listened
with candour and patience to the objections which I made
occasionally. You do Master Bridgenorth less than justice in
confounding him with the unreasonable bigots in policy and
religion, who can listen to no argument but what favours their
own prepossessions.'

'Julian,' replied Alice, 'it is you who misjudge my father's
powers, and his purpose with respect to you, and who overrate
your own powers of resistance. I am but a girl, but I have
been taught by circumstances to think for myself, and to
consider the character of those around me. My father's
views in ecclesiastical and civil policy are as dear to him as
the life which he cherishes only to advance them. They
have been, with little alteration, his companions through life.
They brought him at one period into prosperity, and when they
suited not the times, he suffered for having held them. They
have become not only a part, but the very dearest part, of his
existence. If he shows them not to you at first in the inflexible strength which they have acquired over his mind, do
not believe that they are the less powerful. He who desires
to make converts must begin by degrees. But that he should
sacrifice to an inexperienced young man, whose ruling motive
he will term a childish passion, any part of those treasured
principles which he has maintained through good repute and
bad repute — Oh, do not dream of such an impossibility! If
you meet at all, you must be the wax, he the seal: you must
receive, he must bestow, an absolute impression.'

'That,' said Peveril, 'were unreasonable. I will frankly avow
to you, Alice, that I am not a sworn bigot to the opinions entertained by my father, much as I respect his person. I could
wish that our Cavaliers, or whatsoever they are pleased to call
themselves, would have some more charity towards those who
differ from them in church and state. But to hope that I
would surrender the principles in which I have lived were to
suppose me capable of deserting my benefactress, and breaking
the hearts of my parents.'

'Even so I judged of you,' answered Alice; 'and, therefore,
I asked this interview, to conjure that you will break off all
intercourse with our family — return to your parents — or, what
will be much safer, visit the Continent once more, and abide
till God sends better days to England, for these are black with
many a storm.'

'And can you bid me go, Alice,' said the young man, taking

her unresisting hand — 'can you bid me go, and yet own an
interest in my fate ?   Can you bid me, for fear of dangers
which, as a man, as a gentleman, and a loyal one, I am bound
to show my face to, meanly abandon my parents, my friends,
my country, suffer the existence of evils which I might aid to
prevent, forego the prospect of doing such little good as might
be in my power, fall from an active and honourable station
into the condition of a fugitive and time-server.   Can you bid
me do all this, Alice ? — can you bid me do all this, and, in the
same breath, bid farewell for ever to you and happiness ?   It is
impossible : I cannot surrender at once my love and my honour.'
    'There is no remedy,' said Alice, but she could not suppress
a sigh while she said so — 'there is no remedy, none whatever.
What we might have been to each other, placed in more favourable circumstances, it avails not to think of now ; and, circumstanced as we are, with open war about to break out betwixt
our parents and friends, we can be but well-wishers — cold and
distant well-wishers, who must part on this spot, and at this
hour, never to meet again.'
    'No, by Heaven !' said Peveril, animated at the same time
by his own feelings and by the sight of the emotions which his
companion in vain endeavoured to suppress — 'no, by Heaven !'
he exclaimed, 'we part not — Alice, we part not.   If I am to
leave my native land, you shall be my companion in my exile.
What have you to lose ?   Whom have you to abandon ?   Your
father ?   The good old cause, as it is termed, is dearer to him
than a thousand daughters ; and setting him aside, what tie is
there between you and this barren isle — between my Alice and
any spot of the British dominions where her Julian does not
sit by her ?'
    'O Julian,' answered the maiden, 'why make my duty more
painful by visionary projects, which you ought not to name or
I to listen to ?   Your parents ! my father ! it cannot be.'
    'Fear not for my parents, Alice,' replied Julian, and pressing
close to his companion's side, he ventured to throw his arm
around her ; 'they love me, and they will soon learn to love in
Alice the only being on earth who could have rendered their
son happy.   And for your own father, when state and church
intrigues allow him to bestow a thought upon you, will he not
think that your happiness, your security, is better cared for
when you are my wife than were you to continue under the
mercenary charge of yonder foolish woman ?   What could his
pride desire better for you than the establishment which will

one day be mine ? Come then, Alice, and since you condemn
me to banishment — since you deny me a share in those stirring
achievements which are about to agitate England — come ! do
you, for you only can — do you reconcile me to exile and in-
action, and give happiness to one who, for your sake, is willing
to resign honour ! '

'It cannot — it cannot be,' said Alice, faltering as she uttered her negative. 'And yet,' she said, 'how many in my
place — left alone and unprotected as I am —— But I must
not — I must not — for your sake, Julian, I must not ! '

'Say not for my sake you must not, Alice,' said Peveril,
eagerly ; 'this is adding insult to cruelty. If you will do aught
for my sake, you will say "yes " ; or you will suffer this dear
head to drop on my shoulder — the slightest sign — the moving of an eyelid, shall signify consent. All shall be prepared
within an hour ; within another the priest shall unite us ; and
within a third we leave the isle behind us, and seek our fortunes on the Continent.' But while he spoke, in joyful anticipation of the consent which he implored, Alice found means
to collect together her resolution, which, staggered by the
eagerness of her lover, the impulse of her own affections, and
the singularity of her situation — seeming, in her case, to justify what would have been most blameable in another — had
more than half abandoned her.

The result of a moment's deliberation was fatal to Julian's
proposal. She extricated herself from the arm which had
pressed her to his side, arose, and repelling his attempts to
approach or detain her, said, with a simplicity not unmingled
with dignity, 'Julian, I always knew I risked much in inviting you to this meeting ; but I did not guess that I could have
been so cruel both to you and to myself as to suffer you to
discover what you have to-day seen too plainly — that I love
you better than you love me. But since you do know it, I
will show you that Alice's love is disinterested. She will not
bring an ignoble name into your ancient house. If hereafter,
in your line, there should arise some who may think the claims
of the hierarchy too exorbitant, the powers of the crown too
extensive, men shall not say these ideas were derived from
Alice Bridgenorth, their whig grand-dame.'

'Can you speak thus, Alice ? ' said her lover — ' can you use
such expressions ? and are you not sensible that they show
plainly it is your own pride, not regard for me, that makes
you resist the happiness of both ? '

'Not so, Julian — not so,' answered Alice, with tears in her eyes ; 'it is the command of duty to us both — of duty, which we cannot transgress without risking our happiness here and hereafter. Think what I, the cause of all, should feel when your father frowns, your mother weeps, your noble friends stand aloof, and you, even you yourself, shall have made the painful discovery that you have incurred the contempt and resentment of all to satisfy a boyish passion ; and that the poor beauty, once sufficient to mislead you, is gradually declining under the influence of grief and vexation ! This I will not risk. I see distinctly it is best we should here break off and part ; and I thank God, who gives me light enough to perceive, and strength enough to withstand, your folly as well as my own. Farewell then, Julian ; but first take the solemn advice which I called you hither to impart to you : Shun my father ; you cannot walk in his paths and be true to gratitude and to honour. What he doth from pure and honourable motives you cannot aid him in, except upon the suggestion of a silly and interested passion, at variance with all the engagements you have formed at coming into life.'

'Once more, Alice,' answered Julian, 'I understand you not. If a course of action is good, it needs no vindication from the actor's motives ; if bad, it can derive none.'

'You cannot blind me with your sophistry, Julian,' replied Alice Bridgenorth, 'any more than you can overpower me with your passion. Had the patriarch destined his son to death upon any less ground than faith and humble obedience to a Divine commandment, he had meditated a murder and not a sacrifice. In our late bloody and lamentable wars, how many drew swords on either side from the purest and most honourable motives ? How many from the culpable suggestions of ambition, self-seeking, and love of plunder ? Yet, while they marched in the same ranks, and spurred their horses at the same trumpet-sound, the memory of the former is dear to us as patriots or loyalists ; that of those who acted on mean or unworthy promptings is either execrated or forgotten. Once more, I warn you, avoid my father ; leave this island, which will be soon agitated by strange incidents ; while you stay, be on your guard : distrust everything, be jealous of every one, even of those to whom it may seem almost impossible, from circumstances, to attach a shadow of suspicion ; trust not the very stones of the most secret apartment in Holm-Peel, for that which hath wings shall carry the matter.'

Here Alice broke off suddenly, and with a faint shriek ; for,
stepping from behind the stunted copse which had concealed
him, her father stood unexpectedly before them.

The reader cannot have forgotten that this was the second
time in which the stolen interviews of the lovers had been
interrupted by the unexpected apparition of Major Bridgenorth.
On this second occasion his countenance exhibited anger mixed
with solemnity, like that of the spirit to a ghost-seer, whom he
upbraids with having neglected a charge imposed at their first
meeting.   Even his anger, however, produced no more violent
emotion than a cold sternness of manner in his speech and
action.   ' I thank you, Alice,' he said to his daughter, ' for the
pains you have taken to traverse my designs towards this young
man and towards yourself.   I thank you for the hints you
have thrown out before my appearance, the suddenness of which
alone has prevented you from carrying your confidence to a
pitch which would have placed my life and that of others at
the discretion of a boy, who, when the cause of God and his
country is laid before him, has not leisure to think of them, so
much is he occupied with such a baby-face as thine.'   Alice,
pale as death, continued motionless, with her eyes fixed on the
ground, without attempting the slightest reply to the ironical
reproaches of her father.

' And you,' continued Major Bridgenorth, turning from his
daughter to her lover — ' you, sir, have well repaid the liberal
confidence which I placed in you with so little reserve.   You
I have to thank also for some lessons, which may teach me to
rest satisfied with the churl's blood which nature has poured
into my veins, and with the rude nurture which my father
allotted to me.'

' I understand you not, sir,' replied Julian Peveril, who,
feeling the necessity of saying something, could not, at the
moment, find anything more fitting to say.

' Yes, sir, I thank you,' said Major Bridgenorth, in the same
cold, sarcastic tone, ' for having shown me that breach of hospitality, infringement of good faith, and such-like peccadilloes,
are not utterly foreign to the mind and conduct of the heir of
a knightly house of twenty descents.   It is a great lesson to
me, sir ; for hitherto I had thought with the vulgar that gentle
manners went with gentle blood.   But perhaps courtesy is too
chivalrous a quality to be wasted in intercourse with a Roundheaded fanatic like myself.'

' Major Bridgenorth,' said Julian, ' whatever has happened

in this interview which may have displeased you has been the result of feelings suddenly and strongly animated by the crisis of the moment : nothing was premeditated.'

'Not even your meeting, I suppose ? ' replied Bridgenorth, in the same cold tone. ' You, sir, wandered hither from Holm-Peel, my daughter strolled forth from the Black Fort ; and chance, doubtless, assigned you a meeting by the stone of Goddard Crovan ? Young man, disgrace yourself by no more apologies ; they are worse than useless. And you, maiden, who, in your fear of losing your lover, could verge on betraying what might have cost a father his life, begone to your home. I will talk with you at more leisure, and teach you practically those duties which you seem to have forgotten.'

'On my honour, sir,' said Julian, 'your daughter is guilt-less of all that can offend you : she resisted every offer which the headstrong violence of my passion urged me to press upon her.'

'And, in brief,' said Bridgenorth, ' I am not to believe that you met in this remote place of rendezvous by Alice's special appointment ? '

Peveril knew not what to reply, and Bridgenorth again signed with his hand to his daughter to withdraw.

'I obey you, father,' said Alice, who had by this time re-covered from the extremity of her surprise — 'I obey you ; but Heaven is my witness that you do me more than injustice in suspecting me capable of betraying your secrets, even had it been necessary to save my own life or that of Julian. That you are walking in a dangerous path I well know ; but you do it with your eyes open, and are actuated by motives of which you can estimate the worth and value. My sole wish was, that this young man should not enter blindfold on the same perils ; and I had a right to warn him, since the feelings by which he is hoodwinked had a direct reference to me.'

' 'T is well, minion,' said Bridgenorth, 'you have spoken your say. Retire, and let me complete the conference which you have so considerately commenced.'

' I go, sir,' said Alice. ' Julian, to you my last words are, and I would speak them with my last breath — "Farewell, and caution " ! '

She turned from them, disappeared among the underwood, and was seen no more.

'A true specimen of womankind,' said her father, looking after her, 'who would give the cause of nations up, rather than

endanger a hair of her lover's head.   You, Master Peveril,
doubtless, hold her opinion, that the best love is a safe love ? '

'Were danger alone in my way,' said Peveril, much surprised
at the softened tone in which Bridgenorth made this observation, 'there are few things which I would not face to — to —
deserve your good opinion.'

'Or rather to win my daughter's hand,' said Bridgenorth.
'Well, young man, one thing has pleased me in your conduct,
though of much I have my reasons to complain — one thing
has pleased me.   You have surmounted that bounding wall of
aristocratical pride, in which your father, and, I suppose, his
fathers, remained imprisoned, as in the precincts of a feudal
fortress — you have leaped over this barrier, and shown yourself not unwilling to ally yourself with a family whom your
father spurns as low-born and ignoble.'

However favourable this speech sounded towards success in
his suit, it so broadly stated the consequences of that success
so far as his parents were concerned, that Julian felt it in the
last degree difficult to reply.   At length, perceiving that Major
Bridgenorth seemed resolved quietly to await his answer, he
mustered up courage to say, 'The feelings which I entertain
towards your daughter, Master Bridgenorth, are of a nature to
supersede many other considerations, to which, in any other
case, I should feel it my duty to give the most reverential attention.   I will not disguise from you, that my father's prejudices against such a match would be very strong ; but I devoutly
believe they would disappear when he came to know the merit
of Alice Bridgenorth, and to be sensible that she only could
make his son happy.'

'In the meanwhile, you are desirous to complete the union
which you propose without the knowledge of your parents, and
take the chance of their being hereafter reconciled to it ?   So I
understand, from the proposal which you made but lately to
my daughter.'

The turns of human nature, and of human passion, are so
irregular and uncertain, that, although Julian had but a few
minutes before urged to Alice a private marriage, and an elope-
ment to the Continent, as measures upon which the whole
happiness of his life depended, the proposal seemed not to him
half so delightful when stated by the calm, cold, dictatorial
accents of her father.   It sounded no longer like the impulses
of ardent passion, throwing all other considerations aside, but
as a distinct surrender of the dignity of his house to one who

seemed to consider their relative situation as the triumph of
Bridgenorth over Peveril. He was mute for a moment, in the
vain attempt to shape his answer so as at once to intimate
acquiescence in what Bridgenorth stated and a vindication
of his own regard for his parents and for the honour of his
house.

This delay gave rise to suspicion, and Bridgenorth's eye
gleamed and his lip quivered while he gave vent to it. 'Hark
ye, young man — deal openly with me in this matter, if you
would not have me think you the execrable villain who would
have seduced an unhappy girl under promises which he never
designed to fulfil. Let me but suspect this, and you shall see,
on the spot, how far your pride and your pedigree will preserve
you against the just vengeance of a father.'

'You do me wrong,' said Peveril — 'you do me infinite
wrong, Major Bridgenorth. I am incapable of the infamy which
you allude to. The proposal I made to your daughter was as
sincere as ever was offered by man to woman. I only hesitated,
because you think it necessary to examine me so very closely,
and to possess yourself of all my purposes and sentiments, in
their fullest extent, without explaining to me the tendency of
your own.'

'Your proposal, then, shapes itself thus,' said Bridgenorth :
'you are willing to lead my only child into exile from her
native country, to give her a claim to kindness and protection
from your family, which you know will be disregarded, on
condition I consent to bestow her hand on you, with a fortune
sufficient to have matched that of your ancestors, when they
had most reason to boast of their wealth. This, young man,
seems no equal bargain. And yet,' he continued, after a momentary pause, 'so little do I value the goods of this world,
that it might not be utterly beyond thy power to reconcile me
to the match which you have proposed to me, however unequal
it may appear.'

'Show me but the means which can propitiate your favour,
Major Bridgenorth,' said Peveril, 'for I will not doubt that
they will be consistent with my honour and duty, and you shall
soon see how eagerly I will obey your directions, or submit to
your conditions.'

'They are summed in few words,' answered Bridgenorth :
'be an honest man, and the friend of your country.'

'No one has ever doubted,' replied Peveril, 'that I am
both.'

'Pardon me,' replied the major; 'no one has as yet seen you show yourself either. Interrupt me not — I question not your will to be both; but you have hitherto neither had the light nor the opportunity necessary for the display of your principles or the service of your country. You have lived when an apathy of mind, succeeding to the agitations of the Civil War, had made men indifferent to state affairs, and more willing to cultivate their own ease than to stand in the gap when the Lord was pleading with Israel. But we are Englishmen; and with us such unnatural lethargy cannot continue long. Already, many of those who most desired the return of Charles Stewart regard him as a king whom Heaven, importuned by our entreaties, gave to us in His anger. His unlimited license — an example so readily followed by the young and the gay around him — has disgusted the minds of all sober and thinking men. I had not now held conference with you in this intimate fashion, were I not aware that you, Master Julian, were free from such stain of the times. Heaven, that rendered the King's course of license fruitful, had denied issue to his bed of wedlock; and in the gloomy and stern character of his bigoted successor we already see what sort of monarch shall succeed to the crown of England. This is a critical period, at which it necessarily becomes the duty of all men to step forward, each in his degree, and aid in rescuing the country which gave us birth.' Peveril remembered the warning which he had received from Alice, and bent his eyes on the ground, without returning any reply. 'How is it, young man,' continued Bridgenorth, after a pause, 'so young as thou art, and bound by no ties of kindred profligacy with the enemies of your country, you can be already hardened to the claims she may form on you at this crisis?'

'It were easy to answer you generally, Major Bridgenorth,' replied Peveril — 'it were easy to say that my country cannot make a claim on me which I will not promptly answer at the risk of lands and life. But in dealing thus generally, we should but deceive each other. What is the nature of this call? By whom is it to be sounded? And what are to be the results? for I think you have already seen enough of the evils of civil war to be wary of again awakening its terrors in a peaceful and happy country.'

'They that are drenched with poisonous narcotics,' said the major, 'must be awakened by their physicians, though it were with the sound of the trumpet. Better that men should die bravely, with their arms in their hands, like free-born English-

men, than that they should slide into the bloodless but dishonoured grave which slavery opens for its vassals. But it is
not of war that I was about to speak,' he added, assuming a
milder tone. 'The evils of which England now complains are
such as can be remedied by the wholesome administration of
her own laws, even in the state in which they are still suffered
to exist. Have these laws not a right to the support of every
individual who lives under them ? Have they not a right to
yours ? '

As he seemed to pause for an answer, Peveril replied, ' I
have to learn, Major Bridgenorth, how the laws of England have
become so far weakened as to require such support as mine.
When that is made plain to me, no man will more willingly
discharge the duty of a faithful liegeman to the law as well as
the king. But the laws of England are under the guardianship
of upright and learned judges and of a gracious monarch.'

'And of a House of Commons,' interrupted Bridgenorth, 'no
longer doting upon restored monarchy, but awakened, as with
a peal of thunder, to the perilous state of our religion and of
our freedom. I appeal to your own conscience, Julian Peveril,
whether this awakening hath not been in time, since you yourself know, and none better than you, the secret but rapid
strides which Rome has made to erect her Dagon of idolatry
within our Protestant land.'

Here Julian, seeing, or thinking he saw, the drift of Bridgenorth's suspicions, hastened to exculpate himself from the
thought of favouring the Roman Catholic religion. 'It is true,'
he said, ' I have been educated in a family where that faith is
professed by one honoured individual, and that I have since
travelled in Popish countries ; but even for these very reasons
I have seen Popery too closely to be friendly to its tenets.
The bigotry of the laymen, the persevering arts of the priesthood, the perpetual intrigue for the extension of the forms
without the spirit of religion, the usurpation of that church
over the consciences of men, and her impious pretensions to
infallibility, are as inconsistent to my mind as they can seem
to yours with common sense, rational liberty, freedom of conscience, and pure religion.'

'Spoken like the son of your excellent mother !' said Bridgenorth, grasping his hand, 'for whose sake I have consented
to endure so much from your house unrequited, even when the
means of requital were in my own hand.'

'It was indeed from the instructions of that excellent parent,' said Peveril, 'that I was enabled, in my early youth, to resist and repel the insidious attacks made upon my religious faith by the Catholic priests into whose company I was necessarily thrown. Like her, I trust to live and die in the faith of the Reformed Church of England.'

'The Church of England!' said Bridgenorth, dropping his young friend's hand, but presently resuming it. 'Alas! that church, as now constituted, usurps scarcely less than Rome herself upon men's consciences and liberties; yet, out of the weakness of this half-reformed church, may God be pleased to work out deliverance to England and praise to Himself. I must not forget that one whose services have been in the cause incalculable wears the garb of an English priest, and hath had Episcopal ordination. It is not for us to challenge the instrument, so that our escape is achieved from the net of the fowler. Enough, that I find thee not as yet enlightened with the purer doctrine, but prepared to profit by it when the spark shall reach thee. Enough in especial, that I find thee willing to uplift thy testimony, to cry aloud and spare not, against the errors and arts of the Church of Rome. But, remember, what thou hast now said, thou wilt soon be called upon to justify, in a manner the most solemn — the most awful.'

'What I have said,' replied Julian Peveril, 'being the unbiassed sentiments of my heart, shall, upon no proper occasion, want the support of my open avowal; and I think it strange you should doubt me so far.'

'I doubt thee not, my young friend,' said Bridgenorth; 'and I trust to see thy name rank high amongst those by whom the prey shall be rent from the mighty. At present thy prejudices occupy thy mind like the strong keeper of the house mentioned in Scripture. But there shall come a stronger than he, and make forcible entry, displaying on the battlements that sign of faith in which alone there is found salvation. Watch, hope, and pray, that the hour may come!'

There was a pause in the conversation, which was first broken by Peveril. 'You have spoken to me in riddles, Major Bridgenorth; and I have asked you for no explanation. Listen to a caution on my part, given with the most sincere good-will. Take a hint from me, and believe it, though it is darkly expressed. You are here — at least are believed to be here — on an errand dangerous to the lord of the island. That danger will be retorted on yourself, if you make Man long your place of residence. Be warned, and depart in time.'

'And leave my daughter to the guardianship of Julian Peveril? Runs not your counsel so, young man?' answered Bridgenorth. 'Trust my safety, Julian, to my own prudence. I have been accustomed to guide myself through worse dangers than now environ me. But I thank you for your caution, which I am willing to believe was at least partly disinterested.'

'We do not, then, part in anger?' said Peveril.

'Not in anger, my son,' said Bridgenorth, 'but in love and strong affection. For my daughter, thou must forbear every thought of seeing her, save through me. I accept not thy suit, neither do I reject it; only this I intimate to you, that he who would be my son must first show himself the true and loving child of his oppressed and deluded country. Farewell! Do not answer me now; thou art yet in the gall of bitterness, and it may be that strife, which I desire not, should fall between us. Thou shalt hear of me sooner than thou thinkest for.'

He shook Peveril heartily by the hand, and again bid him farewell, leaving him under the confused and mingled impression of pleasure, doubt, and wonder. Not a little surprised to find himself so far in the good graces of Alice's father that his suit was even favoured with a sort of negative encouragement, he could not help suspecting, as well from the language of the daughter as of the father, that Bridgenorth was desirous, as the price of his favour, that he should adopt some line of conduct inconsistent with the principles in which he had been educated.

'You need not fear, Alice,' he said in his heart; 'not even your hand would I purchase by aught which resembled unworthy or truckling compliance with tenets which my heart disowns; and well I know, were I mean enough to do so, even the authority of thy father were insufficient to compel thee to the ratification of so mean a bargain. But let me hope better things. Bridgenorth, though strong-minded and sagacious, is haunted by the fears of Popery, which are the bugbears of his sect. My residence in the family of the Countess of Derby is more than enough to inspire him with suspicions of my faith, from which, thank Heaven, I can vindicate myself with truth and a good conscience.'

So thinking, he again adjusted the girths of his palfrey, replaced the bit which he had slipped out of its mouth that it might feed at liberty, and mounting, pursued his way back to the Castle of Holm-Peel, where he could not help fearing that something extraordinary might have happened in his absence.

But the old pile soon rose before him, serene and sternly still, amid the sleeping ocean. The banner, which indicated that the Lord of Man held residence within its ruinous precincts, hung motionless by the ensign-staff. The sentinels walked to and fro on their posts, and hummed or whistled their Manx airs. Leaving his faithful companion, Fairy, in the village as before, Julian entered the castle, and found all within in the same state of quietness and good order which external appearances had announced.

CHAPTER XVIII

Now rede me, rede me, brother dear,
Throughout Merry England,
Where will I find a messenger,
Betwixt us two to send.

Ballad of King Estmere.

JULIAN'S first rencounter, after re-entering the castle, was with its young lord, who received him with his usual kindness and lightness of humour.

'Thrice welcome, Sir Knight of Dames,' said the earl; 'here you rove gallantly, and at free will, through our dominions, fulfilling of appointments and achieving amorous adventures; while we are condemned to sit in our royal halls, as dull and as immovable as if our Majesty was carved on the stern of some Manx smuggling dogger, and christened the "King Arthur" of Ramsey.'

'Nay, in that case you would take the sea,' said Julian, 'and so enjoy travel and adventure enough.'

'Oh, but suppose me wind-bound, or detained in harbour by a revenue pink, or ashore, if you like it, and lying high and dry upon the sand. Imagine the royal image in the dullest of all predicaments, and you have not equalled mine.'

'I am happy to hear, at least, that you have had no disagreeable employment,' said Julian; 'the morning's alarm has blown over, I suppose?'

'In faith it has, Julian; and our close inquiries cannot find any cause for the apprehended insurrection. That Bridgenorth is in the island seems certain; but private affairs of consequence are alleged as the cause of his visit; and I am not desirous to have him arrested unless I could prove some malpractices against him and his companions. In fact, it would seem we had taken the alarm too soon. My mother speaks of consulting you on the subject, Julian; and I will not anticipate her solemn communication. It will be partly apologetical, I suppose; for

we begin to think our retreat rather unroyal, and that, like
the wicked, we have fled when no man pursued. This idea
afflicts my mother, who, as a queen-dowager, a queen-regent, a
heroine, and a woman in general, would be extremely mortified
to think that her precipitate retreat hither had exposed her to
the ridicule of the islanders ; and she is disconcerted and out of
humour accordingly. In the meanwhile, my sole amusement
has been the grimaces and fantastic gestures of that ape Fenella,
who is more out of humour, and more absurd in consequence,
than you ever saw her. Morris says it is because you pushed
her downstairs, Julian — how is that ? '

'Nay, Morris has misreported me,' answered Julian ; 'I did
but lift her *up*stairs to be rid of her importunity ; for she
chose, in her way, to contest my going abroad in such an
obstinate manner that I had no other mode of getting rid of
her.'

'She must have supposed your departure, at a moment so
critical, was dangerous to the state of our garrison,' answered
the earl ; 'it shows how dearly she esteems my mother's safety,
how highly she rates your prowess. But, thank Heaven, there
sounds the dinner-bell. I would the philosophers, who find a
sin and waste of time in good cheer, could devise us any pastime
half so agreeable.'

The meal which the young earl had thus longed for, as a
means of consuming a portion of the time which hung heavy
on his hands, was soon over ; as soon, at least, as the habitual
and stately formality of the countess's household permitted.
She herself, accompanied by her gentlewomen and attendants,
retired early after the tables were drawn ; and the young gentlemen were left to their own company. Wine had, for the
moment, no charms for either ; for the earl was out of spirits
from *ennui*, and impatience of his monotonous and solitary
course of life ; and the events of the day had given Peveril
too much matter for reflection to permit his starting amusing
or interesting topics of conversation. After having passed the
flask in silence betwixt them once or twice, they withdrew
each to a separate embrasure of the windows of the dining-
apartment, which, such was the extreme thickness of the wall,
were deep enough to afford a solitary recess, separated, as it
were, from the chamber itself. In one of these sat the Earl
of Derby, busied in looking over some of the new publications
which had been forwarded from London ; and at intervals
confessing how little power or interest these had for him, by

yawning fearfully as he looked out on the solitary expanse of
waters, which, save for the flight of a flock of sea-gulls or of a
solitary cormorant, offered so little of variety to engage his
attention.

Peveril, on his part, held a pamphlet also in his hand, without giving, or affecting to give, it even his occasional attention.
His whole soul turned upon the interview which he had had
that day with Alice Bridgenorth and with her father; while
he in vain endeavoured to form any hypothesis which could
explain to him why the daughter, to whom he had no reason to
think himself indifferent, should have been so suddenly desirous
of their eternal separation, while her father, whose opposition
he so much dreaded, seemed to be at least tolerant of his addresses. He could only suppose, in explanation, that Major
Bridgenorth had some plan in prospect which it was in his own
power to further or to impede; while, from the demeanour, and
indeed the language, of Alice, he had but too much reason to
apprehend that her father's favour could only be conciliated
by something, on his own part, approaching to dereliction of
principle. But by no conjecture which he could form could he
make the least guess concerning the nature of that compliance
of which Bridgenorth seemed desirous. He could not imagine,
notwithstanding Alice had spoken of treachery, that her father
would dare to propose to him uniting in any plan by which
the safety of the countess, or the security of her little kingdom
of Man, was to be endangered. This carried such indelible
disgrace in the front, that he could not suppose the scheme
proposed to him by any who was not prepared to defend with
his sword, upon the spot, so flagrant an insult offered to his
honour. And such a proceeding was totally inconsistent with
the conduct of Major Bridgenorth in every other respect,
besides his being too calm and cold-blooded to permit of his
putting a mortal affront upon the son of his old neighbour, to
whose mother he confessed so much of obligation.

While Peveril in vain endeavoured to extract something like
a probable theory out of the hints thrown out by the father
and by the daughter — not without the additional and lover-like
labour of endeavouring to reconcile his passion to his honour
and conscience — he felt something gently pull him by the cloak.
He unclasped his arms, which, in meditation, had been folded
on his bosom; and withdrawing his eyes from the vacant prospect of sea-coast and sea which they perused, without much
consciousness upon what they rested, he beheld beside him the

"He beheld beside him the little dumb maiden, the elfin Fenella."

little dumb maiden, the elfin Fenella. She was seated on a low
cushion or stool, with which she had nestled close to Peveril's
side, and had remained there for a short space of time, expecting, no doubt, he would become conscious of her presence ; until,
tired of remaining unnoticed, she at length solicited his attention in the manner which we have described. Startled out of
his reverie by this intimation of her presence, he looked down,
and could not, without interest, behold this singular and helpless being.

Her hair was unloosened, and streamed over her shoulders
in such length, that much of it lay upon the ground, and in
such quantity, that it formed a dark veil, or shadow, not only
around her face, but over her whole slender and minute form.
From the profusion of her tresses looked forth her small and
dark, but well-formed, features, together with the large and
brilliant black eyes ; and her whole countenance was composed
into the imploring look of one who is doubtful of the reception
she is about to meet with from a valued friend, while she confesses a fault, pleads an apology, or solicits a reconciliation. In
short, the whole face was so much alive with expression, that
Julian, though her aspect was so familiar to him, could hardly
persuade himself but that her countenance was entirely new.
The wild, fantastic, elvish vivacity of the features seemed
totally vanished, and had given place to a sorrowful, tender,
and pathetic cast of countenance, aided by the expression of the
large dark eyes, which, as they were turned up towards Julian,
glistened with moisture, that, nevertheless, did not overflow
the eyelids.

Conceiving that her unwonted manner arose from a recollection of the dispute which had taken place betwixt them in the
morning, Peveril was anxious to restore the little maiden's
gaiety, by making her sensible that there dwelt on his mind
no unpleasing recollection of their quarrel. He smiled kindly,
and shook her hand in one of his ; while, with the familiarity
of one who had known her from childhood, he stroked down
her long dark tresses with the other. She stooped her head, as
if ashamed and, at the same time, gratified with his caresses ;
and he was thus induced to continue them, until, under the
veil of her rich and abundant locks, he suddenly felt his other
hand, which she still held fast in hers, slightly touched with
her lips, and, at the same time, moistened with a tear.

At once, and for the first time in his life, the danger of being
misinterpreted in his familiarity with a creature to whom the

usual modes of explanation were a blank occurred to Julian's
mind; and, hastily withdrawing his hand and changing his
posture, he asked of her, by a sign which custom had rendered
familiar, whether she brought any message to him from the countess. In an instant Fenella's whole deportment was changed.
She started up and arranged herself in her seat with the rapid-
ity of lightning; and at the same moment, with one turn of her
hand, braided her length of locks into a natural head-dress of
the most beautiful kind. There was, indeed, when she looked
up, a blush still visible on her dark features; but their melancholy and languid expression had given place to that of wild
and restless vivacity, which was most common to them. Her
eyes gleamed with more than their wonted fire, and her
glances were more piercingly wild and unsettled than usual.
To Julian's inquiry, she answered, by laying her hand on her
heart — a motion by which she always indicated the countess — and rising and taking the direction of her apartment,
she made a sign to Julian to follow her.

The distance was not great betwixt the dining-apartment
and that to which Peveril now followed his mute guide; yet,
in going thither, he had time enough to suffer cruelly from the
sudden suspicion that this unhappy girl had misinterpreted
the uniform kindness with which he had treated her, and hence
come to regard him with feelings more tender than those which
belong to friendship. The misery which such a passion was
likely to occasion to a creature in her helpless situation, and
actuated by such lively feelings, was great enough to make
him refuse credit to the suspicion which pressed itself upon his
mind; while, at the same time, he formed the internal resolution so to conduct himself towards Fenella as to check such
misplaced sentiments, if indeed she unhappily entertained them
towards him.

When they reached the countess's apartment, they found
her with writing-implements and many sealed letters before her.
She received Julian with her usual kindness; and having caused
him to be seated, beckoned to the mute to resume her needle. In
an instant Fenella was seated at an embroidering-frame, where,
but for the movement of her dexterous fingers, she might have
seemed a statue, so little did she move from her work either
head or eye. As her infirmity rendered her presence no bar to
the most confidential conversation, the countess proceeded to
address Peveril as if they had been literally alone together.

'Julian,' she said, 'I am not now about to complain to you

of the sentiments and conduct of Derby. He is your friend —
he is my son. He has kindness of heart and vivacity of talent;
and yet——'

'Dearest lady,' said Peveril, 'why will you distress yourself
with fixing your eye on deficiencies which arise rather from a
change of times and manners than any degeneracy of my noble
friend? Let him be once engaged in his duty, whether in
peace or war, and let me pay the penalty if he acquits not
himself becoming his high station.'

'Ay,' replied the countess; 'but when will the call of duty
prove superior to that of the most idle or trivial indulgence
which can serve to drive over the lazy hour? His father was
of another mould; and how often was it my lot to entreat that
he would spare, from the rigid discharge of those duties which
his high station imposed, the relaxation absolutely necessary
to recruit his health and his spirits!'

'Still, my dearest lady,' said Peveril, 'you must allow that
the duties to which the times summoned your late honoured
lord were of a more stirring, as well as a more peremptory, cast
than those which await your son.'

'I know not that,' said the countess. 'The wheel appears
to be again revolving; and the present period is not unlikely
to bring back such scenes as my younger years witnessed.
Well, be it so; they will not find Charlotte de la Tremouille
broken in spirit, though depressed by years. It was even on
this subject I would speak with you, my young friend. Since
our first early acquaintance, when I saw your gallant behaviour
as I issued forth to your childish eye, like an apparition, from
my place of concealment in your father's castle, it has pleased
me to think you a true son of Stanley and Peveril. I trust
your nurture in this family has been ever suited to the esteem
in which I hold you. Nay, I desire no thanks. I have to require of you, in return, a piece of service, not perhaps entirely
safe to yourself, but which, as times are circumstanced, no
person is so well able to render to my house.'

'You have been ever my good and noble lady,' answered
Peveril, 'as well as my kind, and I may say maternal, protectress. You have a right to command the blood of Stanley
in the veins of every one; you have a thousand rights to command it in mine.'[1]

'My advices from England,' said the countess, 'resemble

[1] The reader cannot have forgotten that the Earl of Derby was head of
the great house of Stanley.

more the dreams of a sick man than the regular information
which I might have expected from such correspondents as mine ;
their expressions are like those of men who walk in their sleep,
and speak by snatches of what passes in their dreams.   It is
said a plot, real or fictitious, has been detected among the
Catholics, which has spread far wider and more uncontrollable
terror than that of the fifth of November.   Its outlines seem
utterly incredible, and are only supported by the evidence of
wretches the meanest and most worthless in the creation ; yet
it is received by the credulous people of England with the most
undoubting belief.'

'This is a singular delusion to rise without some real ground,'
answered Julian.

'I am no bigot, cousin, though a Catholic,' replied the countess.   'I have long feared that the well-meant zeal of our priests
for increasing converts would draw on them the suspicion of
the English nation.   These efforts have been renewed with
double energy since the Duke of York conformed to the Catholic
faith ; and the same event has doubled the hate and jealousy
of the Protestants.   So far, I fear, there may be just cause for
suspicion that the duke is a better Catholic than an Englishman, and that bigotry has involved him, as avarice, or the
needy greed of a prodigal, has engaged his brother, in relations
with France, whereof England may have too much reason to
complain.   But the gross, thick, and palpable fabrications of
conspiracy and murder, blood and fire — the imaginary armies
— the intended massacres — form a collection of falsehoods that
one would have thought indigestible even by the coarse appetite
of the vulgar for the marvellous and horrible ; but which are,
nevertheless, received as truth by both Houses of Parliament,
and questioned by no one who is desirous to escape the odious
appellation of friend to the bloody Papists, and favourer of
their infernal schemes of cruelty.'

'But what say those who are most likely to be affected by
these wild reports ?' said Julian.   'What say the English Catholics themselves — a numerous and wealthy body, comprising
so many noble names ?'

'Their hearts are dead within them,' said the countess.
'They are like sheep penned up in the shambles, that the
butcher may take his choice among them.   In the obscure and
brief communications which I have had by a secure hand, they
do but anticipate their own utter ruin and ours, so general is
the depression, so universal the despair.'

'But the King,' said Peveril — 'the King and the Protestant Royalists — what say they to this growing tempest ? '

'Charles,' replied the countess, 'with his usual selfish prudence, truckles to the storm; and will let cord and axe do their work on the most innocent men in his dominions rather than lose an hour of pleasure in attempting their rescue. And for the Royalists, either they have caught the general delirium which has seized on Protestants in general, or they stand aloof and neutral, afraid to show any interest in the unhappy Catholics, lest they be judged altogether such as themselves, and abettors of the fearful conspiracy in which they are alleged to be engaged. In fact, I cannot blame them. It is hard to expect that mere compassion for a persecuted sect, or, what is yet more rare, an abstract love of justice, should be powerful enough to engage men to expose themselves to the awakened fury of a whole people; for, in the present state of general agitation, whoever disbelieves the least tittle of the enormous improbabilities which have been accumulated by these wretched informers is instantly hunted down, as one who would smother the discovery of the plot. It is indeed an awful tempest; and, remote as we lie from its sphere, we must expect soon to feel its effects.'

'Lord Derby already told me something of this,' said Julian; 'and that there were agents in this island whose object was to excite insurrection.'

'Yes,' answered the countess, and her eye flashed fire as she spoke; 'and had my advice been listened to, they had been apprehended in the very fact, and so dealt with as to be a warning to all others how they sought this independent principality on such an errand. But my son, who is generally so culpably negligent of his own affairs, was pleased to assume the management of them upon this crisis.'

'I am happy to learn, madam,' answered Peveril, 'that the measures of precaution which my kinsman has adopted have had the complete effect of disconcerting the conspiracy.'

'For the present, Julian; but they should have been such as would have made the boldest tremble to think of such infringement of our rights in future. But Derby's present plan is fraught with greater danger; and yet there is something in it of gallantry, which has my sympathy.'

'What is it, madam ? ' inquired Julian, anxiously; 'and in what can I aid it, or avert its dangers ? '

'He purposes,' said the countess, 'instantly to set forth for

London. He is, he says, not merely the feudal chief of a small island, but one of the noble peers of England, who must not remain in the security of an obscure and distant castle when his name, or that of his mother, is slandered before his prince and people. He will take his place, he says, in the House of Lords, and publicly demand justice for the insult thrown on his house by perjured and interested witnesses.'

'It is a generous resolution, and worthy of my friend,' said Julian Peveril. 'I will go with him and share his fate, be it what it may.'

'Alas, foolish boy!' answered the countess, 'as well may you ask a hungry lion to feel compassion as a prejudiced and furious people to do justice. They are like the madman at the height of frenzy, who murders without compunction his best and dearest friend ; and only wonders and wails over his own cruelty when he is recovered from his delirium.'

'Pardon me, dearest lady,' said Julian, 'this cannot be. The noble and generous people of England cannot be thus strangely misled. Whatever prepossessions may be current among the more vulgar, the Houses of Legislature cannot be deeply infected by them ; they will remember their own dignity.'

'Alas ! cousin,' answered the countess, 'when did Englishmen, even of the highest degree, remember anything when hurried away by the violence of party feeling ? Even those who have too much sense to believe in the incredible fictions which gull the multitude, will beware how they expose them, if their own political party can gain a momentary advantage by their being accredited. It is amongst such, too, that your kinsman has found friends and associates. Neglecting the old friends of his house, as too grave and formal companions for the humour of the times, his intercourse has been with the versatile Shaftesbury, the mercurial Buckingham — men who would not hesitate to sacrifice to the popular Moloch of the day whatsoever or whomsoever whose ruin could propitiate the deity. Forgive a mother's tears, kinsman ; but I see the scaffold at Bolton again erected. If Derby goes to London while these bloodhounds are in full cry, obnoxious as he is, and I have made him by my religious faith and my conduct in this island, he dies his father's death. And yet upon what other course to resolve —— !'

'Let me go to London, madam,' said Peveril, much moved by the distress of his patroness; 'your ladyship was wont to rely something on my judgment. I will act for the best — will communicate with those whom you point out to me, and only with them; and I trust soon to send you information that this delusion, however strong it may now be, is in the course of passing away; at the worst, I can apprize you of the danger, should it menace the earl or yourself; and may be able also to point out the means by which it may be eluded.'

The countess listened with a countenance in which the anxiety of maternal affection, which prompted her to embrace Peveril's generous offer, struggled with her native disinterested and generous disposition. 'Think what you ask of me, Julian,' she replied, with a sigh. 'Would you have me expose the life of my friend's son to those perils to which I refuse my own? No, never!'

'Nay, but, madam,' replied Julian, 'I do not run the same risk : my person is not known in London ; my situation, though not obscure in my own country, is too little known to be noticed in that huge assemblage of all that is noble and wealthy. No whisper, I presume, however indirect, has connected my name with the alleged conspiracy. I am a Protestant, above all; and can be accused of no intercourse, direct or indirect, with the Church of Rome. My connexions also lie amongst those who, if they do not, or cannot, befriend me, cannot at least be dangerous to me. In a word, I run no danger where the earl might incur great peril.'

'Alas!' said the Countess of Derby, 'all this generous reasoning may be true; but it could only be listened to by a widowed mother. Selfish as I am, I cannot but reflect that my kinswoman has, in all events, the support of an affectionate husband; such is the interested reasoning to which we are not ashamed to subject our better feelings!'

'Do not call it so, madam,' answered Peveril; 'think of me as the younger brother of my kinsman. You have ever done by me the duties of a mother; and have a right to my filial service, were it at a risk ten times greater than a journey to London, to inquire into the temper of the times. I will instantly go and announce my departure to the earl.'

'Stay, Julian,' said the countess; 'if you must make this journey in our behalf — and, alas! I have not generosity enough to refuse your noble proffer — you must go alone, and without communication with Derby. I know him well : his lightness of mind is free from selfish baseness; and for the world, would he not suffer you to leave Man without his company. And if

he went with you, your noble and disinterested kindness would
be of no avail; you would but share his ruin, as the swimmer
who attempts to save a drowning man is involved in his fate,
if he permit the sufferer to grapple with him.'

'It shall be as you please, madam,' said Peveril; 'I am
ready to depart upon half an hour's notice.'

'This night, then,' said the countess, after a moment's
pause — 'this night I will arrange the most secret means of
carrying your generous project into effect; for I would not
excite that prejudice against you which will instantly arise
were it known you had so lately left this island and its Popish lady. You will do well, perhaps, to use a feigned name in
London.'

'Pardon me, madam,' said Julian; 'I will do nothing that
can draw on me unnecessary attention; but to bear a feigned
name, or affect any disguise beyond living with extreme
privacy, would, I think, be unwise as well as unworthy, and
what, if challenged, I might find some difficulty in assigning a
reason for, consistent with perfect fairness of intentions.'

'I believe you are right,' answered the countess, after a
moment's consideration; and then added, 'You propose, doubtless, to pass through Derbyshire and visit Martindale Castle?'

'I should wish it, madam, certainly,' replied Peveril, 'did
time permit and circumstances render it advisable.'

'Of that,' said the countess, 'you must yourself judge.
Despatch is, doubtless, desirable; on the other hand, arriving
from your own family seat, you will be less an object of doubt
and suspicion than if you posted up from hence, without even
visiting your parents. You must be guided in this — in all — by
your own prudence. Go, my dearest son — for to me you should
be dear as a son — go, and prepare for your journey. I will get
ready some despatches and a supply of money. Nay, do not
object. Am I not your mother; and are you not discharging
a son's duty? Dispute not my right of defraying your ex-
penses. Nor is this all; for, as I must trust your zeal and
prudence to act in our behalf when occasion shall demand, I
will furnish you with effectual recommendations to our friends
and kindred, entreating and enjoining them to render whatever
aid you may require, either for your own protection or the
advancement of what you may propose in our favour.'

Peveril made no farther opposition to an arrangement which
in truth the moderate state of his own finances rendered almost indispensable, unless with his father's assistance; and the

countess put into his hand bills of exchange to the amount of two hundred pounds, upon a merchant in the city. She then dismissed Julian for the space of an hour; after which, she said, she must again require his presence.

The preparations for his journey were not of a nature to divert the thoughts which speedily pressed on him. He found that half an hour's conversation had once more completely changed his immediate prospects and plans for the future. He had offered to the Countess of Derby a service which her uniform kindness had well deserved at his hand; but, by her accepting it, he was upon the point of being separated from Alice Bridgenorth, at a time when she was become dearer to him than ever, by her avowal of mutual passion. Her image rose before him, such as he had that day pressed her to his bosom; her voice was in his ear, and seemed to ask whether he could desert her in the crisis which everything seemed to announce as impending. But Julian Peveril, his youth considered, was strict in judging his duty, and severely resolved in executing it. He trusted not his imagination to pursue the vision which presented itself; but resolutely seizing his pen, wrote to Alice the following letter, explaining his situation, as far as justice to the countess permitted him to do so : —

'I leave you, dearest Alice,' thus ran the letter — 'I leave you; and though, in doing so, I but obey the command you have laid on me, yet I can claim little merit for my compliance, since, without additional and most forcible reasons in aid of your orders, I fear I should have been unable to comply with them. But family affairs of importance compel me to absent myself from this island, for, I fear, more than one week. My thoughts, hopes, and wishes will be on the moment that shall restore me to the Black Fort and its lovely valley. Let me hope that yours will sometimes rest on the lonely exile, whom nothing could render such but the command of honour and duty. Do not fear that I mean to involve you in a private correspondence, and let not your father fear it. I could not love you so much, but for the openness and candour of your nature; and I would not that you concealed from Major Bridgenorth one syllable of what I now avow. Respecting other matters, he himself cannot desire the welfare of our common country with more zeal than I do. Differences may occur concerning the mode in which that is to be obtained; but, in the principle, I am convinced there can be only one mind between us; nor can I refuse to listen to his experience and wisdom, even where they may ultimately fail to convince me. Farewell, Alice — farewell! Much might be added to that melancholy word, but nothing that could express the bitterness with which it is written. Yet I could transcribe it again and again, rather than conclude the last communication which I can have with you for some time. My sole comfort is, that my stay will scarce be so long as to permit you to forget one who never can forget you.'

He held the paper in his hand for a minute after he had folded, but before he had sealed, it, while he hurriedly debated in his own mind whether he had not expressed himself towards Major Bridgenorth in so conciliating a manner as might excite hopes of proselytism which his conscience told him he could not realise with honour. Yet, on the other hand, he had no right, from what Bridgenorth had said, to conclude that their principles were diametrically irreconcilable; for though the son of a high Cavalier, and educated in the family of the Countess of Derby, he was himself, upon principle, an enemy of prerogative and a friend to the liberty of the subject. And with such considerations he silenced all internal objections on the point of honour; although his conscience secretly whispered that these conciliatory expressions towards the father were chiefly dictated by the fear that, during his absence, Major Bridgenorth might be tempted to change the residence of his daughter, and perhaps to convey her altogether out of his reach.

Having sealed his letter, Julian called his servant, and directed him to carry it, under cover of one addressed to Mrs. Debbitch, to a house in the town of Rushin, where packets and messages intended for the family at Black Fort were usually deposited; and for that purpose to take horse immediately. He thus got rid of an attendant who might have been in some degree a spy on his motions. He then exchanged the dress he usually wore for one more suited to travelling; and, having put a change or two of linen into a small cloakbag, selected as arms a strong double-edged sword and an excellent pair of pistols, which last he carefully loaded with double bullets. Thus appointed, and with twenty pieces in his purse, and the bills we have mentioned secured in a private pocket-book, he was in readiness to depart as soon as he should receive the countess's commands.

The buoyant spirit of youth and hope, which had, for a moment, been chilled by the painful and dubious circumstances

in which he was placed, as well as the deprivation which he
was about to undergo, now revived in full vigour. Fancy,
turning from more painful anticipations, suggested to him that
he was now entering upon life at a crisis when resolution
and talents were almost certain to make the fortune of their
possessor. How could he make a more honourable entry on
the bustling scene than sent by, and acting in behalf of, one
of the noblest houses in England; and should he perform what
his charge might render incumbent with the resolution and
the prudence necessary to secure success, how many occurrences
might take place to render his mediation necessary to Bridgenorth; and thus enable him, on the most equal and honourable
terms, to establish a claim to his gratitude and to his daughter's
hand.

Whilst he was dwelling on such pleasing, though imaginary,
prospects, he could not help exclaiming aloud — 'Yes, Alice, I
will win thee nobly!' The words had scarce escaped his lips,
when he heard at the door of his apartment, which the servant
had left ajar, a sound like a deep sigh, which was instantly
succeeded by a gentle tap. 'Come in,' replied Julian, somewhat ashamed of his exclamation, and not a little afraid that
it had been caught up by some eavesdropper. 'Come in,' he
again repeated. But his command was not obeyed; on the
contrary, the knock was repeated somewhat louder. He opened
the door, and Fenella stood before him.

With eyes that seemed red with recent tears, and with a
look of the deepest dejection, the little mute, first touching
her bosom and beckoning with her finger, made to him the
usual sign that the countess desired to see him, then turned, as
if to usher him to her apartment. As he followed her through
the long, gloomy, vaulted passages which afforded communication betwixt the various apartments of the castle, he could
not but observe that her usual light trip was exchanged for
a tardy and mournful step, which she accompanied with
low, inarticulate moaning (which she was probably the less
able to suppress, because she could not judge how far it was
audible), and also with wringing of the hands, and other
marks of extreme affliction.

At this moment a thought came across Peveril's mind, which,
in spite of his better reason, made him shudder involuntarily.
As a Peaksman, and a long resident in the Isle of Man, he
was well acquainted with many a superstitious legend, and
particularly with a belief which attached to the powerful

family of the Stanleys, for their peculiar demon, a banshie, or female spirit, who was wont to shriek, 'foreboding evil times'; and who was generally seen weeping and bemoaning herself before the death of any person of distinction belonging to the family.   For an instant, Julian could scarcely divest himself of the belief that the wailing, gibbering form, which glided before him, with a lamp in her hand, was the genius of his mother's race come to announce to him his predestined doom.   It instantly occurred to him as an analogous reflection, that, if the suspicion which had crossed his mind concerning Fenella was a just one, her ill-fated attachment to him, like that of the prophetic spirit to his family, could bode nothing but disaster, and lamentation, and woe.

CHAPTER XIX

Now, hoist the anchor, mates, and let the sails
Give their broad bosom to the buxom wind,
Like lass that woos a lover.
Anonymous.

THE presence of the countess dispelled the superstitious
feeling which, for an instant, had encroached on Julian's
imagination, and compelled him to give attention to
the matters of ordinary life. 'Here are your credentials,' she
said, giving him a small packet carefully put up in a sealskin
cover; 'you had better not open them till you come to London.
You must not be surprised to find that there are one or two
addressed to men of my own persuasion. These, for all our
sakes, you will observe caution in delivering.'

'I go your messenger, madam,' said Peveril; 'and whatever
you desire me to charge myself with, of that I undertake the
care. Yet allow me to doubt whether an intercourse with
Catholics will at this moment forward the purposes of my
mission.'

'You have caught the general suspicion of this wicked sect
already,' said the countess, smiling, 'and are the fitter to go
amongst Englishmen in their present mood. But, my cautious
friend, these letters are so addressed, and the persons to whom
they are addressed so disguised, that you will run no danger in
conversing with them. Without their aid, indeed, you will not
be able to obtain the accurate information you go in search of.
None can tell so exactly how the wind sets as the pilot whose
vessel is exposed to the storm. Besides, though you Protestants
deny our priesthood the harmlessness of the dove, you are ready
enough to allow us a full share of the wisdom of the serpent;
in plain terms, their means of information are extensive, and
they are not deficient in the power of applying it. I therefore
wish you to have the benefit of their intelligence and advice, if
possible.'

'Whatever you impose upon me as a part of my duty, madam, rely on its being discharged punctually,' answered Peveril. 'And now, as there is little use in deferring the execution of a purpose when once fixed, let me know your ladyship's wishes concerning my departure.'

'It must be sudden and secret,' said the countess; 'the island is full of spies; and I would not wish that any of them should have notice that an envoy of mine was about to leave Man for London. Can you be ready to go on board to-morrow?'

'To-night — this instant if you will,' said Julian; 'my little preparations are complete.'

'Be ready, then, in your chamber, at two hours after midnight. I will send one to summon you, for our secret must be communicated, for the present, to as few as possible. A foreign sloop is engaged to carry you over; then make the best of your way to London, by Martindale Castle or otherwise, as you find most advisable. When it is necessary to announce your absence, I will say you are gone to see your parents. But stay — your journey will be on horseback, of course, from Whitehaven. You have bills of exchange, it is true; but are you provided with ready money to furnish yourself with a good horse?'

'I am sufficiently rich, madam,' answered Julian; 'and good nags are plenty in Cumberland. There are those among them who know how to come by them good and cheap.'

'Trust not to that,' said the countess. 'Here is what will purchase for you the best horse on the Borders. Can you be simple enough to refuse it?' she added, as she pressed on him a heavy purse, which he saw himself obliged to accept.

'A good horse, Julian,' continued the countess, 'and a good sword, next to a good heart and head, are the accomplishments of a cavalier.'

'I kiss your hands, then, madam,' said Peveril, 'and humbly beg you to believe that, whatever may fail in my present undertaking, my purpose to serve you, my noble kinswoman and benefactress, can at least never swerve or falter.'

'I know it, my son — I know it; and may God forgive me if my anxiety for your friend has sent you on dangers which should have been his! Go — go. May saints and angels bless you! Fenella shall acquaint him that you sup in your own apartment. So indeed will I; for to-night I should be unable to face my son's looks. Little will he thank me for sending you on his errand; and there will be many to ask whether it

was like the Lady of Latham to thrust her friend's son on the
danger which should have been braved by her own. But oh !
Julian, I am now a forlorn widow, whom sorrow has made
selfish ! '

'Tush, madam,' answered Peveril; 'it is more unlike the
Lady of Latham to anticipate dangers which may not exist at
all, and to which, if they do indeed occur, I am less obnoxious
than my noble kinsman. Farewell! All blessings attend you,
madam. Commend me to Derby, and make him my excuses.
I shall expect a summons at two hours after midnight.'

They took an affectionate leave of each other ; the more
affectionate, indeed, on the part of the countess, that she could
not entirely reconcile her generous mind to exposing Peveril to
danger on her son's behalf; and Julian betook himself to his
solitary apartment.

His servant soon afterwards brought him wine and refreshments ; to which, notwithstanding the various matters he had
to occupy his mind, he contrived to do reasonable justice. But
when this needful occupation was finished, his thoughts began
to stream in upon him like a troubled tide — at once recalling
the past and anticipating the future. It was in vain that he
wrapped himself in his riding-cloak, and, lying down on his
bed, endeavoured to compose himself to sleep. The uncertainty
of the prospect before him, the doubt how Bridgenorth might
dispose of his daughter during his absence, the fear that the
major himself might fall into the power of the vindictive
countess, besides a numerous train of vague and half-formed
apprehensions, agitated his blood, and rendered slumber impossible. Alternately to recline in the old oaken easy-chair
and listen to the dashing of the waves under the windows,
mingled, as the sound was, with the scream of the sea-birds,
or to traverse the apartment with long and slow steps, pausing
occasionally to look out on the sea, slumbering under the
influence of a full moon, which tipped each wave with silver —
such were the only pastimes he could invent, until midnight
had passed for one hour ; the next was wasted in anxious
expectation of the summons of departure.

At length it arrived : a tap at his door was followed by
a low murmur, which made him suspect that the countess
had again employed her mute attendant as the most secure
minister of her pleasure on this occasion. He felt something
like impropriety in this selection ; and it was with a feeling of
impatience alien to the natural generosity of his temper that,

when he opened the door, he beheld the dumb maiden standing before him. The lamp which he held in his hand showed his features distinctly, and probably made Fenella aware of the expression which animated them. She cast her large dark eyes mournfully on the ground ; and, without again looking him in the face, made him a signal to follow her. He delayed no longer than was necessary to secure his pistols in his belt, wrap his cloak closer around him, and take his small portmanteau under his arm. Thus accoutred, he followed her out of the keep, or inhabited part of the castle, by a series of obscure passages leading to a postern gate, which she unlocked with a key, selected from a bundle which she carried at her girdle.

They now stood in the castle-yard, in the open moonlight, which glimmered white and ghastly on the variety of strange and ruinous objects to which we have formerly alluded, and which gave the scene rather the appearance of some ancient cemetery than of the interior of a fortification. The round and elevated tower, the ancient mount, with its quadrangular sides facing the ruinous edifices which once boasted the name of cathedral, seemed of yet more antique and anomalous form when seen by the pale light which now displayed them. To one of these churches Fenella took the direct course, and was followed by Julian ; although he at once divined, and was superstitious enough to dislike, the path which she was about to adopt. It was by a secret passage through this church that in former times the guard-room of the garrison, situated at the lower and external defences, communicated with the keep of the castle ; and through this passage were the keys of the castle every night carried to the governor's apartment, so soon as the gates were locked and the watch set. The custom was given up in James the First's time, and the passage abandoned, on account of the well-known legend of the *Mauthe Dog* — a fiend, or demon, in the shape of a large, shaggy, black mastiff, by which the church was said to be haunted. It was devoutly believed that in former times this spectre became so familiar with mankind as to appear almost nightly in the guard-room, issuing from the passage which we have mentioned at night, and retiring to it at daybreak. The soldiers became partly familiarised to its presence ; yet not so much so as to use any license of language while the apparition was visible ; until one fellow, rendered daring by intoxication, swore he would know whether it was dog or devil, and, with his drawn sword, followed the spectre when it retreated by the usual passage. The man returned in a few minutes, sobered by terror, his mouth gaping, and his hair standing on end, under which horror he died; but, unhappily for the lovers of the marvellous, altogether unable to disclose the horrors which he had seen. Under the evil repute arising from this tale of wonder, the guard-room was abandoned and a new one constructed. In like manner, the guards after that period held another and more circuitous communication with the governor or seneschal of the castle; and that which lay through the ruinous church was entirely abandoned.[1]

In defiance of the legendary terrors which tradition had attached to the original communication, Fenella, followed by Peveril, now boldly traversed the ruinous vaults through which it lay; sometimes only guided over heaps of ruins by the precarious light of the lamp borne by the dumb maiden; sometimes having the advantage of a gleam of moonlight, darting into the dreary abyss through the shafted windows, or through breaches made by time. As the path was by no means a straight one, Peveril could not but admire the intimate acquaintance with the mazes which his singular companion displayed, as well as the boldness with which she traversed them. He himself was not so utterly void of the prejudices of the times, but that he contemplated, with some apprehension, the possibility of their intruding on the lair of the phantom-hound, of which he had heard so often; and in every remote sigh of the breeze among the ruins he thought he heard him baying at the mortal footsteps which disturbed his gloomy realm. No such terrors, however, interrupted their journey; and in the course of a few minutes they attained the deserted and now ruinous guard-house. The broken walls of the little edifice served to conceal them from the sentinels, one of whom was keeping a drowsy watch at the lower gate of the castle; whilst another, seated on the stone steps which communicated with the parapet of the bounding and exterior wall, was slumbering, in full security, with his musket peacefully grounded by his side. Fenella made a sign to Peveril to move with silence and caution, and then showed him, to his surprise, from the window of the deserted guard-room, a boat, for it was now high water, with four rowers, lurking under the cliff on which the castle was built; and made him farther sensible that he was to have

---

[1] This curious legend, and many others, in which the Isle of Man is perhaps richer than even Ireland, Wales, or the Highlands of Scotland, will be found in Note 11 at the end of the volume.

access to it by a ladder of considerable height placed at the
window of the ruin.

Julian was both displeased and alarmed by the security and
carelessness of the sentinels, who had suffered such preparations
to be made without observation or alarm given; and he hesitated whether he should not call the officer of the guard,
upbraid him with negligence, and show him how easily Holm-
Peel, in spite of its natural strength, and although reported
impregnable, might be surprised by a few resolute men.   Fenella
seemed to guess his thoughts with that extreme acuteness of
observation which her deprivations had occasioned her acquiring.
She laid one hand on his arm, and a finger of the other on her
own lips, as if to enjoin forbearance; and Julian, knowing that
she acted by the direct authority of the countess, obeyed her
accordingly; but with the internal resolution to lose no time
in communicating his sentiments to the earl, concerning the
danger to which the castle was exposed on this point.

In the meantime, he descended the ladder with some precaution, for the steps were unequal, broken, wet, and slippery;
and having placed himself in the stern of the boat, made a
signal to the men to push off, and turned to take farewell of
his guide.   To his utter astonishment, Fenella rather slid
down than descended regularly the perilous ladder, and the
boat being already pushed off, made a spring from the last step
of it with incredible agility, and seated herself beside Peveril,
ere he could express either remonstrance or surprise.   He
commanded the men once more to pull in to the precarious landing place; and throwing into his countenance a part of the
displeasure which he really felt, endeavoured to make her comprehend the necessity of returning to her mistress.   Fenella
folded her arms and looked at him with a haughty smile, which
completely expressed the determination of her purpose.   Peveril
was extremely embarrassed; he was afraid of offending the
countess, and interfering with her plan, by giving alarm, which
otherwise he was much tempted to have done.   On Fenella, it
was evident, no species of argument which he could employ
was likely to make the least impression; and the question remained how, if she went on with him, he was to rid himself of
so singular and inconvenient a companion, and provide, at the
same time, sufficiently for her personal security.

The boatmen brought the matter to a decision; for, after
lying on their oars for a minute and whispering among themselves in Low Dutch or German, they began to pull stoutly,

and were soon at some distance from the castle. The possibility of the sentinels sending a musket-ball, or even a cannon-shot, after them was one of the contingencies which gave Peveril momentary anxiety; but they left the fortress, as they must have approached it, unnoticed, or at least unchallenged — a carelessness on the part of the garrison which, notwithstanding that the oars were muffled and that the men spoke little, and in whispers, argued, in Peveril's opinion, great negligence on the part of the sentinels. When they were a little way from the castle, the men began to row briskly towards a small vessel which lay at some distance. Peveril had, in the meantime, leisure to remark that the boatmen spoke to each other doubtfully, and bent anxious looks on Fenella, as if uncertain whether they had acted properly in bringing her off.

After about a quarter of an hour's rowing, they reached the little sloop, where Peveril was received by the skipper, or captain, on the quarter-deck, with an offer of spirits or refreshments. A word or two among the seamen withdrew the captain from his hospitable cares, and he flew to the ship's side, apparently to prevent Fenella from entering the vessel. The men and he talked eagerly in Dutch, looking anxiously at Fenella as they spoke together; and Peveril hoped the result would be that the poor young woman should be sent ashore again. But she baffled whatever opposition could be offered to her; and when the accommodation-ladder, as it is called, was withdrawn, she snatched the end of a rope, and climbed on board with the dexterity of a sailor, leaving them no means of preventing her entrance, save by actual violence, to which apparently they did not choose to have recourse. Once on deck, she took the captain by the sleeve, and led him to the head of the vessel, where they seemed to hold intercourse in a manner intelligible to both.

Peveril soon forgot the presence of the mute, as he began to muse upon his own situation, and the probability that he was separated for some considerable time from the object of his affections. 'Constancy,' he repeated to himself — 'constancy.' And, as if in coincidence with the theme of his reflections, he fixed his eyes on the polar star, which that night twinkled with more than ordinary brilliancy. Emblem of pure passion and steady purpose — the thoughts which arose as he viewed its clear and unchanging light were disinterested and noble. To seek his country's welfare, and secure the blessings of domestic peace; to discharge a bold and perilous duty to his friend and patron; to regard his passion for Alice Bridgenorth as the load-star which was to guide him to noble deeds — were the resolutions which thronged upon his mind, and which exalted his spirits to that state of romantic melancholy which perhaps is ill exchanged even for feelings of joyful rapture.

He was recalled from these contemplations by something which nestled itself softly and closely to his side — a woman's sigh sounded so near him as to disturb his reverie; and as he turned his head, he saw Fenella seated beside him, with her eyes fixed on the same star which had just occupied his own. His first emotion was that of displeasure; but it was impossible to persevere in it towards a being so helpless in many respects, so interesting in others; whose large dark eyes were filled with dew, which glistened in the moonlight; and the source of whose emotions seemed to be in a partiality which might well claim indulgence, at least, from him who was the object of it. At the same time, Julian resolved to seize the present opportunity for such expostulations with Fenella on the strangeness of her conduct as the poor maiden might be able to comprehend. He took her hand with great kindness, but at the same time with much gravity, pointed to the boat, and to the castle, whose towers and extended walls were now scarce visible in the distance; and thus intimated to her the necessity of her return to Holm-Peel. She looked down and shook her head, as if negativing his proposal with obstinate decision. Julian renewed his expostulation by look and gesture — pointed to his own heart, to intimate the countess, and bent his brows, to show the displeasure which she must entertain; to all which, the maiden only answered by her tears.

At length, as if driven to explanation by his continued remonstrances, she suddenly seized him by the arm, to arrest his attention; cast her eye hastily around, as if to see whether she was watched by any one; then drew the other hand, edge-wise, across her slender throat, pointed to the boat and to the castle, and nodded.

On this series of signs, Peveril could put no interpretation excepting that he was menaced with some personal danger, from which Fenella seemed to conceive that her presence was a protection. Whatever was her meaning, her purpose seemed unalterably adopted; at least, it was plain he had no power to shake it. He must therefore wait till the end of their short voyage to disembarrass himself of his companion; and, in the meanwhile, acting on the idea of her having harboured a mis-

placed attachment to him, he thought he should best consult
her interest and his own character in keeping at as great a distance from her as circumstances admitted. With this purpose,
he made the sign she used for going to sleep, by leaning his
head on his palm ; and having thus recommended to her to go
to rest, he himself desired to be conducted to his berth.

The captain readily showed him a hammock in the after-
cabin, into which he threw himself, to seek that repose which
the exercise and agitation of the preceding day, as well as the
lateness of the hour, made him now feel desirable. Sleep, deep
and heavy, sunk down on him in a few minutes, but it did not
endure long. In his sleep, he was disturbed by female cries ;
and at length, as he thought, distinctly heard the voice of Alice
Bridgenorth call on his name.

He awoke, and, starting up to quit his bed, became sensible,
from the motion of the vessel and the swinging of the hammock,
that his dream had deceived him. He was still startled by its
extreme vivacity and liveliness. 'Julian Peveril, help ! — Julian
Peveril !' The sounds still rung in his ears ; the accents were
those of Alice, and he could scarce persuade himself that his
imagination had deceived him. Could she be in the same
vessel ? The thought was not altogether inconsistent with her
father's character and the intrigues in which he was engaged ;
but then, if so, to what peril was she exposed, that she invoked
his name so loudly ?

Determined to make instant inquiry, he jumped out of his
hammock, half-dressed as he was, and stumbling about the
little cabin, which was as dark as pitch, at length, with considerable difficulty, reached the door. The door, however, he
was altogether unable to open ; and was obliged to call loudly to
the watch upon deck. The skipper, or captain, as he was called,
being the only person aboard who could speak English, answered
to the summons, and replied to Peveril's demand, what noise
that was ? — that a boat was going off with the young woman,
that she whimpered a little as she left the vessel, and 'dat
vaas all.'

This explanation satisfied Julian, who thought it probable
that some degree of violence might have been absolutely necessary to remove Fenella ; and although he rejoiced at not having
witnessed it, he could not feel sorry that such had been employed. Her pertinacious desire to continue on board, and the
difficulty of freeing himself, when he should come ashore, from
so singular a companion, had given him a good deal of anxiety

on the preceding night, which he now saw removed by this bold stroke of the captain.

His dream was thus fully explained. Fancy had caught up the inarticulate and vehement cries with which Fenella was wont to express resistance or displeasure, had coined them into language, and given them the accents of Alice Bridgenorth. Our imagination plays wilder tricks with us almost every night.

The captain now undid the door, and appeared with a lantern ; without the aid of which Peveril could scarce have regained his couch, where he now slumbered secure and sound, until day was far advanced, and the invitation of the captain called him up to breakfast.

CHAPTER XX

Now, what is this that haunts me like my shadow,
Frisking and mumming, like an elf in moonlight?
                                    BEN JONSON.

PEVERIL found the master of the vessel rather less rude
than those in his station of life usually are, and received
from him full satisfaction concerning the fate of Fenella,
upon whom the captain bestowed a hearty curse, for obliging
him to lay-to until he had sent his boat ashore and had her
back again.

'I hope,' said Peveril, 'no violence was necessary to reconcile
her to go ashore? I trust she offered no foolish resistance?'

'Resist! *mein Gott*,' said the captain, 'she did resist like a
troop of horse; she did cry, you might hear her at Whitehaven;
she did go up the rigging like a cat up a chimney — but dat
vas *ein* trick of her old trade.'

'What trade do you mean?' said Peveril.

'Oh,' said the seaman, 'I vas know more about her than you,
Meinherr. I vas know that she vas a little — very little girl,
and prentice to one *seiltanzer*, when my lady yonder had the
good luck to buy her.'

'A *seiltanzer*!' said Peveril; 'what do you mean by that?'

'I mean a rope-danzer, a mountebank, a Hans Pickelharing.
I vas know Adrian Brackel vell; he sell de powders dat empty
men's stomach and fill him's own purse. Not know Adrian
Brackel, mein Gott! I have smoked many a pound of tabak
with him.'

Peveril now remembered that Fenella had been brought into
the family when he and the young earl were in England, and
while the countess was absent on an expedition to the Continent. Where the countess found her, she never communicated
to the young men; but only intimated that she had received
her out of compassion, in order to relieve her from a situation
of extreme distress.

He hinted so much to the communicative seaman, who

replied, 'That for distress he knew nocht's on 't; only, that
Adrian Brackel beat her when she would not dance on the
rope, and starved her when she did, to prevent her growth.'
The bargain between the countess and the mountebank, he
said, he had made himself; because the countess had hired his
brig upon her expedition to the Continent. None else knew
where she came from. The countess had seen her on a public
stage at Ostend, compassionated her helpless situation and
the severe treatment she received, and had employed him to
purchase the poor creature from her master, and charged him
with silence towards all her retinue.[1]   'And so I do keep
silence,' continued the faithful confidant, 'van I am in the
havens of Man; but when I am on the broad seas, den my
tongue is mine own, you know. *Die* foolish beoples in the
island, they say she is a *wechselbalg* — what you call a fairy-
elf changeling. My faith, they do not never have seen *ein
wechselbalg;* for I saw one myself at Cologne, and it was twice
as big as yonder girl, and did break the poor people, with eating them up, like de great big cuckoo in the sparrow's nest;
but this Venella eat no more than other girls: it was no
wechselbalg in the world.'

By a different train of reasoning, Julian had arrived at the
same conclusion; in which, therefore, he heartily acquiesced.
During the seaman's prosing he was reflecting within himself
how much of the singular flexibility of her limbs and move-
ments the unfortunate girl must have derived from the discipline and instructions of Adrian Brackel; and also how far
the germs of her wilful and capricious passions might have
been sown during her wandering and adventurous childhood.
Aristocratic, also, as his education had been, these anecdotes
respecting Fenella's original situation and education rather
increased his pleasure at having shaken off her company; and
yet he still felt desirous to know any farther particulars which
the seaman could communicate on the same subject. But he
had already told all he knew. Of her parents he knew nothing,
except that 'her father must have been a damned *hundsfoot*
and a *schelm*, for selling his own flesh and blood to Adrian
Brackel'; for by such a transaction had the mountebank become possessed of his pupil.

This conversation tended to remove any passing doubts
which might have crept on Peveril's mind concerning the
fidelity of the master of the vessel, who appeared from thence

---

[1] See Sale of a Dancing-Girl. Note 14.

to have been a former acquaintance of the countess, and to have enjoyed some share of her confidence. The threatening motion used by Fenella he no longer considered as worthy of any notice, excepting as a new mark of the irritability of her temper.

He amused himself with walking the deck and musing on his past and future prospects, until his attention was forcibly arrested by the wind, which began to rise in gusts from the north-west, in a manner so unfavourable to the course they intended to hold, that the master, after many efforts to beat against it, declared his bark, which was by no means an excellent sea-boat, was unequal to making Whitehaven; and that he was compelled to make a fair wind of it, and run for Liverpool. To this course Peveril did not object. It saved him some land journey, in case he visited his father's castle; and the countess's commission would be discharged as effectually the one way as the other.

The vessel was put, accordingly, before the wind, and ran with great steadiness and velocity. The captain, notwithstanding, pleading some nautical hazards, chose to lie off, and did not attempt the mouth of the Mersey until morning, when Peveril had at length the satisfaction of being landed upon the quay of Liverpool, which even then showed symptoms of the commercial prosperity that has since been carried to such a height.

The master, who was well acquainted with the port, pointed out to Julian a decent place of entertainment, chiefly frequented by seafaring people; for, although he had been in the town formerly, he did not think it proper to go anywhere at present where he might have been unnecessarily recognised. Here he took leave of the seaman, after pressing upon him with difficulty a small present for his crew. As for his passage, the captain declined any recompense whatever; and they parted upon the most civil terms.

The inn to which he was recommended was full of strangers, seamen and mercantile people, all intent upon their own affairs, and discussing them with noise and eagerness peculiar to the business of a thriving seaport. But although the general clamour of the public room, in which the guests mixed with each other, related chiefly to their own commercial dealings, there was a general theme mingling with them, which was alike common and interesting to all; so that, amidst disputes about freight, tonnage, demurrage, and such-like, were heard the

emphatic sounds of 'Deep, damnable, accursed plot.' 'Bloody
Papist villains.' 'The King in danger — the gallows too good
for them,' and so forth.

The fermentation excited in London had plainly reached
even this remote seaport, and was received by the inhabitants
with the peculiar stormy energy which invests men in their situation with the character of the winds and waves with which they
are chiefly conversant. The commercial and nautical interests
of England were indeed particularly anti-Catholic ; although it is
not, perhaps, easy to give any distinct reason why they should
be so, since theological disputes in general could scarce be
considered as interesting to them. But zeal, amongst the lower
orders at least, is often in an inverse ratio to knowledge ; and
sailors were not probably the less earnest and devoted Protestants that they did not understand the controversy between the
churches. As for the merchants, they were almost necessarily
inimical to the gentry of Lancashire and Cheshire, many of
whom still retained the faith of Rome, which was rendered ten
times more odious to the men of commerce, as the badge of
their haughty aristocratic neighbours.

From the little which Peveril heard of the sentiments of the
people of Liverpool, he imagined he should act most prudently
in leaving the place as soon as possible, and before any suspicion
should arise of his having any connexion with the party which
appeared to have become so obnoxious.

In order to accomplish his journey, it was first necessary
that he should purchase a horse ; and for this purpose he resolved to have recourse to the stables of a dealer well known
at the time, and who dwelt in the outskirts of the place ; and
having obtained directions to his dwelling, he went thither to
provide himself.

Joe Bridlesley's stables exhibited a large choice of good
horses ; for that trade was in former days more active than at
present. It was an ordinary thing for a stranger to buy a
horse for the purpose of a single journey, and to sell him, as
well as he could, when he had reached the point of his destina-
tion ; and hence there was a constant demand, and a corresponding supply ; upon both of which Bridlesley, and those of
his trade, contrived, doubtless, to make handsome profits.

Julian, who was no despicable horse-jockey, selected for his
purpose a strong, well-made horse, about sixteen hands high,
and had him led into the yard, to see whether his paces corresponded with his appearance. As these also gave perfect

satisfaction to the customer, it remained only to settle the
price with Bridlesley, who of course swore his customer had
pitched upon the best horse ever darkened the stable-door since
he had dealt that way; that no such horses were to be had
nowadays, for that the mares were dead that foaled them;
and having named a corresponding price, the usual haggling
commenced betwixt the seller and purchaser for adjustment of
what the French dealers call *le prix juste*.

The reader, if he be at all acquainted with this sort of
traffic, well knows it is generally a keen encounter of wits, and
attracts the notice of all the idlers within hearing, who are
usually very ready to offer their opinions or their evidence.
Amongst these, upon the present occasion, was a thin man,
rather less than the ordinary size, and meanly dressed; but
whose interference was in a confident tone, and such as showed
himself master of the subject on which he spoke. The price
of the horse being settled to about fifteen pounds, which was
very high for the period, that of the saddle and bridle had
next to be adjusted, and the thin, mean-looking person before
mentioned found nearly as much to say on this subject as on the
other. As his remarks had a conciliating and obliging tendency
towards the stranger, Peveril concluded he was one of those
idle persons who, unable or unwilling to supply themselves with
the means of indulgence at their own cost, do not scruple to
deserve them at the hands of others by a little officious complaisance; and considering that he might acquire some useful
information from such a person, was just about to offer him
the courtesy of a morning draught, when he observed he had
suddenly left the yard. He had scarce remarked this circumstance, before a party of customers entered the place,
whose haughty assumption of importance claimed the instant
attention of Bridlesley and all his militia of grooms and stable-
boys.

'Three good horses,' said the leader of the party, a tall bulky
man, whose breath was drawn full and high, under a consciousness of fat and of importance — 'three good and able-bodied
horses, for the service of the Commons of England.'

Bridlesley said he had some horses which might serve the
Speaker himself at need; but that, to speak Christian truth, he
had just sold the best in his stable to that gentleman present,
who, doubtless, would give up the bargain if the horse was
needed for the service of the state.

'You speak well, friend,' said the important personage; and

advancing to Julian, demanded, in a very haughty tone, the surrender of the purchase which he had just made.

Peveril, with some difficulty, subdued the strong desire which he felt to return a round refusal to so unreasonable a request, but, fortunately, recollecting that the situation in which he at present stood required, on his part, much circumspection, he replied simply that, upon showing him any warrant to seize upon horses for the public service, he must of course submit to resign his purchase.

The man, with an air of extreme dignity, pulled from his pocket, and thrust into Peveril's hands, a warrant subscribed by the Speaker of the House of Commons, empowering Charles Topham, their officer of the Black Rod, to pursue and seize upon the persons of certain individuals named in the warrant; and of all other persons who are, or should be, accused by competent witnesses of being accessary to, or favourers of, the hellish and damnable Popish Plot at present carried on within the bowels of the kingdom; and charging all men, as they loved their allegiance, to render the said Charles Topham their readiest and most effective assistance, in execution of the duty entrusted to his care.

On perusing a document of such weighty import, Julian had no hesitation to give up his horse to this formidable functionary, whom somebody compared to a lion, which, as the House of Commons was pleased to maintain such an animal, they were under the necessity of providing for by frequent commitments; until 'Take him, Topham,' became a proverb, and a formidable one, in the mouth of the public.

The acquiescence of Peveril procured him some grace in the sight of the emissary, who, before selecting two horses for his attendants, gave permission to the stranger to purchase a grey horse, much inferior indeed to that which he had resigned, both in form and in action, but very little lower in price; as Mr. Bridlesley, immediately on learning the demand for horses upon the part of the Commons of England, had passed a private resolution in his own mind, augmenting the price of his whole stud by an imposition of at least twenty per cent *ad valorem*.

Peveril adjusted and paid the price with much less argument than on the former occasion; for, to be plain with the reader, he had noticed in the warrant of Mr. Topham the name of his father, Sir Geoffrey Peveril of Martindale Castle, engrossed at full length, as one of those subjected to arrest by that officer.

When aware of this material fact, it became Julian's business

to leave Liverpool directly and carry the alarm to Derbyshire,
if, indeed, Mr. Topham had not already executed his charge in
that county, which he thought unlikely, as it was probable
they would commence by securing those who lived nearest to
the seaports. A word or two which he overheard strengthened
his hopes.

'And hark ye, friend,' said Mr. Topham, 'you will have the
horses at the door of Mr. Shortell, the mercer, in two hours, as
we shall refresh ourselves there with a cool tankard, and learn
what folks live in the neighbourhood that may be concerned in
my way. And you will please to have that saddle padded, for
I am told the Derbyshire roads are rough. And you, Captain
Dangerfield, and Master Everett, you must put on your Protestant spectacles, and show me where there is the shadow of
a priest or of a priest's favourer; for I am come down with
a broom in my cap to sweep this north country of such-like
cattle.'

One of the persons he thus addressed, who wore the garb
of a broken-down citizen, only answered, 'Ay, truly, Master
Topham, it is time to purge the garner.'

The other, who had a formidable pair of whiskers, a red
nose, and a tarnished laced coat, together with a hat of Pistol's
dimensions, was more loquacious. 'I take it on my damnation,'
said this zealous Protestant witness, 'that I will discover the
marks of the beast on every one of them betwixt sixteen and
seventy, as plainly as if they had crossed themselves with ink
instead of holy water. Since we have a king willing to do
justice, and a House of Commons to uphold prosecutions, why,
damn me, the cause must not stand still for lack of evidence.'

'Stick to that, noble captain,' answered the officer; 'but,
prithee, reserve thy oaths for the court of justice; it is but
sheer waste to throw them away, as you do, in your ordinary
conversation.'

'Fear you nothing, Master Topham,' answered Dangerfield;
'it is right to keep a man's gifts in use; and were I altogether
to renounce oaths in my private discourse, how should I know
how to use one when I needed it? But you hear me use none
of your Papist abjurations. I swear not by the mass, or before
George, or by anything that belongs to idolatry; but such
downright oaths as may serve a poor Protestant gentleman,
who would fain serve Heaven and the king.'

'Bravely spoken, most noble Festus,' said his yoke-fellow.
'But do not suppose that, although I am not in the habit of

garnishing my words with oaths out of season, I shall be wanting, when called upon, to declare the height and the depth, the width and the length, of this hellish plot against the king and the Protestant faith.'

Dizzy, and almost sick, with listening to the undisguised brutality of these fellows, Peveril, having with difficulty prevailed on Bridlesley to settle his purchase, at length led forth his grey steed ; but was scarce out of the yard, when he heard the following alarming conversation pass, of which he seemed himself the object : —

'Who is that youth ? ' said the slow soft voice of the more precise of the two witnesses. 'Methinks I have seen him somewhere before. Is he from these parts ? '

'Not that I know of,' said Bridlesley, who, like all the other inhabitants of England at the time, answered the interrogatories of these fellows with the deference which is paid in Spain to the questions of an inquisitor. 'A stranger — entirely a stranger — never saw him before ; a wild young colt, I warrant him ; and knows a horse's mouth as well as I do.'

'I begin to bethink me I saw such a face as his at the Jesuits' consult, in the White Horse Tavern,' answered Everett.

'And I think I recollect,' said Captain Dangerfield——

'Come — come, master and captain,' said the authoritative voice of Topham ; 'we will have none of your recollections at present. We all know what these are likely to end in. But I will have you know, you are not to run till the leash is slipped. The young man is a well-looking lad, and gave up his horse handsomely for the service of the House of Commons. He knows how to behave himself to his betters, I warrant you ; and I scarce think he has enough in his purse to pay the fees.' [1]

This speech concluded the dialogue, which Peveril, finding himself so much concerned in the issue, thought it best to hear to an end. Now, when it ceased, to get out of the town unobserved, and take the nearest way to his father's castle, seemed his wisest plan. He had settled his reckoning at the inn and brought with him to Bridlesley's the small portmanteau which contained his few necessaries, so that he had no occasion to return thither. He resolved, therefore, to ride some miles before he stopped, even for the purpose of feeding his horse ; and being pretty well acquainted with the country, he hoped to be able to push forward to Martindale Castle sooner than the worshipful Master Topham, whose saddle was, in the first

---

[1] See Witnesses of the Popish Plot. Note 15.

place, to be padded, and who, when mounted, would, in all probability, ride with the precaution of those who require such security against the effects of a hard trot.

Under the influence of these feelings, Julian pushed for Warrington, a place with which he was well acquainted ; but, without halting in the town, he crossed the Mersey, by the bridge built by an ancestor of his friend the Earl of Derby, and continued his route towards Dishley, on the borders of Derbyshire. He might have reached this latter village easily had his horse been fitter for a forced march ; but in the course of the journey he had occasion, more than once, to curse the official dignity of the person who had robbed him of his better steed, while taking the best direction he could through a country with which he was only generally acquainted.

At length, near Altringham, a halt became unavoidable ; and Peveril had only to look for some quiet and sequestered place of refreshment. This presented itself in the form of a small cluster of cottages, the best of which united the characters of an alehouse and a mill, where the sign of the Cat (the landlord's faithful ally in defence of his meal-sacks), booted as high as Grimalkin in the fairy tale, and playing on the fiddle for the more grace, announced that John Whitecraft united the two honest occupations of landlord and miller ; and, doubtless, took toll from the public in both capacities.

Such a place promised a traveller, who journeyed incognito, safer, if not better, accommodation than he was like to meet with in more frequented inns ; and at the door of the Cat and Fiddle Julian halted accordingly.

CHAPTER XXI

In these distracted times, when each man dreads
The bloody stratagems of busy heads.

                                                    OTWAY.

AT the door of the Cat and Fiddle, Julian received the
usual attention paid to the customers of an inferior
house of entertainment. His horse was carried by a
ragged lad, who acted as hostler, into a paltry stable; where,
however, the nag was tolerably supplied with food and litter.

Having seen the animal on which his comfort, perhaps his
safety, depended properly provided for, Peveril entered the
kitchen, which indeed was also the parlour and hall of the
little hostelry, to try what refreshment he could obtain for
himself. Much to his satisfaction, he found there was only one
guest in the house besides himself; but he was less pleased
when he found that he must either go without dinner or share
with that single guest the only provisions which chanced to be
in the house, namely, a dish of trouts and eels, which their host,
the miller, had brought in from his mill-stream.

At the particular request of Julian, the landlady undertook
to add a substantial dish of eggs and bacon, which perhaps she
would not have undertaken for, had not the sharp eye of
Peveril discovered the flitch hanging in its smoky retreat,
when, as its presence could not be denied, the hostess was
compelled to bring it forward as a part of her supplies.

She was a buxom dame about thirty, whose comely and
cheerful countenance did honour to the choice of the jolly
miller, her loving mate; and was now stationed under the
shade of an old-fashioned huge projecting chimney, within
which it was her province to 'work i' the fire,' and provide for
the wearied wayfaring man the good things which were to send
him rejoicing on his course. Although, at first, the honest
woman seemed little disposed to give herself much additional

trouble on Julian's account, yet the good looks, handsome
figure, and easy civility of her new guest soon bespoke the
principal part of her attention; and while busy in his service,
she regarded him, from time to time, with looks where something like pity mingled with complacency. The rich smoke of
the rasher, and the eggs with which it was flanked, already
spread itself through the apartment; and the hissing of these
savoury viands bore chorus to the simmering of the pan, in
which the fish were undergoing a slower decoction. The table
was covered with a clean huckaback napkin, and all was in
preparation for the meal, which Julian began to expect with a
good deal of impatience, when the companion who was destined
to share it with him entered the apartment.

At the first glance, Julian recognised, to his surprise, the
same indifferently-dressed, thin-looking person who, during the
first bargain which he had made with Bridlesley, had officiously
interfered with his advice and opinion. Displeased at having
the company of any stranger forced upon him, Peveril was still
less satisfied to find one who might make some claim of acquaintance with him, however slender, since the circumstances in
which he stood compelled him to be as reserved as possible.
He therefore turned his back upon his destined messmate, and
pretended to amuse himself by looking out of the window,
determined to avoid all intercourse until it should be inevitably
forced upon him.

In the meanwhile, the other stranger went straight up to
the landlady, where she toiled on household cares intent, and
demanded of her what she meant by preparing bacon and
eggs, when he had positively charged her to get nothing ready
but the fish.

The good woman, important as every cook in the discharge
of her duty, deigned not for some time so much as to acknowledge that she heard the reproof of her guest; and when she
did so, it was only to repel it in a magisterial and authoritative
tone. 'If he did not like bacon — bacon from their own hutch,
well fed on pease and bran — if he did not like bacon and eggs
— new-laid eggs, which she had brought in from the hen-roost
with her own hands — why so put case — it was the worse for
his honour and the better for those who did.'

'The better for those who like them!' answered the guest;
'that is as much as to say, I am to have a companion, good
woman.'

'Do not "good woman" me, sir,' replied the miller's wife,

'till I call you good man; and, I promise you, many would
scruple to do that to one who does not love eggs and bacon
of a Friday.'

'Nay, my good lady,' said her guest, 'do not fix any misconstruction upon me. I daresay the eggs and the bacon
are excellent; only, they are rather a dish too heavy for my
stomach.'

'Ay, or your conscience perhaps, sir,' answered the hostess.
'And now, I bethink me, you must needs have your fish fried
with oil, instead of the good drippings I was going to put to
them. I would I could spell the meaning of all this now; but
I warrant John Bigstaff, the constable, could conjure something
out of it.'

There was a pause here; but Julian, somewhat alarmed at
the tone which the conversation assumed, became interested in
watching the dumb show which succeeded. By bringing his
head a little towards the left, but without turning round or
quitting the projecting latticed window where he had taken
his station, he could observe that the stranger, secured, as he
seemed to think himself, from observation, had sidled close up
to the landlady, and, as he conceived, had put a piece of money
into her hand. The altered tone of the miller's moiety corresponded very much with this supposition.

'Nay, indeed, and forsooth,' she said, 'her house was Liberty
Hall; and so should every publican's be. What was it to her
what gentlefolks ate or drank, providing they paid for it
honestly? There were many honest gentlemen whose stomachs
could not abide bacon, grease, or dripping, especially on a
Friday; and what was that to her, or any one in her line,
so gentlefolks paid honestly for the trouble? Only, she would
say that her bacon and eggs could not be mended betwixt this
and Liverpool; and that she would live and die upon.'

'I shall hardly dispute it,' said the stranger; and turning
towards Julian, he added, 'I wish this gentleman, who I suppose is my trencher-companion, much joy of the dainties which
I cannot assist him in consuming.'

'I assure you, sir,' answered Peveril, who now felt himself
compelled to turn about and reply with civility, 'that it was
with difficulty I could prevail on my landlady to add my cover
to yours, though she seems now such a zealot for the consump-
tion of eggs and bacon.'

'I am zealous for nothing,' said the landlady, 'save that
men would eat their victuals and pay their score; and if there

be enough in one dish to serve two guests, I see little purpose in dressing them two; however, they are ready now, and done to a nicety. Here, Alice!—Alice!'

The sound of that well-known name made Julian start; but the Alice who replied to the call ill resembled the vision which his imagination connected with the accents, being a dowdy, slip-shod wench, the drudge of the low inn which afforded him shelter. She assisted her mistress in putting on the table the dishes which the latter had prepared; and a foaming jug of home-brewed ale, being placed betwixt them, was warranted by Dame Whitecraft as excellent; 'for,' said she, 'we know by practice that too much water drowns the miller, and we spare it on our malt as we would in our mill-dam.'

'I drink to your health in it, dame,' said the elder stranger; 'and a cup of thanks for these excellent fish; and to the drowning of all unkindness between us.'

'I thank you, sir,' said the dame, 'and wish you the like; but I dare not pledge you, for our gaffer says the ale is brewed too strong for women; so I only drink a glass of canary at a time with a gossip or any gentleman guest that is so minded.'

'You shall drink one with me then, dame,' said Peveril, 'so you will let me have a flagon.'

'That you shall, sir, and as good as ever was broached; but I must to the mill, to get the key from the goodman.'

So saying, and tucking her clean gown through the pocket-holes, that her steps might be the more alert and her dress escape dust, off she tripped to the mill, which lay close adjoining.

'A dainty dame, and dangerous, is the miller's wife,' said the stranger, looking at Peveril. 'Is not that old Chaucer's phrase?'

'I—I believe so,' said Peveril, not much read in Chaucer, who was then even more neglected than at present; and much surprised at a literary quotation from one of the mean appearance exhibited by the person before him.

'Yes,' answered the stranger, 'I see that you, like other young gentlemen of the time, are better acquainted with Cowley and Waller than with the "well of English undefiled." I cannot help differing. There are touches of nature about the old bard of Woodstock that to me are worth all the turns of laborious wit in Cowley, and all the ornate and artificial simplicity of his courtly competitor. The description, for instance, of his country coquette —

> Wincing she was, as is a wanton colt,
> Sweet as a flower, and upright as a bolt.

Then again, for pathos, where will you mend the dying scene of Arcite?

> Alas, my heartis queen! alas, my wife!
> Giver at once, and ender of my life.
> What is this world? What axen men to have?
> Now with his love, now in his cold grave
> Alone, withouten other company.

But I tire you, sir; and do injustice to the poet, whom I remember but by halves.'

'On the contrary, sir,' replied Peveril, 'you make him more intelligible to me in your recitation than I have found him when I have tried to peruse him myself.'

'You were only frightened by the antiquated spelling and "the letters black,"' said his companion. 'It is many a scholar's case, who mistakes a nut, which he could crack with a little exertion, for a bullet, which he must needs break his teeth on; but yours are better employed. Shall I offer you some of this fish?'

'Not so, sir,' replied Julian, willing to show himself a man of reading in his turn; 'I hold with old Caius, and profess to fear judgment, to fight where I cannot choose, and to eat no fish.'

The stranger cast a startled look around him at this observation, which Julian had thrown out on purpose to ascertain, if possible, the quality of his companion, whose present language was so different from the character he had assumed at Bridlesley's. His countenance, too, although the features were of an ordinary, not to say mean, cast, had that character of intelligence which education gives to the most homely face; and his manners were so easy and disembarrassed as plainly showed a complete acquaintance with society, as well as the habit of mingling with it in the higher stages. The alarm which he had evidently shown at Peveril's answer was but momentary; for he almost instantly replied, with a smile, 'I promise you, sir, that you are in no dangerous company; for, notwithstanding my fish dinner, I am much disposed to trifle with some of your savoury mess, if you will indulge me so far.'

Peveril accordingly reinforced the stranger's trencher with what remained of the bacon and eggs, and saw him swallow a mouthful or two with apparent relish; but presently after, he began to dally with his knife and fork, like one whose appetite

was satiated; then took a long draught of the black-jack, and
handed his platter to the large mastiff dog, who, attracted by
the smell of the dinner, had sat down before him for some
time, licking his chops, and following with his eye every morsel
which the guest raised to his head.

'Here, my poor fellow,' said he, 'thou hast had no fish, and
needest this supernumerary trencher-load more than I do. I
cannot withstand thy mute supplication any longer.'

The dog answered these courtesies by a civil shake of the
tail, while he gobbled up what was assigned him by the
stranger's benevolence, in the greater haste, that he heard his
mistress's voice at the door.

'Here is the canary, gentlemen,' said the landlady; 'and the
goodman has set off the mill, to come to wait on you himself.
He always does so, when company drink wine.'

'That he may come in for the host's, that is, for the lion's,
share,' said the stranger, looking at Peveril.

'The shot is mine,' said Julian; 'and if mine host will share
it, I will willingly bestow another quart on him, and on you,
sir. I never break old customs.'

These sounds caught the ear of Gaffer Whitecraft, who had
entered the room — a strapping specimen of his robust trade,
prepared to play the civil or the surly host as his company
should be acceptable or otherwise. At Julian's invitation, he
doffed his dusty bonnet, brushed from his sleeve the looser
particles of his professional dust, and sitting down on the end
of a bench, about a yard from the table, filled a glass of canary
and drank to his guests, and 'especially to this noble gentleman,' indicating Peveril, who had ordered the canary.

Julian returned the courtesy by drinking his health, and
asking what news were about in the country.

'Nought, sir — I hears on nought, except this plot, as they
call it, that they are pursuing the Papishers about; but it
brings water to my mill, as the saying is. Between expresses
hurrying hither and thither, and guards and prisoners riding
to and again, and the custom of the neighbours, that come to
speak over the news of an evening, nightly I may say, instead
of once a-week, why the spigot is in use, gentlemen, and your
landlord thrives; and then I serving as constable, and being a
known Protestant, I have tapped, I may venture to say, it may
be ten stands of ale extraordinary, besides a reasonable sale of
wine for a country corner. Heaven make us thankful, and keep
all good Protestants from plot and Popery!'

'I can easily conceive, my friend,' said Julian, 'that curiosity is a passion which runs naturally to the alehouse; and that anger, and jealousy, and fear are all of them thirsty passions, and great consumers of home-brewed. But I am a perfect stranger in these parts, and I would willingly learn, from a sensible man like you, a little of this same plot, of which men speak so much and appear to know so little.'

'Learn a little of it! Why, it is the most horrible — the most damnable, bloodthirsty beast of a plot —— But hold — hold, my good master; I hope, in the first place, you believe there is a plot? for, otherwise, the justice must have a word with you, as sure as my name is John Whitecraft.'

'It shall not need,' said Peveril; 'for I assure you, mine host, I believe in the plot as freely and fully as a man can believe in anything he cannot understand.'

'God forbid that anybody should pretend to understand it,' said the implicit constable; 'for his worship the justice says it is a mile beyond him, and he be as deep as most of them. But men may believe though they do not understand; and that is what the Romanists say themselves. But this I am sure of, it makes a rare stirring time for justices, and witnesses, and constables. So here's to your health again, gentlemen, in a cup of neat canary.'

'Come — come, John Whitecraft,' said his wife, 'do not you demean yourself by naming witnesses along with justices and constables. All the world knows how they come by their money.'

'Ay, but all the world knows that they *do* come by it, dame; and that is a great comfort. They rustle in their canonical silks, and swagger in their buff and scarlet, who but they? Ay — ay, the cursed fox thrives — and not so cursed neither. Is there not Doctor Titus Oates, the saviour of the nation — does he not live at Whitehall, and eat off plate, and have a pension of thousands a-year, for what I know? and is he not to be Bishop of Litchfield so soon as Dr. Doddrum dies?'

'Then I hope Dr. Doddrum's reverence will live these twenty years; and I daresay I am the first that ever wished such a wish,' said the hostess. 'I do not understand these doings, not I; and if a hundred Jesuits came to hold a consult at my house, as they did at the White Horse Tavern, I should think it quite out of the line of business to bear witness against them, provided they drank well and paid their score.'

' Very true, dame,' said her elder guest; 'that is what I call keeping a good publican conscience; and so I will pay my score presently, and be jogging on my way.'

Peveril, on his part, also demanded a reckoning, and discharged it so liberally that the miller flourished his hat as he bowed, and the hostess courtesied down to the ground.

The horses of both guests were brought forth; and they mounted, in order to depart in company. The host and hostess stood in the doorway to see them depart. The landlord proffered a stirrup-cup to the elder guest, while the landlady offered Peveril a glass from her own peculiar bottle. For this purpose, she mounted on the horse-block, with flask and glass in hand; so that it was easy for the departing guest, although on horseback, to return the courtesy in the most approved manner, namely, by throwing his arm over his landlady's shoulder and saluting her at parting.

Dame Whitecraft did not decline this familiarity; for there is no room for traversing upon a horse-block, and the hands which might have served her for resistance were occupied with glass and bottle — matters too precious to be thrown away in such a struggle. Apparently, however, she had something else in her head; for, as, after a brief affectation of reluctance, she permitted Peveril's face to approach hers, she whispered in his ear, ' Beware of trepans!' an awful intimation, which, in those days of distrust, suspicion, and treachery, was as effectual in interdicting free and social intercourse as the advertisement of ' man-traps and spring-guns ' to protect an orchard. Pressing her hand, in intimation that he comprehended her hint, she shook his warmly in return, and bade God speed him. There was a cloud on John Whitecraft's brow; nor did his final farewell sound half so cordial as that which had been spoken within doors. But then Peveril reflected that the same guest is not always equally acceptable to landlord and landlady; and unconscious of having done anything to excite the miller's displeasure, he pursued his journey without thinking farther of the matter.

Julian was a little surprised, and not altogether pleased, to find that his new acquaintance held the same road with him. He had many reasons for wishing to travel alone; and the hostess's caution still rung in his ears. If this man, possessed of so much shrewdness as his countenance and conversation intimated, versatile, as he had occasion to remark, and disguised beneath his condition, should prove, as was likely, to be a

concealed Jesuit or seminary priest, travelling upon their great
task of the conversion of England, and rooting out of the
Northern heresy — a more dangerous companion, for a person
in his own circumstances, could hardly be imagined, since
keeping society with him might seem to authorise whatever
reports had been spread concerning the attachment of his
family to the Catholic cause. At the same time, it was very
difficult, without actual rudeness, to shake off the company of
one who seemed determined, whether spoken to or not, to
remain alongside of him.

Peveril tried the experiment of riding slow; but his companion, determined not to drop him, slackened his pace so as
to keep close by him. Julian then spurred his horse to a full
trot; and was soon satisfied that the stranger, notwithstanding
the meanness of his appearance, was so much better mounted
than himself as to render vain any thoughts of out-riding him.
He pulled up his horse to a more reasonable pace, therefore, in
a sort of despair. Upon his doing so, his companion, who had
been hitherto silent, observed, that Peveril was not so well
qualified to try speed upon the road as he would have been
had he abode by his first bargain of horse-flesh that morning.

Peveril assented drily, but observed, that the animal would
serve his immediate purpose, though he feared it would render
him indifferent company for a person better mounted.

'By no means,' answered his civil companion; 'I am one of
those who have travelled so much as to be accustomed to
make my journey at any rate of motion which may be most
agreeable to my company.'

Peveril made no reply to this polite intimation, being too
sincere to tender the thanks which, in courtesy, were the
proper answer. A second pause ensued, which was broken by
Julian asking the stranger whether their roads were likely to
lie long together in the same direction.

'I cannot tell,' said the stranger, smiling, 'unless I knew
which way you were travelling.'

'I am uncertain how far I shall go to-night,' said Julian,
willingly misunderstanding the purport of the reply.

'And so am I,' replied the stranger; 'but though my horse
goes better than yours, I think it will be wise to spare him;
and in case our road continues to lie the same way, we are
likely to sup, as we have dined, together.'

Julian made no answer whatever to this round intimation,
but continued to ride on, turning, in his own mind, whether it

would not be wisest to come to a distinct understanding with his pertinacious attendant, and to explain, in so many words, that it was his pleasure to travel alone. But, besides that the sort of acquaintance which they had formed during dinner rendered him unwilling to be directly uncivil towards a person of gentlemanlike manners, he had also to consider that he might very possibly be mistaken in this man's character and purpose; in which case, the cynically refusing the society of a sound Protestant would afford as pregnant matter of suspicion as travelling in company with a disguised Jesuit.

After brief reflection, therefore, he resolved to endure the encumbrance of the stranger's society until a fair opportunity should occur to rid himself of it; and, in the meantime, to act with as much caution as he possibly could in any communication that might take place between them, for Dame White-craft's parting caution still rang anxiously in his ears, and the consequences of his own arrest upon suspicion must deprive him of every opportunity of serving his father, or the countess, or Major Bridgenorth, upon whose interest, also, he had promised himself to keep an eye.

While he revolved these things in his mind, they had journeyed several miles without speaking; and now entered upon a more waste country and worse roads than they had hitherto found, being, in fact, approaching the more hilly district of Derbyshire. In travelling on a very stony and uneven lane, Julian's horse repeatedly stumbled; and, had he not been supported by the rider's judicious use of the bridle, must at length certainly have fallen under him.

'These are times which crave wary riding, sir,' said his companion; 'and by your seat in the saddle, and your hand on the rein, you seem to understand it to be so.'

'I have been long a horseman, sir,' answered Peveril.

'And long a traveller, too, sir, I should suppose; since, by the great caution you observe, you seem to think the human tongue requires a curb, as well as the horse's jaws.'

'Wiser men than I have been of opinion,' answered Peveril, 'that it were a part of prudence to be silent when men have little or nothing to say.'

'I cannot approve of their opinion,' answered the stranger. 'All knowledge is gained by communication, either with the dead, through books, or, more pleasingly, through the conversation of the living. The *deaf and dumb*, alone, are excluded from improvement; and surely their situation is not so enviable that we should imitate them.'

At this illustration, which awakened a startling echo in Peveril's bosom, the young man looked hard at his companion; but in the composed countenance and calm blue eye he read no consciousness of a farther meaning than the words immediately and directly implied. He paused a moment, and then answered, 'You seem to be a person, sir, of shrewd apprehension; and I should have thought it might have occurred to you that, in the present suspicious times, men may, without censure, avoid communication with strangers. You know not me; and to me you are totally unknown. There is not room for much discourse between us, without trespassing on the general topics of the day, which carry in them seeds of quarrel between friends, much more betwixt strangers. At any other time, the society of an intelligent companion would have been most acceptable upon my solitary ride; but at present——'

'At present!' said the other, interrupting him, 'you are like the old Romans, who held that *hostis* meant both a stranger and an enemy. I will therefore be no longer a stranger. My name is Ganlesse; by profession I am a Roman Catholic priest. I am travelling here in dread of my life; and I am very glad to have you for a companion.'

'I thank you for the information with all my heart,' said Peveril; 'and to avail myself of it to the uttermost, I must beg of you to ride forward, or lag behind, or take a side-path, at your own pleasure; for as I am no Catholic, and travel upon business of high concernment, I am exposed both to risk and delay, and even to danger, by keeping such suspicious company. And so, Master Ganlesse, keep your own pace, and I will keep the contrary; for I beg leave to forbear your company.'

As Peveril spoke thus, he pulled up his horse and made a full stop.

The stranger burst out a-laughing. 'What!' he said, 'you forbear my company for a trifle of danger? St. Anthony! how the warm blood of the Cavaliers is chilled in the young men of the present day! This young gallant, now, has a father, I warrant, who has endured as many adventures for hunted priests as a knight-errant for distressed damsels.'

'This raillery avails nothing, sir,' said Peveril. 'I must request you will keep your own way.'

'My way is yours,' said the pertinacious Master Ganlesse, as

he called himself; 'and we will both travel the safer that we
journey in company. I have the receipt of fern-seed, man, and
walk invisible. Besides, you would not have me quit you in
this lane, where there is no turn to right or left?'

Peveril moved on, desirous to avoid open violence; for which
the indifferent tone of the traveller, indeed, afforded no apt
pretext; yet highly disliking his company, and determined to
take the first opportunity to rid himself of it.

The stranger proceeded at the same pace with him, keeping
cautiously on his bridle hand, as if to secure that advantage in
case of a struggle. But his language did not intimate the least
apprehension. 'You do me wrong,' he said to Peveril, 'and
you equally wrong yourself. You are uncertain where to lodge
to-night; trust to my guidance. Here is an ancient hall,
within four miles, with an old knightly pantaloon for its lord,
an all-be-ruffed Dame Barbara for the lady gay, a Jesuit in a
butler's habit to say grace, an old tale of Edgehill and Worster
fights to relish a cold venison pasty and a flask of claret mantled
with cobwebs, a bed for you in the priest's hiding-hole, and,
for aught I know, pretty Mistress Betty, the dairymaid, to
make it ready.'

'This has no charms for me, sir,' said Peveril, who, in spite
of himself, could not but be amused with the ready sketch
which the stranger gave of many an old mansion in Cheshire
and Derbyshire, where the owners retained the ancient faith of
Rome.

'Well, I see I cannot charm you in this way,' continued his
companion; 'I must strike another key. I am no longer Ganlesse, the seminary priest, but (changing his tone, and snuffling
in the nose) Simon Canter, a poor preacher of the Word, who
travels this way to call sinners to repentance, and to strengthen,
and to edify, and to fructify, among the scattered remnant who
hold fast the truth. What say you to this, sir?'

'I admire your versatility, sir, and could be entertained
with it at another time. At present, sincerity is more in
request.'

'Sincerity!' said the stranger. 'A child's whistle, with but
two notes in it — yea, yea and nay, nay. Why, man, the very
Quakers have renounced it, and have got in its stead a gallant
recorder, called hypocrisy, that is somewhat like sincerity in
form, but of much greater compass, and combines the whole
gamut. Come, be ruled — be a disciple of Simon Canter for
the evening, and we will leave the old tumble-down castle of

the knight aforesaid, on the left hand, for a new brick-built
mansion, erected by an eminent salt-boiler from Namptwich,
who expects the said Simon to make a strong spiritual pickle
for the preservation of a soul somewhat corrupted by the evil
communications of this wicked world.   What say you ?   He has
two daughters — brighter eyes never beamed under a pinched
hood ; and for myself, I think there is more fire in those who
live only to love and to devotion than in your court beauties,
whose hearts are running on twenty follies besides.   You know
not the pleasure of being conscience-keeper to a pretty precisian,
who in one breath repeats her foibles and in the next confesses
her passion.   Perhaps, though, you may have known such in
your day ?   Come, sir, it grows too dark to see your blushes ;
but I am sure they are burning on your cheek.'
   ' You take great freedom, sir,' said Peveril, as they now
approached the end of the lane, where it opened on a broad
common ; 'and you seem rather to count more on my forbearance than you have room to do with safety.   We are now nearly
free of the lane which has made us companions for this last half-
hour.   To avoid your farther company, I will take the turn to
the left upon that common ; and if you follow me, it shall be
at your peril.   Observe, I am well armed ; and you will fight
at odds.'
   ' Not at odds,' returned the provoking stranger, ' while I
have my brown jennet, with which I can ride round and round
you at pleasure ; and this text, of a handful in length (showing
a pistol which he drew from his bosom), which discharges very
convincing doctrine on the pressure of a forefinger, and is apt
to equalise all odds, as you call them, of youth and strength.
Let there be no strife between us, however ; the moor lies before
us — choose your path on it ; I take the other.'
   ' I wish you good-night, sir,' said Peveril to the stranger.
' I ask your forgiveness, if I have misconstrued you in anything ; but the times are perilous, and a man's life may depend
on the society in which he travels.'
   'True,' said the stranger ; ' but in your case the danger is
already undergone, and you should seek to counteract it.   You
have travelled in my company long enough to devise a handsome branch of the Popish Plot.   How will you look when you
see come forth, in comely folio form, *The Narrative of Simon
Canter, otherwise called Richard Ganlesse, concerning the Horrid
Popish Conspiracy for the Murder of the King and Massacre of
all Protestants, as given on oath to the Honourable House of*

*Commons; setting forth how far Julian Peveril, Younger, of
Martindale Castle, is concerned in carrying on the same* —— ' [1]
    ' How, sir ?   What mean you ? ' said Peveril, much startled.
    ' Nay, sir,' replied his companion, ' do not interrupt my title-
page.   Now that Oates and Bedloe have drawn the great prizes,
the subordinate discoverers get little but by the sale of their
Narrative; and Janeway, Newman, Simmons, and every book-
seller of them will tell you that the title is half the narrative.
Mine shall therefore set forth the various schemes you have
communicated to me, of landing ten thousand soldiers from the
Isle of Man upon the coast of Lancashire ; and marching into
Wales, to join the ten thousand pilgrims who are to be shipped
from Spain ; and so completing the destruction of the Protestant
religion, and of the devoted city of London.   Truly, I think
such a *Narrative*, well spiced with a few horrors, and published
cum privilegio Parliamenti, might, though the market be somewhat overstocked, be still worth some twenty or thirty pieces.'
    ' You seem to know me, sir,' said Peveril ; ' and if so, I think
I may fairly ask you your purpose in thus bearing me company,
and the meaning of all this rhapsody.   If it be mere banter, I
can endure it within proper limit, although it is uncivil on the
part of a stranger.   If you have any farther purpose, speak it
out ; I am not to be trifled with.'
    ' Good, now,' said the stranger, laughing ; ' into what an
unprofitable chafe you have put yourself !   An Italian *fuorus-
cito*, when he desires a parley with you, takes aim from behind
a wall with his long gun, and prefaces his conference with " *Posso
tirare.*"   So does your man-of-war fire a gun across the bows of
a Hans-mogan Indiaman, just to bring her to ; and so do I
show Master Julian Peveril that, if I were one of the honourable society of witnesses and informers, with whom his imagination has associated me for these two hours past, he is as much
within my danger now as what he is ever likely to be.'   Then
suddenly changing his tone to serious, which was in general
ironical, he added, ' Young man, when the pestilence is diffused
through the air of a city, it is in vain men would avoid the
disease by seeking solitude and shunning the company of their
fellow-sufferers.'
    ' In what, then, consists their safety ? ' said Peveril, willing
to ascertain, if possible, the drift of his companion's purpose.
    ' In following the counsels of wise physicians ' ; such was
the stranger's answer.

---

¹ See Narratives of the Plot.   Note 16.

'And as such,' said Peveril, 'you offer me your advice?'

'Pardon me, young man,' said the stranger, haughtily, 'I see no reason I should do so. I am not,' he added, in his former tone, 'your fee'd physician. I offer no advice; I only say it would be wise that you sought it.'

'And from whom or where can I obtain it?' said Peveril. 'I wander in this country like one in a dream; so much a few months have changed it. Men who formerly occupied themselves with their own affairs are now swallowed up in matters of state policy; and those tremble under the apprehension of some strange and sudden convulsion of empire who were formerly only occupied by the fear of going to bed supperless. And to sum up the matter, I meet a stranger, apparently well acquainted with my name and concerns, who first attaches himself to me whether I will or no, and then refuses me an explanation of his business, while he menaces me with the strangest accusations.'

'Had I meant such infamy,' said the stranger, 'believe me, I had not given you the thread of my intrigue. But be wise, and come on with me. There is hard by a small inn, where, if you can take a stranger's warrant for it, we shall sleep in perfect security.'

'Yet you yourself,' said Peveril, 'but now were anxious to avoid observation; and in that case, how can you protect me?'

'Pshaw! I did but silence that tattling landlady, in the way in which such people are most readily hushed; and for Topham and his brace of night-owls, they must hawk at other and lesser game than I should prove.'

Peveril could not help admiring the easy and confident indifference with which the stranger seemed to assume a superiority to all the circumstances of danger around him; and after hastily considering the matter with himself, came to the resolution to keep company with him for this night, at least; and to learn, if possible, who he really was, and to what party in the estate he was attached. The boldness and freedom of his talk seemed almost inconsistent with his following the perilous, though at that time the gainful, trade of an informer. No doubt, such persons assumed every appearance which could insinuate them into the confidence of their destined victims; but Julian thought he discovered in this man's manner a wild and reckless frankness, which he could not but connect with the idea of sincerity in the present case. He therefore answered, after a moment's recollection, 'I embrace your proposal, sir; although, by doing so, I am reposing a sudden, and perhaps an unwary, confidence.'

'And what am I, then, reposing in you?' said the stranger. 'Is not our confidence mutual?'

'No; much the contrary. I know nothing of you whatever; you have named me; and, knowing me to be Julian Peveril, know you may travel with me in perfect security.'

'The devil I do!' answered his companion. 'I travel in the same security as with a lighted petard, which I may expect to explode every moment. Are you not the son of Peveril of the Peak, with whose name Prelacy and Popery are so closely allied, that no old woman of either sex in Derbyshire concludes her prayer without a petition to be freed from all three? And do you not come from the Popish Countess of Derby, bringing, for aught I know, a whole army of Manxmen in your pocket, with full complement of arms, ammunition, baggage, and a train of field artillery?'

'It is not very likely I should be so poorly mounted,' said Julian, laughing, 'if I had such a weight to carry. But lead on, sir. I see I must wait for your confidence till you think proper to confer it; for you are already so well acquainted with my affairs, that I have nothing to offer you in exchange for it.'

'*Allons*, then,' said his companion; 'give your horse the spur, and raise the curb rein, lest he measure the ground with his nose, instead of his paces. We are not now more than a furlong or two from the place of entertainment.'

They mended their pace accordingly, and soon arrived at the small solitary inn which the traveller had mentioned. When its light began to twinkle before them, the stranger, as if recollecting something he had forgotten, 'By the way, you must have a name to pass by; for it may be ill travelling under your own, as the fellow who keeps this house is an old Cromwellian. What will you call yourself? My name is — for the present — Ganlesse.'

'There is no occasion to assume a name at all,' answered Julian. 'I do not incline to use a borrowed one, especially as I may meet with some one who knows my own.'

'I will call you Julian, then,' said Master Ganlesse; 'for Peveril will smell, in the nostrils of mine host, of idolatry, conspiracy, Smithfield fagots, fish on Fridays, the murder of Sir Edmondsbury Godfrey, and the fire of purgatory.'

As he spoke thus, they alighted under the great broad-branched oak-tree that served to canopy the ale-bench, which, at an earlier hour, had groaned under the weight of a frequent conclave of rustic politicians. Ganlesse,[1] as he dismounted, whistled in a particularly shrill note, and was answered from within the house.

---

[1] See Note 17.

CHAPTER XXII

He was a fellow in a peasant's garb ;
Yet one could censure you a woodcock's carving,
Like any courtier at the ordinary.

The Ordinary.

THE person who appeared at the door of the little inn to
receive Ganlesse, as we mentioned in our last chapter,
sung as he came forward this scrap of an old ballad —

'Good even to you, Diccon ;
And how have you sped ?
Bring you the bonny bride
To banquet and bed ? '

To which Ganlesse answered, in the same tone and tune —

'Content thee, kind Robin ;
He need little care,
Who brings home a fat buck
Instead of a hare.'

'You have missed your blow, then ? ' said the other, in
reply.

'I tell you, I have not,' answered Ganlesse ; 'but you will
think of nought but your own thriving occupation. May the
plague that belongs to it stick to it, though it hath been the
making of thee.'

'A man must live, Diccon Ganlesse,' said the other.

'Well — well,' said Ganlesse, 'bid my friend welcome, for my
sake. Hast thou got any supper ? '

'Reeking like a sacrifice ; Chaubert has done his best. That
fellow is a treasure ! give him a farthing candle, and he will
cook a good supper out of it. Come in, sir. My friend's friend
is welcome, as we say in my country.'

'We must have our horses looked to first,' said Peveril,
who began to be considerably uncertain about the character
of his companions ; 'that done, I am for you.'

Ganlesse gave a second whistle ; a groom appeared, who took charge of both their horses, and they themselves entered the inn.

The ordinary room of a poor inn seemed to have undergone some alterations, to render it fit for company of a higher description. There were a beaufet, a couch, and one or two other pieces of furniture, of a style inconsistent with the appearance of the place. The tablecloth, which was already laid, was of the finest damask ; and the spoons, forks, etc., were of silver. Peveril looked at this apparatus with some surprise ; and again turning his eyes attentively upon his travelling-companion Ganlesse, he could not help discovering (by the aid of imagination, perhaps) that, though insignificant in person, plain in features, and dressed like one in indigence, there lurked still about his person and manners that indefinable ease of manner which belongs only to men of birth and quality, or to those who are in the constant habit of frequenting the best company. His companion, whom he called Will Smith, although tall and rather good-looking, besides being much better dressed, had not, nevertheless, exactly the same ease of demeanour, and was obliged to make up for the want by an additional proportion of assurance. Who these two persons could be, Peveril could not attempt even to form a guess. There was nothing for it but to watch their manner and conversation.

After speaking a moment in whispers, Smith said to his companion, ' We must go look after our nags for ten minutes, and allow Chaubert to do his office.'

' Will not he appear and minister before us, then ? ' said Ganlesse.

' What, he ! — he shift a trencher — he hand a cup ! No, you forget whom you speak of. Such an order were enough to make him fall on his own sword ; he is already on the borders of despair, because no craw-fish are to be had.'

' Alack-a-day ! ' replied Ganlesse. ' Heaven forbid I should add to such a calamity ! To stable, then, and see we how our steeds eat their provender, while ours is getting ready.'

They adjourned to the stable accordingly, which, though a poor one, had been hastily supplied with whatever was necessary for the accommodation of four excellent horses ; one of which, that from which Ganlesse was just dismounted, the groom we have mentioned was cleaning and dressing by the light of a huge wax candle.

' I am still so far Catholic,' said Ganlesse, laughing, as he saw that Peveril noticed this piece of extravagance.   'My horse is my saint, and I dedicate a candle to him.'

'Without asking so great a favour for mine, which I see standing behind yonder old hen-coop,' replied Peveril, 'I will at least relieve him of his saddle and bridle.'

'Leave him to the lad of the inn,' said Smith; 'he is not worthy any other person's handling; and I promise you, if you slip a single buckle, you will so flavour of that stable duty that you might as well eat roast-beef as ragouts, for any relish you will have of them.'

'I love roast-beef as well as ragouts at any time,' said Peveril, adjusting himself to a task which every young man should know how to perform when need is; 'and my horse, though it be but a sorry jade, will champ better on hay and corn than on an iron bit.'

While he was unsaddling his horse and shaking down some litter for the poor wearied animal, he heard Smith observe to Ganlesse — 'By my faith, Dick, thou hast fallen into poor Slender's blunder: missed Anne Page and brought us a great lubberly postmaster's boy.'

'Hush! he will hear thee,' answered Ganlesse; 'there are reasons for all things — it is well as it is.   But, prithee, tell thy fellow to help the youngster.'

'What!' replied Smith, 'd'ye think I am mad?   Ask Tom Beacon — Tom of Newmarket — Tom of ten thousand, to touch such a four-legged brute as that?   Why, he would turn me away on the spot — discard me, i' faith.   It was all he would do to take in hand your own, my good friend; and if you consider him not the better, you are like to stand groom to him yourself to-morrow.'

'Well, Will,' answered Ganlesse, 'I will say that for thee, thou hast a set of the most useless, scoundrelly, insolent vermin about thee that ever eat up a poor gentleman's revenues.'

'Useless!   I deny it,' replied Smith.   'Every one of my fellows does something or other so exquisitely that it were sin to make him do anything else; it is your jacks-of-all-trades who are masters of none.   But hark to Chaubert's signal!   The coxcomb is twangling it on the lute, to the tune of *Éveillez-vous, belle endormie.*   Come, Master What-d'ye-Call (addressing Peveril), "get ye some water and wash this filthy witness from your hand," as Betterton says in the play; for Chaubert's cookery is like Friar Bacon's head — time is — time was — time will soon be no more.'

So saying, and scarce allowing Julian time to dip his hands
in a bucket and dry them on a horse-cloth, he hurried him
from the stable back to the supper-chamber.

Here all was prepared for their meal with an epicurean delicacy which rather belonged to the saloon of a palace than the
cabin in which it was displayed. Four dishes of silver, with
covers of the same metal, smoked on the table ; and three seats
were placed for the company.   Beside the lower end of the
board was a small side-table, to answer the purpose of what is
now called a dumb waiter ; on which several flasks reared their
tall, stately, and swan-like crests, above glasses and rummers.
Clean covers were also placed within reach ; and a small
travelling-case of morocco, hooped with silver, displayed a
number of bottles, containing the most approved sauces that
culinary ingenuity had then invented.

Smith, who occupied the lower seat, and seemed to act as
president of the feast, motioned the two travellers to take their
places and begin.   'I would not stay a grace-time,' he said,
'to save a whole nation from perdition.   We could bring no
chauffettes with any convenience, and even Chaubert is nothing
unless his dishes are tasted in the very moment of projection.
Come, uncover and let us see what he has done for us.   Hum ! —
ha ! — ay — squab pigeons — wild-fowl — young chickens —
venison cutlets — and a space in the centre, wet, alas ! by a
gentle tear from Chaubert's eye, where should have been the
soupe aux écrevisses.   The zeal of that poor fellow is ill repaid
by his paltry ten louis per month.'

'A mere trifle,' said Ganlesse ; 'but, like yourself, Will, he
serves a generous master.'

The repast now commenced ; and Julian, though he had
seen his young friend the Earl of Derby and other gallants
affect a considerable degree of interest and skill in the science
of the kitchen, and was not himself either an enemy or a
stranger to the pleasures of a good table, found that, on the
present occasion, he was a mere novice.   Both his companions,
but Smith in especial, seemed to consider that they were now
engaged in the only true and real business of life, and weighed
all its minutiæ with a proportional degree of accuracy.   To
carve the morsel in the most delicate manner, and to appor-
tion the proper seasoning with the accuracy of the chemist ;
to be aware, exactly, of the order in which one dish should
succeed another, and to do plentiful justice to all — was a minute-
ness of science to which Julian had hitherto been a stranger.

Smith accordingly treated him as a mere novice in epicurism, cautioning him 'to eat his soup before the bouilli, and to forget the Manx custom of bolting the boiled meat before the broth, as if Cutlar MacCulloch[1] and all his whingers were at the door.' Peveril took the hint in good part, and the entertainment proceeded with animation.

At length Ganlesse paused, and declared the supper exquisite. 'But, my friend Smith,' he added, 'are your wines curious? When you brought all that trash of plates and trumpery into Derbyshire, I hope you did not leave us at the mercy of the strong ale of the shire, as thick and muddy as the squires who drink it?'

'Did I not know that *you* were to meet me, Dick Ganlesse?' answered their host, 'and can you suspect me of such an omission? It is true, you must make champagne and claret serve, for my burgundy would not bear travelling. But if you have a fancy for sherry or Vin de Cahors, I have a notion Chaubert and Tom Beacon have brought some for their own drinking.'

'Perhaps the gentlemen would not care to impart,' said Ganlesse.

'Oh, fie! anything in the way of civility,' replied Smith. 'They are, in truth, the best-natured lads alive, when treated respectfully; so that if you would prefer ——'

'By no means,' said Ganlesse — 'a glass of champagne will serve in a scarcity of better.'

'The cork shall start obsequious to my thumb,'

said Smith; and as he spoke, he untwisted the wire, and the cork struck the roof of the cabin. Each guest took a large rummer glass of the sparkling beverage, which Peveril had judgment and experience enough to pronounce exquisite.

'Give me your hand, sir,' said Smith; 'it is the first word of sense you have spoken this evening.'

'Wisdom, sir,' replied Peveril, 'is like the best ware in the pedlar's pack, which he never produces till he knows his customer.'

'Sharp as mustard,' returned the *bon vivant*; 'but be wise, most noble pedlar, and take another rummer of this same flask, which you see I have held in an oblique position for your service, not permitting it to retrograde to the perpendicular. Nay, take it off before the bubble bursts on the rim and the zest is gone.'

---

[1] See Note 18.

'You do me honour, sir,' said Peveril, taking the second glass. 'I wish you a better office than that of my cup-bearer.'

'You cannot wish Will Smith one more congenial to his nature,' said Ganlesse. 'Others have a selfish delight in the objects of sense. Will thrives, and is happy, by imparting them to his friends.'

'Better help men to pleasures than to pains, Master Ganlesse,' answered Smith, somewhat angrily.

'Nay, wrath thee not, Will,' said Ganlesse; 'and speak no words in haste, lest you may have cause to repent at leisure. Do I blame thy social concern for the pleasures of others? Why, man, thou dost therein most philosophically multiply thine own. A man has but one throat, and can but eat, with his best efforts, some five or six times a-day; but thou dinest with every friend that cuts up a capon, and art quaffing wine in other men's gullets from morning to night — *et sic de cæteris.*'

'Friend Ganlesse,' returned Smith, 'I prithee beware; thou knowest I can cut gullets as well as tickle them.'

'Ay, Will,' answered Ganlesse, carelessly; 'I think I have seen thee wave thy whinyard at the throat of a Hogan-mogan — a Netherlandish weasand, which expanded only on thy natural and mortal objects of aversion — Dutch cheese, rye-bread, pickled herring, onions, and Geneva.'

'For pity's sake, forbear the description!' said Smith; 'thy words overpower the perfumes, and flavour the apartment like a dish of salmagundi!'

'But for an epiglottis like mine,' continued Ganlesse, 'down which the most delicate morsels are washed by such claret as thou art now pouring out, thou couldst not, in thy bitterest mood, wish a worse fate than to be necklaced somewhat tight by a pair of white arms.'

'By a tenpenny cord,' answered Smith; 'but not till you were dead; that thereafter you be presently embowelled, you being yet alive; that your head be then severed from your body, and your body divided into quarters, to be disposed of at his Majesty's pleasure. How like you that, Master Richard Ganlesse?'

'E'en as you like the thoughts of dining on bran-bread and milk-porridge — an extremity which you trust never to be reduced to. But all this shall not prevent me from pledging you in a cup of sound claret.'

As the claret circulated, the glee of the company increased; and Smith, placing the dishes which had been made use of upon the side-table, stamped with his foot on the floor, and the table sinking down a trap, again rose, loaded with olives, sliced neat's tongue, caviare, and other provocatives for the circulation of the bottle.

'Why, Will,' said Ganlesse, 'thou art a more complete mechanist than I suspected; thou hast brought thy scene-shifting inventions to Derbyshire in marvellously short time.'

'A rope and pulleys can be easily come by,' answered Will; 'and with a saw and a plane, I can manage that business in half a day. I love that knack of clean and secret conveyance; thou knowest it was the foundation of my fortunes.'

'It may be the wreck of them too, Will,' replied his friend.

'True, Diccon,' answered Will; 'but *dum vivimus, vivamus* — that is my motto; and therewith I present you a brimmer to the health of the fair lady you wot of.'

'Let it come, Will,' replied his friend; and the flask circulated briskly from hand to hand.

Julian did not think it prudent to seem a check on their festivity, as he hoped in its progress something might occur to enable him to judge of the character and purposes of his companions. But he watched them in vain. Their conversation was animated and lively, and often bore reference to the literature of the period, in which the elder seemed particularly well skilled. They also talked freely of the court, and of that numerous class of gallants who were then described as 'men of wit and pleasure about town'; and to which it seemed probable they themselves appertained.

At length the universal topic of the Popish Plot was started, upon which Ganlesse and Smith seemed to entertain the most opposite opinions. Ganlesse, if he did not maintain the authority of Oates in its utmost extent, contended that at least it was confirmed in a great measure by the murder of Sir Edmondsbury Godfrey, and the letters written by Coleman [1] to the confessor of the French king.

With much more noise and less power of reasoning, Will Smith hesitated not to ridicule and run down the whole discovery, as one of the wildest and most causeless alarms which had ever been sounded in the ears of a credulous public. 'I shall never forget,' he said, 'Sir Godfrey's most original funeral. Two bouncing parsons, well armed with sword and pistol, mounted the pulpit to secure the third fellow who preached from being murdered in the face of the congregation. Three

---

[1] See Note 19.

parsons in one pulpit — three suns in one hemisphere — no wonder men stood aghast at such a prodigy.'[1]

'What then, Will,' answered his companion, 'you are one of those who think the good knight murdered himself, in order to give credit to the Plot?'

'By my faith, not I,' said the other; 'but some true blue Protestant might do the job for him, in order to give the thing a better colour. I will be judged by our silent friend whether that be not the most feasible solution of the whole.'

'I pray you, pardon me, gentlemen,' said Julian; 'I am but just landed in England, and am a stranger to the particular circumstances which have thrown the nation into such a ferment. It would be the highest degree of assurance in me to give my opinion betwixt gentlemen who argue the matter so ably; besides, to say truth, I confess weariness; your wine is more potent than I expected, or I have drank more of it than I meant to do.'

'Nay, if an hour's nap will refresh you,' said the elder of the strangers, 'make no ceremony with us. Your bed — all we can offer as such — is that old-fashioned Dutch-built sofa, as the last new phrase calls it. We shall be early stirrers to-morrow morning.'

'And that we may be so,' said Smith, 'I propose that we do sit up all this night. I hate lying rough, and detest a pallet-bed. So have at another flask, and the newest lampoon to help it out —

> Now a plague of their votes
> Upon Papists and plots,
> And be d—d Doctor Oates !
>   Tol de rol.'

'Nay, but our Puritanic host,' said Ganlesse.

'I have him in my pocket, man : his eyes, ears, nose, and tongue,' answered his boon companion, 'are all in my possession.'

'In that case, when you give him back his eyes and nose, I pray you keep his ears and tongue,' answered Ganlesse. 'Seeing and smelling are organs sufficient for such a knave; to hear and tell are things he should have no manner of pretensions to.'

'I grant you it were well done,' answered Smith; 'but it were a robbing of the hangman and the pillory; and I am an

---

[1] See Funeral Service of Sir Edmondsbury Godfrey. Note 20.

honest fellow, who would give Dun [1] and the devil his due.
So,

> All joy to great Cæsar,
> Long life, love, and pleasure ;
> May the King live for ever !
>   'T is no matter for us, boys.

While this Bacchanalian scene proceeded, Julian had wrapt
himself closely in his cloak and stretched himself on the couch
which they had shown to him.   He looked towards the table
he had left ; the tapers seemed to become hazy and dim as he
gazed ; he heard the sound of voices, but they ceased to convey
any impression to his understanding ; and in a few minutes he
was faster asleep than he had ever been in the whole course of
his life.

---

[1] See Dun the Hangman.   Note 21.

CHAPTER XXIII

The Gordon then his bugle blew,
    And said, ' Awa, awa ;
The House of Rhodes is all on flame,
    I hauld it time to ga'.'
                                        Old Ballad.

WHEN Julian awakened the next morning, all was still
and vacant in the apartment. The rising sun, which
shone through the half-closed shutters, showed some
relics of the last night's banquet, which his confused and throbbing head assured him had been carried into a debauch.

Without being much of a boon companion, Julian, like other
young men of the time, was not in the habit of shunning wine,
which was then used in considerable quantities ; and he could
not help being surprised that the few cups he had drank over
night had produced on his frame the effects of excess. He
rose up, adjusted his dress, and sought in the apartment for
water to perform his morning ablutions, but without success.
Wine there was on the table ; and beside it one stool stood
and another lay, as if thrown down in the heedless riot of the
evening. 'Surely,' he thought to himself, 'the wine must
have been very powerful which rendered me insensible to the
noise my companions must have made ere they finished their
carouse.'

With momentary suspicion, he examined his weapons, and
the packet which he had received from the countess, and kept
in a secret pocket of his upper coat, bound close about his
person. All was safe ; and the very operation reminded him
of the duties which lay before him. He left the apartment
where they had supped and went into another, wretched
enough, where, in a truckle-bed, were stretched two bodies,
covered with a rug, the heads belonging to which were amicably deposited upon the same truss of hay. The one was the
black shock-head of the groom ; the other, graced with a long

thrum nightcap, showed a grizzled pate, and a grave caricatured countenance, which the hook-nose and lantern-jaws proclaimed to belong to the Gallic minister of good cheer whose praises he had heard sung forth on the preceding evening. These worthies seemed to have slumbered in the arms of Bacchus as well as of Morpheus, for there were broken flasks on the floor ; and their deep snoring alone showed that they were alive.

Bent upon resuming his journey, as duty and expedience alike dictated, Julian next descended the trap-stair and essayed a door at the bottom of the steps. It was fastened within. He called ; no answer was returned. It must be, he thought, the apartment of the revellers, now probably sleeping as soundly as their dependants still slumbered, and as he himself had done a few minutes before. Should he awake them ? To what purpose ? They were men with whom accident had involved him against his own will ; and, situated as he was, he thought it wise to take the earliest opportunity of breaking off from society which was suspicious, and might be perilous. Ruminating thus, he essayed another door, which admitted him to a bedroom, where lay another harmonious slumberer. The mean utensils, pewter measures, empty cans and casks, with which this room was lumbered, proclaimed it that of the host, who slept surrounded by his professional implements of hospitality and stock-in-trade.

This discovery relieved Peveril from some delicate embarrassment which he had formerly entertained. He put upon the table a piece of money, sufficient, as he judged, to pay his share of the preceding night's reckoning ; not caring to be indebted for his entertainment to the strangers, whom he was leaving without the formality of an adieu.

His conscience cleared of this gentlemanlike scruple, Peveril proceeded with a light heart, though somewhat a dizzy head, to the stable, which he easily recognised among a few other paltry outhouses. His horse, refreshed with rest, and perhaps not unmindful of his services the evening before, neighed as his master entered the stable ; and Peveril accepted the sound as an omen of a prosperous journey. He paid the augury with a sieveful of corn ; and, while his palfrey profited by his attention, walked into the fresh air to cool his heated blood, and consider what course he should pursue in order to reach the Castle of Martindale before sunset. His acquaintance with the country in general gave him confidence that he could not have greatly deviated from the nearest road ; and with his horse in good condition, he conceived he might easily reach Martindale before nightfall.

Having adjusted his route in his mind, he returned into the stable to prepare his steed for the journey, and soon led him into the ruinous courtyard of the inn, bridled, saddled, and ready to be mounted. But as Peveril's hand was upon the mane and his left foot in the stirrup, a hand touched his cloak, and the voice of Ganlesse said, 'What, Master Peveril, is this your foreign breeding? or have you learned in France to take French leave of your friends?'

Julian started like a guilty thing, although a moment's reflection assured him that he was neither wrong nor in danger. 'I cared not to disturb you,' he said, 'although I did come as far as the door of your chamber. I supposed your friend and you might require, after our last night's revel, rather sleep than ceremony. I left my own bed, though a rough one, with more reluctance than usual; and as my occasions oblige me to be an early traveller, I thought it best to depart without leave-taking. I have left a token for mine host on the table of his apartment.'

'It was unnecessary,' said Ganlesse: 'the rascal is already overpaid. But are you not rather premature in your purpose of departing? My mind tells me that Master Julian Peveril had better proceed with me to London than turn aside for any purpose whatever. You may see already that I am no ordinary person, but a master-spirit of the time. For the cuckoo I travel with, and whom I indulge in his prodigal follies, he also has his uses. But you are of a different cast; and I not only would serve you, but even wish you to be my own.'

Julian gazed on this singular person when he spoke. We have already said his figure was mean and slight, with very ordinary and unmarked features, unless we were to distinguish the lightnings of a keen grey eye, which corresponded, in its careless and prideful glance, with the haughty superiority which the stranger assumed in his conversation. It was not till after a momentary pause that Julian replied, 'Can you wonder, sir, that in my circumstances — if they are indeed known to you so well as they seem — I should decline unnecessary confidence on the affairs of moment which have called me hither, or refuse the company of a stranger, who assigns no reason for desiring mine?'

'Be it as you list, young man,' answered Ganlesse; 'only remember hereafter, you had a fair offer; it is not every one to whom I would have made it. If we should meet hereafter on other, and on worse, terms, impute it to yourself, and not to me.'

'I understand not your threat,' answered Peveril, 'if a threat be indeed implied. I have done no evil — I feel no apprehension ; and I cannot, in common sense, conceive why I should suffer for refusing my confidence to a stranger, who seems to require that I should submit me blindfold to his guidance.'

'Farewell, then, Sir Julian of the Peak — that may soon be,' said the stranger, removing the hand which he had as yet left carelessly on the horse's bridle.

'How mean you by that phrase ?' said Julian ; 'and why apply such a title to me ?'

The stranger smiled, and only answered, 'Here our conference ends. The way is before you. You will find it longer and rougher than that by which I would have guided you.'

So saying, Ganlesse turned his back and walked toward the house. On the threshold he turned about once more, and seeing that Peveril had not yet moved from the spot, he again smiled and beckoned to him ; but Julian, recalled by that sign to recollection, spurred his horse and set forward on his journey.

It was not long ere his local acquaintance with the country enabled him to regain the road to Martindale, from which he had diverged on the preceding evening for about two miles. But the roads, or rather the paths, of this wild country, so much satirised by their native poet, Cotton, were so complicated in some places, so difficult to be traced in others, and so unfit for hasty travelling in almost all, that, in spite of Julian's utmost exertions, and though he made no longer delay upon the journey than was necessary to bait his horse at a small hamlet through which he passed at noon, it was nightfall ere he reached an eminence from which an hour sooner the battlements of Martindale Castle would have been visible ; and where, when they were hid in night, their situation was indicated by a light constantly maintained in a lofty tower called the Warder's Turret, and which domestic beacon had acquired through all the neighbourhood the name of Peveril's Pole-star.

This was regularly kindled at curfew-toll, and supplied with as much wood and charcoal as maintained the light till sunrise ; and at no period was the ceremonial omitted saving during the space intervening between the death of a lord of the castle and his interment. When this last event had taken place, the nightly beacon was rekindled with some ceremony, and continued till fate called the successor to sleep with his fathers.

It is not known from what circumstance the practice of maintaining this light originally sprung. Tradition spoke of it doubtfully. Some thought it was the signal of general hospitality, which, in ancient times, guided the wandering knight or the weary pilgrim to rest and refreshment. Others spoke of it as a 'love-lighted watchfire,' by which the provident anxiety of a former lady of Martindale guided her husband homeward through the terrors of a midnight storm. The less favourable construction of unfriendly neighbours of the dissenting persuasion ascribed the origin and continuance of this practice to the assuming pride of the family of Peveril, who thereby chose to intimate their ancient *suzerainté* over the whole country, in the manner of the admiral, who carries the lantern in the poop, for the guidance of the fleet. And in the former times our old friend, Master Solsgrace, dealt from the pulpit many a hard hit against Sir Geoffrey, as he that had raised his horn and set up his candlestick on high. Certain it is, that all the Peverils, from father to son, had been especially attentive to the maintenance of this custom, as something intimately connected with the dignity of their family; and in the hands of Sir Geoffrey the observance was not likely to be omitted.

Accordingly, the polar star of Peveril had continued to beam more or less brightly during all the vicissitudes of the Civil War; and glimmered, however faintly, during the subsequent period of Sir Geoffrey's depression. But he was often heard to say, and sometimes to swear, that, while there was a perch of woodland left to the estate, the old beacon-grate should not lack replenishing. All this his son Julian well knew; and therefore it was with no ordinary feelings of surprise and anxiety that, looking in the direction of the castle, he perceived that the light was not visible. He halted, rubbed his eyes, shifted his position, and endeavoured in vain to persuade himself that he had mistaken the point from which the polar star of his house was visible, or that some newly intervening obstacle — the growth of a plantation, perhaps, or the erection of some building — intercepted the light of the beacon. But a moment's reflection assured him that, from the high and free situation which Martindale Castle bore in reference to the surrounding country, this could not have taken place; and the inference necessarily forced itself upon his mind that Sir Geoffrey, his father, was either deceased or that the family must have been disturbed by some strange calamity, under the pressure of which their wonted custom and solemn usage had been neglected.

Under the influence of undefinable apprehension, young
Peveril now struck the spurs into his jaded steed, and forcing
him down the broken and steep path at a pace which set safety
at defiance, he arrived at the village of Martindale-Moultrassie,
eagerly desirous to ascertain the cause of this ominous eclipse.
The street through which his tired horse paced slow and reluctantly was now deserted and empty ; and scarcely a candle
twinkled from a casement, except from the latticed window of
the little inn, called the Peveril Arms, from which a broad
light shone, and several voices were heard in rude festivity.

Before the door of this inn the jaded palfrey, guided by the
instinct or experience which makes a hackney well acquainted
with the outside of a house of entertainment, made so sudden
and determined a pause that, notwithstanding his haste, the
rider thought it best to dismount, expecting to be readily supplied with a fresh horse by Roger Raine, the landlord, the
ancient dependant of his family.   He also wished to relieve his
anxiety, by inquiring concerning the state of things at the
castle, when he was surprised to hear, bursting from the
taproom of the loyal old host, a well-known song of the Commonwealth time, which some Puritanical wag had written in
reprehension of the Cavaliers and their dissolute courses, and
in which his father came in for a lash of the satirist.

'Ye thought in the world there was no power to tame ye,
So you tippled and drabb'd till the saints overcame ye ;
"Forsooth," and "Ne'er stir," sir, have vanquish'd "G—d—n me,"
            Which nobody can deny.

There was bluff old Sir Geoffrey loved brandy and mum well,
And to see a beer-glass turn'd over the thumb well ;
But he fled like the wind, before Fairfax and Cromwell,
            Which nobody can deny.'

Some strange revolution, Julian was aware, must have taken
place, both in the village and in the castle, ere these sounds of
unseemly insult could have been poured forth in the very inn
which was decorated with the armorial bearings of his family ;
and not knowing how far it might be advisable to intrude on
these unfriendly revellers, without the power of repelling or
chastising their insolence, he led his horse to a back-door, which,
as he recollected, communicated with the landlord's apartment,
having determined to make private inquiry of him concerning
the state of matters at the castle.   He knocked repeatedly, and
as often called on Roger Raine with an earnest but stifled voice.

At length a female voice replied by the usual inquiry, ' Who is there ? '

' It is I, Dame Raine — I, Julian Peveril ; tell your husband to come to me presently.'

' Alack, and a well-a-day, Master Julian, if it be really you — you are to know my poor goodman has gone where he can come to no one ; but, doubtless, we shall all go to him, as Matthew Chamberlain says.'

' He is dead, then ? ' said Julian. ' I am extremely sorry —— '

' Dead six months and more, Master Julian ; and let me tell you, it is a long time for a lone woman, as Matt Chamberlain says.'

' Well, do you or your chamberlain undo the door. I want a fresh horse ; and I want to know how things are at the castle.'

' The castle — lack-a-day ! Chamberlain — Matthew Chamberlain — I say, Matt ! '

Matt Chamberlain apparently was at no great distance, for he presently answered her call ; and Peveril, as he stood close to the door, could hear them whispering to each other, and distinguish in a great measure what they said. And here it may be noticed that Dame Raine, accustomed to submit to the authority of old Roger, who vindicated as well the husband's domestic prerogative as that of the monarch in the state, had, when left a buxom widow, been so far incommoded by the exercise of her newly acquired independence, that she had recourse, upon all occasions, to the advice of Matt Chamberlain ; and as Matt began no longer to go slipshod, and in a red nightcap, but wore Spanish shoes and a high-crowned beaver, at least of a Sunday, and moreover was called ' Master Matthew ' by his fellow-servants, the neighbours in the village argued a speedy change of the name on the sign-post — nay, perhaps, of the very sign itself, for Matthew was a bit of a Puritan, and no friend to Peveril of the Peak.

' Now counsel me, an you be a man, Matt Chamberlain,' said Widow Raine ; ' for never stir, if here be not Master Julian's own self, and he wants a horse, and what not, and all as if things were as they wont to be.'

' Why, dame, an ye will walk by my counsel,' said the chamberlain, ' e'en shake him off : let him be jogging while his boots are green. This is no world for folks to scald their fingers in other folks' broth.'

' And that is well spoken, truly,' answered Dame Raine ; ' but then, look you, Matt, we have eaten their bread, and, as my poor goodman used to say —— '

'Nay — nay, dame, they that walk by the counsel of the dead shall have none of the living; and so you may do as you list; but if you will walk by mine, drop latch, and draw bolt, and bid him seek quarters farther — that is my counsel.'

'I desire nothing of you, sirrah,' said Peveril, 'save but to know how Sir Geoffrey and his lady do ? '

'Lack-a-day ! — lack-a-day ! ' in a tone of sympathy, was the only answer he received from the landlady ; and the conversation betwixt her and her chamberlain was resumed, but in a tone too low to be overheard.

At length, Matt Chamberlain spoke aloud, and with a tone of authority : ' We undo no doors at this time of night, for it is against the justices' orders, and might cost us our license ; and for the castle, the road up to it lies before you, and I think you know it as well as we do.'

'And I know you,' said Peveril, remounting his wearied horse, 'for an ungrateful churl, whom, on the first opportunity, I will assuredly cudgel to a mummy.'

To this menace Matthew made no reply, and Peveril presently heard him leave the apartment, after a few earnest words betwixt him and his mistress.

Impatient at this delay, and at the evil omen implied in these people's conversation and deportment, Peveril, after some vain spurring of his horse, which positively refused to move a step farther, dismounted once more, and was about to pursue his journey on foot, notwithstanding the extreme disadvantage under which the high riding-boots of the period laid those who attempted to walk with such encumbrances, when he was stopped by a gentle call from the window.

Her counsellor was no sooner gone than the good-nature and habitual veneration of the dame for the house of Peveril, and perhaps some fear for her counsellor's bones, induced her to open the casement, and cry, but in a low and timid tone, 'Hist ! hist ! Master Julian — be you gone ? '

'Not yet, dame,' said Julian ; 'though it seems my stay is unwelcome.'

'Nay, but, good young master, it is because men counsel so differently ; for here was my poor old Roger Raine would have thought the chimney-corner too cold for you ; and here is Matt Chamberlain thinks the cold courtyard is warm enough.'

'Never mind that, dame,' said Julian; ' do but only tell me what has happened at Martindale Castle? I see the beacon is extinguished.'

'Is it in troth? — ay, like enough; then good Sir Geoffrey has gone to Heaven with my old Roger Raine!'

'Sacred Heaven!' exclaimed Peveril; 'when was my father taken ill?'

'Never, as I knows of,' said the dame; 'but, about three hours since, arrived a party at the castle, with buff-coats and bandeliers, and one of the Parliament's folks, like in Oliver's time. My old Roger Raine would have shut the gates of the inn against them, but he is in the church-yard, and Matt says it is against law; and so they came in and refreshed men and horses, and sent for Master Bridgenorth, that is at Moultrassie Hall even now; and so they went up to the castle, and there was a fray, it is like, as the old knight was no man to take napping, as poor Roger Raine used to say. Always the officers had the best on 't; and reason there is, since they had the law on their side, as our Matthew says. But since the pole-star of the castle is out, as your honour says, why, doubtless, the old gentleman is dead.'

'Gracious Heaven! Dear dame, for love or gold, let me have a horse to make for the castle!'

'The castle!' said the dame. 'The Roundheads, as my poor Roger called them, will kill you as they have killed your father. Better creep into the woodhouse, and I will send Bett with a blanket and some supper. Or stay — my old Dobbin stands in the little stable beside the hen-coop — e'en take him, and make the best of your way out of the country, for there is no safety here for you. Hear what songs some of them are singing at the tap! So take Dobbin, and do not forget to leave your own horse instead.'

Peveril waited to hear no farther, only that, just as he turned to go off to the stable, the compassionate female was heard to exclaim — ' O Lord! what will Matthew Chamberlain say?' but instantly added, 'Let him say what he will, I may dispose of what 's my own.'

With the haste of a double-fee'd hostler did Julian exchange the equipments of his jaded brute with poor Dobbin, who stood quietly tugging at his rackful of hay, without dreaming of the business which was that night destined for him. Notwithstanding the darkness of the place, Julian succeeded marvellous quickly in preparing for his journey; and leaving his own horse to find its way to Dobbin's rack by instinct, he leaped upon his new acquisition, and spurred him sharply against the hill, which rises steeply from the village to the castle. Dobbin, little accustomed to such exertions, snorted, panted, and trotted as briskly as he could, until at length he brought his rider before the entrance-gate of his father's ancient seat.

The moon was now rising, but the portal was hidden from its beams, being situated, as we have mentioned elsewhere, in a deep recess betwixt two large flanking towers. Peveril dismounted, turned his horse loose, and advanced to the gate, which, contrary to his expectation, he found open. He entered the large courtyard ; and could then perceive that lights yet twinkled in the lower part of the building, although he had not before observed them, owing to the height of the outward walls. The main door, or great hall-gate, as it was called, was, since the partially decayed state of the family, seldom opened, save on occasions of particular ceremony. A smaller postern door served the purpose of ordinary entrance ; and to that Julian now repaired. This also was open — a circumstance which would of itself have alarmed him, had he not already had so many causes for apprehension. His heart sunk within him as he turned to the left, through a small outward hall, towards the great parlour, which the family usually occupied as a sitting-apartment ; and his alarm became still greater when, on a nearer approach, he heard proceeding from thence the murmur of several voices. He threw the door of the apartment wide ; and the sight which was thus displayed warranted all the evil bodings which he had entertained.

In front of him stood the old knight, whose arms were strongly secured, over the elbows, by a leathern belt drawn tight round them, and made fast behind ; two ruffianly-looking men, apparently his guards, had hold of his doublet. The scabbardless sword which lay on the floor, and the empty sheath which hung by Sir Geoffrey's side, showed the stout old Cavalier had not been reduced to this state of bondage without an attempt at resistance. Two or three persons, having their backs turned towards Julian, sat round a table, and appeared engaged in writing ; the voices which he had heard were theirs, as they murmured to each other. Lady Peveril — the emblem of death, so pallid was her countenance — stood at the distance of a yard or two from her husband, upon whom her eyes were fixed with an intenseness of gaze like that of one who looks her last on the object which she loves the best. She was the first to perceive Julian, and she exclaimed, 'Merciful Heaven! my son! — the misery of our house is complete!'

'My son!' echoed Sir Geoffrey, starting from the sullen state of dejection, and swearing a deep oath; 'thou art come in the right time, Julian. Strike me one good blow — cleave me that traitorous thief from the crown to the brisket! and that done, I care not what comes next.'

The sight of his father's situation made the son forget the inequality of the contest which he was about to provoke.

'Villains,' he said, 'unhand him!' and, rushing on the guards with his drawn sword, compelled them to let go Sir Geoffrey and stand on their own defence.

Sir Geoffrey, thus far liberated, shouted to his lady, 'Undo the belt, dame, and we will have three good blows for it yet; they must fight well that beat both father and son!'

But one of those men who had started up from the writing-table when the fray commenced prevented Lady Peveril from rendering her husband this assistance; while another easily mastered the hampered knight, though not without receiving several severe kicks from his heavy boots — his condition permitting him no other mode of defence. A third, who saw that Julian, young, active, and animated with the fury of a son who fights for his parents, was compelling the two guards to give ground, seized on his collar, and attempted to master his sword. Suddenly dropping that weapon and snatching one of his pistols, Julian fired it at the head of the person by whom he was thus assailed. He did not drop, but, staggering back as if he had received a severe blow, showed Peveril, as he sunk into a chair, the features of old Bridgenorth, blackened with the explosion, which had even set fire to a part of his grey hair. A cry of astonishment escaped from Julian; and in the alarm and horror of the moment he was easily secured and disarmed by those with whom he had been at first engaged.

'Heed it not, Julian,' said Sir Geoffrey — 'heed it not, my brave boy; that shot has balanced all accompts. But how — what the devil — he lives! Was your pistol loaded with chaff, or has the foul fiend given him proof against lead?'

There was some reason for Sir Geoffrey's surprise, since, as he spoke, Major Bridgenorth collected himself, sat up in the chair as one who recovers from a stunning blow, then rose, and wiping with his handkerchief the marks of the explosion from his face, he approached Julian, and said, in the same cold unaltered tone in which he usually expressed himself, 'Young

"Julian fired at the head of the person by whom he was assailed."

man, you have reason to bless God, who has this day saved
you from the commission of a great crime.'

'Bless the devil, ye crop-eared knave!' exclaimed Sir Geoffrey; 'for nothing less than the father of all fanatics saved
your brains from being blown about like the rinsings of Beelzebub's porridge-pot!'

'Sir Geoffrey,' said Major Bridgenorth, 'I have already told
you, that with you I will hold no argument; for to you I am
not accountable for any of my actions.'

'Master Bridgenorth,' said the lady, making a strong effort
to speak, and to speak with calmness, 'whatever revenge your
Christian state of conscience may permit you to take on my
husband — I — I, who have some right to experience compassion
at your hand — for most sincerely did I compassionate you when
the hand of Heaven was heavy on you — I implore you not to
involve my son in our common ruin! Let the destruction of
the father and mother, with the ruin of our ancient house,
satisfy your resentment for any wrong which you have ever
received at my husband's hand.'

'Hold your peace, housewife,' said the knight; 'you speak
like a fool, and meddle with what concerns you not. Wrong at
my hand? The cowardly knave has ever had but even too much
right. Had I cudgelled the cur soundly when he first bayed
at me, the cowardly mongrel had been now crouching at my
feet, instead of flying at my throat. But if I get through this
action, as I have got through worse weather, I will pay off old
scores, as far as tough crab-tree and cold iron will bear me out.'

'Sir Geoffrey,' replied Bridgenorth, 'if the birth you boast
of has made you blind to better principles, it might have at
least taught you civility. What do you complain of? I am a
magistrate; and I execute a warrant, addressed to me by the
first authority in the state. I am a creditor also of yours; and
law arms me with powers to recover my own property from the
hands of an improvident debtor.'

'You a magistrate!' said the knight; 'much such a magistrate as Noll was a monarch. Your heart is up, I warrant,
because you have the King's pardon, and are replaced on the
bench, forsooth, to persecute the poor Papist. There was never
turmoil in the state, but knaves had their vantage by it;
never pot boiled, but the scum was cast uppermost.'

'For God's sake, my dearest husband,' said Lady Peveril,
'cease this wild talk! It can but incense Master Bridgenorth,
who might otherwise consider that in common charity ——'

'Incense him!' said Sir Geoffrey, impatiently interrupting her; 'God's death, madam, you will drive me mad! Have you lived so long in this world, and yet expect consideration and charity from an old starved wolf like that? And if he had it, do you think that I, or you, madam, as my wife, are subjects for his charity? Julian, my poor fellow, I am sorry thou hast come so unluckily, since thy petronel was not better loaded; but thy credit is lost for ever as a marksman.'

This angry colloquy passed so rapidly on all sides, that Julian, scarce recovered from the extremity of astonishment with which he was overwhelmed at finding himself suddenly plunged into a situation of such extremity, had no time to consider in what way he could most effectually act for the succour of his parents. To speak Bridgenorth fair seemed the more prudent course; but to this his pride could hardly stoop; yet he forced himself to say, with as much calmness as he could assume, 'Master Bridgenorth, since you act as a magistrate, I desire to be treated according to the laws of England, and demand to know of what we are accused, and by whose authority we are arrested?'

'Here is another howlet for ye!' exclaimed the impetuous old knight; 'his mother speaks to a Puritan of charity; and thou must talk of law to a Roundheaded rebel, with a wannion to you! What warrant hath he, think ye, beyond the Parliament's or the devil's?'

'Who speaks of the Parliament?' said a person entering, whom Peveril recognised as the official person whom he had before seen at the horse-dealer's, and who now bustled in with all the conscious dignity of plenary authority — 'who talks of the Parliament?' he exclaimed. 'I promise you, enough has been found in this house to convict twenty plotters. Here be arms, and that good store. Bring them in, captain.'

'The very same,' exclaimed the captain, approaching, 'which I mention in my printed Narrative of Information, lodged before the Honourable House of Commons; they were commissioned from old Vander Huys of Rotterdam, by orders of Don John of Austria, for the service of the Jesuits.'

'Now, by this light,' said Sir Geoffrey, 'they are the pikes, musketoons, and pistols that have been hidden in the garret ever since Naseby fight!'

'And here,' said the captain's yoke-fellow, Everett, 'are proper priest's trappings — antiphoners, and missals, and copes, I warrant you — ay, and proper pictures, too, for Papists to mutter and bow over.'

'Now, plague on thy snuffling whine,' said Sir Geoffrey; 'here is a rascal will swear my grandmother's old farthingale to be priest's vestments, and the story-book of *Owlenspiegel* a Popish missal!'

'But how 's this, Master Bridgenorth?' said Topham, addressing the magistrate. 'Your honour has been as busy as we have; and you have caught another knave while we recovered these toys.'

'I think, sir,' said Julian, 'if you look into your warrant, which, if I mistake not, names the persons whom you are directed to arrest, you will find you have no title to apprehend me.'

'Sir,' said the officer, puffing with importance, 'I do not know who you are; but I would you were the best man in England, that I might teach you the respect due to the warrant of the House. Sir, there steps not the man within the British seas but I will arrest him on authority of this bit of parchment; and I do arrest you accordingly. What do you accuse him of, gentlemen?'

Dangerfield swaggered forward, and peeping under Julian's hat, 'Stop my vital breath,' he exclaimed, 'but I have seen you before, my friend, an I could but think where; but my memory is not worth a bean, since I have been obliged to use it so much of late, in the behalf of the poor state. But I do know the fellow; and I have seen him amongst the Papists — I 'll take that on my assured damnation.'

'Why, Captain Dangerfield,' said the captain's smoother but more dangerous associate, 'verily, it is the same youth whom we saw at the horse-merchant's yesterday; and we had matter against him then, only Master Topham did not desire us to bring it out.'

'Ye may bring out what ye will against him now,' said Topham, 'for he hath blasphemed the warrant of the House. I think ye said ye saw him somewhere?'

'Ay, verily,' said Everett, 'I have seen him amongst the seminary pupils at St. Omer's; he was who but he with the regents there.'

'Nay, Master Everett, collect yourself,' said Topham; 'for, as I think, you said you saw him at a consult of the Jesuits in London.'

'It was I said so, Master Topham,' said the undaunted Dangerfield; 'and mine is the tongue that will swear it.'

'Good Master Topham,' said Bridgenorth, 'you may suspend

farther inquiry at present, as it doth but fatigue and perplex
the memory of the king's witnesses.'

'You are wrong, Master Bridgenorth — clearly wrong.   It
doth but keep them in wind — only breathes them, like grey-
hounds before a coursing-match.'

'Be it so,' said Bridgenorth, with his usual indifference of
manner ; 'but at present this youth must stand committed
upon a warrant, which I will presently sign, of having assaulted
me while in discharge of my duty as a magistrate, for the
rescue of a person legally attached.   Did you not hear the
report of a pistol ? '

'I will swear to it,' said Everett.

'And I,' said Dangerfield.   'While we were making search
in the cellar, I heard something very like a pistol-shot ; but I
conceived it to be the drawing of a long-corked bottle of sack,
to see whether there were any Popish relics in the inside on 't.'

'A pistol-shot ! ' exclaimed Topham ; 'here might have been
a second Sir Edmondsbury Godfrey's matter.   Oh, thou real
spawn of the red old dragon ! for he too would have resisted
the House's warrant, had we not taken him something at
unawares.   Master Bridgenorth, you are a judicious magistrate
and a worthy servant of the state ; I would we had many such
sound Protestant justices.   Shall I have this young fellow away
with his parents — what think you ? or will you keep him for
re-examination ? '

'Master Bridgenorth,' said Lady Peveril, in spite of her
husband's efforts to interrupt her, 'for God's sake, if ever you
knew what it was to love one of the many children you have
lost, or her who is now left to you, do not pursue your vengeance to the blood of my poor boy !   I will forgive you all the
rest — all the distress you have wrought — all the yet greater
misery with which you threaten us ; but do not be extreme
with one who never can have offended you.   Believe, that if
your ears are shut against the cry of a despairing mother, those
which are open to the complaint of all who sorrow will hear
my petition and your answer.'

The agony of mind and of voice with which Lady Peveril
uttered these words seemed to thrill through all present,
though most of them were but too much inured to such scenes.
Every one was silent when, ceasing to speak, she fixed on
Bridgenorth her eyes, glistening with tears, with the eager
anxiety of one whose life or death seemed to depend upon the
answer to be returned.   Even Bridgenorth's inflexibility seemed

to be shaken; and his voice was tremulous, as he answered,
'Madam, I would to God I had the present means of relieving
your great distress otherwise than by recommending to you a
reliance upon Providence; and that you take heed to your
spirit, that it murmur not under this crook in your lot. For
me, I am but as a rod in the hand of the strong man, which
smites not of itself, but because it is wielded by the arm of
him who holds the same.'

'Even as I and my black rod are guided by the Commons
of England,' said Master Topham, who seemed marvellously
pleased with the illustration.

Julian now thought it time to say something in his own
behalf; and he endeavoured to temper it with as much composure as it was possible for him to assume. 'Master Bridgenorth,' he said, 'I neither dispute your authority nor this
gentleman's warrant ——'

'You do not?' said Topham. 'Oh, ho, master youngster, I
thought we should bring you to your senses presently!'

'Then, if you so will it, Master Topham,' said Bridgenorth,
'thus it shall be. You shall set out with early day, taking
with you, towards London, the persons of Sir Geoffrey and
Lady Peveril; and that they may travel according to their
quality, you will allow them their coach, sufficiently guarded.'

'I will travel with them myself,' said Topham; 'for these
rough Derbyshire roads are no easy riding; and my very eyes
are weary with looking on these bleak hills. In the coach I
can sleep as sound as if I were in the House, and Master
Bodderbrains on his legs.'

'It will become you so to take your ease, Master Topham,'
answered Bridgenorth. 'For this youth, I will take him under
my charge and bring him up myself.'

'I may not be answerable for that, worthy Master Bridgenorth,' said Topham, 'since he comes within the warrant of the
House.'

'Nay, but,' said Bridgenorth, 'he is only under custody for
an assault, with the purpose of a rescue; and I counsel you
against meddling with him, unless you have stronger guard.
Sir Geoffrey is now old and broken, but this young fellow is in
the flower of his youth, and hath at his beck all the debauched
young Cavaliers of the neighbourhood. You will scarce cross
the country without a rescue.'

Topham eyed Julian wistfully, as a spider may be supposed
to look upon a stray wasp which has got into his web, and

which he longs to secure, though he fears the consequences of attempting him.

Julian himself replied, 'I know not if this separation be well or ill meant on your part, Master Bridgenorth; but on mine, I am only desirous to share the fate of my parents; and therefore I will give my word of honour to attempt neither rescue nor escape, on condition you do not separate me from them.'

'Do not say so, Julian,' said his mother. 'Abide with Master Bridgenorth; my mind tells me he cannot mean so ill by us as his rough conduct would now lead us to infer.'

'And I,' said Sir Geoffrey, 'know, that between the doors of my father's house and the gates of hell there steps not such a villain on the ground. And if I wish my hands ever to be unbound again, it is because I hope for one downright blow at a grey head that has hatched more treason than the whole Long Parliament.'

'Away with thee!' said the zealous officer; 'is Parliament a word for so foul a mouth as thine? Gentlemen,' he added, turning to Everett and Dangerfield, 'you will bear witness to this.'

'To his having reviled the House of Commons — by G—d, that I will!' said Dangerfield; 'I will take it on my damnation.'

'And verily,' said Everett, 'as he spoke of Parliament generally, he hath contemned the House of Lords also.'

'Why, ye poor insignificant wretches,' said Sir Geoffrey, 'whose very life is a lie, and whose bread is perjury, would you pervert my innocent words almost as soon as they have quitted my lips? I tell you the country is well weary of you; and should Englishmen come to their senses, the jail, the pillory, the whipping-post, and the gibbet will be too good preferment for such base blood-suckers. And now, Master Bridgenorth, you and they may do your worst; for I will not open my mouth to utter a single word while I am in the company of such knaves.'

'Perhaps, Sir Geoffrey,' answered Bridgenorth, 'you would better have consulted your own safety in adopting that resolution a little sooner: the tongue is a little member, but it causes much strife. You, Master Julian, will please to follow me, and without remonstrance or resistance; for you must be aware that I have the means of compelling.'

Julian was, indeed, but too sensible that he had no other course but that of submission to superior force; but ere he left the apartment he kneeled down to receive his father's blessing, which the old man bestowed not without a tear in his eye, and in the emphatic words, 'God bless thee, my boy, and keep thee good and true to church and king, whatever wind shall bring foul weather!'

His mother was only able to pass her hand over his head, and to implore him, in a low tone of voice, not to be rash or violent in any attempt to render them assistance. 'We are innocent,' she said, 'my son — we are innocent ; and we are in God's hands. Be the thought our best comfort and protection.'

Bridgenorth now signed to Julian to follow him, which he did, accompanied, or rather conducted, by the two guards who had first disarmed him. When they had passed from the apartment, and were at the door of the outward hall, Bridgenorth asked Julian whether he should consider him as under parole; in which case, he said, he would dispense with all other security but his own promise.

Peveril, who could not help hoping somewhat from the favourable and unresentful manner in which he was treated by one whose life he had so recently attempted, replied, without hesitation, that he would give his parole for twenty-four hours, neither to attempt to escape by force nor by flight.

'It is wisely said,' replied Bridgenorth; 'for though you might cause bloodshed, be assured that your utmost efforts could do no service to your parents. Horses there — horses to the courtyard!'

The trampling of the horses was soon heard ; and in obedience to Bridgenorth's signal, and in compliance with his promise, Julian mounted one which was presented to him, and prepared to leave the house of his fathers, in which his parents were now prisoners, and to go, he knew not whither, under the custody of one known to be the ancient enemy of his family. He was rather surprised at observing that Bridgenorth and he were about to travel without any other attendants.

When they were mounted, and as they rode slowly towards the outer gate of the courtyard, Bridgenorth said to him, 'It is not every one who would thus unreservedly commit his safety, by travelling at night and unaided, with the hot-brained youth who so lately attempted his life.'

'Master Bridgenorth,' said Julian, 'I might tell you truly, that I knew you not at the time when I directed my weapon against you ; but I must also add, that the cause in which I used it might have rendered me, even had I known you, a slight respecter of your person. At present, I do know you, and have neither malice against your person nor the liberty of a parent to fight for. Besides, you have my word; and when was a Peveril known to break it?'

'Ay,' replied his companion, 'a Peveril — a Peveril of the Peak! — a name which has long sounded like a war-trumpet in the land; but which has now perhaps sounded its last loud note. Look back, young man, on the darksome turrets of your father's house, which uplift themselves as proudly on the brow of the hill as their owners raised themselves above the sons of their people. Think upon your father, a captive — yourself, in some sort a fugitive — your light quenched — your glory abased — your estate wrecked and impoverished. Think that Providence has subjected the destinies of the race of Peveril to one whom, in their aristocratic pride, they held as a plebeian upstart. Think of this; and when you again boast of your ancestry, remember, that He who raiseth the lowly can also abase the high in heart.'

Julian did indeed gaze for an instant, with a swelling heart, upon the dimly-seen turrets of his paternal mansion, on which poured the moonlight, mixed with long shadows of the towers and trees. But while he sadly acknowledged the truth of Bridgenorth's observation, he felt indignant at his ill-timed triumph. 'If fortune had followed worth,' he said, 'the Castle of Martindale and the name of Peveril had afforded no room for their enemy's vainglorious boast. But those who have stood high on Fortune's wheel must abide by the consequence of its revolutions. This much I will at least say for my father's house, that it has not stood unhonoured; nor will it fall — if it is to fall — unlamented. Forbear, then, if you are indeed the Christian you call yourself, to exult in the misfortunes of others, or to confide in your own prosperity. If the light of our house be now quenched, God can rekindle it in His own good time.'

Peveril broke off in extreme surprise; for, as he spake the last words, the bright red beams of the family beacon began again to glimmer from its wonted watch-tower, checkering the pale moonbeam with a ruddier glow. Bridgenorth also gazed on this unexpected illumination with surprise, and not, as it seemed, without disquietude. 'Young man,' he resumed, 'it can scarcely be but that Heaven intends to work great things by your hand, so singularly has that augury followed on your words.'

So saying, he put his horse once more in motion; and looking back, from time to time, as if to assure himself that the beacon of the castle was actually rekindled, he led the way through the well-known paths and alleys, to his own house of Moultrassie, followed by Peveril, who, although sensible that the light might be altogether accidental, could not but receive as a good omen an event so intimately connected with the traditions and usages of his family.

They alighted at the hall-door, which was hastily opened by a female; and while the deep tone of Bridgenorth called on the groom to take their horses, the well-known voice of his daughter Alice was heard to exclaim in thanksgiving to God, who had restored her father in safety.

CHAPTER XXIV

We meet, as men see phantoms in a dream,
Which glide, and sigh, and sign, and move their lips,
But make no sound ; or, if they utter voice,
'T is but a low and undistinguish'd moaning,
Which has nor word nor sense of utter'd sound.

The Chieftain.

WE said, at the conclusion of the last chapter, that a female form appeared at the door of Moultrassie Hall ; and that the well-known accents of Alice Bridgenorth were heard to hail the return of her father, from what she naturally dreaded as a perilous visit to the Castle of Martindale.

Julian, who followed his conductor with a throbbing heart into the lighted hall, was therefore prepared to see her whom he best loved with her arms thrown around her father. The instant she had quitted his paternal embrace, she was aware of the unexpected guest who had returned in his company. A deep blush, rapidly succeeded by deadly paleness, and again by a slighter suffusion, showed plainly to her lover that his sudden appearance was anything but indifferent to her. He bowed profoundly, a courtesy which she returned with equal formality, but did not venture to approach more nearly, feeling at once the delicacy of his own situation and of hers.

Major Bridgenorth turned his cold, fixed, grey, melancholy glance first on the one of them and then on the other. 'Some,' he said, gravely, 'would, in my case, have avoided this meeting ; but I have confidence in you both, although you are young, and beset with the snares incidental to your age. There are those within who should not know that ye have been acquainted. Wherefore, be wise, and be as strangers to each other.'

Julian and Alice exchanged glances as her father turned from them, and, lifting a lamp which stood in the entrance-hall, led the way to the interior apartment. There was little of consolation in this exchange of looks ; for the sadness of Alice's glance was mingled with fear, and that of Julian clouded by an anxious sense of doubt. The look also was but momentary; for Alice, springing to her father, took the light out of his hand, and, stepping before him, acted as the usher of both into the large oaken parlour, which has been already mentioned as the apartment in which Bridgenorth had spent the hours of dejection which followed the death of his consort and family. It was now lighted up as for the reception of company; and five or six persons sat in it, in the plain, black, stiff dress which was affected by the formal Puritans of the time, in evidence of their contempt of the manners of the luxurious court of Charles the Second, amongst whom excess of extravagance in apparel, like excess of every other kind, was highly fashionable.

Julian at first glanced his eyes but slightly along the range of grave and severe faces which composed this society — men, sincere perhaps in their pretensions to a superior purity of conduct and morals, but in whom that high praise was somewhat chastened by an affected austerity in dress and manners allied to those Pharisees of old who made broad their phylacteries, and would be seen of man to fast, and to discharge with rigid punctuality the observances of the law. Their dress was almost uniformly a black cloak and doublet, cut straight and close, and undecorated with lace or embroidery of any kind, black Flemish breeches and hose, square-toed shoes, with large roses made of serge ribbon. Two or three had huge loose boots of calf-leather, and almost every one was begirt with a long rapier, which was suspended by leathern thongs to a plain belt of buff or of black leather. One or two of the elder guests, whose hair had been thinned by time, had their heads covered with a skullcap of black silk or velvet, which, being drawn down betwixt the ears and the skull, and permitting no hair to escape, occasioned the former to project in the ungraceful manner which may be remarked in old pictures, and which procured for the Puritans the term of 'prick-eared Roundheads,' so unceremoniously applied to them by their contemporaries.

These worthies were ranged against the wall, each in his ancient, high-backed, long-legged chair; neither looking towards, nor apparently discoursing with, each other; but plunged in their own reflections, or awaiting, like an assembly of Quakers, the quickening power of Divine inspiration.

Major Bridgenorth glided along this formal society with noiseless step, and a composed severity of manner resembling their own. He paused before each in succession, and apparently communicated, as he passed, the transactions of the evening, and the circumstances under which the heir of Martindale Castle was now a guest at Moultrassie Hall. Each seemed to stir at his brief detail, like a range of statues in an enchanted hall, starting into something like life as a talisman is applied to them successively. Most of them, as they heard the narrative of their host, cast upon Julian a look of curiosity, blended with haughty scorn and the consciousness of spiritual superiority ; though, in one or two instances, the milder influences of compassion were sufficiently visible. Peveril would have undergone this gauntlet of eyes with more impatience had not his own been for the time engaged in following the motions of Alice, who glided through the apartment, and, only speaking very briefly, and in whispers, to one or two of the company who addressed her, took her place beside a treble-hooded old lady, the only female of the party, and addressed herself to her in such earnest conversation as might dispense with her raising her head or looking at any others in the company.

Her father put a question, to which she was obliged to return an answer — ' Where was Mistress Debbitch ? '

' She had gone out,' Alice replied, ' early after sunset, to visit some old acquaintances in the neighbourhood, and she was not yet returned.'

Major Bridgenorth made a gesture indicative of displeasure ; and, not content with that, expressed his determined resolution that Dame Deborah should no longer remain a member of his family. ' I will have those,' he said aloud, and without regarding the presence of his guests, ' and those only, around me, who know to keep within the sober and modest bounds of a Christian family. Who pretends to more freedom must go out from among us, as not being of us.'

A deep and emphatic humming noise, which was at that time the mode in which the Puritans signified their applause, as well of the doctrines expressed by a favourite divine in the pulpit as of those delivered in private society, ratified the approbation of the assessors, and seemed to secure the dismission of the unfortunate governante, who stood thus detected of having strayed out of bounds. Even Peveril, although he had reaped considerable advantages, in his early acquaintance with Alice, from the mercenary and gossiping disposition of her governess, could not hear of her dismissal without approbation, so much was he desirous that, in the hour of difficulty, which might soon approach, Alice might have the benefit of counte-

nance and advice from one of her own sex of better manners and
less suspicious probity than Mistress Debbitch.

Almost immediately after this communication had taken
place, a servant in mourning showed his thin, pinched, and
wrinkled visage in the apartment, announcing, with a voice
more like a passing bell than the herald of a banquet, that refreshments were provided in an adjoining apartment. Gravely
leading the way, with his daughter on one side and the Puritanical female whom we have distinguished on the other, Bridgenorth himself ushered his company, who followed with little
attention to order or ceremony, into the eating-room, where a
substantial supper was provided.

In this manner, Peveril, although entitled, according to ordinary ceremonial, to some degree of precedence — a matter at
that time considered of much importance, although now little
regarded — was left among the last of those who quitted the
parlour; and might indeed have brought up the rear of all,
had not one of the company, who was himself late in the
retreat, bowed and resigned to Julian the rank in the company
which had been usurped by others.

This act of politeness naturally induced Julian to examine
the features of the person who had offered him this civility;
and he started to observe, under the pinched velvet cap and
above the short band-strings, the countenance of Ganlesse, as
he called himself — his companion on the preceding evening. He
looked again and again, especially when all were placed at the
supper-board, and when, consequently, he had frequent opportunities of observing this person fixedly, without any breach of
good manners. At first he wavered in his belief, and was much
inclined to doubt the reality of his recollection; for the difference
of dress was such as to effect a considerable change of appearance; and the countenance itself, far from exhibiting anything
marked or memorable, was one of those ordinary visages which
we see almost without remarking them, and which leave our
memory so soon as the object is withdrawn from our eyes. But
the impression upon his mind returned, and became stronger,
until it induced him to watch with peculiar attention the manners
of the individual who had thus attracted his notice.

During the time of a very prolonged grace before meat, which
was delivered by one of the company, who, from his Geneva
band and serge doublet, presided, as Julian supposed, over some
dissenting congregation, he noticed that this man kept the
same demure and severe cast of countenance usually affected by

the Puritans, and which rather caricatured the reverence unquestionably due upon such occasions. His eyes were turned
upward, and his huge penthouse hat, with a high crown and
broad brim, held in both hands before him, rose and fell with
the cadences of the speaker's voice; thus marking time, as it
were, to the periods of the benediction. Yet when the slight
bustle took place which attends the adjusting of chairs, etc., as
men sit down to table, Julian's eye encountered that of the
stranger; and as their looks met, there glanced from those of
the latter an expression of satirical humour and scorn, which
seemed to intimate internal ridicule of the gravity of his present
demeanour.

Julian again sought to fix his eye, in order to ascertain that
he had not mistaken the tendency of this transient expression,
but the stranger did not allow him another opportunity. He
might have been discovered by the tone of his voice; but the
individual in question spoke little, and in whispers, which was
indeed the fashion of the whole company, whose demeanour at
table resembled that of mourners at a funeral feast.

The entertainment itself was coarse, though plentiful; and
must, according to Julian's opinion, be distasteful to one so
exquisitely skilled in good cheer, and so capable of enjoying,
critically and scientifically, the genial preparations of his companion, Smith, as Ganlesse had shown himself on the preceding
evening. Accordingly, upon close observation, he remarked
that the food which he took upon his plate remained there
unconsumed; and that his actual supper consisted only of a
crust of bread with a glass of wine.

The repast was hurried over with the haste of those who
think it shame, if not sin, to make mere animal enjoyments
the means of consuming time or of receiving pleasure; and
when men wiped their mouths and mustachios, Julian remarked
that the object of his curiosity used a handkerchief of the finest
cambric — an article rather inconsistent with the exterior plain-
ness, not to say coarseness, of his appearance. He used also
several of the more minute refinements, then only observed at
tables of the higher rank; and Julian thought he could discern
at every turn something of courtly manners and gestures, under
the precise and rustic simplicity of the character which he had
assumed.[1]

----

[1] A Scottish gentleman *in hiding*, as it was emphatically termed, for
some concern in a Jacobite insurrection or plot, was discovered among a
number of ordinary persons by the use of his toothpick.

But if this were indeed that same Ganlesse with whom Julian had met on the preceding evening, and who had boasted the facility with which he could assume any character which he pleased to represent for the time, what could be the purpose of his present disguise? He was, if his own words could be credited, a person of some importance, who dared to defy the danger of those officers and informers before whom all ranks at that time trembled; nor was he likely, as Julian conceived, without some strong purpose, to subject himself to such a masquerade as the present, which could not be otherwise than irksome to one whose conversation proclaimed him of light life and free opinions. Was his appearance here for good or for evil? Did it respect his father's house, or his own person, or the family of Bridgenorth? Was the real character of Ganlesse known to the master of the house, inflexible as he was in all which concerned morals as well as religion? If not, might not the machinations of a brain so subtle affect the peace and happiness of Alice Bridgenorth?

These were questions which no reflection could enable Peveril to answer. His eyes glanced from Alice to the stranger; and new fears, and undefined suspicions, in which the safety of that beloved and lovely girl was implicated, mingled with the deep anxiety which already occupied his mind on account of his father and his father's house.

He was in this tumult of mind when, after a thanksgiving as long as the grace, the company arose from table, and were instantly summoned to the exercise of family worship. A train of domestics, grave, sad, and melancholy as their superiors, glided in to assist at this act of devotion, and ranged themselves at the lower end of the apartment. Most of these men were armed with long tucks, as the straight stabbing swords, much used by Cromwell's soldiery, were then called. Several had large pistols also; and the corslets or cuirasses of some were heard to clank as they seated themselves to partake in this act of devotion. The ministry of him whom Julian had supposed a preacher was not used on this occasion. Major Bridgenorth himself read and expounded a chapter of Scripture with much strength and manliness of expression, although so as not to escape the charge of fanaticism. The nineteenth chapter of Jeremiah was the portion of Scripture which he selected; in which, under the type of breaking a potter's vessel, the prophet presages the desolation of the Jews. The lecturer was not naturally eloquent; but a strong, deep, and sincere conviction of the truth of what he said supplied him with language of energy and fire, as he drew a parallel between the abominations of the worship of Baal and the corruptions of the Church of Rome — so favourite a topic with the Puritans of that period ; and denounced against the Catholics, and those who favoured them, that hissing and desolation which the prophet directed against the city of Jerusalem. His hearers made a yet closer application than the lecturer himself suggested ; and many a dark proud eye intimated, by a glance on Julian, that on his father's house were already, in some part, realised those dreadful maledictions.

The lecture finished, Bridgenorth summoned them to unite with him in prayer ; and on a slight change of arrangements amongst the company, which took place as they were about to kneel down, Julian found his place next to the single-minded and beautiful object of his affection, as she knelt, in her loveliness, to adore her Creator. A short time was permitted for mental devotion, during which Peveril could hear her half-breathed petition for the promised blessings of peace on earth and good-will towards the children of men.

The prayer which ensued was in a different tone. It was poured forth by the same person who had officiated as chaplain at the table, and was in the tone of a Boanerges, or Son of Thunder — a denouncer of crimes, an invoker of judgments, almost a prophet of evil and of destruction. The testimonies and the sins of the day were not forgotten : the mysterious murder of Sir Edmondsbury Godfrey was insisted upon ; and thanks and praise were offered, that the very night on which they were assembled had not seen another offering of a Protestant magistrate to the bloodthirsty fury of the revengeful Catholics.

Never had Julian found it more difficult, during an act of devotion, to maintain his mind in a frame befitting the posture and the occasion ; and when he heard the speaker return thanks for the downfall and devastation of his family, he was strongly tempted to have started upon his feet and charged him with offering a tribute stained with falsehood and calumny at the throne of truth itself. He resisted, however, an impulse which it would have been insanity to have yielded to, and his patience was not without its reward ; for when his fair neighbour arose from her knees, the lengthened and prolonged prayer being at last concluded, he observed that her eyes were streaming with tears ; and one glance with which she looked at him in that

moment showed more of affectionate interest for him in his
fallen fortunes and precarious condition than he had been able
to obtain from her when his worldly estate seemed so much the
more exalted of the two.

Cheered and fortified with the conviction that one bosom in
the company, and that in which he most eagerly longed to secure an interest, sympathised with his distress, he felt strong
to endure whatever was to follow, and shrunk not from the
stern still smile with which, one by one, the meeting regarded
him, as, gliding to their several places of repose, they indulged
themselves at parting with a look of triumph on one whom
they considered as their captive enemy.

Alice also passed by her lover, her eyes fixed on the ground,
and answered his low obeisance without raising them. The
room was now empty, but for Bridgenorth and his guest, or
prisoner, for it is difficult to say in which capacity Peveril
ought to regard himself. He took an old brazen lamp from the
table, and, leading the way, said at the same time, 'I must be
the uncourtly chamberlain who am to usher you to a place of
repose more rude, perhaps, than you have been accustomed to
occupy.'

Julian followed him, in silence, up an old-fashioned winding
staircase, within a turret. At the landing-place on the top was
a small apartment, where an ordinary pallet bed, two chairs,
and a small stone table, were the only furniture. 'Your bed,'
continued Bridgenorth, as if desirous to prolong their interview,
'is not of the softest; but innocence sleeps as sound upon straw
as on down.'

'Sorrow, Major Bridgenorth, finds little rest on either,'
replied Julian. 'Tell me, for you seem to await some question
from me, what is to be the fate of my parents, and why you
separate me from them ?'

Bridgenorth, for answer, indicated with his finger the mark
which his countenance still showed from the explosion of
Julian's pistol.

'That,' replied Julian, 'is not the real cause of your proceedings against me. It cannot be that you, who have been a
soldier, and are a man, can be surprised or displeased by my
interference in the defence of my father. Above all, you cannot, and I must needs say you do not, believe that I would
have raised my hand against you personally, had there been a
moment's time for recognition.'

'I may grant all this,' said Bridgenorth; 'but what the

better are you for my good opinion, or for the ease with which I can forgive you the injury which you aimed at me ? You are in my custody as a magistrate, accused of abetting the foul, bloody, and heathenish plot for the establishment of Popery, the murder of the King, and the general massacre of all true Protestants.'

'And on what grounds, either of fact or suspicion, dare any one accuse me of such a crime ?' said Julian. 'I have hardly heard of the plot, save by the mouth of common rumour, which, while it speaks of nothing else, takes care to say nothing distinctly even on that subject.'

'It may be enough for me to tell you,' replied Bridgenorth, 'and perhaps it is a word too much, that you are a discovered intriguer, a spied spy, who carries tokens and messages betwixt the Popish Countess of Derby and the Catholic party in London. You have not conducted your matters with such discretion but that this is well known, and can be sufficiently proved. To this charge, which you are well aware you cannot deny, these men, Everett and Dangerfield, are not unwilling to add, from the recollection of your face, other passages, which will certainly cost you your life when you come before a Protestant jury.'

'They lie like villains,' said Peveril, 'who hold me accessory to any plot either against the King, the nation, or the state of religion ; and for the countess, her loyalty has been too long and too highly proved to permit her being implicated in such injurious suspicions.'

'What she has already done,' said Bridgenorth, his face darkening as he spoke, 'against the faithful champions of pure religion hath sufficiently shown of what she is capable. She hath betaken herself to her rock, and sits, as she thinks, in security, like the eagle reposing after his bloody banquet. But the arrow of the fowler may yet reach her : the shaft is whetted, the bow is bended, and it will be soon seen whether Amalek or Israel shall prevail. But for thee, Julian Peveril — why should I conceal it from thee ? — my heart yearns for thee as a woman's for her first-born. To thee I will give, at the expense of my own reputation, perhaps at the risk of personal suspicion, for who, in these days of doubt, shall be exempted from it ? — to thee, I say, I will give means of escape, which else were impossible to thee. The staircase of this turret descends to the gardens, the postern gate is unlatched, on the right hand lie the stables, where you will find your own horse, take it, and make for Liverpool. I will give you credit with a friend under the name of Simon Simonson, one persecuted by the prelates ; and he will expedite your passage from the kingdom.'

'Major Bridgenorth,' said Julian, 'I will not deceive you. Were I to accept your offer of freedom, it would be to attend to a higher call than that of mere self-preservation. My father is in danger, my mother in sorrow ; the voices of religion and nature call me to their side. I am their only child — their only hope ; I will aid them, or perish with them ! '

'Thou art mad,' said Bridgenorth ; 'aid them thou canst not, perish with them thou well mayst, and even accelerate their ruin ; for, in addition to the charges with which thy unhappy father is loaded, it would be no slight aggravation that, while he meditated arming and calling together the Catholics and High Churchmen of Cheshire and Derbyshire, his son should prove to be the confidential agent of the Countess of Derby, who aided her in making good her stronghold against the Protestant commissioners, and was despatched by her to open secret communication with the Popish interest in London.'

'You have twice stated me as such an agent,' said Peveril, resolved that his silence should not be construed into an admission of the charge, though he felt that it was in some degree well founded. 'What reason have you for such an allegation ?'

'Will it suffice for a proof of my intimate acquaintance with your mystery,' replied Bridgenorth, 'if I should repeat to you the last words which the countess used to you when you left the castle of that Amalekitish woman ? Thus she spoke : " I am now a forlorn widow," she said, "whom sorrow has made selfish." '

Peveril started, for these were the very words the countess had used ; but he instantly recovered himself, and replied, 'Be your information of what nature it will, I deny and I defy it so far as it attaches aught like guilt to me. There lives not a man more innocent of a disloyal thought or of a traitorous purpose. What I say for myself, I will, to the best of my knowledge, say and maintain on account of the noble countess, to whom I am indebted for nurture.'

'Perish, then, in thy obstinacy ! ' said Bridgenorth ; and turning hastily from him, he left the room, and Julian heard him hasten down the narrow staircase, as if distrusting his own resolution.

With a heavy heart, yet with that confidence in an overruling Providence which never forsakes a good and brave man, Peveril betook himself to his lowly place of repose.

CHAPTER XXV

The course of human life is changeful still,
As is the fickle wind and wandering rill ;
Or, like the light dance which the wild breeze weaves
Amidst the faded race of fallen leaves,
Which now its breath bears down, now tosses high,
Beats to the earth, or wafts to middle sky.
Such, and so varied, the precarious play
Of fate with man, frail tenant of a day !

Anonymous.

WHILST, overcome with fatigue and worn out by
anxiety, Julian Peveril slumbered as a prisoner in
the house of his hereditary enemy, Fortune was
preparing his release by one of those sudden frolics with which
she loves to confound the calculations and expectancies of humanity ; and as she fixes on strange agents for such purposes,
she condescended to employ, on the present occasion, no less a
personage than Mistress Deborah Debbitch.

Instigated, doubtless, by the pristine reminiscences of former
times, no sooner had that most prudent and considerate dame
found herself in the vicinity of the scenes of her earlier days
than she bethought herself of a visit to the ancient housekeeper
of Martindale Castle, Dame Ellesmere by name, who, long retired from active service, resided at the keeper's lodge, in the
west thicket, with her nephew, Lance Outram, subsisting upon
the savings of her better days, and on a small pension allowed
by Sir Geoffrey to her age and faithful services.

Now, Dame Ellesmere and Mistress Deborah had not by
any means been formerly on so friendly a footing as this haste
to visit her might be supposed to intimate. But years had
taught Deborah to forget and forgive ; or perhaps she had no
special objection, under cover of a visit to Dame Ellesmere, to
take the chance of seeing what changes time had made on her
old admirer the keeper. Both inhabitants were in the cottage
when, after having seen her master set forth on his expedition

to the castle, Mistress Debbitch, dressed in her very best gown, footed it through gutter, and over stile, and by pathway green, to knock at their door, and to lift the latch at the hospitable invitation which bade her come in.

Dame Ellesmere's eyes were so often dim that, even with the aid of spectacles, she failed to recognise, in the portly and mature personage who entered their cottage, the tight, well-made lass who, presuming on her good looks and flippant tongue, had so often provoked her by insubordination; and her former lover, the redoubted Lance, not being conscious that ale had given rotundity to his own figure, which was formerly so slight and active, and that brandy had transferred to his nose the colour which had once occupied his cheeks, was unable to discover that Deborah's French cap, composed of sarsenet and Brussels lace, shaded the features which had so often procured him a rebuke from Dr. Dummerar, for suffering his eyes, during the time of prayers, to wander to the maid-servants' bench.

In brief, the blushing visitor was compelled to make herself known; and when known, was received by aunt and nephew with the most sincere cordiality.

The home-brewed was produced; and, in lieu of more vulgar food, a few slices of venison presently hissed in the frying-pan, giving strong room for inference that Lance Outram, in his capacity of keeper, neglected not his own cottage when he supplied the larder at the castle. A modest sip of the excellent Derbyshire ale and a taste of the highly-seasoned hash soon placed Deborah entirely at home with her old acquaintance.

Having put all necessary questions, and received all suitable answers, respecting the state of the neighbourhood, and such of her own friends as continued to reside there, the conversation began rather to flag, until Deborah found the art of again renewing its interest by communicating to her friends the dismal intelligence that 'They must soon look for deadly bad news from the castle; for that her present master, Major Bridgenorth, had been summoned by some great people from London to assist in taking her old master, Sir Geoffrey; and that all Master Bridgenorth's servants, and several other persons whom she named, friends and adherents of the same interest, had assembled a force to surprise the castle; and that as Sir Geoffrey was now so old, and gouty withal, it could not be expected he should make the defence he was wont; and then he was known to be so stout-hearted, that it was not to be supposed that he would yield up without stroke of sword; and then if he was

killed, as he was like to be, amongst them that liked never a
bone of his body, and now had him at their mercy, why, in that
case, she, Dame Deborah, would look upon Lady Peveril as little
better than a dead woman ; and undoubtedly there would be a
general mourning through all that country, where they had
such great kin ; and silks were likely to rise on it, as Master
Lutestring, the mercer of Chesterfield, was like to feel in his
purse bottom.   But for her part, let matters wag how they
would, an if Master Julian Peveril was to come to his own, she
could give as near a guess as e'er another who was likely to be
lady at Martindale.'

The text of this lecture, or, in other words, the fact that
Bridgenorth was gone with a party to attack Sir Geoffrey
Peveril in his own Castle of Martindale, sounded so stunningly
strange in the ears of those old retainers of his family, that
they had no power either to attend to Mistress Deborah's in-
ferences or to interrupt the velocity of speech with which she
poured them forth.   And when at length she made a breathless pause, all that poor Dame Ellesmere could reply was the
emphatic question, 'Bridgenorth brave Peveril of the Peak !
Is the woman mad ?'

'Come — come, dame,' said Deborah, 'woman me no more
than I woman you.   I have not been called "Mistress" at the
head of the table for so many years, to be woman'd here by
you.   And for the news, it is as true as that you are sitting
there in a white hood, who will wear a black one ere long.'

'Lance Outram,' said the old woman, 'make out, if thou
be'st a man, and listen about if aught stirs up at the castle.'

'If there should,' said Outram, 'I am even too long here ' ;
and he caught up his cross-bow and one or two arrows and
rushed out of the cottage.

'Well-a-day !' said Mistress Deborah, 'see if my news have
not frightened away Lance Outram too, whom they used to say
nothing could start.   But do not take on so, dame ; for I daresay, if the castle and the lands pass to my new master, Major
Bridgenorth, as it is like they will — for I have heard that he
has powerful debts over the estate — you shall have my good
word with him, and I promise you he is no bad man ; something
precise about preaching and praying, and about the dress
which one should wear, which, I must own, beseems not a
gentleman, as, to be sure, every woman knows best what
becomes her.   But for you, dame, that wear a Prayer Book at
your girdle with your housewife-case, and never change the

fashion of your white hood, I daresay he will not grudge you
the little matter you need, and are not able to win.'

'Out, sordid jade!' exclaimed Dame Ellesmere, her very
flesh quivering betwixt apprehension and anger, 'and hold
your peace this instant, or I will find those that shall flay the
very hide from thee with dog-whips. Hast thou eat thy noble
master's bread, not only to betray his trust and fly from his
service, but wouldst thou come here, like an ill-omened bird as
thou art, to triumph over his downfall?'

'Nay, dame,' said Deborah, over whom the violence of the
old woman had obtained a certain predominance; 'it is not I
that say it, only the warrant of the Parliament folks.'

'I thought we had done with their warrants ever since
the blessed twenty-ninth of May,' said the old housekeeper
of Martindale Castle; 'but this I tell thee, sweetheart, that I
have seen such warrants crammed, at the sword's point, down
the throats of them that brought them; and so shall this be,
if there is one true man left to drink of the Dove.'

As she spoke, Lance Outram re-entered the cottage. 'Naunt,'
he said in dismay, 'I doubt it is true what she says. The beacon tower is as black as my belt. No pole-star of Peveril. What
does that betoken?'

'Death, ruin, and captivity,' exclaimed old Ellesmere. 'Make
for the castle, thou knave. Thrust in thy great body. Strike
for the house that bred thee and fed thee; and if thou art
buried under the ruins, thou diest a man's death.'

'Nay, naunt, I shall not be slack,' answered Outram. 'But
here comes folks that I warrant can tell us more on 't.'

One or two of the female servants, who had fled from the
castle during the alarm, now rushed in with various reports
of the case; but all agreeing that a body of armed men were
in possession of the castle, and that Major Bridgenorth had
taken young Master Julian prisoner, and conveyed him down
to Moultrassie Hall, with his feet tied under the belly of the
nag — a shameful sight to be seen, and he so well born and so
handsome.

Lance scratched his head; and though feeling the duty
incumbent upon him as a faithful servant, which was indeed
specially dinned into him by the cries and exclamations of his
aunt, he seemed not a little dubious how to conduct himself.
'I would to God, naunt,' he said at last, 'that old Whitaker
were alive now, with his long stories about Marston Moor and
Edge Hill, that made us all yawn our jaws off their hinges, in

spite of broiled rashers and double-beer! When a man is
missed, he is moaned, as they say; and I would rather than a
broad piece he had been here to have sorted this matter, for it
is clean out of my way as a woodsman, that have no skill of
war. But dang it, if old Sir Geoffrey go to the wall without a
knock for it! Here you, Nell (speaking to one of the fugitive
maidens from the castle) — but no, you have not the heart of
a cat, and are afraid of your own shadow by moonlight. But,
Cis, you are a stout-hearted wench, and know a buck from a
bullfinch. Hark thee, Cis, as you would wish to be married,
get up to the castle again, and get thee in — thou best knowest
where, for thou hast oft gotten out of postern to a dance,
or junketing, to my knowledge. Get thee back to the castle,
as ye hope to be married; see my lady — they cannot hinder
thee of that — my lady has a head worth twenty of ours; if I
am to gather force, light up the beacon for a signal, and spare
not a tar barrel on 't. Thou mayst do it safe enough. I warrant the Roundheads busy with drink and plunder. And, hark
thee, say to my lady I am gone down to the miners' houses at
Bonadventure. The rogues were mutinying for their wages
but yesterday; they will be all ready for good or bad. Let her
send orders down to me; or do you come yourself, your legs
are long enough.'

'Whether they are or not, Master Lance — and you know
nothing of the matter — they shall do your errand to-night, for
love of the old knight and his lady.'

So Cisly Sellok, a kind of Derbyshire Camilla, who had won the
smock at the foot-race at Ashbourne, sprung forward towards
the castle, with a speed which few could have equalled.

'There goes a mettled wench,' said Lance; 'and now, naunt,
give me the old broadsword — it is above the bed-head — and
my wood-knife; and I shall do well enough.'

'And what is to become of me?' bleated the unfortunate
Mistress Deborah Debbitch.

'You must remain here with my aunt, Mistress Deb; and,
for old acquaintance' sake, she will take care no harm befalls
you; but take heed how you attempt to break bounds.'

So saying, and pondering in his own mind the task which
he had undertaken, the hardy forester strode down the moonlight glade, scarcely hearing the blessings and cautions which
Dame Ellesmere kept showering after him. His thoughts were
not altogether warlike. 'What a tight ankle the jade hath!
she trips it like a doe in summer over the dew. Well, but here

are the huts. Let us to this gear. Are ye all asleep, ye dammers, sinkers, and drift-drivers? Turn out, ye subterranean badgers. Here is your master, Sir Geoffrey, dead, for aught ye know or care. Do not you see the beacon is unlit, and you sit there like so many asses?'

'Why,' answered one of the miners, who now began to come out of their huts,

> 'An he be dead,
> He will eat no more bread.'

And you are like to eat none neither,' said Lance; 'for the works will be presently stopped, and all of you turned off.'

'Well, and what of it, Master Lance? As good play for nought as work for nought. Here is four weeks we have scarce seen the colour of Sir Geoffrey's coin; and you ask us to care whether he be dead or in life? For you, that goes about, trotting upon your horse, and doing for work what all men do for pleasure, it may be well enough; but it is another matter to be leaving God's light, and burrowing all day and night in darkness, like a toad in a hole — that's not to be done for nought, I trow; and if Sir Geoffrey is dead, his soul will suffer for't; and if he's alive, we'll have him in the barmoot court.'

'Hark ye, gaffer,' said Lance, 'and take notice, my mates, all of you,' for a considerable number of these rude and subterranean people had now assembled to hear the discussion — 'Has Sir Geoffrey, think you, ever put a penny in his pouch out of this same Bonadventure mine?'

'I cannot say as I think he has,' answered old Ditchley, the party who maintained the controversy.

'Answer on your conscience, though it be but a leaden one. Do not you know that he hath lost a good penny?'

'Why, I believe he may,' said Gaffer Ditchley. 'What then? Lose to-day, win to-morrow; the miner must eat in the meantime.'

'True; but what will you eat when Master Bridgenorth gets the land, that will not hear of a mine being wrought on his own ground? Will he work on at dead loss, think ye?' demanded trusty Lance.

'Bridgenorth! — he of Moultrassie Hall, that stopped the great Felicity work, on which his father laid out, some say, ten thousand pounds, and never got in a penny? Why, what has he to do with Sir Geoffrey's property down here at Bonadventure? It was never his, I trow.'

'Nay, what do I know?' answered Lance, who saw the impression he had made. 'Law and debt will give him half Derbyshire, I think, unless you stand by old Sir Geoffrey.'

'But if Sir Geoffrey be dead,' said Ditchley, cautiously, 'what good will our standing by do to him?'

'I did not say he was dead but only as bad as dead : in the hands of the Roundheads — a prisoner up yonder at his own castle,' said Lance ; 'and will have his head cut off, like the good Earl of Derby's, at Bolton-le-Moors.'

'Nay, then, comrades,' said Gaffer Ditchley, 'an it be as Master Lance says, I think we should bear a hand for stout old Sir Geoffrey, against a low-born, mean-spirited fellow like Bridgenorth, who shut up a shaft had cost thousands, without getting a penny profit on 't. So hurra for Sir Geoffrey, and down with the Rump! But hold ye a blink — hold (and the waving of his hand stopped the commencing cheer). Hark ye, Master Lance, it must be all over, for the beacon is as black as night ; and you know yourself that marks the lord's death.'

'It will kindle again in an instant,' said Lance ; internally adding, 'I pray to God it may! It will kindle in an instant — lack of fuel, and the confusion of the family!'

'Ay, like enow — like enow,' said Ditchley ; 'but I winna budge till I see it blazing.'

'Why then, there a goes!' said Lance. 'Thank thee, Cis — thank thee, my good wench. Believe your own eyes, my lads, if you will not believe me ; and now hurra for Peveril of the Peak — the King and his friends — and down with Rumps and Roundheads!'

The sudden rekindling of the beacon had all the effect which Lance could have desired upon the minds of his rude and ignorant hearers, who, in their superstitious humour, had strongly associated the polar star of Peveril with the fortunes of the family. Once moved, according to the national character of their countrymen, they soon became enthusiastic ; and Lance found himself at the head of thirty stout fellows and upwards, armed with their pick-axes, and ready to execute whatever task he should impose on them.

Trusting to enter the castle by the postern, which had served to accommodate himself and other domestics upon an emergency, his only anxiety was to keep his march silent ; and he earnestly recommended to his followers to reserve their shouts for the moment of the attack. They had not advanced far on their road to the castle when Cisly Sellok met them, so breathless with haste that the poor girl was obliged to throw herself into Master Lance's arms.

'Stand up, my mettled wench,' said he, giving her a sly kiss at the same time, 'and let us know what is going on up at the castle.'

'My lady bids you, as you would serve God and your master, not to come up to the castle, which can but make bloodshed; for she says Sir Geoffrey is lawfully in hand, and that he must bide the issue; and that he is innocent of what he is charged with, and is going up to speak for himself before King and Council, and she goes up with him. And besides, they have found out the postern, the Roundhead rogues; for two of them saw me when I went out of door, and chased me; but I showed them a fair pair of heels.'

'As ever dashed dew from the cowslip,' said Lance. 'But what the foul fiend is to be done? for if they have secured the postern, I know not how the dickens we can get in.'

'All is fastened with bolt and staple, and guarded with gun and pistol, at the castle,' quoth Cisly; 'and so sharp are they, that they nigh caught me coming with my lady's message, as I told you. But my lady says, if you could deliver her son, Master Julian, from Bridgenorth, that she would hold it good service.'

'What!' said Lance, 'is young master at the castle? I taught him to shoot his first shaft. But how to get in!'

'He was at the castle in the midst of the ruffle, but old Bridgenorth has carried him down prisoner to the hall,' answered Cisly. 'There was never faith nor courtesy in an old Puritan, who never had pipe and tabor in his house since it was built.'

'Or who stopped a promising mine,' said Ditchley, 'to save a few thousand pounds, when he might have made himself as rich as the Lord of Chatsworth, and fed a hundred good fellows all the whilst.'

'Why, then,' said Lance, 'since you are all of a mind, we will go draw the cover for the old badger; and I promise you that the hall is not like one of your real houses of quality, where the walls are as thick as whinstone dikes, but foolish brickwork, that your pick-axes will work through as if it were cheese. Huzza once more for Peveril of the Peak! down with Bridgenorth and all upstart cuckoldy Roundheads!'

Having indulged the throats of his followers with one buxom huzza, Lance commanded them to cease their clamours, and proceeded to conduct them, by such paths as seemed the least likely to be watched, to the courtyard of Moultrassie Hall. On the road they were joined by several stout yeomen farmers, either followers of the Peveril family or friends to the High Church and Cavalier party ; most of whom, alarmed by the news which began to fly fast through the neighbourhood, were armed with sword and pistol.

Lance Outram halted his party, at the distance, as he himself described it, of a flight-shot from the house, and advanced alone, and in silence, to reconnoitre ; and having previously commanded Ditchley and his subterranean allies to come to his assistance whenever he should whistle, he crept cautiously forward, and soon found that those whom he came to surprise, true to the discipline which had gained their party such decided superiority during the Civil War, had posted a sentinel, who paced through the courtyard piously chanting a psalm-tune, while his arms, crossed on his bosom, supported a gun of formidable length.

'Now, a true soldier,' said Lance Outram to himself, 'would put a stop to thy snivelling ditty, by making a broad arrow quiver in your heart, and no great alarm given. But, dang it, I have not the right spirit for a soldier : I cannot fight a man till my blood's up ; and for shooting him from behind a wall, it is cruelly like to stalking a deer. I'll e'en face him and try what to make of him.'

With this doughty resolution, and taking no farther care to conceal himself, he entered the courtyard boldly, and was making forward to the front door of the hall, as a matter of course. But the old Cromwellian who was on guard had not so learned his duty. 'Who goes there ? Stand, friend — stand ; or, verily, I will shoot thee to death !' were challenges which followed each other quick, the last being enforced by the levelling and presenting the said long-barrelled gun with which he was armed.

'Why, what a murrain !' answered Lance. 'Is it your fashion to go a-shooting at this time o'night ? Why, this is but a time for bat-fowling.'

'Nay, but hark thee, friend,' said the experienced sentinel, 'I am none of those who do this work negligently. Thou canst not snare me with thy crafty speech, though thou wouldst make it to sound simple in mine ear. Of a verity I will shoot, unless thou tell thy name and business.'

'Name !' said Lance ; 'why, what a dickens should it be but

Robin Round — honest Robin of Redham; and for business, an you must needs know, I come on a message from some Parliament man up yonder at the castle, with letters for worshipful Master Bridgenorth of Moultrassie Hall, and this be the place, as I think; though why ye be marching up and down at his door, like the sign of the Red Man, with your old firelock there, I cannot so well guess.'

'Give me the letters, my friend,' said the sentinel, to whom this explanation seemed very natural and probable, 'and I will cause them forthwith to be delivered into his worship's own hand.'

Rummaging in his pockets, as if to pull out the letters which never existed, Master Lance approached within the sentinel's piece, and, before he was aware, suddenly seized him by the collar, whistled sharp and shrill, and exerting his skill as a wrestler, for which he had been distinguished in his youth, he stretched his antagonist on his back — the musket for which they struggled going off in the fall.

The miners rushed into the courtyard at Lance's signal; and, hopeless any longer of prosecuting his design in silence, Lance commanded two of them to secure the prisoner, and the rest to cheer loudly, and attack the door of the house. Instantly the courtyard of the mansion rang with the cry of 'Peveril of the Peak for ever!' with all the abuse which the Royalists had invented to cast upon the Roundheads during so many years of contention; and at the same time, while some assailed the door with their mining implements, others directed their attack against the angle, where a kind of porch joined to the main front of the building; and there, in some degree protected by the projection of the wall and of a balcony which overhung the porch, wrought in more security, as well as with more effect, than the others; for the doors being of oak, thickly studded with nails, offered a more effectual resistance to violence than the brickwork.

The noise of this hubbub on the outside soon excited wild alarm and tumult within. Lights flew from window to window, and voices were heard demanding the cause of the attack; to which the party cries of those who were in the courtyard afforded a sufficient, or at least the only, answer, which was vouchsafed. At length the window of a projecting staircase opened, and the voice of Bridgenorth himself demanded authoritatively what the tumult meant, and commanded the rioters to desist, upon their own proper and immediate peril.

'We want our young master, you canting old thief,' was the reply; 'and if we have him not instantly, the topmost stone of your house shall lie as low as the foundation!'

'We will try that presently,' said Bridgenorth; 'for if there is another blow struck against the walls of my peaceful house, I will fire my carabine among you, and your blood be upon your own head. I have a score of friends, well armed with musket and pistol, to defend my house; and we have both the means and heart, with Heaven's assistance, to repay any violence you can offer.'

'Master Bridgenorth,' replied Lance, who, though no soldier, was sportsman enough to comprehend the advantage which those under cover, and using firearms, must necessarily have over his party, exposed to their aim, in a great measure, and without means of answering their fire — 'Master Bridgenorth, let us crave parley with you, and fair conditions. We desire to do you no evil, but will have back our young master; it is enough that you have got our old one and his lady. It is foul chasing, to kill hart, hind, and fawn; and we will give you some light on the subject in an instant.'

This speech was followed by a great crash amongst the lower windows of the house, according to a new species of attack which had been suggested by some of the assailants.

'I would take the honest fellow's word, and let young Peveril go,' said one of the garrison, who, carelessly yawning, approached on the inside the post at which Bridgenorth had stationed himself.

'Are you mad?' said Bridgenorth; 'or do you think me poor enough in spirit to give up the advantages I now possess over the family of Peveril for the awe of a parcel of boors, whom the first discharge will scatter like chaff before the whirlwind?'

'Nay,' answered the speaker, who was the same individual that had struck Julian by his resemblance to the man who called himself Ganlesse, 'I love a dire revenge, but we shall buy it somewhat too dear if these rascals set the house on fire, as they are like to do, while you are parleying from the window. They have thrown torches or firebrands into the hall; and it is all our friends can do to keep the flame from catching the wainscoting, which is old and dry.'

'Now, may Heaven judge thee for thy lightness of spirit,' answered Bridgenorth; 'one would think mischief was so properly thy element that to thee it was indifferent whether friend or foe was the sufferer.'

So saying, he ran hastily downstairs towards the hall, into which, through broken casements, and betwixt the iron bars, which prevented human entrance, the assailants had thrust lighted straw, sufficient to excite much smoke and some fire, and to throw the defenders of the house into great confusion; insomuch, that of several shots fired hastily from the windows little or no damage followed to the besiegers, who, getting warm in the onset, answered the hostile charges with loud shouts of 'Peveril for ever!' and had already made a practicable breach through the brick wall of the tenement, through which Lance, Ditchley, and several of the most adventurous among their followers, made their way into the hall.

The complete capture of the house remained, however, as far off as ever. The defenders mixed with much coolness and skill that solemn and deep spirit of enthusiasm which sets life at less than nothing in comparison to real or supposed duty. From the half-opened doors which led into the hall, they maintained a fire which began to grow fatal. One miner was shot dead; three or four were wounded; and Lance scarce knew whether he should draw his forces from the house and leave it a prey to the flames, or, making a desperate attack on the posts occupied by the defenders, try to obtain unmolested possession of the place. At this moment his course of conduct was determined by an unexpected occurrence, of which it is necessary to trace the cause.

Julian Peveril had been, like other inhabitants of Moultrassie Hall on that momentous night, awakened by the report of the sentinel's musket, followed by the shouts of his father's vassals and followers; of which he collected enough to guess that Bridgenorth's house was attacked with a view to his liberation. Very doubtful of the issue of such an attempt, dizzy with the slumber from which he had been so suddenly awakened, and confounded with the rapid succession of events to which he had been lately a witness, he speedily put on a part of his clothes and hastened to the window of his apartment. From this he could see nothing to relieve his anxiety, for it looked towards a quarter different from that on which the attack was made. He attempted his door; it was locked on the outside; and his perplexity and anxiety became extreme, when suddenly the lock was turned, and in an undress hastily assumed in the moment of alarm, her hair streaming on her shoulders, her eyes gleaming betwixt fear and resolution, Alice Bridgenorth rushed into his apartment, and seized his hand with the fervent exclamation, 'Julian, save my father!'

The light which she bore in her hand served to show those features which could rarely have been viewed by any one without emotion, but which bore an expression irresistible to a lover.

'Alice,' he said, 'what means this? What is the danger? Where is your father?'

'Do not stay to question,' she answered; 'but if you would save him, follow me!'

At the same time she led the way, with great speed, halfway down the turret staircase which led to his room, thence turning through a side door, along a long gallery, to a larger and wider stair, at the bottom of which stood her father, surrounded by four or five of his friends, scarce discernible through the smoke of the fire which began to take hold in the hall, as well as that which arose from the repeated discharge of their own firearms.

Julian saw there was not a moment to be lost, if he meant to be a successful mediator. He rushed through Bridgenorth's party ere they were aware of his approach, and throwing himself amongst the assailants, who occupied the hall in considerable numbers, he assured them of his personal safety, and conjured them to depart.

'Not without a few more slices at the Rump, master,' answered Lance. 'I am principally glad to see you safe and well; but here is Joe Rimegap shot as dead as a buck in season, and more of us are hurt; and we 'll have revenge, and roast the Puritans like apples for lambswool!'

'Then you shall roast me along with them,' said Julian; 'for I vow to God, I will not leave the hall, being bound by parole of honour to abide with Major Bridgenorth till lawfully dismissed.'

'Now out on you, an you were ten times a Peveril!' said Ditchley; 'to give so many honest fellows loss and labour on your behalf, and to show them no kinder countenance. I say, beat up the fire and burn all together!'

'Nay — nay; but peace, my masters, and hearken to reason,' said Julian; 'we are all here in evil condition, and you will only make it worse by contention. Do you help to put out this same fire, which will else cost us all dear. Keep yourselves under arms. Let Master Bridgenorth and me settle some grounds of accommodation, and I trust all will be favourably made up on both sides; and if not, you shall have my consent and countenance to fight it out; and come on it what will, I will never forget this night's good service.'

He then drew Ditchley and Lance Outram aside, while the rest stood suspended at his appearance and words, and expressing the utmost thanks and gratitude for what they had already done, urged them, as the greatest favour which they could do towards him and his father's house, to permit him to negotiate the terms of his emancipation from thraldom ; at the same time forcing on Ditchley five or six gold pieces, that the brave lads of Bonadventure might drink his health ; whilst to Lance he expressed the warmest sense of his active kindness, but protested he could only consider it as good service to his house if he was allowed to manage the matter after his own fashion.

'Why,' answered Lance, 'I am well out on it, Master Julian ; for it is matter beyond my mastery. All that I stand to is, that I will see you safe out of this same Moultrassie Hall ; for our old naunt Ellesmere will else give me but cold comfort when I come home. Truth is, I began unwillingly ; but when I saw the poor fellow Joe shot beside me, why, I thought we should have some amends. But I put it all in your honour's hands.'

During this colloquy both parties had been amicably employed in extinguishing the fire, which might otherwise have been fatal to all. It required a general effort to get it under ; and both parties agreed on the necessary labour with as much unanimity as if the water they brought in leathern buckets from the well to throw upon the fire had some effect in slaking their mutual hostility.

CHAPTER XXVI

Necessity, thou best of peacemakers,
As well as surest prompter of invention,
Help us to composition !
                                    Anonymous.

WHILE the fire continued, the two parties laboured in active union, like the jarring factions of the Jews during the siege of Jerusalem, when compelled to unite in resisting an assault of the besiegers. But when the last bucket of water had hissed on the few embers that continued to glimmer; when the sense of mutual hostility, hitherto suspended by a feeling of common danger, was in its turn rekindled, the parties, mingled as they had hitherto been in one common exertion, drew off from each other, and began to arrange themselves at opposite sides of the hall, and handle their weapons, as if for a renewal of the fight.

Bridgenorth interrupted any further progress of this menaced hostility. 'Julian Peveril,' he said, 'thou art free to walk thine own path, since thou wilt not walk with me that road which is more safe, as well as more honourable. But if you do by my counsel, you will get soon beyond the British seas.'

'Ralph Bridgenorth,' said one of his friends, 'this is but evil and feeble conduct on thine own part. Wilt thou withhold thy hand from the battle, to defend, from these sons of Belial, the captive of thy bow and of thy spear? Surely we are enow to deal with them in the security of our good old cause; nor should we part with this spawn of the old serpent until we essay whether the Lord will not give us victory therein.'

A hum of stern assent followed; and had not Ganlesse now interfered, the combat would probably have been renewed. He took the advocate for war apart into one of the window recesses, and apparently satisfied his objections; for as he returned to his companions, he said to them, 'Our friend hath so well argued this matter that, verily, since he is of the same mind with the worthy Major Bridgenorth, I think the youth may be set at liberty.'

As no further objection was offered, it only remained with Julian to thank and reward those who had been active in his assistance. Having first obtained from Bridgenorth a promise of indemnity to them for the riot they had committed, a few kind words conveyed his sense of their services; and some broad pieces, thrust into the hand of Lance Outram, furnished the means for affording them a holiday. They would have remained to protect him; but, fearful of farther disorder, and relying entirely on the good faith of Major Bridgenorth, he dismissed them all excepting Lance, whom he detained to attend upon him for a few minutes, till he should depart from Moultrassie. But, ere leaving the hall, he could not repress his desire to speak with Bridgenorth in secret; and advancing towards him, he expressed such a desire.

Tacitly granting what was asked of him, Bridgenorth led the way to a small summer saloon adjoining to the hall, where, with his usual gravity and indifference of manner, he seemed to await in silence what Peveril had to communicate.

Julian found it difficult, where so little opening was afforded him, to find a tone in which to open the subjects he had at heart, that should be at once dignified and conciliating. 'Major Bridgenorth,' he said at length, 'you have been a son, and an affectionate one. You may conceive my present anxiety. My father! What has been designed for him?'

'What the law will,' answered Bridgenorth. 'Had he walked by the counsels which I procured to be given to him, he might have dwelt safely in the house of his ancestors. His fate is now beyond my control — far beyond yours. It must be with him as his country shall decide.'

'And my mother?' said Peveril.

'Will consult, as she has ever done, her own duty; and create her own happiness by doing so,' replied Bridgenorth. 'Believe, my designs towards your family are better than they may seem through the mist which adversity has spread around your house. I may triumph as a man; but as a man I must also remember, in my hour, that mine enemies have had theirs. Have you aught else to say?' he added, after a momentary pause. 'You have rejected once, yea and again, the hand I stretched out to you. Methinks little more remains between us.'

These words, which seemed to cut short farther discussion,

were calmly spoken ; so that, though they appeared to discourage farther question, they could not interrupt that which
still trembled on Julian's tongue. He made a step or two
towards the door ; then suddenly returned. 'Your daughter!'
he said — 'Major Bridgenorth — I should ask — I *do* ask forgiveness for mentioning her name — but may I not inquire after
her ?   May I not express my wishes for her future happiness ?'

'Your interest in her is but too flattering,' said Bridgenorth ;
'but you have already chosen your part ; and you must be,
in future, strangers to each other. I may have wished it
otherwise, but the hour of grace is passed, during which your
compliance with my advice might — I will speak it plainly —
have led to your union. For her happiness — if such a word
belongs to mortal pilgrimage — I shall care for it sufficiently.
She leaves this place to-day, under the guardianship of a sure
friend.'

'Not of —— ' exclaimed Peveril, and stopped short ; for he
felt he had no right to pronounce the name which came to his
lips.

'Why do you pause ?' said Bridgenorth ; 'a sudden thought
is often a wise, almost always an honest, one. With whom did
you suppose I meant to entrust my child, that the idea called
forth so anxious an expression ?'

'Again I should ask your forgiveness,' said Julian, 'for meddling where I have little right to interfere. But I saw a face
here that is known to me ; the person calls himself Ganlesse.
Is it with him that you mean to entrust your daughter ?'

'Even to the person who calls himself Ganlesse,' said Bridgenorth, without expressing either anger or surprise.

'And do you know to whom you commit a charge so
precious to all who know her and so dear to yourself ?' said
Julian.

'Do *you* know, who ask me the question ?' answered Bridgenorth.

'I own I do not,' answered Julian ; 'but I have seen him
in a character so different from that he now wears, that I feel
it my duty to warn you how you entrust the charge of your
child to one who can alternately play the profligate or the
hypocrite, as it suits his own interest or humour.'

Bridgenorth smiled contemptuously. 'I might be angry,'
he said, 'with the officious zeal which supposes that its green
conceptions can instruct my grey hairs ; but, good Julian, I do
but only ask from you the liberal construction that I, who

have had much converse with mankind, know with whom I trust what is dearest to me. He of whom thou speakest hath one visage to his friends, though he may have others to the world, living amongst those before whom honest features should be concealed under a grotesque vizard ; even as in the sinful sports of the day, called maskings and mummeries, where the wise, if he show himself at all, must be contented to play the apish and fantastic fool.'

'I would only pray your wisdom to beware,' said Julian, 'of one who, as he has a vizard for others, may also have one which can disguise his real features from you yourself.'

'This is being over careful, young man,' replied Bridgenorth, more shortly than he had hitherto spoken ; 'if you would walk by my counsel, you will attend to your own affairs, which, credit me, deserve all your care, and leave others to the management of theirs.'

This was too plain to be misunderstood ; and Peveril was compelled to take his leave of Bridgenorth and of Moultrassie Hall without farther parley or explanation. The reader may imagine how oft he looked back, and tried to guess, amongst the lights which continued to twinkle in various parts of the building, which sparkle it was that gleamed from the bower of Alice. When the road turned into another direction, he sunk into a deep reverie, from which he was at length roused by the voice of Lance, who demanded where he intended to quarter for the night. He was unprepared to answer the question ; but the honest keeper himself prompted a solution of the problem, by requesting that he would occupy a spare bed in the lodge, to which Julian willingly agreed. The rest of the inhabitants had retired to rest when they entered ; but Dame Ellesmere, apprised by a messenger of her nephew's hospitable intent, had everything in the best readiness she could for the son of her ancient patron. Peveril betook himself to rest ; and, notwithstanding so many subjects of anxiety, slept soundly till the morning was far advanced.

His slumbers were first broken by Lance, who had been long up, and already active in his service. He informed him that his horse, arms, and small cloak-bag had been sent from the castle by one of Major Bridgenorth's servants, who brought a letter, discharging from the major's service the unfortunate Deborah Debbitch, and prohibiting her return to the hall. The officer of the House of Commons, escorted by a strong guard, had left Martindale Castle that morning early, travelling in Sir

Geoffrey's carriage — his lady being also permitted to attend on him. To this he had to add, that the property at the castle was taken possession of by Master Win-the-Fight, the attorney, from Chesterfield, with other officers of law, in name of Major Bridgenorth, a large creditor of the unfortunate knight.

Having told these Job's tidings, Lance paused ; and, after a moment's hesitation, declared he was resolved to quit the country and go up to London along with his young master. Julian argued the point with him ; and insisted he had better stay to take charge of his aunt, in case she should be disturbed by these strangers. Lance replied, 'She would have one with her who would protect her well enough ; for there was where-withal to buy protection amongst them. But for himself, he was resolved to follow Master Julian to the death.'

Julian heartily thanked him for his love.

'Nay, it is not altogether out of love neither,' said Lance, 'though I am as loving as another ; but it is, as it were, partly out of fear, lest I be called over the coals for last night's matter ; for as for the miners, they will never trouble them, as the creatures only act after their kind.'

'I will write in your behalf to Major Bridgenorth, who is bound to afford you protection, if you have such fear,' said Julian.

'Nay, for that matter, it is not altogether fear, more than altogether love,' answered the enigmatical keeper ; 'although it hath a tasting of both in it. And, to speak plain truth, thus it is — Dame Debbitch and Naunt Ellesmere have resolved to set up their houses together, and have made up all their quarrels. And of all ghosts in the world, the worst is, when an old true-love comes back to haunt a poor fellow like me. Mistress Deborah, though distressed enow for the loss of her place, has been already speaking of a broken sixpence, or some such token, as if a man could remember such things for so many years, even if she had not gone over seas, like a woodcock, in the meanwhile.'

Julian could scarce forbear laughing. 'I thought you too much of a man, Lance, to fear a woman marrying you whether you would or no.'

'It has been many an honest man's luck, for all that,' said Lance ; 'and a woman in the very house has so many deuced opportunities. And then there would be two upon one ; for naunt, though high enough when any of *your* folks are concerned, hath some look to the main chance; and it seems Mistress Deb is as rich as a Jew.'

'And you, Lance,' said Julian, 'have no mind to marry for cake and pudding?'

'No, truly, master,' answered Lance, 'unless I knew of what dough they were baked. How the devil do I know how the jade came by so much? And then if she speaks of tokens and love-passages, let her be the same tight lass I broke the sixpence with, and I will be the same true lad to her. But I never heard of true love lasting ten years; and hers, if it lives at all, must be nearer twenty.'

'Well, then, Lance,' said Julian, 'since you are resolved on the thing, we will go to London together; where, if I cannot retain you in my service, and if my father recovers not these misfortunes, I will endeavour to promote you elsewhere.'

'Nay — nay,' said Lance, 'I trust to be back to bonny Martindale before it is long, and to keep the greenwood, as I have been wont to do; for, as to Dame Debbitch, when they have not me for their common butt, naunt and she will soon bend bows on each other. So here comes old Dame Ellesmere with your breakfast. I will but give some directions about the deer to Rough Ralph, my helper, and saddle my forest pony, and your honour's horse, which is no prime one, and we will be ready to trot.'

Julian was not sorry for this addition to his establishment; for Lance had shown himself, on the preceding evening, a shrewd and bold fellow, and attached to his master. He therefore set himself to reconcile his aunt to parting with her nephew for some time. Her unlimited devotion for 'the family' readily induced the old lady to acquiesce in his proposal, though not without a gentle sigh over the ruins of a castle in the air, which was founded on the well-saved purse of Mistress Deborah Debbitch. 'At any rate,' she thought, 'it was as well that Lance should be out of the way of that bold, long-legged, beggarly trollop, Cis Sellok.' But to poor Deb herself, the expatriation of Lance, whom she had looked to as a sailor to a port under his lee, for which he can run if weather becomes foul, was a second severe blow, following close on her dismissal from the profitable service of Major Bridgenorth.

Julian visited the disconsolate damsel, in hopes of gaining some light upon Bridgenorth's projects regarding his daughter, the character of this Ganlesse, and other matters, with which her residence in the family might have made her acquainted;

but he found her by far too much troubled in mind to afford him the least information. The name of Ganlesse she did not seem to recollect, that of Alice rendered her hysterical, that of Bridgenorth furious. She numbered up the various services she had rendered in the family; and denounced the plague of swartness to the linen, of leanness to the poultry, of dearth and dishonour to the housekeeping, and of lingering sickness and early death to Alice — all which evils, she averred, had only been kept off by her continued, watchful, and incessant cares. Then again turning to the subject of the fugitive Lance, she expressed such a total contempt of that mean-spirited fellow, in a tone between laughing and crying, as satisfied Julian it was not a topic likely to act as a sedative; and that, therefore, unless he made a longer stay than the urgent state of his affairs permitted, he was not likely to find Mistress Deborah in such a state of composure as might enable him to obtain from her any rational or useful information.

Lance, who good-naturedly took upon himself the whole burden of Dame Debbitch's mental alienation, or 'taking on,' as such fits of *passio hysterica* are usually termed in the country, had too much feeling to present himself before the victim of her own sensibility and of his obduracy. He therefore intimated to Julian, by his assistant Ralph, that the horses stood saddled behind the lodge, and that all was ready for their departure.

Julian took the hint, and they were soon mounted, and clearing the road at a rapid trot in the direction of London; but not by the most usual route. Julian calculated that the carriage in which his father was transported would travel slowly; and it was his purpose, if possible, to get to London before it should arrive there, in order to have time to consult with the friends of his family what measures should be taken in his father's behalf.

In this manner, they advanced a day's journey towards London; at the conclusion of which, Julian found his resting-place in a small inn upon the road. No one came, at the first call, to attend upon the guests and their horses, although the house was well lighted up; and there was a prodigious chattering in the kitchen, such as can only be produced by a French cook, when his mystery is in the very moment of projection. It instantly occurred to Julian — so rare was the ministry of these Gallic artists at that time — that the clamour he heard must necessarily be produced by the Sieur Chaubert, on whose *plats* he had lately feasted, along with Smith and Ganlesse.

One or both of these were therefore probably in the little inn; and if so, he might have some opportunity to discover their real purpose and character. How to avail himself of such a meeting he knew not; but chance favoured him more than he could have expected.

'I can scarce receive you, gentlefolks,' said the landlord, who at length appeared at the door; 'here be a sort of quality in my house to-night whom less than all will not satisfy; nor all neither, for that matter.'

'We are but plain fellows, landlord,' said Julian; 'we are bound for Moseley market, and can get no farther to-night. Any hole will serve us, no matter what.'

'Why,' said the honest host, 'if that be the case, I must e'en put one of you behind the bar, though the gentlemen have desired to be private; the other must take heart of grace, and help me at the tap.'

'The tap for me,' said Lance, without waiting his master's decision. 'It is an element which I could live and die in.'

'The bar, then, for me,' said Peveril; and stepping back, whispered to Lance to exchange cloaks with him, desirous, if possible, to avoid being recognised.

The exchange was made in an instant; and presently afterwards the landlord brought a light; and as he guided Julian into his hostelry, cautioned him to sit quiet in the place where he should stow him; and if he was discovered, to say that he was one of the house, and leave him to make it good. 'You will hear what the gallants say,' he added; 'but I think thou wilt carry away but little on it; for when it is not French it is court gibberish, and that is as hard to construe.'

The bar, into which our hero was inducted on these conditions, seemed formed, with respect to the public room, upon the principle of a citadel, intended to observe and bridle a rebellious capital. Here sat the host on the Saturday evenings, screened from the observation of his guests, yet with the power of observing both their wants and their behaviour, and also that of overhearing their conversation — a practice which he was much addicted to, being one of that numerous class of philanthropists to whom their neighbours' business is of as much consequence, or rather more, than their own.

Here he planted his new guest, with a repeated caution not to disturb the gentlemen by speech or motion; and a promise that he should be speedily supplied with a cold buttock of beef and a tankard of home-brewed. And here he left him, with no other light than that which glimmered from the well-illuminated apartment within, through a sort of shuttle which accommodated the landlord with a view into it.

This situation, inconvenient enough in itself, was, on the present occasion, precisely what Julian would have selected. He wrapped himself in the weather-beaten cloak of Lance Outram, which had been stained, by age and climate, into a thousand variations from its original Lincoln green ; and, with as little noise as he could, set himself to observe the two inmates, who had engrossed to themselves the whole of the apartment, which was usually open to the public. They sat by a table, well covered with such costly rarities as could only have been procured by much forecast, and prepared by the exquisite Mons. Chaubert ; to which both seemed to do much justice.

Julian had little difficulty in ascertaining that one of the travellers was, as he had anticipated, the master of the said Chaubert, or, as he was called by Ganlesse, Smith ; the other, who faced him, he had never seen before. This last was dressed like a gallant of the first order. His periwig, indeed, as he travelled on horseback, did not much exceed in size the bar-wig of a modern lawyer ; but then the essence which he shook from it with every motion impregnated a whole apart-ment which was usually only perfumed by that vulgar herb, tobacco. His riding-coat was laced in the newest and most courtly style ; and Grammont himself might have envied the embroidery of his waistcoat, and the peculiar cut of his breeches, which buttoned above the knee, permitting the shape of a very handsome leg to be completely seen. This, by the proprietor thereof, had been stretched out upon a stool, and he contemplated its proportions, from time to time, with infinite satisfaction.

The conversation between these worthies was so interesting, that we propose to assign to it another chapter.